THE AGENT'S DEMON

LOCKE & STEEL BOOK ONE

L. E. MEDLOCK

STONE SOUL PUBLISHING

For Mum

CHAPTER ONE

The professor's demon lurks in the shadows at the back of the room. His shaggy hair and three-day-old beard look scruffy against Professor Monaghan's starched cravat and perfectly aligned cuff links. Tigerish amber eyes alight on me and I drop my gaze. Demons don't like it if you look at them too long.

"How may I help, professor?" I ask the golden freckles scattered over my knuckles. Monaghan must have summoned me for a reason, but calling me here alone, less than an hour before the ritual—it's not a good sign.

Not quite alone: at the sound of my voice, the other man in the room glances at me. I hunch my shoulders, the collar of my white shirt squeezing my throat. The man looks away, but not before a quick check over my shoulder, searching for a demon I don't have.

"Miss Locke is not a field agent," the professor says, catching the look too. "She's Agent Turner's apprentice." He'd risen when I entered, and now he takes a seat. His burgundy suit is pristine, his fair skin pale from too many days behind a desk. "Miss Locke, this is Mr. Pemberton."

The Legal Secretary to the Home Office. I swallow. What's Turner done now?

Pemberton's disdain is clear in the downward slant of his mouth under his moustache. "Exactly how many women do you employ here, Monaghan?"

"Not enough, sir, if I'm honest. We only have two Hound agents for the whole of Britain. If you would allow me to recruit just *one* more—"

"You have plenty of agents, Monaghan. You don't need any more."

"Seven, in total," the other man persists. "Seven agents to cover thirty million people, and only two of those are equipped to—"

The Secretary raises his hand. He studiously avoids looking anywhere near Monaghan's demon, Tiberius. "The Home Office has already made its position on this clear. I did not come to debate it with you."

Monaghan's lips thin, but he says nothing. I keep quiet, feeling big and awkward and like I'm taking up too much space. I don't know if my presence is helping or hindering this conversation. Hindering, probably, given the Secretary's reaction.

Tiberius watches the Secretary. A few more minutes under that pitiless gaze and the Secretary will be crossing himself and backing out muttering a prayer.

"Miss Locke," the professor says.

"Sir?"

"Tell me what you're working on for Turner."

So, she *is* in trouble. I pause—a pause that does not go unnoticed, by the slight lift of Monaghan's brows—and clear my throat. "Agent Turner is investigating the murder of Martha Tabram, sir, who died on the seventh of this month." That was the case the last I'd heard, at least. Has something changed?

"Our police have been all over that crime scene," Pemberton interjects. "There's no evidence that points towards—" He flicks a glance at Tiberius, who remains as inscrutable as ever, "*unnatural* involvement. I appreciate your efforts, Monaghan, but it's been three weeks. You can call off your dog."

"Sir, if my agent deems an investigation worth continuing, then I see no reason to halt it."

The Secretary clasps the arms of his chair, his face flushing. "Frankly, Monaghan, your agent is making the CID uncomfortable. To have a woman in the station is insult enough, let alone the fact that she's Jewish, but with one of those *creatures*—" He does cross himself, then. I dig my nails into my palms to repress a flash of unholy amusement. "It's too much for any decent man to withstand. No," Pemberton continues, warming to the topic, "I think you should consider retiring her. The demon, as well. They're too old to do any more good."

I inhale. Even Monaghan looks surprised.

"We *could* retire Turner," he says, slowly, not looking at me. I struggle to keep my face straight. Retirement for a human agent means their apprentice would inherit the role. The demon, too. "But as for the Hound—sir, we cannot afford to lose any of our demons. Lavender has been with the agency for years; her experience is incredibly valuable. Besides, Miss Locke is not ready to take Turner's place." A quick glance at me as he says it, but I don't protest. I'm *not* ready.

"We haven't had any *serious* unnatural activity in over a decade," Pemberton says. "You can do well enough with six agents. And that other Hound agent you have—what's her name; the Indian? She'll do, I suppose."

"Agent Khurana," I correct, without thinking.

"What do you need more than one Hound for, anyway?" he continues, as if I hadn't spoken.

I bite the inside of my lip. No male agent can summon a Hound, and the demons themselves are always female. Their high-tuned senses and their ability to detect the unique energy that other demons emit make them invaluable. Having only two is challenging enough; going down to one would be impossible.

Not to mention that if Turner *and* her demon were retired, there'd be no need for an apprentice. I'd be back in the workhouse breaking my back and choking on cotton, and this time with no Monaghan to pluck me out. I subtly wipe my palms on my skirt.

The professor looks over his shoulder at Tiberius. Without a word exchanged, the demon gets up and pads to the door. He opens it and murmurs something to the assistant, Miller. The study is no more than fifteen feet in width and breadth, even with the overflowing bookcases lining the walls, and Tiberius has no difficulty moving around the perimeter.

"I've asked Turner to join us," Monaghan says. "She can tell us what evidence she has so far. If there is none, I will assign her to another case. Even if we *are* experiencing a lull, we cannot afford to give away good agents."

Pemberton doesn't look appeased, and I can't entirely blame him. Hound demons are of little use after the first few days of a murder. By then, any trace of the demon would have been overridden by the comings and goings of the local community. In the East End of London, that time might be shortened to a few hours. If Turner was still investigating after three weeks, she must have found something worth pursuing. Or she was just being stubborn.

Knowing Turner, I suspect the latter.

Tiberius returns to his spot in the corner, brushing against Pemberton as he goes. The man flinches and Monaghan throws the demon a warning look. Tiberius leans against the window overlooking the gas-lit street and looks placidly back.

I know better than to give him the same look, but I want to. The last thing we need is to antagonise the Secretary, and being taunted by the agency's most powerful demon is not going to set him at ease.

"You're retiring another agent soon, aren't you?" Pemberton asks, his voice shrewd.

Monaghan nods as if he'd expected this. "Agent Stewart. Horner is his apprentice; he'll take on the demon. We will carry out the transfer this evening, in fact. Reaper demons are the best we have," he adds, as the Secretary opens his mouth, "and Tiberius is constrained to my side in London. We need him."

Monaghan had sent a request to the Home Office to recruit another Reaper. The word had come back an hour later; a polite but firm 'no'.

A knock comes before Pemberton can argue the point. Turner sweeps in without waiting for an invitation. Her grey hair is scraped into a bun, like mine, and the lines around her eyes are visibly strained. Behind her comes Lavender, pale and severe in a high-collared black dress. Lavender's gaze snags on the Secretary. She looks at me and her thin mouth quirks. My own softens, though I'm too tightly wound to return the smile.

Turner flounces into the centre of the study and shakes out her skirt so it folds gracefully over her wide hips. "Well?" she demands, raising her chin. "I'm quite busy, Monaghan, so this had better be good."

I can't help it; I cough into my fist to cover a snort. Lavender comes to stand beside me. As tall as the demon is, I'm taller than her by three inches. But then, I dwarf everyone. I was the only one in my family to inherit my father's height. Advantageous in a son, shameful in a daughter.

"Agent Turner." The title is almost a rebuke and I wince on Turner's behalf. She doesn't seem to hear it. "This is the Legal Secretary, Mr. Edward Leigh Pemberton."

She turns on the man and her gaze sharpens into a glare as he remains sitting. Pemberton reddens and lurches to his feet. "Ma'am," he says, reaching for a hat that isn't there.

She greets him with a nod. "I assume you want an update on the case?"

That needles Pemberton. "I have an update on the case from Commissioner Warren. All possible leads are being pursued."

"That's a lot of words to say the good Commissioner doesn't *have* any leads," Turner replies.

I wince again. If Monaghan's goal in summoning her was to further Pemberton's cause, it's working.

"We'd like to know what evidence you have to believe in demonic involvement." Monaghan regards Turner with steady eyes, the green dulled by the oil lamp on his desk. "The Secretary has some concerns."

"No doubt," she replies, tartly. "*I'd* be concerned if there was a murderer ripping up my city."

"*Turner*. What progress have you made?"

She puts her hands on her hips and sighs. "It's a tricky one. Whatever stabbed poor Martha has gone to ground. Lavender's not had much luck hunting him."

"But you remain on the case?"

"I'm not going to give up as easily as that. That's not what we do, is it?"

Pemberton stops listening. "This murder has already caused enough unrest. If we're to find the killer—the *human* killer," he says, with a sideways glance at Turner, "then the police need to be given the freedom to continue their investigations without being disturbed."

"Perhaps some disturbance might get them to work harder," Turner interjects.

"We do not need demons stalking through the streets causing havoc."

"Yes," Turner says, sarcastically, "Lavender is clearly a force of evil."

Despite Lavender's age—advanced, even for a demon—her slender frame and narrow waist is the height of fashion. With my height, my freckles and my unfashionable yellow hair, *I* am more likely to draw attention than she is.

"You have no definitive evidence that a demon committed this murder?" Monaghan asks, quietly redirecting the conversation.

Turner sucks her teeth. "No," she admits. "Not yet."

Pemberton snorts. "The East End is in a precarious state. This murder has tipped it towards unrest. If it slides any further, we'll have a riot on our hands. I have to balance the needs of the city, Monaghan. Let the police do their job. And consider what I said about retirement."

Turner's eyes flash. She says nothing, though, perhaps sensing how close to the limit Pemberton is.

I find I'm kneading the folds of my wool skirt and clasp my fingers together instead. Lavender tilts her head towards me as if scenting my nerves. Perhaps she does; I don't yet know the limits of a Hound's nose, if there are any.

"Turner," Monaghan says, "stay at the agency and await my orders. Hand over any relevant case notes to Miss Locke to file."

"Professor—"

He lowers his head fractionally; enough to silence Turner.

"I'm glad we could see eye to eye on this, Monaghan," Pemberton says. He offers his hand, and the professor stands to shake it.

"Of course, sir. I'm happy to assist as best I can."

Pemberton picks up his hat and gloves, nods at Turner and me, and departs, leaving the door open behind him.

Monaghan eyes it for a moment, then looks at Turner. "If you haven't discovered anything by now, you're unlikely to."

"Lavender will find the killer," she replies. "We just need more time."

"We must pick our battles, Turner." The words carry the ring of repetition. "Better that you come off the case now, before the Secretary presses me for the alternative."

The woman exhales, her expression rigid. "If we keep losing the battles, professor, we won't stand a chance in the war." She strides from the room, taking Lavender with her.

Monaghan takes a minute to smooth out a crease in his jacket sleeve, frowning. "Take whatever notes she has, if she has any," he advises, finally. "And get her to drop the case. I do not wish to retire her. Or you," he adds, with a tired smile.

I can't return it. The workhouse doesn't need girls who can read Latin or crack a Caesar's code. Without the agency, I'm nothing.

"Yes, sir," I reply. "I'll do my best."

He glances over his shoulder at the dark window. "I had better ensure that Pemberton has left, before we get started," he says. "I will meet you downstairs shortly."

I curtsy, the closest thing to a salute Monaghan will permit, and hurry after Turner.

CHAPTER TWO

The ground floor of the agency teems with activity: two of our three regional agents and their demons have come to London for the ritual. Promoting a Reaper agent is an important moment. And a dangerous one.

Everyone clusters around the grandiose doors that lead to the underground room where we perform the ritual. The wood shimmers with latent magical energy, remnants of hundreds of spells performed over hundreds of years; a violent death to anyone who tries to open it without the key.

I find Turner with Agent Stewart and Jacob, close to the doors. Stewart clucks his tongue soothingly while Jacob paces like a spooked horse.

"I can't help it," the apprentice says, his hands flashing in pale punctuation as he talks. "What if something goes wrong? What if it doesn't work? What if it doesn't stick?"

"Don't worry," Turner says, her voice taking on the matronly air she reserves for small children and young men. "Stupider men than you have gone through this ritual, and they've all succeeded, so you've got nothing to worry about."

"Um, thank you?"

"That's not helpful," Stewart mutters. "You'll be all right, Horner."

Jacob rubs at his temples, dislodging his mop of dark blond hair, and doesn't reply.

"Turner," I interrupt. "Can I speak to you for a moment?"

"Of course," she replies, and I draw her out of earshot of the others. Lavender trails after us, close enough to Turner to stay within the boundaries of their bond.

"I spoke to the professor," I begin.

"He sent you to persuade me not to do anything stupid, didn't he?"

"He's worried about what the Home Office will do," I reply, in a quieter voice than the one she used. "They're threatening to retire you."

"It's been almost a month since the last time they did that," she says. "I was starting to think they'd given up."

Lavender folds her hands at the small of her back, and casts Turner an arch glance. "Perhaps you could try *not* antagonising their workforce."

"I have no patience for stupidity."

I try again. "He asked me—"

"To get me to drop the case," Turner interrupts. "I'm sure he did. And I'm *also* sure that we have better things to do right now than talk about work. This is Horner's night."

"But earlier, you said—"

"Ah," she says, cutting me off a second time as the professor approaches with the key. "Here's Monaghan. About bloody time, too. Shall we?"

"Turner—" My voice disappears into a babble of noise as all the agents, demons and apprentices fall in behind Monaghan. Turner doesn't—or pretends not to—hear me. Sighing, I shelve the conversation for later.

The ritual room spreads under the entirety of the building, and the tunnel that leads down to it has a low, arched ceiling. I hold my breath as I descend.

As head of the agency, Monaghan leads the way with Tiberius. Jacob goes next, as the focus of the ritual, with Stewart and his demon Maximus. No one begrudges the Reaper second place—it's difficult not to respect a demon who can lift a horse over his head with one hand. Next are the Phantom agents; Dominic Rayne and his demon Cassius as vanguard, then the regional agents, Moss for Scotland and Peters for the North, with their Phantom demons. Each of them will return to their hub in the morning, enabling the agency to reach every corner of Britain. Only Williamson, our agent for the West, isn't here.

The Hounds come last; Khurana, her demon, Isis, and her apprentice, Eve, and then Turner, Lavender and I to bring up the rear.

Pebbles clatter over stone. "For god's sake," Turner mutters. "They could have put some lamps down here. Are we so hard done by we can't afford new oil?"

"Peace," Lavender says. In the gloom, I just make out the demon looping her arm under Turner's, supporting her. "Look, we're nearly there."

"One of these days someone is going to fall and break their neck. Or maybe that's the idea," Turner says, her voice dripping with irony, "get rid of us old folk so they can bring in new stock."

"I doubt that's Monaghan's intention," I mutter, but all thought of Monaghan and the Secretary fades from my mind as the narrow passage opens up. I exhale and my breath frosts the air in front of my face. And not just from the cold: a strange, heavy aura hangs in the room.

The chamber is wide, its cracked stone walls shadowed beyond the reach of the torches that are fastened to thick columns in a circle wide enough to contain fifty people. My heels thud softly on the floor: packed earth instead of hard flagstones.

Tiberius finishes lighting the torches and Jacob goes to the centre of the room with Stewart and Maximus. The demon holds himself with wary stillness; the torchlight turns his tawny skin amber and his sable hair bronze.

I examine the floor to keep from noticing how wan Jacob looks. Most of the stone is bare except for the large round space within the columns. There, scarlet shapes stain the earth, loops and angles and symbols that look like writing, but a language I've never seen before. A crimson pentacle surrounds the glyphs, far more faded than the rest: the foundation of the ritual. At its centre sits a large, shallow bowl.

The agents spread out between the columns, encircling Maximus and the two agents; a barrier should something go wrong. I check for Eve and find her standing behind her agent. Khurana's thick glossy braid hangs over her shoulder. Even in the torchlight her large grey eyes are startling against her brown skin and straight brows. Her white-haired demon is a ghost in the shadows, alabaster skin stark against her black bodice and skirts. Both of them watch Maximus.

Old records speak of the agency's first attempts at the summons ritual: one ended with an escaped demon and his prospective agent in bloody pieces all over the floor. Another resulted in the deaths of half a dozen agency members. Fewer pieces; the demon ate most of them. That was nearly three hundred years ago, though. Now, the precautions are just that: precautions.

Somehow, the reminder isn't very reassuring.

Low whispers catch my attention. Agent Peters stands near the door, but Clara is with him. The maid murmurs something to him from behind her hand. How did she get in here?

I look at Turner, who makes a cutting motion with her hand. "Leave her," she says. "If she wants to worm her way in here, let her. Maybe we'll get lucky, and *she'll* get eaten."

Lavender tuts but says nothing.

I suppose Clara has to know what to expect. Unlike male agents, who are recruited as apprentices, the agency takes on women as maids, first. A way to get around the Home Office's regulations and to accustom us to the supernatural more gradually, which is apparently something female agents need.

Eventually, it'll be Clara's turn to take up the role of Hound agent. Whether she'll be replacing me or Eve, I don't know. Nor do I care to imagine.

Small stone plinths cluster around the northernmost column, each crowned with a handful of black ritual bags. The velvet on some has frayed, and others are merely a shard of bone where the bag and the components have rotted away over the years. Jacob crosses the bloodwriting to pick up his, and the tension in the room thickens.

I hug the nearest column, my breath in my throat. It *will* work.

He returns and stands by the bowl, within the northern spike of the pentacle, back straight and head high.

"Good lad," says Turner. "Don't let them smell your fear."

I'm not sure if *them* is supposed to mean the demons, or the agents.

He gives a jerky nod, and Agent Stewart stands by the bowl not far from him. Maximus joins them, until they each stand within three of the five prongs of the pentacle.

"Do get on with it," someone in the ring mutters. Rayne, I realise, sparing him a glance. The Phantom agent looks bored, his thin brows arched and his eyes lidded. Cassius leans against a column beside him, not even looking at the ritual. In the flickering torchlight, the demon's red hair looks like blood. He catches my gaze with his ice blue eyes, and smirks. I look away quickly.

Stewart leans over the bowl and makes a sharp movement. The tinder in the urn sparks, and, within minutes, flames lick up the sides of the brass basin. The agents around me stay silent, waiting. The fire leaps higher and Agent Stewart creeps back a little. Jacob does not move.

Good. Maximus hasn't moved, either, and he watches Jacob with a level expression. I hope Jacob's three years as an apprentice has been enough to earn the demon's trust.

Monaghan has his gaze on his pocket watch. We wait, and after a while he nods. Jacob holds the ritual bag over the fire. His mouth moves, but with the crackle of the fire I can't make out the words of the spell.

The spell components tumble into the flames. Orange-red shimmers to white, then yellow, then back to orange-red. The faint scent of flowers permeates the air.

Beneath Jacob's feet, the crimson symbols glow. Softly, and barely visible with the torches all lit. But I see it. My breath hangs in the air like a cloud of tiny snowdrops. I shiver and pull my wool jacket tighter around me.

Across the room, Jacob shudders. A jolt of fear goes through me; if he stops partway through the ritual, disrupts it... But he straightens, and relief ripples through the circle of agents. I look at Turner.

She gives a short, satisfied nod. "He did well. Best we get upstairs, now, let the magic dissipate." She hustles me out of the circle towards the passage.

Other agents follow, walking slowly but steadily away from the markings. I hesitate and glance back. Khurana and Rayne flank Maximus with their demons. The Reaper does not look perturbed, and strides with us back to the agency. I look for Jacob, but then we're in the tunnel and I have to concentrate on my feet.

It's a tense walk that only seems to take a few seconds. Turner emerges first and the rest of us spill into the hall. I stand out of the way.

Eve joins me. Her springy black curls are pulled into a loose bun and she's taken care with her dress, choosing the dove grey that brings out the warmth in her deep brown skin. "That was anticlimactic," she murmurs. "Was it supposed to end like that?"

"It hasn't ended yet." Now comes the hard part; the test that will determine if the spell is in place. The test to confirm that Maximus is safe, that even under attack he would never hurt an agent.

Rayne and Khurana take Maximus into the dining hall, out of sight. Jacob follows. He's biting his lip, the skin white under his teeth. Stewart goes in last, his expression downcast. Once this test is complete, he won't be an agent any longer. A pang of sympathy goes through me. Monaghan and Tiberius go in last, closing the door behind them.

"I'll keep my fingers crossed," Eve mutters.

The group in the lobby dissipates, each regional agent and their detachment heading upstairs, back to their quarters. The test is always private, witnessed only by those with the skill and experience to subdue the demon in case he breaks free.

"You were gone for a while," Eve adds. "What did Monaghan want?"

I tell her about the Secretary, about the professor's orders, and she huffs.

"The Home Office will never shut us down. They can't afford to. If they were to get rid of every agent in the country, they'd be overrun by demons. And they know that very well. They just want to keep us on a short leash." Given the lack of prominent demonic cases over the last few years, I'm not sure the Home Office see it the same way.

I change the subject, unwilling to think about the consequences Pemberton had threatened. "Are you and Khurana staying in London?"

Eve smooths a few strands of her curly hair and shakes her head. "We're going to Bristol in the morning. The local police force found a body in the river."

"Murder?"

"Yes, but—worse." Eve looks grim and I brace myself. "Infanticide."

I close my eyes momentarily. No wonder they're sending Khurana; Monaghan will want the best. "The water will have done a number on the body," I say. Perhaps I should be offering comfort instead of pointing out the decaying state of the corpse, but it's the first thing I think of.

Eve nods, used to our macabre conversations. "I'm going to look at a map, see if I can track the location back to a crime scene." Her smile returns, dimmer than it normally is. "At least it's a case; a *real* case. All we've had lately are assaults and rumours. I can't wait to work on something important."

"If you need any help..." I offer.

"I'll be fine."

The door to the dining room opens, cutting short any further conversation. Khurana and Isis emerge, unruffled, and walk past us. Rayne and Cassius follow and I hold my breath until Jacob appears. He looks as though he could be blown over by a stiff wind.

"It worked," he says, with a shaky smile. He's supporting Maximus, who looks even worse.

The professor looms behind him. "Well done, Agent Horner."

"Thank you, sir."

"Normally I'd assign you an apprentice straight away," he continues, "but I don't think it's right that you get one before Rayne does. You'll have to wait, I'm afraid."

Jacob bobs his head. "Of course."

"Make sure you get some rest." Monaghan pats him on the shoulder and leaves with Tiberius.

I frown. "You're more likely to need an apprentice than Rayne is. We have other Phantoms, but if something happens to you—"

"I just became an agent, Hazel, I don't want to think about dying yet," he says, not without humour. "Besides, I don't mind. Domin—Rayne's been here longer than I have. Come on," he adds, to Maximus. The demon looks dazzled, and blood stains his shirtfront. "Let's get you upstairs." He wraps one arm around Maximus as though the Reaper is a doddering grandmother and escorts him from the room.

"I'll go with them," Eve tells me. Before I can follow, Turner marches out of the lobby, towards the entrance that leads to Temple Avenue and Blackfriars Bridge.

"See you later," I tell Eve, then pivot and lengthen my stride to reach Turner. Lavender pauses as I reach them and lets me dart in front. "Are you going back to Whitechapel?" I ask.

"Are you going to tell me that I shouldn't?" she counters.

"Monaghan wants you to stay here."

"I heard him." Turner's voice holds the brisk tone that masks her frustration. "A woman has been stabbed to death and all that lot seem to care about is the comfort of their officers. If they cared more about getting the job done, we might have caught the killer by now."

"I don't disagree," I reply, "but Monaghan's right: it's been three weeks. What can we do?"

"I intend to find out."

"I can take down your findings," I suggest. "Whatever you've already got. I'll write a report and we can give it to the police. They can take it from here."

Turner's mouth pinches. Her ruddy cheeks are pale, and I wonder if she's been eating. "There is work to do. I'm not wasting my time taking bloody notes."

My face grows hot.

Lavender pats my arm. "The report can wait," she says, in her gentle voice. "We promise we won't disturb the authorities."

"Speak for yourself," Turner mutters.

The Hound shrugs daintily. "Besides, it's just us. No Phantoms or Reapers to get in the way. Or report back," she adds, her eyes twinkling.

"You shouldn't be working on a case alone," I object, but I can predict Turner's response before it comes.

"The last thing we need is one of the boys getting in our way." She snatches an umbrella from the stand by the door and tucks it under her arm. "Once they learn that us *dogs* can handle our own cases, we'll all be better off. And we might actually solve a few, for a change," she says, with a bitterness that has never waned, even in the seven years I've worked for her. "You need to look at the bigger picture, Locke," she continues. "Monaghan has to balance the whims of the Home Office with the dangers that we face on a daily basis. It's not an easy thing to do, but it's something you'll need to learn to be a good field agent."

I nod, not entirely sure how to learn that but tucking away the words to dwell on later. Other agents sit their apprentices down and talk them through a lesson from beginning to end. Turner drops pearls of knowledge in my path and leaves me to pick them up. At least, I hope they're pearls.

"Besides, I might have something." She raises a hand as I open my mouth. "Before you tell me what I should and should not be reporting to my superiors, I said I *might* have something. It might be nothing, but we'll only find out when we know something."

I frown as I attempt to parse that. "What kind of something?"

"There's a regiment of Coldstream Guards near Whitechapel. Get me background on the officers there—ties to the agency, paranormal run-ins, skeletons in the ancestral closet—the usual."

There'd been something about the guards in the papers, a week ago, but I can't recall what. It wasn't a priority, then. "When do you need it by?" I ask, reluctantly. This is not how the conversation was supposed to go.

"Couple of days. Can you handle that?"

"Of course I can."

She smirks, and I realise the jibe had been deliberate. "Glad to hear it."

"What about the professor?" I ask, unable to shake the meeting from my mind. "If he finds out you're still on the case—or if Pemberton finds out—"

"You're worrying again," Turner cuts in. "What did I tell you?"

"Right," I reply, sighing. "The bigger picture."

"Monaghan will be occupied with regional placements for the next few days," Lavender says. "He won't notice one apprentice doing a little research."

Turner's always flirted with authority but she's never gone against a direct order before. And neither have I.

Turner thwacks me on the arm affectionately. "I'll be back soon." She sweeps out of the door without saying goodbye.

"When exactly are you returning?" I ask Lavender.

"You know Turner; 'soon' could be a few days or a few weeks." She's drifting towards the door, Turner's pace drawing the invisible tether between them taut. "I'll try to make it the former. I would prefer not to stay in Whitechapel for long." Another fond smile and Lavender floats out of the door after Turner.

When they're gone, I head for the stairs. We have regiment records in the agency library, everything from the last government census to genealogy records. I'll start now. Get it over with.

"Miss Locke."

I stiffen. "Professor Monaghan."

He meets me as I ascend, immaculate in his three-piece suit and ivory cravat. Tiberius follows, less dignified in an open jacket and wool trousers.

"I'm pleased the ritual went well," he says. He looks it; a line of strain I hadn't realised was there is gone, and his stance is loose, relaxed. Stewart is nearing fifty, his reflexes slowing with age. It must have been a lot of pressure, the fear of losing him. "I expect Jacob is delighted," he adds.

"He is," I agree. "He was very nervous."

"No doubt. And you; I assume Turner has something else for you to work on?"

It comes so quickly after Turner's order that I wonder if he suspects. I take a deep breath, as if I'm being deliberate with my answer. If I tell him the truth, either Monaghan will punish her, or he'll be forced to lie to Pemberton. If Monaghan doesn't know, then at least he can claim ignorance if he's asked.

That's what I tell myself.

"She does," I say. "I'm investigating a potential lead on a London case. Nothing to disclose yet."

He nods. "Send me your report when it's ready."

"Yes, sir."

He continues on his way and I climb past Tiberius, who doesn't give me a second glance. The lie sits heavily in my chest. If there's one thing Monaghan values, it's honesty.

I hope Turner's right.

CHAPTER THREE

The morning dawns foggy and cold, the first real autumnal day. I dart out of bed and shiver when my feet touch the icy floor. It's too early for the fire to have been lit; the apprentice rooms are always left until last. I wash quickly and pull on my drawers under my nightgown, then throw that off and hastily don a chemise and my blouse and skirt. When I'm buttoning my jacket and can spare a thought beyond getting warm, I realise that Eve's bed is empty; only a bottle of hair oil and a stack of dog-eared penny dreadfuls to tell me she was here. I make my bed and step around the two unoccupied bunks to the door.

I find Eve in the kitchen, surrounded by papers. Her eyes are red-rimmed, and a lamp sits on the table, burnt to the wick. The sky through the window is overcast and even the large kitchen fire doesn't do much to brighten the room.

"Have you been up all night?" I ask.

"I have to finish this map before we leave," she replies, her forehead in her palm as she stares down at the paper. Her fingernails are jagged and torn.

"Do you need any help?"

"I do not need help." The words come with a snap. I pause, and she sighs and rubs her face. "Forgive me. I'm just tired. Khurana...she's relying on me."

"You work harder than any other apprentice," I say, indicating the collection of plans and diagrams spread out over the table. "Than any *agent*. Khurana would never be disappointed."

"I have to work ten times harder than anyone else just so they take me seriously," Eve replies, glaring at her map. "Otherwise, they look at me and see..." She stops and flops her hands on the table with a sigh.

I can imagine what she was going to say. Eve has the features of her Ghanaian mother. Beautiful features, but some people only see beauty when it reflects their own face. Not that Eve cares a fig for beauty; the work has always come first.

"Monaghan wouldn't have recruited you if he thought you couldn't do this," I tell her.

"It's not Monaghan I want to impress."

I want to say the same for Khurana, but at the end of the day they're just words, they don't mean much. "If I can't help," I say, "can I at least make you some tea?" Tea might not fix everything, but it's a good start.

Eve smiles at me. "That would be lovely."

Maia has tea leaves in small tin canisters in the larder, a different canister for each blend. Some are British, some come from China, and some she brought with her from India years ago. Those she dishes out only on special occasions. One of the Chinese jasmine blends is particularly delicious, and Eve needs something delicious this morning. Hoping Maia forgives me for the expense, I set about brewing a pot.

Eve and I are halfway through our cups by the time Jacob sneaks in. Sneaks, as though he's a serving boy trying to steal a biscuit. Maximus comes with him.

I tense in surprise. Agents and their demons don't come to the kitchen unless they need something.

"Is that the jasmine blend?" he asks.

"There's some left in the pot."

He helps himself, pouring the tea through a strainer. Then, to my surprise, he turns to the demon. "Would you like some?"

Maximus hesitates. His gaze flicks to me and Eve. After a moment, he nods, and Jacob pours him a cup. The demon accepts it with grace, cradling the porcelain carefully in his large hands. His nails are pointed and much darker than his skin. Talons.

I return my gaze to Jacob. "How was your night?"

He sits on the bench opposite. "It went well," he replies, seeming to understand what I mean. Maximus stands behind him, a gap of six feet between them, holding his tea with both hands. Jacob turns his head and pats the bench beside him. "Come sit down, Max."

My brows soar up. "Max?"

Jacob flushes and shifts in his seat. "Well, Maximus is such a mouthful, you know, and I didn't get to name him. I asked what he would prefer, and he said he was happy with Max."

I stare at the demon, who folds onto the bench without looking up. He's only a little taller than Jacob, but he has the same broad, muscled build as Tiberius. It's a sign that they're getting along, surely, if this big demon is letting Jacob call him by a diminutive.

"Max," I repeat. "Pleased to meet you."

The demon glances at me shyly and my expression softens. No wonder Jacob wanted to give him a name with less historical weight.

"Do you have orders yet?" I ask, and Jacob shakes his head.

"Nothing. I thought I'd teach Max how to play whist. Would you like to play with us?"

I'm smiling, now, and I see Eve trying to suppress one as she studies. "No, thank you."

"When are you heading to Bristol?" he asks Eve.

"Less than an hour," she replies. "So, no whist for me, either."

"Just as well," Jacob says, "you still owe me from our last match."

Eve raises a single finger, not looking up. "I maintain that you cheated."

"I did not cheat. You're a sore loser."

"There's no such thing. You either win, or you lose. If I'd won, you wouldn't have called me a sore winner, would you?"

"I might have, if you went on about it the way you did when you lost."

"If you keep on like that, I'll have to beat you again."

"Are you sure you mean *again*? Were you dreaming when you beat me the first time?"

Max watches this back and forth as though he's been transported to a country where he doesn't understand the language.

"Good morning." Maia sweeps into the room, tying her apron. She eyes the four of us. "Breakfast?"

Jacob dimples at her. "Yes, please."

"Would you like some help?" I ask.

Maia pushes her headscarf back with her wrist, letting a few grey-black hairs escape to fall against her weathered cheek. She gives me her don't-be-ridiculous look. "Boiling eggs? I think that I can manage."

"Thank you, Maia."

"Yes, well, I know you will eat it, at least. If the professor sends me back one more full plate, I will go up there and force feed him myself." She slaps down a tray of fresh brown eggs and glares at them as though they'd insulted her personally.

"He must be meeting with the Secretary." The others glance at me. "He never eats when he meets someone from the Home Office," I explain. Eve gives me a narrow look and I flush.

"He should not meet the man so often, then," Maia grumbles.

Our young runner jogs into the room, his broad face dusty but wearing a grin. "Mornin', Miss Bhatt."

"You are late, Mister Doyle."

"Sorry, Miss. The Prof wanted to read through the 'eadlines. I had to wait for 'im to finish before I could get copies out. 'Ere they are: *Times, Chronicle,* and the *Standard.*" He hands her a stack of newspapers and takes the tuppence she gives him in return.

"Do not be late again. What do I bribe you for if not to be here early?"

Doyle salutes cheekily. "Pleasure doin' business with ya, Miss Bhatt." He tosses another grin in our direction and lopes away.

Maia spreads out the newspapers on her table. Bigger cases usually show up in the paper within a day of the crime, and sometimes it's quicker to read the report from *The Times* than to wait for the police to let us in on the case.

The housekeeper goes still. The kind of still that makes my muscles go rigid. "What is it?"

Wordlessly she drops a newspaper on the table. We all hunch over it to read.

HORRIBLE MURDER IN WHITECHAPEL

Scarcely has the horror and sensation caused by the discovery of the murdered woman in Whitechapel some short time ago had time to abate, than another discovery is made, which; for the brutality exercised on the victim, is even more shocking, and will no doubt create as great a sensation in the vicinity as its predecessor. The affair, up to the present, is enveloped in complete mystery, and the police have as yet no evidence to trace the perpetrators of the horrible deed.

"Another one," Eve mutters, and Jacob sits back, shaking his head.

I pull the paper closer and read on. Another woman, dead, found in the early hours of yesterday morning with her throat cut and her lower body ripped open. I file away the injuries in a section of my mind that is not appalled at the words I'm reading, that is already considering how the thing was done.

The woman was wearing workhouse clothes when she was murdered. As though it isn't enough for workers to slave away every day of their life in fear of what happens if they do not, now they must fear the streets as well.

"Have you seen Turner?" I ask, looking up.

Maia's face is taut, her mouth held tightly. I forget, sometimes, that Maia and Clara aren't agents themselves. They aren't used to the things the rest of us see on a daily basis. "No," she replies. "She has not returned yet."

Terror sweeps through me. Turner had been in Whitechapel, what if she—

No, the murder was yesterday morning. Too early. Then she must have heard, by now; she must be working the case. If it's not *already* her case. It can't be a coincidence that two horrific murders happened less than a month apart, surely?

Tabram's murder was nothing like this, though. This...mutilation the paper references, this wasn't Tabram's fate.

"How could someone do this?" Jacob murmurs. "What kind of monster would take someone's life and then...and then...?" He trails off, no words to put to the horror described in the newspaper.

"Turner thinks the first murder was connected to a demon," I say. "This would support that theory."

Maia brings us plates of eggs and sliced bread. Jacob grimaces, his skin shaded with a grey cast, and waves it away. I have none of his delicacy, and I eat quickly.

"I thought she was off the case," Eve says, digging into her meal with pragmatism.

"She was. More or less."

I finish eating. If Monaghan's seen the headlines, he'll want to know that Turner's still on the case. Hopefully he'll overlook the fact that I lied to him about it.

"I'm going to see the professor," I tell the others.

"I'll be here if he needs me," Jacob says, wryly. Reapers are called in to remove a target, so unless we have a suspect confirmed, it's unlikely he'll be needed, and he knows as much.

I nod anyway, reassured at the offer.

"I'm leaving in a few minutes," Eve adds. "Come say goodbye when you're done."

I make my way quickly through the agency, my boot heels clacking against the stone. The day has cast off its chill and sweat prickles at the back of my neck and under my arms, part heat and part nerves. Homicide cases in London are normally small, single incidents; a Sentinel gone rogue or a Blood Drinker who thought they could get away with draining a body in the crowded capital. None of them like this.

The professor's assistant, Miller, is already at his desk outside the main office. He glances up when I arrive. "Purpose?" he snaps. I hope his irritability is due to Monaghan turfing him out of bed at dawn rather than any specific grudge against me.

"The Whitechapel murder. *Murders*," I correct.

He nods and waves me in. Monaghan is fully dressed, although his demon is still in shirtsleeves. I avert my gaze.

The professor notices. "Tiberius, put on your jacket," he orders. The demon does as bid without comment. "My apologies, Miss Locke. It has been a long morning." Newspapers are spread over his desk, the article I read earlier lying front and centre.

"It's not a problem, sir."

He sits behind the desk and lays his hands on the papers, though I have his whole attention. "How can I help you?"

I pause and consider my words. Perhaps it would be better to see his state of mind before I reveal the truth. "Have you read the article?"

"I have. A nasty business. And following so soon after the first murder…" He gestures me to the chair in front of his desk and I take a seat, folding my hands in my lap. "The nature of this one might indicate a demon is at fault. I've not seen horror like this for some time." His gaze drops to a framed photo that is turned away from me and he doesn't elaborate. I stay quiet, but I try to express sympathy in my expression. "I want an agent in there," he mutters.

"Has the Office invited us to attend the inquest?"

"Not yet, though I expect a letter today." He drums his fingers on the paper. "What about Turner?" Guilt flashes through me. It must seep into my face: Monaghan leans both elbows on the desk and sighs. "You had better tell me all of it."

"Turner went to stay in Whitechapel for a few days," I admit readily. "She thought there might be a lead in the Coldstream regiment based near there. She asked me to investigate any links to the paranormal among their officers."

"When does she return from the East End?"

"I don't know. She didn't say."

"I see." His expression doesn't change, but Tiberius shifts and looks away. Sometimes the demon seems a better reflection of the professor's emotions than his own face; I wonder if that's a result of the spell that binds them or merely a side effect of their thirteen years of partnership. "Do you know where she's staying?"

I shift in my own seat. "I don't. She—"

"Didn't say?" he finishes. "No, she rarely does. Very well. Sit tight for now, and don't go into Whitechapel. Until we have an established presence there, I don't want any agents going in alone. Especially not..." He trails off.

"My gender makes me a target," I guess.

"Exactly." He taps his fingers on the desk. "I have a dinner tonight with some members of the House of Lords. I will find out what I can about the current state of the investigation. Turner will return soon," he adds, reassuringly. "She always does."

I nod. Monaghan turns his attention to the newspapers, so I rise and show myself out.

Frustration thrums through my blood. I won't be much use to Turner or the victims sitting at the agency. But what else can I do? Even if I was allowed into Whitechapel, I wouldn't know where to start. I have little choice but to stay where I'm ordered. I push it to the back of my mind.

Eve is in the lobby, struggling with a valise in one hand and a stack of reports in the other. Khurana and Isis are deep in conversation with Maia, no doubt saying their own farewells.

"Let me," I say, taking the valise. I know better than to touch the reports. Eve grins at me, as if reading my mind. "Are you taking a coach?"

"It's outside, come on." In the street a hansom carriage waits, its horses stamping with impatience. "Maia got a telegram while you were with the professor," Eve explains, hefting the reports. "Williamson wants discharge records for the London asylums."

"He thinks the target was committed?" I keep my voice low, mindful of the driver perched atop the coach like a raven.

She helps me lash the valise to the rear of the coach. "It's a theory. A good one, I think, given the youth of the victim."

I think of what she told me last night. A case like this won't be easy. I don't envy her.

Khurana and Isis emerge and Eve pulls her bonnet down, tying the ribbons in a quick messy knot under her chin. I sigh and reach out to tug the ends into a bow. "Be careful," I order. With Khurana, she's as safe as the rest of us, but having either Jacob or Eve out of London always makes worry twist in the pit of my stomach.

"I'm always careful." Eve hops into the coach before Khurana, winks at me, then slides over to the far corner.

I step back respectfully as the agent and her demon sweep past. Khurana spares me little more than a glance, but Isis' light blue eyes examine my expression, as though she sees something there worth suspicion. I give a shallow curtsy, dropping my gaze, and the demon moves past me.

When they enter, Khurana gives a sharp word to the driver, and he whips up his horses. They ramble off in the direction of the station, and I turn back to the building.

Inside, Maia has been replaced by Rayne. "Was that Khurana, leaving?" he asks.

"Yes. *Sir*," I add. Rayne is the highest-ranking Phantom agent. He prefers that apprentices demonstrate respect.

"Where did she go?"

"Bristol, sir. She's joining Williamson on a case."

"I see." His mouth forms a moue of distaste or disappointment. With Khurana gone, he'll have to work with Turner if he needs a Hound. Perhaps he isn't happy about that.

Loyalty to Turner makes me draw my shoulders back and look down at him. But internally, I can't help but agree. As a

Hound agent, Khurana never works alone, but when the number of solved cases is tallied, it's always Khurana's name that ends up on top. Though she's not a man, her record is so good most of us think Monaghan will name her his heir. Except Rayne. He still thinks she can be beaten.

"Let me know when they come back, won't you?" He doesn't wait for an answer.

His lanky, red-headed demon slinks up to me. "Yes," Cassius murmurs, a smirk on his pale lips, "do tell us, won't you, little Hound?" There's a breath more emphasis on the word *little*, and it stings.

I don't react. Words alone can't hurt me. I won't let them.

The refrain seems to have grown less meaningful over the years, or perhaps it's that I'm no longer facing children who might not know their words carry barbs. This demon knows that very well.

He chuckles as he passes me, reading my reaction even as I repress it. I bite the inside of my cheek. *The report*, I remind myself, and get to work. The sting in my chest, however, doesn't ease.

CHAPTER FOUR

It's another day before any word comes out of the Home Office, and when it does it's in the physical form of Edward Leigh Pemberton.

"Miss Locke, isn't it? Is Monaghan in?" he asks, as I curtsy.

"This way, sir." He doesn't need me to direct him—he knows the way—but I'm eager for news. And if the Home Office is sending the Legal Secretary here, in person, there must be news.

I lead him to Monaghan's study on the first floor. Miller looks at me, then at Pemberton, and gets up to announce us. At his nod, I walk inside and stop just in the entrance.

"The Legal Secretary, sir."

Monaghan displays no surprise. "Show him in, Miss Locke, thank you. And you may as well stay. I imagine Agent Turner will want a debrief of this conversation, when she returns."

I step aside and take up a position in the corner, as unobtrusive as possible. The Secretary gives me a look as he enters, one that says he's not happy about the audience. He ignores Tiberius.

"Please have a seat, sir." Pemberton is settled before the sentence is over. The fabric of his jacket pinches over his wide middle. "I assume you're here to discuss the recent developments in Whitechapel," Monaghan continues.

"That's one word for it. I call it cold-blooded murder," the man says, in disgust. His whiskers practically quiver with the force of his words.

Monaghan had stood at our entrance, and he remains standing, his arms clasped behind his back. "I don't disagree. How is the department handling the murder?"

"In the normal way," Pemberton replies. "If you can call anything about this case normal. The CID are working under the Home Office with Commissioner Warren. They've begun interviewing the witnesses, but trouble is, there aren't that many witnesses."

"I understand the inquest will begin on Monday?"

"That's right. Baxter's our coroner."

The name means nothing to me, but Monaghan nods. "Good man."

Pemberton snorts. "If he stops complaining long enough to get the job done. As if we can afford a new morgue in the East End. Really, Monaghan, you wouldn't believe the letters he sends." He goes on for a while, listing the Coroner's evidently sensible complaints.

I let my gaze wander. The Legal Secretary grips the chair's armrest, his thumb moving back and forth against the fine grain of the wood. Nervous, perhaps. Uncomfortable, certainly. I don't know if that's because of the topic of conversation, or because Tiberius stands in the opposite corner, staring at the man.

"Look, Monaghan," Pemberton says, finally. "The Secretary of State has concerns."

"Concerns?" the professor repeats. I think he does well not to colour the word with disbelief.

"The CID think this murder is related to that other woman."

"Martha Tabram."

"Yes, that one. There's no proof yet, but it seems clear that someone—or some *people*—are targeting these unfortunates. The Prime Minister wants to ensure that the Home Office are doing as much as possible to assist in the investigation. You know. The usual drill."

"Of course," Monaghan replies, politely.

I glance at the brass-plated clock on the far wall. It's been fifteen minutes and Pemberton still hasn't come to the point. I stay silent. Just because Monaghan invited me to stay does not mean that he wants or needs my contribution.

"Of course, the Minister asked about your agency," Pemberton continues. "I told him that you're assisting the CID in whatever capacity they need. That you will have agents on the case by the end of the day."

The professor inclines his head. "I will put my best investigative agent on the case."

"And that—that Hound agent, you still have her?"

My skin prickles with awareness and I hold myself still so as to better hear the answer.

"I will put Agent Turner back on the case immediately, sir."

"I hope I don't have to tell you, Monaghan, that your agents need to behave with the utmost discretion. Most of the junior officers in the force have no idea about..." He makes an expansive gesture that incorporates Tiberius and most of the adjacent bookshelf. I think the latter is by accident, although the majority of shelves in this room are laden with lexicons on demons and the paranormal. "Whatever creatures your agents take in with them need to stay out of the public eye."

"I will ensure that my agents are discreet," the professor says in a hard, level voice. "It would not assist our investigation if our true nature were discovered."

Pemberton stands and shakes the professor's hand. "I'll leave you to it, then, Monaghan." He brushes his hand on his trousers as he leaves, less discreetly than he thinks.

I wait for the door to click shut before I speak. "Your orders, sir?"

"Talk to Rayne," he says. "Have him and Cassius attend the police station tomorrow. And tell me when Turner reports in; I want to know as soon as she's back."

"Yes, sir." I hurry out to find Rayne.

Turner will want my Coldstream Guard report when she returns. As I search, I mentally run through my notes, checking for holes or inaccuracies. I can't find any, but I resolve to go over them again tonight, to be sure.

I find Rayne in the morning room, a neat little parlour set up to entertain less formal guests. He lounges by a lit fire, smoking. His demon sits in an armchair, flipping through a book.

"Excuse me, Agent Rayne," I call, stopping in the doorway.

"Yes?" he asks, without getting up.

Cassius abandons whatever book he was pretending to read and watches me. I keep my gaze on Rayne's face. "There's been another murder in Whitechapel. The professor would like you to investigate."

"It's about time." He discards his pipe and stands. In his sleek suit, checked in the same colours as the professor's, he looks as tall as me. He keeps his distance, as if reluctant to test that theory by getting any closer. "Where's Turner?" he asks.

"She's in Whitechapel. I'm...not sure where," I admit, and hate the flush that heats my cheeks. "She had me investigate a lead among the Coldstream regiment. I have a report. I could make you a copy—"

"No, that won't be necessary," he interrupts. "What I want you to do is compile a list of brothels in Whitechapel."

I tilt my chin, regarding him in surprise. "Brothels?"

"And lodging houses, for that matter. Once we have the victim's identity and whereabouts for the last week, I want to know which of those are closest and which have been operating the longest."

It's not a bad idea, but that kind of research will take time, and it's nothing the police aren't already doing. "But the regiment—"

"We can't afford to waste time pursuing vague leads." Rayne gestures to Cassius, who stands and lopes after him. "You'll have that report to me by tomorrow?"

That'll take me all night. I check my irritation and respond in the affirmative.

"Monaghan said you were good," says Rayne, his brows rising at my response. "I admit I didn't believe him. Tomorrow, then." A nod, and he and Cassius are gone before I can react to his backhanded compliment.

I wonder what Turner will think of Rayne dumping her theory for his own and wince. If I start now, I should be able to make a copy of Turner's report anyway, and still compile the information Rayne needs. I'm used to late nights. I make my way to the library, inwardly drafting a few requests to the Department of Records as I walk.

CHAPTER FIVE

S omeone shakes me awake. I rub my eyes. It's dark; the oil lantern on my desk is burnt out, without even a wisp of smoke to say it died recently. A piece of paper sticks to my cheek. I must have fallen asleep in the library.

"Hazel-ji." It's Maia; her hand is warm on my back.

I scrub my face. "Maia." My voice is rough. She hands me a glass of water and I drink it gratefully. "What time is it?" I ask, my throat clearer after the drink.

"A little after three."

I glance at the window: the sky is pitch black. "What's going on?" I ask, sitting upright.

Maia hesitates. "A body has been found in the West India Docks."

"Another murder?" The docks are in east London, but not in Whitechapel. What does that mean for our killer?

"Yes, but...you need to go," Maia says. "You need to help identify the body."

"Why me? Who do they think it is?" A sick feeling explodes in my stomach. I know the answer. It's written in the lines of Maia's face. "It's Turner, isn't it?"

Her lips go white where they press together. She nods. I put my fist to my mouth. I saw Turner a few days ago, more alive, more *vibrant* than ever. She can't be dead.

"Will you go?"

I nod unsteadily. "What about Lavender? Is she here?"

"I do not know. She has not returned. The professor waits downstairs. Can you—will you come?"

I shake myself. All we know at the moment is that a body has been found. Whether it's Turner or not is something we'll have to determine. Then I can worry about what happens next. I just need to hold myself together until we have the facts.

"Yes. Yes, I'll come." I get up and straighten my blouse. Maia has a jacket for me, my navy wool with its close-fitting sleeves. I slip it on, grateful for the warmth; even in early September the nights are cool. At the workhouse, I was lucky to find a scrap of blanket to wrap myself in.

Maia leads me downstairs and waits while I relieve myself and splash water on my face. My eyes, when I look at them in the mirror, are red-rimmed, and the freckles dotting my nose and cheeks stand out in coffee-coloured constellations against my pale skin. I do what I can with my hair, pulling the thick blonde strands into a tight bun, and pinch my cheeks for colour. The overall effect is still a woman who's had far too little sleep, and my broad face reflects my grimace back at me.

We reach the entrance, where Monaghan is standing by the door in a formal black suit and top hat. He must have returned late from his dinner. His arms are straight at his sides, but he rubs his fingers together. Tiberius murmurs something to him and he looks up, sees me.

"Locke," he says. "I'm glad you're here. This isn't going to be easy, if it's true."

Maia hands me a bonnet and I jam it on over my bun. "Who found the body?" I ask, trying to think in terms of what and how and why. Not who. Not yet.

"The dock workers." Monaghan holds the door open for me and I emerge into a chilly breeze. Smog sits above the streets despite the wind, blanketing the city. A coach is waiting, and I spare a thought to be grateful that Monaghan has handled all of these details. I couldn't, not with the way my brain seems untethered from my body.

I climb in first, and Monaghan follows, then Tiberius. I try to think of questions, of what I need to know. My mind is blank. It's all I can do to grip the door of the coach and watch the cobblestones roll by as we make our way east through the city. The streets are quiet save for the occasional shout or loud conversation. As we move further east, the noise increases, and lights spill onto the street from pubs that are still open. We turn off a main road and drive towards the soft rush of the Thames.

The closer we get to the docks, the more I think this must be a mistake. Turner is too quick to be surprised by some thug in the middle of the night. Lavender is too experienced to let her agent be caught by some demon. This isn't Turner's body. This is another Whitechapel victim. It's someone with Turner's hair, or a woman who shares the same name. It's not *my* Turner.

I hear the clang of metal and the cries of the dock. We pull up next to a large warehouse on the bank of the Thames. Black water ripples against the dock walls.

I don't wait for the driver to open the doors. As soon as we stop, I jump out, taking a deep breath. The air is rife with the stench of fish and fuel and the smell of metal.

A handful of policemen loiter at the doors to the warehouse, barring the way against a group of workers. Monaghan gets out of the coach, moving slowly. He sees the police and exhales.

"Come, then," he mutters. "Let's see what needs to be seen." He strides towards them, his greatcoat fluttering behind him. I follow him, my gaze on the warehouse.

"Sir," one of the policemen says, touching the brim of his helmet. "You're the professor?"

"Yes, I'm Monaghan." In the surroundings of the dock warehouse, the professor's shiny top hat and spotless white cravat should look out of place, but somehow, he manages to look as though he spends every evening striding through the dark alleys of London. "You're the officer in charge?"

"Aye. One of the workers found the body and called us in. We found this on her person." The man holds out a thick leather wallet and my breath escapes me.

Monaghan takes it and opens the bifold to reveal a slip of white card. The writing on it is blurred, washed out, but the stamp of the agency and the Home Office seal is stark on the white paper.

"Thought it best to wait until you got here, sir, before alerting the station," the officer says.

"Yes. You did the right thing, Constable." He puts it away with shaking hands. "Can you show us to the body?"

The man hesitates and looks at me. "I don't think it's a sight for a lady, sir, with respect."

"Miss Locke will accompany me to identify the body. If you please, Constable. The night is growing late, and I have much work to do."

The tone in his voice has the constable snapping to attention. "This way, sir."

He leads us into the warehouse. Behind us, the dock workers mutter amongst themselves, a mixture of English and Mandarin. I don't catch much, and I don't try to. I don't want to know what the body looked like when they found it, especially if it *is*—

But it won't be Turner. It won't.

We weave between huge crates and thick coils of rope. The river runs into inlets inside the warehouse, each one big enough to house a large chug or a small steamer. Lamps dangle from wooden beams far over my head. Their light illuminates a flash of movement as a rat scurries across my path.

"I should warn you," the constable says, over his shoulder, "my boys had to fish the body out of the water. And it looks like it rolled along the bottom of the Thames for a mile or two first."

God. *Please* let it not be Turner.

We make our way to a shadowed corner of the warehouse next to an inlet of dark water. The constable's steps falter, and he rolls his shoulders before continuing. I tuck my fingers into fists, squeeze hard.

The officer steps to one side, and the body's there, lying beside the water. I gasp, throttling the sound quickly. It's torn up, legs ripped from feet to thighs, and one arm bent so unnaturally it has to be broken. Black ink marks her collarbone with a small flower I don't recognise. Its face is turned towards us, towards me. I put my hand to my throat, will myself not to vomit. One of her eyes is partially eaten and oozing blood, and the other stares out of a face scarred by jagged tears. But even broken, I recognise it.

"That's her." Monaghan's voice seems to come from a great distance. "Doctor Phillips, I assume?"

I drag my gaze from the body and see a man I hadn't noticed before. He wears a thigh-length coat and a tall hat. He and Monaghan shake hands.

"What can you tell me about the cause of death?"

"I'd say she hit her head and fell into the river about three days ago," the doctor replies, glancing down at the body—at Turner. "No obvious signs of attack, and nothing like what we've seen in the East End. She probably fell."

"That's impossible," I say, quietly. "Not Turner."

The doctor looks at me, frowning, then at the constable. The officer shrugs, a non-verbal, *I warned her.*

"Is it possible that someone could have pushed her?" Monaghan asks.

"I've only been here twenty minutes," the doctor replies, sharply. "You'll know more once I've done the autopsy. Until then, anything's possible."

"I understand. I'd appreciate it if the autopsy could be held discreetly. I don't think we need reports of another body in the papers, especially if the death is accidental."

"I'll have the body taken to a City morgue," Phillips replies. "It won't be connected to the Whitechapel murders."

"Thank you, doctor." There's another shaking of hands and a glint of silver crosses palms.

The constable rubs the back of his neck. "The cart is outside, doctor. I'm sorry to rush you, but we've got a freighter due in from Hong Kong any minute."

"We need a few minutes alone with the body."

They stare at him. "Excuse me?" the officer asks.

Monaghan gazes at them coolly. "My colleagues and I need to make our own examination. We won't be long." His tone doesn't leave room for argument, and Tiberius circles up behind them, escorting them towards the doors. When they're underway, he returns to us.

"Can you sense anything?" I ask the demon. "Any traces of her killer?"

He gazes at me. "That is not my skill," he replies, in his low, gravelly voice.

"Right." Even if Tiberius *was* a Hound, the time Turner's body has spent in the river would have washed away any traces of a demon.

"What about the spell?" Monaghan asks him. "Is Lavender still alive?"

Another icy shock. Lavender. If she isn't here, or dead alongside Turner, then could she be all right?

"I cannot tell," he says. "The spell is broken, but I don't know if she lives."

"She'd go back to the agency, wouldn't she?" She must, it's the only place she could go.

"If Turner's been dead for three days," Monaghan says, glancing at her body, "Lavender should have returned by now."

Trembling, I wipe my mouth. "So, what do we do? How do we find her?" I pray she's alive. I can't lose Turner and Lavender in the same night.

Monaghan looks at me, and the swooping feeling in my stomach goes cold. "If she is alive, we can pull her back by recasting the summons ritual."

When an agent dies and the demon does not, a transfer ritual has to take place. It's cast by the agent's apprentice as part of the ceremony to make them a full-fledged agent, just like Jacob did for Maximus.

"Sir." I have nothing else to say, and just stand, dumbly, waiting for orders.

He turns to face me. The only sounds for a moment are the murmur of the water and the scuttle of rats. "Miss Locke," he says. I straighten. "You have been an apprentice for five years and an agency member for nearly seven. But I'm obliged to ask: are you sure that becoming an agent is what you want?"

This is the only opportunity I'll get to change my mind. Memories of the workhouse flash through my head. I don't want to go back.

But I'm not sure I want to say yes, either. I can't be the person Turner is—was. I don't know how to be.

I look at her body, lying twisted and motionless at my feet. If I say no, Monaghan will release me onto the streets to make my own way. Someone else will be called upon to take up Turner's role, to help solve her murder. Clara, most likely, given that Eve is on the other side of the country.

Clara hasn't been here long enough. She doesn't have the knowledge to catch this killer. And she didn't know Turner the way I did. Didn't know either of them. If I say no—if I leave—I'll be turning my back on them both.

I can't do that. I can't walk away while Turner's murderer is still out there. I have to bring them to justice.

"Yes," I say, and hope to God I don't regret it. "This is what I want."

"I'm glad," Monaghan says, rewarding me with a slight smile. It vanishes with his next words. "I doubt this is accidental. Whatever killed our latest victim in Whitechapel probably killed Turner to cover their tracks."

"So, I can have the case?" I want it, suddenly. I want it with a fierceness that surprises me.

"I'll put you on it with Rayne. It'll be a cold welcome from the Home Office, but you don't need me to tell you that," Monaghan says. "Try not to ruffle any feathers."

Tiberius puts his hands in his pockets, looking at the body. "The Home Office needs to sanction any ritual," he reminds Monaghan.

"By the time they get around to doing so, the murderer may have fled," the professor responds. "*If* they grant it. More likely they'll try to persuade me to wait until Khurana returns, and we cannot afford to lose any time." He does up the top button of his coat. "Let's get back to the agency before the dockhands kick us out. Lavender's file is in the library," he says to me. "I suggest you pull together her summon components. If she is alive, I don't want to lose her. Understood, Agent Locke?"

Agent. I have to swallow before I can reply. "Yes, sir. I'll get started straight away."

He puts a hand on my shoulder. "Rest, first. It's been a long night. And you must be focused for the ceremony."

It's all I can do to nod. My mind races, trying to recall Lavender's file at the same time as it tries to plan, to think. "When, sir?"

"We'll hold a service for Turner, first, so the night after tomorrow."

"I'll be ready."

He smiles, a little sadly. "I'd hoped it wouldn't be so soon, but here we are. I'm happy to welcome you aboard, agent."

I nod, again, feeling adrift. In two days, I'll have my own demon. I'll be a real agent.

I glance again at Turner's body, and the excitement I feel is tempered by fear.

CHAPTER SIX

I'm granted the rest of the day to sleep. Instead, I sit with the sheets wrapped around my shoulders and try to think. My mind is stupid, reiterating that Turner is dead, that Lavender is gone.

I want to go to Turner's room and find her there, have her greet me with her hands on her hips and demand her report. But her room will be empty.

My eyes burn. Tears don't come, not even when I put my hands to my face and pull my lips back from my teeth to snarl. The stone weight that fills me does not move. I want to scream.

I press my fingers to my eyes until stars explode on the backs of my eyelids. Me sitting here, screaming into my hands, will do no good. I need reason, now. Logic. Strength.

Day shifts to night before I realise it. I must sleep, but I don't recall waking. Morning comes, a slow, soft dawn that trembles through the windows. I stare at the pale light creeping over the floor and acknowledge the large portion of my chest given over to grief. It will stay, but I cannot let it keep me from what needs to be done.

Resolved, I rise and dress. Eve's bed is a stark reminder that I'm alone, and I feel a pang. She'd be a better agent than me. She was ready the moment she joined.

Eve's not here, I remind myself.

Maia waits for me in the north-west library. She greets me with a strained smile.

"I didn't think you'd be awake," I say, sitting at the desk I normally use. The desk that will become someone else's, once I take an apprentice.

Me, with an apprentice. Isn't that a thought.

"I thought you would have trouble sleeping." Maia arches her eyebrows at me. "Was I not correct?"

I take the cup of tea she offers, strong but softened with a dash of milk, just as I like it. "It was...difficult." The memory of Turner's body threatens to surge through my mind again, as it did over and over yesterday. I lock it away, push down the horror that comes with it.

Maia puts a hand on my shoulder, briefly, then places a large book in front of me. "Here are the records for the rituals performed over the last one hundred years."

I haven't looked at these records in years, not since I first joined, when I thirsted for knowledge about everything the agency was, everything it did. Lavender's file is a blurry memory. I open the book to its last third and flip to her page. There were only a few summons after her: Cassius, Maximus, and Spurio, Moss' partner. After that the pages are blank, waiting for the next set of agents to call forth their demons.

The agency documents each successful summons for just this situation, to ensure that demons remain within the agency when their human partner dies or retires. The slightest change in the components could upset the spell and target the wrong demon, attracting a new one instead of bringing Lavender back.

"Monaghan thinks she's dead," I say, into silence.

The other woman sits next to me and drags the oil lamp closer, illuminating the black scrawl over the parchment. "It will not hurt to try."

I run my hand over Lavender's name and the name beside it: Turner. The writing is in Lavender's hand, oddly. I didn't think demons were allowed to know their spell components. Protection, I assume, in case some other agency tries to summon them after the agent dies.

I concentrate on the text, the list of components that will summon Lavender to this building. If she lives.

"Wolf fang," I read first. The bone is the central ingredient that narrows the spell's focus to a specific type of demon. Wolves call to the Hounds.

"Agent Peters brought back a skull from his last hunting trip." Maia grimaces. I can't imagine what her expression had been when Peters dumped a wolf's severed head in her kitchen.

Next, the book lists blue iris petals, for wisdom. I should have guessed. But the component underneath takes me by surprise. "Aloe? I didn't know aloe could be used in magic."

Maia looks as blank as I feel. "What does it symbolise?"

"Affection."

We both fall silent. I blink to clear the blurriness from my vision and move on. Holly, for foresight. There's a small annotation in Turner's hand; *Leaves, not berries*. Finally, twelve petals of a violet, for loyalty. I could not ask for a better partner.

"I will send Doyle for the flowers," Maia says. "I expect a greenhouse will have them. Holly and aloe are in the garden. I assume you will want to pack the bag yourself?"

"Yes, thank you." I get out my notebook, a tiny leather-bound thing that Turner gifted me the day I became her apprentice. I pause, put aside the surge of emotion that comes with the memory, and write down the amounts required. "I'll get the fang."

"Are you sure? I do not mind—"

"It's fine," I reply. "It doesn't bother me." Dead things are nothing to be afraid of. It's the living that should be feared.

Maia looks grateful. She runs her hand over the book, her expression remote. "It may be worth considering all possibilities," she says. Her voice is careful, hesitant.

"What do you mean?"

"I mean...in case Lavender does not answer the call." She means in case Lavender is dead.

"I wouldn't know what to choose," I say, deflecting.

"Perhaps you should have a name in mind. Just in case."

Anger flares in me and I stamp it down. It's not an unreasonable suggestion. "I feel as though we're running out of Romans," I say, after a moment.

She snorts. "The Empire is built of colonisers; we do not need to add more. Turner paid no attention to that nonsense, anyway."

"She never told me how Lavender was named."

"She thought the tradition of naming her partner after a Roman was limiting, for Hounds—for women. When the time came, she gave Lavender the option to choose her own." Maia stands with an audible creak and groans. I want to grasp her sleeve so she can't leave. I feel like a child who doesn't want to let go of her skirts, doesn't want to step outside, into the dark. "Choose whatever you like," she says. "At the end of the day, it is the demon who matters, not the name."

"'A rose by any other name,'" I quote, and she smiles.

"We have a saying, in Punjabi," she says. "*Suno sab ki karo man ki.*"

"Don't listen, but do...what you want?" I hazard. It's been a year or so since I took lessons at her table, and I'm rustier than I should be.

"Listen to all, but do what you think is right," she corrects. "Obey your own conscience, not the words of others."

I smile, self-deprecating. "What if my conscience is wrong?"

"Then we have another saying: hindsight has the best eyesight." She winks at me. "I should make sure that Clara has started the fires. I will leave you to your wolf."

"Thank you," I reply, wryly, and make my way to the other end of the library.

The taxidermy room is at the far end of the building, shut off from casual passers-by. I stand in the entrance and regard the still figures. The tiger takes up the most space, its red-black striped fur gleaming in my lamplight, its muzzle wrinkled in a snarl. Two wooden perches hold a number of stuffed birds, from snowy owls to huge eagles, their wings spread in imitation of flight. In a cabinet, large tarantulas lie spread out under glass next to scorpions, whose tails are either poised to strike or are missing completely, taken for a component.

Arachnids haven't been used in the ritual for years; they call to Stalker and Strike demons, whose low-level powers of mimicry are of little use to the agency. After one disastrous ritual when a serpent's fang invoked a Blood Drinker, the stuffed reptiles were left to rot. The birds are missing the most extremities: Phantoms respond best to anything winged, and it's Phantoms that the agency built its investigative strength on. Reapers only respond to one call out of five, and only to a tiger fang. Hounds came last, once the agency understood that the gender of the caster affected the spell as much as the bone core itself.

I move to a box of tools, selecting a pair of small pliers. The wolf carcass stalks the tiger, its mouth open in a howl to allow access to its teeth. I keep its head steady with one hand—marvelling at the softness of its fur, even in death—and select my fang. After a lot of wriggling, it comes loose with a pop. I drop the fang into a little tin, one of many lined up in preparation on the shelves around the room. Satisfied, I put away the pliers and head down to the kitchen.

It's past dawn now, and I find Clara tending the main hearth. She looks up as I enter and glowers at me. I check my stride, frowning, and the expression vanishes.

"Good morning, Miss Agent," the girl says.

It's not an address she's used before, and I doubt she means it as a compliment. If I hadn't said yes to Monaghan's offer, Clara would have taken my place. I can't begrudge her frustration.

"Good morning, Clara."

She wipes her hands on her apron. "Miss Bhatt said I was to tell you that you'd be moving into Turner's rooms tomorrow night, after the funeral."

"Oh. I see." That's logical. There are few rooms set aside for female agents, and I can't stay in the apprentice wing. "Is there a truckle bed set up?" Lavender will need somewhere to sleep, and at least if it's a familiar room, there should be less change for her to adjust to.

Clara huffs. "What, you want me to check? I have to light the fires in the professor's rooms and then I have to get breakfast ready for the agents—"

"Don't worry," I say, hastily, as she builds up steam. "I'll check later. Thank you, Clara."

"'Course, miss." With a sniff, she strides away, and I'm left alone in the empty kitchen.

I fold onto the bench at the table and put my forehead in my hands. Once again, I wish Eve were here. I have no idea what to do, how to step into Turner's shoes. She was brilliant, and I'm...

The sour truth festers within me: I'm not enough.

Sighing, I pack that thought away, fold it down deep, and smooth my expression. There is still work to do. I must focus on that, not on my doubts. However truthful they might be.

CHAPTER SEVEN

The hallway on the ground floor of the agency brims with flowers. Vases top every surface, filled with crimson roses and scarlet anemones. Red, everywhere I look, as though the hall has been splattered with blood.

I wince at the image. It's the anemones: Aphrodite's tears and Adonis' blood. Fitting symbolism for a funeral, though, and I can't deny they look beautiful.

I move towards Jacob and his demon. We're both clad in black—his tailored jacket and black checked waistcoat more fashionable than my wool skirt and coat—and he wears a small skullcap. Monaghan has gone ahead with Rayne and Clara has opted to stay behind and prepare dinner for our return.

"Are you all right?" Jacob asks me, as we wait for our coach.

"I'm fine. Thank you." I hold myself with tension, my stomach tight and my hands clenched together.

"It must have been..." He shakes his head. A few strands of dark blond hair escape their pomade and fall against his brow. "I can't imagine what it was like, seeing her that way."

"I don't want to talk about it." My voice is cold—colder than it needs to be, but the last thing I want to think about today is her corpse. Her *murdered* corpse. I don't care that the coroner's report we received only an hour ago was inconclusive, that the doctor submitted her death as accidental; Turner was murdered. I'm sure of it.

He ducks his head. "I apologise."

Relenting, I raise my hand in a conciliatory gesture. "It's just...not an image that I want in my head right now."

He takes my hand and squeezes softly. "Of course."

I can't think of anything else to say, and I'm so tired I don't want to say anything at all.

I'm saved by Maia. "The coach is here," she says, gesturing us forward. "We should go now."

Outside, rain falls in a light staccato rhythm. Turner would have liked that. She always said funerals were saddest in the rain. She always said the oddest things.

The black coach waits on the busy street, drawn by two dappled greys wearing crowns of black feathers. We get in, Maia and I first with Jacob and Max opposite us.

The trip to the cemetery is silent. I look at my hands instead of the window, instead of the same cobblestones I crossed to get to the docks. It will be over soon.

I shouldn't think that way. This is a chance to say goodbye, a chance to remember Turner as she was when she was alive, not the way she was when Monaghan and I found her. I shouldn't wish for it to end so quickly.

But I do. I want to put this behind me. I want it to stop hurting.

The Jewish cemetery emerges from the rain as a dim shape, mirrored on the other side of the street by a small Christian church. The coach pulls up in front of the cemetery's doors and I get out, letting the rain dampen my jacket and slip under my collar. The wet cold sends a chill through me. It's better than the grief welling in my chest.

We drift into the prayer hall. The only people present are other agency members. No family, no friends. Agency funerals are a secret affair; too many demons in one place to allow unnecessary civilians.

Is this what it'll be like when I die? No one to mourn me except those who managed to survive long enough to do so?

Perhaps that's not so different from the rest of the world. Those who live longest are rewarded by the sight of their family and friends shrivelling and dying.

The service is brief and to the point. The rabbi tears black ribbons for us and leads us behind the coffin in a slow train. The cemetery workers do their duty in silence, and Turner's simple pine coffin is lowered into the ground with little ceremony. A few more words from the rabbi and then he leaves us to mourn.

The night of Jacob's ritual, all twenty-two members of the agency were present: agents and apprentices, humans and demons. For this, there are eight of us.

We stand in the rain around the grave, cemetery workers nearby, waiting for us to leave so they can begin filling it in. Turner's tomb is as simple as the service was, and the stone monument marking her grave sits unveiled. There will be no further ceremonies, no recitation of prayers. This one moment is all we'll have.

The headstone is engraved with a candelabra, a stylised flower, and Turner's name and years. No one would know, looking at it, who she was or what she did for the agency. For London.

After a while, Monaghan sighs. "I need to get back," he says. "Agent Locke, make sure you're prepared for this evening."

I nod and he and Tiberius leave. Rayne and his demon, who haven't said a word, go with them.

Jacob picks up a smooth, pretty pebble and places it atop the grave. He rests his left hand there, for a moment, and murmurs something in Hebrew. When he steps away, he clenches his hands.

"She deserved better than this," he mutters.

"I know." I glance at the skeletal church tower that rises from the other side of the street. No doubt someday my own funeral will be held under its gaze. I take morbid comfort from the fact that I won't be far from Turner's resting place.

Beside me, Maia sighs. "She deserved much more than this."

Letting out a harsh breath, Jacob goes to run his hand through his hair and then seems to remember his skullcap. "I have to go, too," he says. "Monaghan's sending us into Kent for a case. Not even time for a proper *shiva*."

I eye the tight stretch of skin around his mouth, the glassy sheen to his eyes, and try to dredge up something resembling comfort. "They must need you, then. And Turner wouldn't want you to neglect your duty."

Another huff of breath, but his mouth eases. "No, she would not." He glances at Max, who straightens. "All right, then. Do you want me to hold the coach?"

"No. I'll stay for a little longer."

He asks Maia the same, and she declines. I watch him and Max disappear through the grey rain, then gaze back at the tomb, at the simple wood coffin below.

"I don't think I can do it," I murmur, unsure if I'm talking to Maia, or to the grave. Releasing the words into the thrumming rain makes my doubt crystallise into certainty. "I'll never be Turner, or Khurana. I don't know how to be."

Maia folds her hands in front of her, her head inclined so the rain runs off her modest bonnet without spilling into her face. "I joined the agency twenty-one years ago," she says, gazing down at the grave. "The family who hired me as their *ayah* deserted me when I arrived. I had nowhere to go, no friends and no family.

"One night, I was searching for work and I ran into a demon. A Stalker," she adds, and I shudder. Turner ran into a Stalker demon once or twice while I was her apprentice. They hide in the shadows, all legs and eyes. Maia smiles a little at my reaction. "I had seen jinn, in my country, but nothing like this. I called for help, but...no one cared. Except for Turner. She and Lavender were already hunting him. They intervened. They were not supposed to; Hounds are for tracking. But still, she saved my life. And then she saved it again, when she brought me to the agency," Maia says, her eyes foggy.

"You could have gone home long ago," I say, awed. Maia only told me that Turner had introduced her to Monaghan, not this.

"Perhaps I will, someday," she replies. "I have no desire to become an agent, and Monaghan is too fond of my cooking to try and persuade me otherwise. But not yet. There is still work to be done."

Turner's favourite saying. "There always is." I gaze at the tombstone. The police are no closer to identifying the Whitechapel murderer, and if Turner was right and a demon *is* behind the killings, then I might be able to help catch them. "I need Lavender," I murmur. "I can't do this without her."

"They were partners for thirty years. I have never seen as strong a bond." Maia gestures at the flower on the stone, a small bud with almond-shaped petals. Lavender, I realise.

"It must be nice," I say, "to stay with someone you trust for that long."

"Yes." Maia picks up her skirts. "She deserved much more than this," she repeats, bitterly, and turns away.

I regard the tombstone for a moment, then touch my hand to the small stone Jacob put there. "I will do my best," I whisper. It sounds inadequate, aloud, but I can't think of another promise that I can deliver on. This, at least, I can do. I *will* do, for myself as much as for Turner's memory.

CHAPTER EIGHT

Turner's room is less than half the size of the room I share with Eve. It holds a narrow bed, a vanity, two small wardrobes, a single chair and a truckle bed set up in the corner. I have no family items to decorate the space, and the vanity looks bald with their absence.

It's my own room, at least, until Lavender joins me.

My clothes hang in one of the wardrobes. The other must still contain Turner's things. I avoid it and don a fresh blouse. I change my black jacket for my navy one, and hope that will do. Earlier, I packed all of the components into their velvet bag—three times over, until Maia had to pull the thing away from me so Clara could take it to the ritual room.

For the final time, I glance at my notebook, at the words of the spell relayed to me by Monaghan only an hour before. The ritual itself is a zealously guarded secret, kept hidden by the agency and all its branches around the Empire. Monaghan made me repeat the words until I'd memorised them, an odd mix of bastardised Latin and other languages I can only guess the root of. There's little in the agency's library about the origin of demons, and even the lexicons do no more than theorise it.

Whatever this language started as, it must have evolved over the years by absorbing and merging with others.

I'm trying to distract myself. I close my eyes, take a deep breath, and put all thoughts of languages and mysteries out of my head, leaving only the words of the spell. And Lavender.

Straightening my collar one last time, I glance around the room. Satisfied that it provides as welcome a picture as it can, I head downstairs, to the locked door that leads to the ritual room.

I'm early, so it's just Maia, Jacob and Max who wait for me. But the door is already unbarred and open to the darkness that waits.

"I do not think this room has ever been opened twice in such a short space of time," Maia says, half-smiling. I try to summon the coordination to return it, but I can't think beyond the words of the spell.

"Nervous?" Jacob asks, with a chuckle. "Don't worry. You'll do better than I did. I almost soiled myself when the flames went up." Maia and Max both stare at him and he flushes. "That was indelicate. I apologise."

I manage a smile. "I will try to restrain myself." The clock in the hall strikes quarter to midnight. Fifteen minutes. "Are the others coming?"

"They're on the way."

My stomach coils with nerves. I stare at the darkness in the tunnel, willing myself not to quake.

"Agent Locke." Monaghan has dressed modestly in a charcoal suit with a nipped-in waist. Behind him, Rayne is more extravagant in dove grey and maroon. Their demons trail them. "Are you ready?" asks the professor.

I straighten my shoulders and draw myself up to my full height, trying not to stoop when I have to look down a few inches at Monaghan. "Yes, sir. I'm ready."

The lines at the corners of his eyes wrinkle in a smile. "Then let's begin." He takes the first steps into the tunnel. Then there's a pause.

"It's your turn," Jacob whispers. "It's your ritual; you come next."

I look at Maia, and she nods at me, grim but encouraging. It's enough. I turn from her and walk after Monaghan into the dimly lit tunnel.

No one walks beside me. Grief sharpens in my chest like a blade. I breathe through it shallowly. By the time we reach the circular room, it has eased to a dull ache.

Tiberius lights the torches one by one. Jacob and the others fan out among the columns, less than half of the presence that was here during Jacob's ritual. I wish Maia was beside me. I wish I wasn't alone.

It's silent but for the faint crackle of the torches. Slowly, I make my way to the large bowl at the centre of the room. My mouth is bone dry.

As I near the bloodwriting on the floor, I see faint smears among the glyphs that look as though they've been wiped clean. Mistakes, perhaps, made by past summoners. The thought does not fill me with confidence.

My black velvet bag lies on the pedestal, ready for the ritual. I pick it up, rub my thumb over the velvet. The bag is light—lighter than it should be, considering the amount of power it can control. I want to open it again, count each little component, but the others are waiting. I run the spell through my head one more time. I am an agent. I'm as ready as I'll ever be.

Then I realise that, with Turner gone, there's no one to start the fire for me. Another sharp stab in my stomach. I breathe out shakily and return to the bowl. There's wood inside, and tinder and flint. I fumble the flint at first and have to stop to steady my hands. Flushing, I try to ignore the weight of the agency's collective gaze and keep my face expressionless. The sparks take a few minutes to catch, but after a while the flames eat through the wood and lick at the sides of the bowl.

Monaghan is looking at his pocket watch. I keep my gaze on him. Then he lifts his head and nods. It's time.

I cup the bag in my palm and hold it over the crackling flames. The words of the spell roll off my tongue, breaking the thick silence that circles me. There is a strange rhythm to them, a pulse like a drum of a heart. I tip over my hand and shake the spell components into the fire.

Instead of the delicate iris petals I'd counted so carefully, tumbling out of the bag comes a cluster of red anemones and crimson roses, the petals bruised and torn.

The flowers fall into the flames and shrivel, dying. Desperate, I give the bag another shake, but nothing else comes. No aloe, no holly or violet. No wolf fang.

My fingers go white on the black velvet. That wasn't the spell I prepared.

I glance up, my heart pounding through my head. The others are still waiting. They haven't noticed; they're too far away.

I take a deep breath. If I stop now, the bindings will fracture and the magic will unravel, dangerous and free.

Lavender might still come. I hold on, biting my lip until it stings, waiting.

The fire goes white. *Something* has answered.

I scour my mind for the meaning to the flowers. Roses for passion, red anemones for Adonis and Aphrodite, for—for death and forsaken love. God, what kind of demon am I calling?

Around me the bloodwriting lights up, flickering as though someone has dropped a match on oil. I snap my hand away from the flames, the velvet bag dangling from my nerveless fingers. I search the shadows on the other side of the fire, waiting.

The flames snap up, bursting over my vision in white sparks. I blink rapidly. In the next moment, the fire dies away, and red and black ashes fill the urn. A figure stands on the other side of the bowl. I steel myself and look up.

And *up*. The demon is a head taller than me. That realisation sticks in my mind and for a moment I don't realise what has happened, why shocked whispers are ricocheting off the walls. Then I understand.

The demon is male. I haven't called a Hound at all.

CHAPTER NINE

"*L ocke*," comes a whispered command from the columns, and I shake myself. It doesn't matter what the demon is, if I don't seal the spell and name him, he'll be loose in the agency with nothing to keep him from turning on us but his moral code. And unbound demons don't *have* a moral code.

But I have no names. I was so desperate for Lavender that I didn't bother preparing for the worst-case scenario. Even if I'd tried, I couldn't have prepared for *this*.

I scan his face for inspiration. Straight black hair falls over pale skin and angular cheekbones. He has narrow feline eyes, but his pupils are thin black slits. The eyes of a snake. Their colour is bright, startling against the obsidian of his hair. If I had a poetic mind, I might call it silver.

I take in the breadth of his shoulders, the sharpness to that gaze. Silver is too malleable and too delicate a name for this creature. But it gives me an idea.

"I name you Steel," I say, ignoring the ripple that goes around the room. I take care to keep my voice blank. Better for him to think I don't care a jot for his answer, that I have a dozen other demons waiting for me to choose them. "Will you serve?" I ask, and a tingle scuttles over my skin: the magic settling, binding.

His gaze travels over the ash-filled urn and the bloodwriting alight on the floor. A line between his brows grows. He looks up. "Steel," he repeats, in a voice deeper than I expected. "I can hardly refuse."

I feel magic closing around me like cobwebs. It's done.

I step around the urn to face him, to find out exactly what I've allied myself to. He *is* tall, well over six feet, dressed in plain wool trousers and bare shirtsleeves. He has no jacket. Or shoes, for that matter. Maia will need to find him something before we visit Whitechapel.

I realise I'm making plans as if he's a Hound when I have no idea what I've done.

His gaze slips over my worn kid boots and sweeps up my wool skirt to my high-necked jacket. His eyebrows arch in a look born of condescension.

The condescension isn't important. It matters little what he thinks of me, as long as he can do his job. That sharp, lovely face is nothing more than a reminder of what he is: in the devil's children, beauty is not to be trusted.

The size of him may prove an issue. My own height makes me conspicuous enough, and to be accompanied by this towering creature will mean I'll never go unnoticed. He'll be intimidating, though. Perhaps I can work with that.

His expression turns amused: he's caught my slow assessment.

Then a crowd of people reach my elbows. Max and Cassius flank us, their expressions hard.

"We need to get upstairs," Monaghan says, watching the demon—Steel—with an icy gaze. Tiberius lingers behind him, close enough to act, if necessary. "The spell must be left to dissipate."

I can still feel it, crawling over my skin with a thousand velvet legs. Nodding, I go to follow Monaghan.

Everyone shifts towards the door while trying to keep their eyes on Steel. They halt in confusion.

We can't all fit through the tunnel like this. I turn to the demon. "This way," I say, a peace offering.

He glances sideways at his guards, but after a moment he falls into step behind me. I lead the way upstairs and my stomach tightens again. In all my concern over the ritual, I hadn't spared a thought for the test.

When we emerge from the basement, Monaghan and Rayne put us in a small study with Jacob and Max and then disappear. The new demon collapses in an armchair in one corner of the room and I circle around to stand behind another. I place my hands on its back, more to appear in control than to feel as though I am. Max takes centre position and Jacob paces the length of the room and back, keeping an eye on Steel. He does not get too close.

The demon scans the room. "An agency, I assume," he says.

I regard him with as calm an expression as I can muster. "Correct."

"Paris?"

He's looking at a volume of French histories on the bookcase by the door. "London," I reply. "We are not affiliated with the

Sûreté." I don't know why I added that, why I feel the need to fill the silence.

"Ah." Another slow scan, this time taking in Jacob, who he dismisses after a few seconds, then Max, who earns a longer scrutiny but is also eventually dismissed. Then he turns to me. I earn the longest inspection.

I inspect him back, taking in the details I couldn't see earlier. His shirt is clean but ill-fitting, and his trousers are marred by a small tear at the knee, stitched with grey thread that gleams on dark wool; second-hand and cheaply repaired. His feet are dirty and his nails black. I take a second glance, and swallow. The nails are talons, blunted as though he or someone has clipped them. Not built to wear shoes but used to them: he'd spent time passing as a human, without the funds to do so comfortably.

My curiosity gets the better of me. "Why don't you have any shoes?"

"I have shoes," he says, "I just happened to not be wearing them when you brought me here. Don't you warlocks provide footwear, anyway? Part of the package?"

"Warlock?"

"The spell. The bloodwriting. Only warlocks cast that kind of magic."

"I'm not a warlock. I'm an agent."

He shrugs and leans back in the chair, his hands resting on the arms as though he's reclining before a warm fire on a cold evening. "There is little difference, from my perspective."

"Where were you, when you were called?" Jacob shakes his head at me, warning me off this conversation. I ignore him. I want to know how I ended up with this demon.

"I was in Paris." He flexes his feet. "Why did you call me?" he asks, before I can think of another question.

He answered my question, it seems only fair to answer his. "I was looking for a Hound demon called Lavender. Were you with her?"

"I don't know who that is." His expression betrays no sign of a lie, but I don't yet know his tells.

"Why did you come?"

"You summoned me," he says, with a half-smile that reads, *I can't believe you asked.* "It doesn't work the other way around."

So, the spell's components identified him as a match for the ritual, or close enough. Red roses and anemones: love and death.

"I saw a distance limitation in the bloodwriting," he says, after a pause. "Thirty feet?"

"Twenty." Any more than that and the spell will cripple both of us with pain—and, if the distance is far enough, kill the demon.

"That seems inconvenient." He examines the floor between us, and I shift uncomfortably.

"The only way to break it is for me to die," I add, "and you can't kill me." The two things that the agency tests, after a summons; that the distance limit is in place, and that the demon can't willingly hurt their agent.

"Yes, I saw that, too." He laughs; a low, husky sound. "I guess your agency figured that one out pretty quickly."

I don't know what to say to that, but he doesn't seem to expect an answer. We lapse into silence, and I try not to knead the fabric of the armchair. My mind races. If the spell has failed, what will happen? No agent has ever been allowed to perform the ritual twice.

If it *hasn't* failed, then what does *that* mean? Will I keep this serpent-eyed creature as my partner? And was it only the components that focused the spell, or could Lavender have answered if she wanted to? And if that is true and she *chose* not to answer...

I close my mind to the questions. Answers will come, or they won't. Right now, what matters is getting through the next few minutes. So, I remain quiet, and wait.

There is no clock in the room, so I have no idea how long it is before the others return. It feels like an hour, maybe more.

Then Rayne and his demon pour into the room as if they've been desperate to break down the door. Monaghan enters and stands against the wall, his arms folded and his demon close by.

Rayne begins. "What are you?" he asks, displacing Max to stand in front of Steel. "What kind of demon? Copper class? Silver? What?"

The demon rests his chin on his hand and examines Rayne. "I did hear you the first time," he replies, mildly.

"Then, what are you?"

"I am a Hound."

I stare at him. No Hound in the history of the agency has been male.

"Hounds are female," Rayne says, on the tail of my thought. He widens his stance, his hands balled into loose fists at his side. "Male Hounds don't exist."

"How do you think we get little baby Hounds? We don't just come into being, fully formed," Steel replies, and Rayne colours.

"Then why haven't we seen any before?"

"Ask the warlock who drew your ritual."

"What were the ingredients that called you?" Rayne asks, trying another approach.

The demon gives him a long-suffering look. "How would I know what the warlock used?"

Rayne turns to me. "What did you put in there?"

"I didn't put them in," I say, stung into replying quickly. I modify my tone, and add, "I had Lavender's components, but the bag was wrong. It was full of roses and anemones."

Steel tilts his head. "I don't know if that is a compliment or an insult," he murmurs.

"You chose the wrong one?" Rayne doesn't go so far as to claim aloud that the situation is my fault, but I hear it in his voice.

"I—I suppose I must have." Or someone switched the bags. I have no evidence to support that theory, so I can only assume I made a mistake. The thought cuts. "The wolf fang was also missing," I add, returning my gaze to Steel.

Rayne turns on him, too. "Then you cannot be a Hound. Without a focus, the spell wouldn't have been able to summon any class."

"I *was* a Hound," the demon replies. His expression indicates he thinks this whole thing is a game. "I'm not anymore. Well, in a manner of speaking. I have no class—they cast me out."

I've never heard of a demon without a class. From what the lexicons say, there used to be at least eight classes, each one segregating into subsets of demons. Over the centuries, classes were absorbed or destroyed, leaving only three: copper, silver, and diamond. According to the agency's records at least.

"That explains why he was summoned and not one of the normal Hounds," Jacob says. "Perhaps—"

"How do we know you're not lying?" Rayne interrupts. "How do we know that you won't turn on us as soon as you can?"

"Do you have so little faith in your own spells?" Steel replies.

"Can you sense demons?" Monaghan asks, his quiet voice cutting through the room.

A beat as the demon examines him. "All Hounds can. Male or female."

"Then we can still use you."

"Sir," Rayne protests, "the ritual failed. We should try again, with another, worthy agent."

My head jerks to look at him. "Who would you suggest?" I ask, coating my voice in ice.

He glances at me and then away. "I mean nothing by it," he says, gruffly. "But if you mixed up something as simple as the components, I cannot believe you're the right person to hold a partnership with a demon."

I understand his reasoning. I *did* mix up the bags. I *did* fail the spell. My face flushes, all the way down to my collarbones. If they say no to Steel, they'll never let me try again.

"Professor," I begin, "it was not my intention—"

Monaghan raises a hand, and we all fall silent. "I know you would never do this intentionally, Locke. I've never known you to make a mistake on this scale." He regards the demon, who has steepled his hands in front of his face and is watching us as closely. "We need a Hound. Just because this is one is male shouldn't mean that we toss him back."

"I resent the implication that I am a fish," the demon murmurs.

"But before we decide, there is something we must do."

I tense, knowing what's to come. Rayne looks at the demon with a satisfied smile.

"We must test him."

CHAPTER TEN

I take up my stance at one end of the agency's small dining hall. Tiberius shows the new demon a spot not far from me, well within the distance limit.

Jacob touches my elbow. "Are you all right?" he asks, under his breath.

My heart fills my throat and my blood beats so quickly it makes my hands tremble. "Now I know how nervous you were," I murmur; forced levity.

If Steel fails the test, he'll be destroyed, and I'll be removed from the agency. They'll have no use for a failed agent.

"Who wants to begin?" Monaghan offers.

"Maximus and I can test him, sir," Jacob suggests, staying by my side.

"You don't have enough experience." Rayne's already moving to a glass case on one side of the wall. A number of weapons stand on display, from English broadswords to Japanese katanas, even an akrafena that Khurana gifted Eve the day she became her apprentice. Blades only; we're not permitted pistols. The risk to bystanders is too high.

Rayne chooses a pair of French stiletto daggers, as long as his arm from wrist to elbow. Cassius waltzes over to stand between me and Steel. They'll force him to the point of attack, until the only thing restraining him is the spell. I shiver.

"You'll be fine," Jacob whispers, and backs away, leaving the centre of the room clear. All I have to do is watch, but that hardly feels like an easy task.

Steel eyes the daggers and takes a step back, closer to the limit. I raise my head instinctively. He must catch my unconscious warning; Rayne lunges forward and Steel steps sideways. A dagger slices through the air where he'd stood.

Rayne whirls with the movement of his lunge into another attack. Steel evades it. Again, Rayne charges and again Steel slips away. In his shirtsleeves and bare feet, he's practically defenceless against Rayne's weapons, but still he does not fight back.

I spare a glance at Monaghan. The professor is nodding as he watches, whether in approval for Rayne or the demon I don't know.

The agent darts forward, both hands raised for a fast downward slash. Steel ducks underneath, moving with unnatural speed. He sweeps out his foot. Rayne stumbles. Steel wrenches his leg and, with a dull thud, Rayne lands on his backside. One dagger goes clattering across the floor.

The demon smirks, but does nothing to press his advantage. "Are you quite comfortable down there?"

Rayne snarls. He jumps up and charges at Steel. I start forward without thinking; Steel has proved that he won't attack us.

Monaghan raises his hand. "Enough."

Cassius grips Rayne's shoulder, murmuring something in his ear.

"He passed," I say, pleased and oddly proud, though Steel's skills have nothing to do with me.

"He passed the first test," Monaghan agrees. "Now, for the second." He lifts his hand and beckons Tiberius.

The Reaper goes to stand next to Rayne. Steel's eyes narrow as he takes in the three of them: the agent, Tiberius and Cassius. As one, they advance. Rayne holds out his last dagger until the tip touches the slice of skin left bare by Steel's undone collar.

They step forward. He steps back. A muscle clenches in the demon's jaw. Again, they move forward, and Steel is forced back. His bare feet grow closer and closer to the invisible barrier of the spell that binds him to me. I take a deep breath, brace myself.

It thuds into me with the force of a cannonball. I feel like I'm underwater, inches away from the surface and still drowning. If I take one step forward, it'll stop.

I don't move. This is my test, as much as it is the demon's. Gritting my teeth, I take quick shallow breaths, and wait.

Another step. He's breached the barrier. Steel lets out a low, smothered sound, and takes another step. What is he doing? This hurts him, too, worse than it hurts me.

I hiss as the pressure tightens around my chest and glare at him. His mouth quirks at the corner, despite the tension in his jaw. He stops, even when Rayne digs the blade into his flesh.

"I've gone as far as I can," Steel mutters, hoarse. "Do you plan on driving a hole through my sternum?"

"We need to be certain."

"We're finished." Monaghan says. "The demon is safe."

Steel's eyes flash and I get the impression, first, that no one has ever called him 'safe', and second, that he does not like it.

Rayne pulls away. The professor moves from his place at the wall and regards me.

"Take up the Whitechapel investigation," he orders. "Do what you can with the demon—Steel, did you name him?" I blush, but Monaghan makes no comment on the name. "If he offers resistance, he will be removed. Clear?"

I bow. "Sir."

Steel mutters something I don't catch, obviously less happy with these orders.

"It's late," Monaghan adds. "In fact, it's early. Why don't you get some rest, Locke?"

Now that the test is over, the tremble in my hands is winding through my body and I feel a breath away from collapsing. Rest sounds wonderful.

"Oh, and here." He pulls a slim leather wallet from his pocket. "Your credentials."

Inside lies an identification card, stamped with Her Majesty's crest and signed by the Secretary of State. At the top, in bold black font: *Her Majesty's Private Investigation Agency*.

Private is a stand in for *Paranormal*. Proclaiming us as agents of the supernatural would draw unwanted attention from those who don't know what the agency does—the majority of Britain.

"Don't lose it, please; they are not easy to replace. And don't forget to collect your allowance from Miller." He gives me a wry smile and leaves with Tiberius.

Rayne picks up his fallen dagger and follows with Cassius, not giving me a second glance. Jacob, however, lingers.

"Will you be all right?" he asks. Max is giving the new demon a level stare, which Steel ignores in favour of examining the blood on his shirt.

If I say no, I don't doubt Jacob will accompany me to my room and might even try to change Monaghan's decision. Besides, I'll have to face this demon alone sooner or later.

"I'll manage," I reply. With one hard look in Steel's direction, Jacob collects his partner and leaves.

I turn to the demon, and we size each other up. His eyes will take some getting used to. He has a way of tilting his head so his black hair falls into them, making the contrast more vibrant. An affected habit, I suspect.

My gaze falls to the bloody mark on his chest. "Is it deep?"

He pauses before he responds. "No," he says, his lips barely moving to acknowledge the word. To acknowledge me.

No need to let a slight that insignificant get to me. "Then I will show you around, Mr. Steel," I say.

"An interesting choice of name." The tone in his voice says the opposite.

"Would you have preferred Lavinia?" I ask, archly.

"I suppose I should be grateful you did not name me Caligula."

"I might have thought you'd favour such a name, being a demon."

"No doubt you did." There is something in his gaze I can't place. I turn away and lead him to the south wing.

It's only when we reach my room, Turner's old one, that I realise the issue. Clara put up a truckle bed in my room, assuming—all of us assuming—that I'd be returning with a female demon. Not the tall, male Hound behind me.

I pause on the threshold. I can't very well let him sleep in the same room as me. But this is all the accommodation that Hound agents receive. Where else is he going to sleep?

"This is your room?"

I step aside in answer, and he takes the opportunity to walk past me, through the door. Swallowing, I linger on the threshold.

"*This* is your room?" he repeats, incredulous.

"Yes."

He stares at the simple lodging, and I try to see the place through his eyes. No portraits, or jewellery, no mementos well-worn and well loved. Anyone could live here.

"I keep things bare to prevent distractions," I say, into the quiet. It's a half-truth. I own nothing from before the agency, not even a picture of my parents. That part of my life is over. "About where you'll sleep—" I begin, hesitant.

"If this is to be the limit of what you can provide, then I think the corridor is preferable." He breezes past me into the passage, then sets his shoulders to the wall and folds his arms. And stays there, as though he's going to sleep standing upright like a horse.

I eye him. "Are you...certain? I could ask for other accommodation..."

He tucks his chin into his chest and closes his eyes, ending the discussion. His position is within the parameters of the spell, but it looks the furthest thing from comfortable.

Unsure what else to do, I go into my room and close the door. After a moment's thought, I lock it. Just in case. Then I stare at my room, bemused, only a thin wall between me and my new partner.

It seems I have much to learn about this creature before I can hope for the kind of camaraderie that Lavender and Turner shared. If we're ever to reach that point.

With a tired sigh, I strip out of my clothes and into a nightgown, readying myself for bed. I hope this Hound has a good nose. I have a murderer to find.

CHAPTER ELEVEN

I'm woken in what feels like the middle of the night. Someone knocks on the door. I immediately think of Turner and scramble out of bed to unlock it.

Maia stands on the other side. "All is well," she says. "Forgive me, I did not mean to startle you."

"Did something happen?" I ask, sleepy-mouthed and blurry.

"No. I just thought you should eat."

I sit on my bed, rubbing my face. Light streams through the window in bright squares that should have woken me long before now. The night must have taken more out of me than I thought.

I peek through my fingers at the door as Maia closes it behind her. I don't feel the crushing pressure of the spell's limit. "Is he still outside?" I whisper, and then feel foolish for whispering.

"It seems he has been there all morning." Maia hands me a bowl of soup and then places a small box on my dresser.

"Did he sleep?" I ask, after I've taken a mouthful: only carrot and celery, yet rich with flavour. Maia could make a delicious meal from a handful of almonds.

She shrugs. "I could not tell. I gave him a bowl of soup. The poor thing seemed starved."

I imagine Steel's expression if Maia was to call him 'poor thing' to his face.

"Well." Maia pulls up the lone chair and takes a seat, facing me with the stare that drags all of my worries out into the open. "A male Hound."

I swallow another mouthful of soup. It's hot. She must have come straight up after making it. "So he says," I reply.

"I thought we knew everything there was to know about demons," Maia says, thoughtfully. "Of course, it would not be the first time that we were wrong. I assume that you will want to document him," she adds. "For the lexicon."

That hadn't occurred to me. This is a chance to capture information on what differentiates him from other Hounds; his abilities, his limits.

"Later," I decide. "Monaghan's put us on the Whitechapel case. That's my priority."

Maia nods, and her next look is shrewd. "And how do you feel about a male demon as a partner?"

Not easy, but I'd hardly risk the case on such a small matter. "A demon is a demon."

The woman hums. "Let us hope he can do half a good a job as Lavender did."

I lower the bowl and let it rest on my legs, the warmth chasing away a sudden chill. "What do the rest of the agency think?" I ask, instead of dwelling on Lavender.

"Jacob is worried, as usual. Rayne was not content with the test, and if there is one thing I will grant your new demon, it is the ability to put that boy in his place."

"And Monaghan? Is he angry?"

"Angry? Why would he be?"

I fiddle with my spoon, turning up a chunk of carrot from the broth. "That I failed the ritual."

"The ritual was designed to summon and bind a demon," she says, firmly. "And at that, you were successful."

I still *feel* as though I failed. "Any word from Eve?"

"The case they have been given will be difficult. I do not think they will have much time for letters."

Eve will have a few things to say about Steel by then. I'll have to ensure my new partner and I are cordial when she does.

"Ah, there is more. I brought up Turner's things from the library. The professor thought it best you have them." Maia indicates the box she'd put on the once bare dresser.

"That's all there is?" I ask, frowning.

"That, and the clothes in the wardrobe. Turner was not one for material possessions." Maia's mouth turns down and she stands. "Well. Do not forget your dinner. Now that the test has been passed, your demon should become accustomed to Maximus before he becomes territorial."

I nod and Maia slips through the door. I don't look as she does, not sure if I want to catch sight of Steel just yet.

After finishing the soup, I climb out of bed and dress. I stand in front of the second wardrobe and, bracing myself, open it. Inside hang two simple woollen skirts and a plain evening gown.

Turner's dresses. I stroke my hand along one of the sleeves, allow myself a moment of welling grief. Then I let it go.

None of the dresses are big enough to fit me. A few other pieces hang to the side, pressed too closely together for me to make out at a glance. I push them apart and inhale in surprise.

Men's suits; one in grey, one in black and another in brown. I compare the sizing to the dresses. All the same. Men would attract less attention than women, and suits such as these could have belonged to any of a thousand men in the city. In somewhere like Whitechapel, someone in one of these suits wouldn't draw a second glance.

Still, it would take someone with considerable strength of will to risk public ridicule. I close the wardrobe and finish getting dressed.

The small box that Maia left looks old and worn. I open it and flip through its contents: a couple of books; an old portrait of a couple—Turner's parents, perhaps; a sprig of dried lavender that makes my heart squeeze; a small journal, like my own notebook.

I sit on the bed and open it to the last page. A confusing mess of symbols meets my eyes. A code?

I flick through the pages. Sure enough, each one is covered in the same code. Some of the symbols don't look like letters at all.

I look at the books again, searching for a clue to the code she used. They all seem unrelated. I try a generic Caesar's code, shifting the letters through the alphabet, then a few other cyphers, but none of my solutions work. I'll have to give it more thought.

Glancing again at the window, I note the brightness of the day and the position of the sun. I've been stalling. At some point today, I'll need to leave my room.

Resolutely, I stand and shake out my skirt. There's no point putting it off any longer.

The demon sits sprawled across the floor, his back to the wall. His legs reach almost to the other side of the corridor. I clear my throat. He doesn't react. With his chin sunk onto his chest, I can't tell if he's asleep.

I take a step closer, but he doesn't even twitch. Is this an act to lure me closer, before he…before he what? What can he do?

Taking my courage in both hands, I touch his shoulder. Steel groans and lifts his head, blinking. "What is it?"

My eyebrows arch up before I can stop them. "You were asleep?"

He frowns at me. "Was that not evident?"

I stand upright, looking down at him. It's reassuring to do so; it feels more normal than anything else has in the last day. "We should go down for dinner," I tell him. "You do eat, don't you?"

The demon's eyes spark and he lurches to his feet, as if I'd cast a spell with my words. "Lead the way."

It's with trepidation that I approach the kitchen. Maia is at the hearth, speaking to Clara in a low, hard voice. Jacob sits astride the bench with Max.

At my approach, Maia's conversation falls silent, and Clara turns in a whirl of skirts. The maid levels a burning gaze at me and flounces out of the room. I send a searching look Maia's way, but the older woman shrugs.

"You know how Clara is. Sweet as honey one minute, vinegar the next."

"I've done nothing to offend her." The only thing that's changed in the last day is the addition of another demon to the agency. What reason would she have to be angry at that?

My gaze falls on Steel. It's Clara who places the ingredient bags in the ritual room to soak up as much magic as possible. She had opportunity. I drift closer to Maia.

"Where was Clara, before the ritual?"

The housekeeper tilts her head in thought. "Tidying the rooms upstairs. Why do you ask?" She narrows her eyes at me. "You think she had something to do with the spell?"

"I don't know," I say, after a moment. Why would she sabotage an event we all needed? "Perhaps I just made a mistake."

Maia raises one brow at that. "That is possible, I suppose."

Steel gives a soft snort behind me. I ignore it.

"Why do you not confront her?" Maia continues. "If she changed the components, she should be punished for it."

"I have no proof. I won't cause dissent in the agency for no good reason."

"It is your choice." The tone in her voice tells me what she thinks of my decision. "How did you sleep?"

I take a minute to realise that she's addressing Steel. So does he, it seems, as he takes longer to answer. "Badly," is his flat response. I hadn't considered that my demon might be rude.

"I am not surprised," she says, brisk and business-like. "Sleeping on the floor cannot be comfortable. I will see what I can do about getting you a room with a bed."

He displays no sign of gratitude. I remind myself that he has little reason to.

"Thank you," I reply. "That would be appreciated."

"Go on and sit down. I will make you something to eat."

Jacob greets me as I join him, his gaze flicking to Steel.

"All right?" he asks, frowning. "Everything…went well?"

"As well as can be expected," I murmur back, then realise Steel has not sat down, and I twist in my seat to look for him.

He's stopped a few feet behind me, staring across the table at Max. The Reaper stares back. A low vibration reverberates in my chest, a sound without sound. They're facing off like two cats who've come across each other unexpectedly in a dark alley.

"Steel?" I ask, as Jacob says, "Max?"

The Reaper folds first, glancing down at his agent. His mouth shifts into a small smile, and he sits at the table opposite Jacob. He does not look at Steel. The Hound breathes out loud enough that I can hear him, and sits stiffly at the end of the bench, half-turned away from the Reaper. I give him an enquiring look, but he avoids my gaze.

"We haven't met properly." Jacob sounds as bemused as I feel. "I'm Jacob," he says, "and this is Max. That's Maia, of course."

Steel gives no response, and the energy that vibrates off both demons makes the hair on my arms stand on end.

"I'm sure we can all be friends," Jacob continues, with an awkward half-laugh. "Or at least…civil?"

"I will have no fighting in my kitchen." Maia swoops between both demons and lands a plate in front of them. "Eat. Stop behaving like children."

Max takes up his utensils, ignoring Steel, and Steel eventually does the same, eating with focused determination. By the time Maia sets a plate in front of me, his is half empty.

When we've finished, I clear the table and get halfway through cleaning the dishes before Maia catches me at it and ushers me away. Max and Steel start bristling at each other again, so I turn to Jacob.

"Do you know where Rayne is?"

He shakes his head. "I haven't seen him all day."

"He went to the station," Maia calls. "He is talking with the Inspector about the Whitechapel case."

I press my hands on the wood. He must have left while I was still asleep. I've been in the role for less than a day and I'm already behind.

"Are you on this case, too?" I ask Jacob.

"Me?" He gives me an odd look. "You know Tiberius covers London."

"I know. I only..." I want a familiar face. I don't want to walk into this alone.

I glance at Steel and correct that thought. I'm not alone anymore—I won't be alone again for years. The thought is both disconcerting and oddly comforting.

CHAPTER TWELVE

I catch a few hours of sleep that night and wake before dawn. It's chilly again, and I dress quickly, putting my things into a neat pile for Clara to wash. A vague sense of guilt nags at me as I do. Now I'm no longer an apprentice, I don't have to do my own cleaning, but leaving it for someone else feels like I'm taking advantage. It takes me a few attempts to stop straightening the clothes and leave.

"Good morning," I announce loudly to the heap of slumbering demon outside. Maia found him some clothes that fit, so now he has a decent jacket and some shoes.

He glares up at me, his serpentine eyes narrowed. "Morning?" he croaks. "I think you must be mistaken. It's still night."

I glance at the windows that line the corridor. Sure enough, dawn is a pale impression above the cluttered rooftops of the city. "The earlier we rise, the more day we have," I reply. "And we have a lot to accomplish."

I stride to the stairs and pause just inside the spell's limit. I'm impatient, but I don't want to hurt him.

Grumbling comes from behind me, then the rustle of clothes and finally slow, lumbering footsteps. "What, exactly, are we doing?"

"First, breakfast." I turn my head to catch the brightening of his expression. Too easy. "Then, we must speak to Agent Rayne about the case."

"Everyone keeps talking about this case," he says, as we make our way downstairs.

"You haven't seen the newspapers?"

"Why would I be interested in the papers?"

Sighing, I explain. "There's been a series of murders in the Whitechapel district. The agency's investigating."

"Aren't murders commonplace in the East End?" he asks, through a wide yawn.

He knows London, then, and its districts. "It's not the murders themselves," I reply. "It's how they were committed. The perpetrator was—is—either a demon, or unhinged. No one sane could commit these kinds of atrocities."

He raises a brow, looking interested. "Perhaps this won't be a complete waste of my time, after all."

Exasperated, I drop the subject. We're the first to rise, so we have the kitchen to ourselves. I slice some bread and spread it with dripping, serving it to Steel with watercress and a cup of tea. Steel eats everything but wrinkles his nose at the tea.

"Too hot?"

He puts it aside. "Too bitter. Don't you have any sugar?"

"Do you know how expensive sugar is?" I take his cup and I return it full of cool water, setting it down with a click. "Here.

Water." Then I'm annoyed at myself for being offended over tea, of all things.

Steel takes his water mutely, his cheeks sucked in as though he's restraining a smirk.

Rosy light creeps in at the window. "Rayne will be up, soon," I say, once we've finished. "Let's go." He follows me with a grumble, eyeing the rest of the loaf.

The entrance hall has been cleared of flowers, although their cloying scent lingers in the air. Roses and anemones. I frown at a table where a vase of them had stood. It would have been easy enough for Clara to change the spell components, but what would she have gained by doing so?

The answer comes quickly: if I'd failed, she would have been next in line to perform the ritual. She could have bypassed her apprenticeship completely.

It would have been a foolish decision, both for her, and for the agency. Monaghan wouldn't have approved it. Unless he desperately needed a Hound...

No matter how I look at the situation, I can't shake my suspicion. I could have made a mistake and picked up the wrong bag, but for it to be filled with the same flowers that lined the agency's halls that evening... Suspicious, indeed.

Suspicion isn't enough. I can't risk Clara's position, or my own, without solid proof.

I close my eyes and pinch the bridge of my nose. What's done is done. I have Steel, now, and I'm on the Whitechapel case. Anything that's not related to solving the murders is superfluous.

With new determination, I open my eyes. I feel a prickle of awareness and realise Steel is watching me, something calculating in his face. I look at him and the expression disappears behind a smirk.

Footsteps make me turn. Rayne descends the staircase with Cassius, both of them dressed in hats and coats. He glances at me as he reaches the hall.

"Miss Locke," he says, pulling on his gloves. "It's early. What can I do for you?"

"I finished the report you wanted," I reply. "If you're heading into Whitechapel, I can get my coat—"

"Not necessary. We won't need a Hound yet."

I pause. "Would you like the report now, then?"

"Have Clara leave it in my room."

"And the Coldstream Guards?"

He frowns. "I thought we discussed that. The military suspects in the Tabram case were cleared. Pursuing that line of investigation is wasting time."

Jacob appears on the staircase with Max. He and the Reaper also wear coats and hats, and my answer to Rayne dies on my tongue. Jacob gives me a sheepish look.

"Agent Rayne asked me to accompany him," he says, apologetically.

"The police have a suspect," Rayne explains. "Some butcher they're calling Leather Apron. If Cassius can find him, the Reaper can deal with him and we'll close this case once and for all."

I press my tongue to the back of the teeth as I choose my words. "I thought it was a Hound's duty to track a suspect."

"Monaghan can't expect you to go out there searching for this man," Rayne says, as if he's surprised I'd suggest such a thing. "It's too dangerous for a woman to be on the streets right now."

"Max doesn't know how to mask his presence," I reply. It's one of the reasons Reapers aren't sent in until the last possible moment; demons can feel them coming a mile away. Tiberius can cloak his aura, but only for a short time, and Max is too young to do even that much. "Would it not be safer—"

"I know what I'm doing, Locke," Rayne interrupts. "Leave it with me."

"It's just this once," Jacob adds, searching my face. "Max is getting cooped up here, anyway. We need to get out for a bit."

"Of course," I say, my lips a little too pursed. First, I couldn't get the ritual right, and now I can't even do my job. "I will leave the report in your room, sir."

"Good girl."

I flare my tongue between my teeth and bite down to stay silent. Rayne touches the brim of his hat and strides out with Cassius beside him.

"It's just one day," Jacob says. The words are tossed over his shoulder as he follows Rayne out of the door. "We'll be back soon." They vanish and I glare at the closed doors. Some agent I'm turning out to be.

"So, we're left behind to sit here and do nothing?" Steel comments.

"We have a hierarchy." Rayne outranks both of us. Neither Jacob nor I have much choice but to obey.

"How are we supposed to investigate a murder if we can't investigate the *actual murder*? You might as well have left me in Paris."

Despite all his complaints, he's right. Sitting here won't do the victims any favours. But before I can do anything, I need information.

"This way," I call, climbing the staircase.

"Are we going back to bed?"

"No. We have research to do."

There's a pause, and Steel draws level with me. He glances down—the strangeness of that makes me blink, off balance—and says, scornfully, "Research?"

"Research," I confirm. "You didn't think this agency was *all* blood rituals and breakfasts?"

"I'd hoped it was."

"Without the necessary knowledge, even our best agents are useless. That's why we have apprentices."

"So, why can't your apprentice do this?"

I doubt Clara would lift a finger to read a book, even if I asked. "Summoning you wasn't...planned for," I say, evasively.

"That much was evident."

"The previous Hound agent was murdered," I explain. My voice skips on the last word, but the demon doesn't comment. "Monaghan had to promote another quickly, and as her apprentice I was the logical choice."

"Your agency can't be doing a very good job if all these people are getting killed."

I glare at him. He lifts one shoulder in a half-hearted shrug.

"That's why we're here," I tell him. "We're going to stop it."

He hums, non-committal.

In the library, I head to the bookcase that holds Maia's newspapers. The shelves are all full. I pull out the papers from the last month and drop them onto my desk. Steel folds into a winged chair against the wall and throws one leg over the arm.

"How long is this going to take?"

"As long as necessary." I sit down and get to work.

Martha Tabram was killed on the seventh of August. Articles about her murder are scattered throughout the newspapers. I scan each one, looking for any mention of the military, or the Coldstream Guards. Turner must have been on to something. I'm not going to leave her investigation unfinished.

There's not much in the first week after Tabram's death. I move on to the next, scanning through each paper. Finally, I find an inquest report that describes the witnesses. I skim through it, running my finger under each line so I miss nothing.

Here. One of the witnesses identified two soldiers who were with the victim on the night she died. These soldiers must be the ones Turner found, the Coldstream regiment. The witness, Mary Ann Connolly, is described in the report as an "unfortunate" known as Pearly Poll, who lived in the Whitechapel district.

If I can find Mary Ann, she can tell me about the soldiers she saw that night. Of course, that would mean leaving the agency and risking the danger that Rayne ordered me to avoid. I look at Steel. His head is tilted back against the chair, his eyes lidded. With a demon beside me, I shouldn't have any problems. His height alone should intimidate any would-be attackers.

The truth that lies under my excuses is that I don't want to sit here, waiting. Turner is dead, these women are dead, and another day will widen the gap between us and their killer.

I stand. Steel lifts his head, his gaze lighting up with interest. I don't blame him for being restless.

"Maia gave you a coat, did she not?" I ask.

His mouth turns up at one corner. "We're leaving?"

"We're going to find someone. But first let's get something to hide those eyes." I rifle through the shelves until I find a box of someone's effects; a past agent, perhaps. When I turn, Steel is already behind me. "These are for you," I tell him, and hand him a pair of coloured spectacles.

He takes them, arching his eyebrows. "Do you doubt my eyesight, Miss Locke?"

"They're not prescription; they're to hide your eyes." He smirks and I realise he was teasing. "If you put them on, we can get underway."

The frames are silver and the lenses tinted dark grey, dark enough that they obscure the elongated length of his pupils when he slots the arms over his ears.

"You will spoil me with all of these gifts," he says, the sardonic note in his voice evident.

"It's my duty to protect you," I reply automatically, and he blinks. "You'll need a hat, too," I add, and head out of the library, pleased when I hear Steel follow.

CHAPTER THIRTEEN

S mog squats in the city streets, filling the air with the stink of coal. I breathe through my mouth where I can, holding my breath when the foul air becomes too much. Steel is a tall impression of black at my side. A Homburg hat sits at an angle on his head, giving him a rakish air. With his dark spectacles, he could be an aristocrat's son dressed incognito, seeking adventure among the working class of the East End. It's as good a disguise as any.

Nevertheless, this will be a test for him as much as it is for me. I try to keep my eyes on his figure and on the road ahead.

It's an easy walk to the East End. Just as well: there aren't many cabs willing to travel into Whitechapel right now, despite the rich young men who want to test their mettle against the district's killer.

We pass St. Botolph's Church and head into Whitechapel proper, where the houses crowd together and the alleys bloat with people. Raucous shouting from an alleyway indicates a bar fight has spilled into the streets.

A few people glance at us as we pass. My gait lengthens and I inhale the mixture of cooked meat, sweat and refuse that makes up the aroma of east London. Here, I'm just another woman trying to make her way in the world. A weight falls away from my shoulders.

"What are we doing here?" Steel asks.

"We're looking for a woman called Pearly Poll."

He looks around with a clear expression of distaste. "And how are you going to find her in this?"

I raise my eyebrows at him. "*We* are going to *look*."

Without waiting for an answer, I turn down a narrow alley that leads up to Spitalfields Market. It's early afternoon, and the streets are filled with beggars, bare-footed children playing games, and the occasional street juggler.

This part of the city is crammed with more people than it has the space to serve, and most of them will have to barter for a space at a lodging house for the night. Others won't be able to afford even that, and will spend their nights tied to a pew, or out on the streets. I smooth my hand over my simple wool jacket, remind myself that this is no longer my home. I can leave whenever I want.

"These people..." Steel murmurs. "Why are they all here? Don't they have...?" He makes an oblique gesture, as though the words he wants can't fit into one sentence.

"They've nowhere else to go, Mr. Steel," I reply. "The Empire takes chunks of the world for itself, promising protection and safe haven in exchange for the scars it leaves behind. When people draw upon that promise, this is what they're rewarded with."

It's the most I've said to him since he arrived, and he looks surprised at me, or at the words themselves. He makes no reply, and I focus on our hunt. It's not in my power to fix all of London's troubles, but I can attempt to solve this one.

The buildings open up around Mitre Square. It's almost as busy as the market, but I see a couple of women standing on the corner, chatting. Their clothes are well worn, and they stand in a way that displays the curves of their bodies. One calls out to a man who walks by. He curses them and hurries on. I head in their direction.

"Good afternoon," I greet them, drawing their attention.

The nearest, a pretty woman with dark, curly hair, sizes me up. She has a faint bruise under her eye. "Bugger off," she says. "This corner's taken, you hear?"

A soft snicker comes from Steel. I give the woman a rueful smile. "I'm not working. I just wanted to ask you a few questions. About the murder."

Their faces close off. "Move on, luv. We've talked ourselves 'oarse to the coppers. We ain't interested in talking 'bout it no more," the first woman says. Her companion stares warily at Steel.

I turn and gesture at the square. He quirks a brow and moves away, standing at a nearby alley.

"I'll be honest with you," I tell the women. "I'm not working for the police. My colleague and I are with a private organisation."

"Colleague, eh?" the other woman says, smirking. "Must be hard to get any work done, eh, luv?"

"I'll just bet it's hard." This is accompanied by a lascivious wink in Steel's direction.

I don't turn to see how the demon reacts to that. "My name is Hazel," I offer. "I understand that Mary Ann Connolly saw a man with Martha the night she died. I'd like to talk to her."

"The coppers have talked to her already," the dark-haired woman says. "They ain't done nothing about it. That man's gone free and God help the next woman he drags into a dark alley."

"Annie, hush," the other girl says. "You're right," she tells me. "Poll said she saw them with Martha. But she didn't see 'em with Mary Nichols, God bless her soul." Mary was the most recent victim. But just because they weren't seen doesn't mean they weren't present.

"Poor girl," the woman called Annie says. "We'll have a drink for her, tonight." They nod together.

"Is Poll with you?" I ask.

Annie shrugs. "She'll be round 'ere somewhere. If she ain't off with a glass o' gin. She likes her drink, that one."

"Don't we all," comes a murmured agreement.

"What does she look like?"

"Light brown 'air, striped skirt," Annie replies. "She 'as a green necktie she likes to wear." They trail off, scanning the square for a mark, their attention moved on.

"Thank you," I say, and leave them to it.

Turning around, I see no sign of Steel. Tensing, I sweep the square for any hint of danger. No one looks out of place, or aware that a demon was in their midst.

My chest tightens, a slow band of pressure squeezing around my ribs. It takes me a second to realise that the sensation isn't imagined: the limit of the spell has been reached.

I hurry to the shadowed alley and stop in its mouth. Steel stands at the other end, examining the muddy floor.

"Is everything all right?" I ask, cautiously.

He looks up, his expression cool and unconcerned. "I thought I sensed something, but I was mistaken." He wanders back, loose-limbed and casual. The band around my chest eases as he approaches.

I measure the distance between where he was standing and where I had been speaking to Annie and her friend. It was a few feet beyond the limit of the spell. I assess him, and he returns my look with disinterest. He was testing it. Trying to find a way out?

No doubt he expects me to confront him. I don't think playing into his expectations will gain me the truth.

"They don't know where Connolly is," I tell him, watching for a change in expression that might indicate his thought process. Nothing: he's a blank slate. "We'll keep looking."

"All right," he agrees, amiably. Amiably because he's agreeing to my order, or because he wants another opportunity to test the limit of the spell?

I resume our pace, walking side by side. As an apprentice, when I'd considered the possibility of becoming an agent, I hadn't thought that I might have to guard against my own demon. How can he help me solve this case when he wants nothing to do with me?

There seems to be only one option: get him to trust me. Somehow.

For now, I keep walking. Trust will take time, and time I do not have. The case must come first.

The afternoon wanes into evening, and I start to wonder if Annie had been wrong; that Connolly wasn't here at all. My stomach growls, eager for the dinner Maia will be preparing. I listen for the Spitalfields bells that will mark the time. Rayne will return to the agency soon, if he hasn't already. Being here is already disobeying his order; being absent when he returns will not bode well for me.

"Is that her?" Steel asks, pulling me from my thoughts. He tilts his head at a woman with long striped skirts and a green neckerchief.

"Yes. Thank you," I add, cursing inwardly: I'd been so immersed in my thoughts I hadn't seen her. I shouldn't be so distracted.

Bearing in mind the reaction from the two women earlier, I approach Mary Ann cautiously. Steel drops back and leans against the wall, sinking both hands into the pockets of his greatcoat. He puts his chin to his chest, and the roguishly angled hat conceals his eyes.

I step up to the woman's side. "Mary Ann Connolly."

She eyes me, startled. "Do I know you?" she asks, in a low, croaky voice that speaks of long nights with little sleep.

I pull out the warrant card Monaghan gave me. Showing it to Annie and her friend might have led to more questions than I'd like to answer, but Mary Ann is alone, and clearly nervous. This might do more to reassure her than words can. Her eyes widen at the stamp on the card.

"I'm a private investigator, looking into the recent murders on behalf of my employer," I say, keeping the details vague.

"You identified two suspects, the night Martha Tabram was murdered. Can you tell me more about them?"

"I already gave my report to the police," she says, eyes narrowing. "What's it got to do with you and whatever rich asshole is making you wander round 'ere?"

"We're following up on the details, in case there's anything the police missed."

Her gaze sparks. "Aye, they couldn't find their way out of a paper bag." She snorts. "Well. Good to have a woman on it, at any rate. You work for them high and mighties in the City, do you? Fancy that."

"It's a small department," I reply, with a self-deprecating smile, "and my role is unofficial." The ploy seems to work; her posture unbends, and she slants her body to face me. "You told the coroner that you met two soldiers that night," I prompt her.

"That's right. A private and a corporal. They had white bands round their 'ats."

I nod, pulling out my tiny notebook. "And it was the private who went with Martha?"

"S'right. I identified them for the investigator. He said it weren't them." She scowled and shook her head. "But I knows what I saw."

"Could you identify them again for me?"

She laughs at that. "Bless you, luv. You should have seen the Major's face when I first walked in. Me, with all their soldiers? Nah, they won't let that happen again." Mary Ann's eyes are tight, the corners wrinkling as she grimaces. She doesn't want to go through the process again any more than this Major does.

"I understand." The police or the regiment will have a record of her identification; I don't need to force her to revisit that night. "Thank you for your help."

"You just catch the bloke who did this," she replies, grimly. "It's 'ard enough working these streets already. Now we have to worry about a bloody killer, too."

"I'll get him." The words slip out before I can stop them. Promises are for children; Turner taught me that. We don't make them if we can't keep them.

But I can't ignore my conviction. Somehow, I'll find a way to keep this promise.

I return to Steel, who examines me from under the brim of his hat. "What now?" he asks.

The sky is darkening. I wait, and after a moment the bells ring out the hour: six o'clock. Staying any longer is too great a risk, both in terms of the danger that walks these streets, and in disobeying Rayne's orders.

"We return to the agency," I decide.

"Aren't we here to catch a killer?"

"You have good ears."

"Hound," he reminds me. "That's why you called me, isn't it? To sniff out a murderer? So, let's get to it."

I waver, caught between my orders and my desire to do as he says. Common sense blankets my conviction. Wandering the streets of Whitechapel with no leads and no clues is going to have us walking in circles.

"We go back."

Steels pushes off the wall. "As you wish. Lead the way."

I narrow my eyes at him, half in suspicion and half in warning, and sweep in front to start home. Tomorrow, I'll visit the regiment, and I'll find the private who met Martha Tabram. And, hopefully, I'll find her murderer.

CHAPTER FOURTEEN

Rayne is not waiting when we return. I breathe a sigh of relief as I remove my hat and gloves. The grand clock in the hallway strikes half past the hour. Dinner, and then I'll go through the inquest report again, see if I can find any other clues.

Steel turns towards the dining hall once I've put away my things. I hesitate. Normally I eat in the kitchen, the same as the other apprentices; the dining hall is saved for agents. But *I'm* an agent, now.

The demon is already at the door, so I follow him inside. Three long tables stretch across the middle of the room, although only half of one has been set with cutlery and plates. None of the tables are occupied.

"Rayne and Jacob must still be out there," I say, more to fill the silence than to begin a conversation.

"All the better for my stomach," Steel murmurs, making a direct line for the sideboard, which has been laid out with steamed vegetables, baked fish and small buttery potatoes. There's also a dish of Maia's turmeric-spiced rice, dotted with tiny pearl onions. Steel takes some of everything. Amused, I trail after him.

"Did you not eat in Paris?" I ask, wondering if his plate will crack under its load.

"Generally, people prefer that you *buy* food rather than steal it," he replies, dryly. He chooses a chair set against the wall, balancing his plate on his lap. He eats with dedication, leaving no room for conversation.

I sit close enough that it won't strain our bond if he chooses to move. Without conversation I can pay attention to my own thoughts, which puzzle over the murders.

Martha Tabram was stabbed thirty-nine times, whereas Mary Ann Nichols had her throat slit. Why the difference? Why just cut Mary's throat?

Just, as though the horror of the crime isn't enough.

"Here you are." Maia enters the room and takes Steel's plate, who, it seems, has finished first. "I was wondering where you disappeared to."

"I went to speak to someone about the case."

"I see." Maia takes my plate and stacks it on top of Steel's. She doesn't comment on the fact that I ate less than half of my meal. "I am glad you have returned. I have set up some new rooms for you." She puts the plates on the sideboard and wipes her hands on her apron. "Come, I will show you."

"Thank you, Maia. I appreciate it," I reply. I glance at Steel and he rises.

"We cannot have demons sleeping in corridors," Maia says. She leads us up to the third floor, but instead of continuing to the fourth, where Turner and Khurana's rooms are located, she turns onto the corridor that houses the male agents. There are doors all along the passage, more than twice the number of agents.

"We'll be on the third floor?" I ask, doubtfully.

"This floor is the only one that contains adjoining rooms. We cannot permit a man to sleep in the same room as you, demon or not," Maia says, with a snort.

"And Turner's things?" Even if I can't fit into Turner's clothes, I don't want to part with them.

"I have moved them. There is enough space for more dresses, if you like. The agency has a fund to keep its agents clothed and shod."

I'd look like a horse playing dress-up. "I have everything I need," I reply, flatly.

"You will need an evening dress, soon; Her Majesty's agents are often invited to the Home Office's dinner parties. But that can wait. As you say, you have the case to deal with." Maia opens a door and nods to another close by. "That is your room," she tells Steel. "There is an adjoining door between the two. I will give you the key," she adds to me, and enters the room.

I hesitate before following her. "Let me know if the room suits," I say, and Steel gives me a look I can't decipher.

The new room is not quite twice the size of Turner's, but it's close. The bed is a double, swathed in a thick russet blanket, and a rug covers the floor, shielding our feet from the cold. The dresser has a mirror and a matching chair, and the two wardrobes are large and made of oak. My gaze is drawn to the adjoining door, opposite the bed.

"Here is the key." Maia hands it to me, a small iron thing with a circular grip. "Best that you lock it when I leave," she adds, pointedly.

I hesitate. The ritual test was instigated centuries ago, to ensure the loyalty of the summoned demon, but...could there be a chance that Steel cheated? That he's not as safe as I've assumed?

I recall the frustration in Steel's expression as he'd stood with Rayne's blade digging into his chest, the way he'd tested the spell's limits earlier. The binding worked, so there's no reason to think that the limitations around causing harm did not. I take the key from Maia, anyway.

"Turner's books are here." The other woman indicates the box and then a pile of things next to it. "Clara laundered your clothes as well, and I took the liberty of purchasing some new things. Now, I will be in the kitchen if you need me." She squeezes my arm as she leaves, a soft comfort.

When she's gone, I sit on the bed and regard the room. The windows are flanked by heavy purple drapes, blocking the light from the street gas lamps. Anything that might have belonged to the agent who used to own the room has gone, and the place feels unfamiliar and uncomfortable.

Taking a deep breath, I set about rectifying that, putting away my clothes and the new things Maia selected for me: a pretty horsehair brush with a silver handle, a simple copper bowl for washing and a small jar of castor oil for my brows.

Once they're on the dresser, I fold into the chair and rest my elbow on its back. It isn't the room that's making me uncomfortable, it's the adjoining door. It shouldn't be any different than having Steel sleep in the corridor—there's still a wall and a door between us—but it feels much more intimate to know he's so close.

I pick up the key, turn it over in my hand. What would Eve do? What would Khurana do, if she were in my position?

Khurana would not sit here, afraid of her own demon. I tap the key against my chin, regarding the door through narrowed eyes. A few hours ago, I was thinking about how I could get Steel to trust me. This is an opportunity to try.

I grip the key and advance towards the door as though striding into battle. Raising my hand, I tap on the wood, twice, and wait for a response.

None comes. I stand there for a long moment. Perhaps he won't answer. Perhaps all he'll allow me is the tense civility we've built outside these rooms.

The door opens. I blink and Steel stares at me.

"I…" I haven't prepared anything to say. "I thought I'd check that you have everything you need," I finish.

His gaze slides sideways, as if he's watching my words march out of my mouth. He opens the door wider, giving me a view into the room. "It's sufficient."

One wardrobe, instead of two, and the furniture seems more cheaply made, but the bed is equipped with sheets and a warm blanket, and there's even a razor and a shaving bowl on the dresser. Maia thought of everything.

"Good." I search for something else to bridge the gap between us. What do agents talk about with their demons, if not cases? I recall the way Jacob reintroduced me to Max. "How do you feel about the name Steel?" I ask. Although the spell is sealed by a name, I don't have to use it. "Would you prefer a different one?"

He shrugs. "One name is much the same as another."

"Do you have one of your own?" I persist.

"Not that I'm attached to. And yours?" he adds, before I can pursue the point. "What should I call you?"

I hadn't thought to introduce myself to him. "My apologies," I say, hastily. "My name is Hazel Locke."

"Hazel," he says, drawing the word out long and slow in a way that brings a flush to my cheeks and irritation to the rest of me.

I take a breath to remind myself what he is. "You may call me agent or Miss Locke." I keep my voice cool.

His mouth twitches into a smirk. "Why, when such a pretty name exists for my use?"

"Not for your use, Mr. Steel."

"I thought my name was Steel," he says, with a sardonic lift of his eyebrows.

"*Mister* Steel," I repeat.

"You're more stubborn than I expected, Miss Locke," he says, but the purring tone in his voice has vanished.

If I had a point, he has successfully diverted me from it. "So, you're pleased with the room?" I ask, reverting to my original topic.

"A bed is better than cold stone to sleep on."

That's something, at least. "You're welcome," I say, and his eyes narrow, his dark brows slanting downward.

"Am I?" he says, low but no purr; all menace. "Forgive me. Should I have thanked you for trapping me here and binding me to you like a dog? Should I be grateful that you deign to give me a roof and three meals, and forget that I can't go more than twenty feet away from you? Would you like me to thank you for it?"

My eyes have widened. "I—"

He turns away, the ice in his voice melting. "It's late, Agent Locke. I'm tired."

The words and the gesture are as clear a dismissal as he could make. I swallow, his words reverberating through my head. I turn to go, then stop. After a moment's hesitation, I take one step inside and place the key on his dresser. Then I turn and leave, shutting the door behind me. It's not much, not compared to everything he just said, but it's something. It's something, isn't it?

I stay awake for a long time, staring at the ceiling, listening for the click of a lock. I'm not sure if I'll feel better if I hear it, or worse.

CHAPTER FIFTEEN

I fall asleep before I hear anything. In the morning, I try to ignore the adjoining door while I dress, avoid thinking about the previous night. I don't succeed as well as I'd hoped.

Steel is awake and standing in the corridor when I emerge. "I didn't think you'd rise so early," I say, glancing at the dark window.

"I thought you'd prefer not to have to lever me out of bed."

I don't deign to give that a response.

"Whitechapel, again?" he asks, as we walk to breakfast.

"We need to visit the regiment," I reply. "I want to find out more about these soldiers." But first, I'll need to tell Rayne. I'll need his support to arrange a meeting with the Major.

It's too early for breakfast in the dining hall, so I take Steel to the kitchen. He settles at the table, yawning, and eats while I think. Rayne will go back to the station today. We can meet him there.

"Hazel."

I look up, my spoon halfway to my mouth. "Maia?" The housekeeper's face is drawn, and my heart skips. "What is it?"

"You should see Monaghan." Maia holds a newspaper, the pages crumpled in her hand. "He's in his office."

The sun has crept high enough over the roofs to illuminate the kitchen. Monaghan is always up before dawn, but he doesn't usually take meetings at this time.

I lower my spoon. "There's been another murder," I guess.

Steel pauses, and Maia gives a jerky nod. "Yes. Another woman."

Another murder the same night I was looking for clues to the killer's identity. I stand and have to wait as Steel drains his bowl and lumbers up after me. I grip my skirts with both hands and push down the coil of tension bubbling up my throat. What did he do to her? Who was she?

Monaghan's assistant isn't at his desk yet, but the door is open. Monaghan looks up as I reach the study and beckons me in. Tiberius leans against the mahogany desk, his collar unbuttoned and his necktie looped haphazardly around his throat. He straightens when I enter and retreats to the back of the room.

"There's been another murder?" I ask.

Monaghan nods and the tight feeling in my chest squeezes. "A woman was found a few hours ago in Hanbury Street."

Hanbury Street was a few minutes from where we were yesterday. If I'd listened to Steel, I might have saved her. Taking a deep breath, I battle the guilt worming through my stomach and ask, "How was she killed?"

"Her throat was slit, and..." He hesitates.

I stand straighter, try to show I can handle the news. "And?"

"Her intestines were removed."

I wince before I can stop myself. Monaghan's eyes are on my face, so I control my reaction quickly. "Go on."

"The police found her this morning. A few reporters have already been down there, and Doyle managed to get word to us. I think you should visit the crime scene," he adds, his gaze taking in both me and Steel. "Perhaps you will find something, so soon after the murder."

"Yes, sir."

"I understand Rayne visited Whitechapel yesterday," he adds, lacing his fingers on the desk. "And he took Maximus with him."

I hesitate. If I confirm the truth, no doubt Jacob will bear some of the punishment alongside Rayne. Monaghan's expression goes cold and distant: he doesn't need me to confirm it; he already knows.

"That's correct," I admit.

"Rayne needs to understand that Reapers are not investigative agents," Monaghan says, in a hard voice. "If we are going to catch this man, we must use delicacy. A Reaper's energy is not subtle, and Maximus does not have the experience yet to disguise it. Rayne must take a Hound in future." How I'm expected to make Rayne do that is not made clear. But the professor drops his gaze. "Take a cab to Hanbury Street, and see what you and Steel can find," he orders. "I'll send Rayne to you as soon as he wakes."

"Yes, sir." I curtsy and leave.

Steel says nothing as I collect my coat and hat, but I sense his curiosity vibrate in the diminished space between us. Outside, I call a hansom cab and squeeze into it with the demon. The driver clicks his horse into a quick trot. When we're moving and I don't have to do anything but think, my mind turns back to the murder.

"If we had stayed in Whitechapel," I ask, quietly, "could you have sensed the murderer?"

"If it was another demon," Steel replies, "yes."

I clench my hands into fists on my lap. Guilt wars with shame and disappointment. A real agent would have stayed out until dawn, searching for this man. If I had just looked for a little longer...

My vision blurs and I look up at the dull grey sky to ease the tears before they come. I can't let emotion sway me now. Another woman lies dead. I won't let her death be for nothing.

The driver is reluctant to get too close to Whitechapel, so I stop the cab a few minutes' walk away and pay him with two coins from my new allowance. The man whips his horse into a canter, as eager to leave the East End as I am to enter it.

"Hanbury Street is this way," I tell Steel. Even if I didn't know it, the location of the crime scene would be easy to find; Whitechapel throngs with people heading in that direction, craning their necks for a glimpse at the corpse.

"You know this place," Steel says, trailing after me.

There's intent behind the statement, an exploratory probe to nudge me into giving up some detail about myself, or the agency. "Yes," I reply, simply, and add, over my shoulder, "Keep your head down." He makes a sound of acknowledgement and I push my way through the crowd.

The police have cordoned off the entrance to Hanbury Street and huddle around a house. I approach the nearest officer. "Who is the Inspector in charge?"

The man blinks at me, and stammers, "I-Inspector Chandler. Who—"

"He's inside?" I hold his gaze, unblinking. Sometimes a direct gaze can be as intimidating as a fist. Another of Turner's pearls.

"Wh—yes, in the yard, but—"

"Thank you." I sweep past him and into the house before he can do more than gape at me.

At the far end of the passage, the door to the yard is open. Light spills into the cramped interior. The sound of voices comes from upstairs, no doubt the police searching the rooms. I stride through the house and into the yard.

It's full of police, far more than necessary just to keep a crime scene clear. I stop and turn in a circle, examining the space. Blood splatters the wall of the house twenty inches from the ground. More stains the wooden paling to the left, great smears of it. There's no sign of the body: it must have been taken to the morgue. I click my tongue, annoyed. We'll have to learn what we can from the officers.

Most of the police seem to be interviewing the locals they've corralled into the yard. One of them is noticeable only for his lack of a hat; the officer in charge, no doubt. I approach him, my chin up and my shoulders squared.

"Inspector? Are you in charge here?"

He turns from the younger constable he was speaking to and regards me with arched brows. "You'll be interviewed in due course, ma'am. Go on, stand out of the way."

"I'm not here for an interview. I'm here on behalf of the Agency." I proffer my identity card, wincing internally at the look that crosses his face when he reads the title. Clearly, he's one of the few officers who knows what the agency is.

The man spits a white globule of saliva onto the ground. "This ain't the work of some *creature*," he says, confirming my theory.

"Sir," I begin, conscious of the men around us who probably haven't been let in on the secret, "the nature of the murders—"

"The nature of these bloody murders indicates we're dealing with a madman," the man interrupts. "We should be looking in asylums, not churches and graveyards." Behind him, the young constable twitches and peers curiously at me.

"I doubt we'll find what we're looking for on holy ground," Steel mutters, from behind me.

I keep my expression bland, though I want to frown at him. Antagonising the local authorities will not help my investigation. "I appreciate your concern," I say. "We will endeavour to stay out of the way as much as possible."

"You won't get no help here," he grumbles. "Not for that—blasphemy." He crosses himself and leaves us, muttering what are either curses or prayers under his breath. I clench my jaw. Even with Monaghan's warning, I hadn't expected *no* help.

The constable stares at me in blatant curiosity.

"I'm Agent Locke," I tell him. I put on a smile, affable and modest. "May I ask your name, Sergeant?"

"I'm not—it's Constable, actually," the man says, blushing: good, the flattery has disarmed him. "Constable Smith."

"Constable Smith, then," I say, broadening my smile a little, stooping so he doesn't feel overpowered. "Perhaps you could tell me the circumstances of this woman's death?"

He slants his shoulders towards me. "I...shouldn't go against the Inspector's orders."

"Has he ordered you not to communicate with other government departments?" I ask, blandly. "That would be a serious offence, if it's the case."

"No, no, no, of course not." The man shifts his weight. "I suppose...if you're part of a government department..."

I flash him my card, a little too quickly for him to catch the details. "Anything you can tell us would be helpful. Thank you so much, Constable."

"Well," he says, warming, "the body was found in the backyard of this house, at six this morning."

"By the wall?" I ask, indicating the blood.

"Her head lay near the wall. Her throat was cut, and..." His throat bobs.

My smile slips. "And?"

He visibly steels himself. "Her intestines were...outside her stomach. Other parts of her body were sliced off and put above her shoulder." He stops, his face a queer greyish shade, and I nod.

"Thank you, Constable. Has the body been removed?"

"T-to the local morgue."

Perhaps the supervising doctor can give me more information. "Was there anything else of note?"

"I…" He glances at the bloody spots on the wall and looks away. "We found some things with her. A couple of rings. Bit of an envelope. The department is investigating local pawn shops and the like."

"I see."

The constable darts a nervous glance at the house. "I had best go and join the Inspector, miss."

"Yes, of course. Thank you for your help."

He flees the yard before I finish speaking.

I turn to gaze at the blood-smeared paling. Yards like these were not private: anyone could have wandered in. If this woman had also been a prostitute, like Mary Ann Nichols, it would be a nice, quiet place to take a client. Ideal for that kind of work.

But not ideal for a murderer. I examine the area. An enclosed space, bordered by a tall fence on three sides and the building on the fourth. He would have to come through the corridor of the house, as we did—a *populated* house. And at least a dozen flats look out over this yard. Anyone could have woken during the night and seen something through their window. As for escape, it would have been almost impossible, for a human.

Less impossible, if the killer has supernatural powers. Phantom demons can become invisible when they wish, and Reapers have the extraordinary strength that would make tall palings like this an easy climb. Even a Hound could scale these walls with a little effort.

I turn around. "Mr. Steel, could you…?" I pause. The demon's eyes are wide, and he stares at the blood. "Mr. Steel?"

"Her injuries…" He blinks a few times, and his expression goes back to that cool unconcern that I'm more familiar with.

"I didn't know the full extent of her injuries." I frown at him. "This is one of the reasons we believe the perpetrator to be a demon. Otherwise, why remove her organs and then place them so carefully?" It feels like ritual, as though there's some power in the organisation of her corpse. Magic is something I still don't quite comprehend, even after seven years at the agency. The energy that fuels demons is considered worth discussion only in how it applies to the summons ritual. Anything else is forbidden.

"Locke. I've been looking for you." Rayne steps out of the building and walks up to us. Cassius trails behind him, sunlight glinting off his red hair and his smile. "Monaghan said you'd left," Rayne says, giving Steel a narrow-eyed glare. "It's not appropriate for you to be here."

If I'm to be a real agent, this is exactly where I need to be. "The woman was found over there," I say, pointing to the wall and ignoring the statement. "Her throat was cut, and she was disembowelled. Her organs were arranged around her."

"*Arranged*?" Rayne repeats. "How do you mean?"

I relay what the policeman had told us and Rayne grimaces. "Cassius, find out what else our departmental colleagues know." The demon smirks and fades from view, leaving an empty space where he'd just been. I've seen Phantoms exhibit the trick more than once, but it still makes a shiver run up my spine. "You, Steel," Rayne continues. "Search for any traces of demons."

Steel puts his hands in his pockets and tilts his head. "It's *Mister* Steel, actually," he replies. My mouth tries to tick into a smile. I suppress it.

A muscle spasms in Rayne's jaw. "*Mr.* Steel, then. You are a Hound, are you not? Do your duty."

The demon's mouth curls up at the edges, mocking, and I sigh. Orders are clearly not going to work with this Hound. "Cassius doesn't have the ability to sense demons," I say. "He could use some help. And we would both appreciate it." Agent Rayne does not look as if he agrees with my statement.

"It's difficult to smell anything in this place," Steel complains, wrinkling his nose, "let alone another demon."

"Please. If you could try."

He shrugs and slinks away without responding.

"Is this demon a member of the agency or not?" Rayne mutters. "He should listen to us."

I consider pointing out that he *had* listened—to me—but a cold shoulder from Rayne will not help the situation. "He's new," I say, instead, "and arrogant. I think we'll have better results by appealing to his ego."

Rayne looks at me as though I'd just appeared and haven't been standing here for the last five minutes. "That's...insightful. Well," he adds, his expression turning grim, "let's hope we get some results. Were they able to identify the body?"

"Not yet. All they've told me is how she was murdered. And that she was found at about six this morning."

"Given the place and the time of discovery, I assume she was an unfortunate."

I nod, eyeing the yard again. "I expect so."

"Are they being targeted because they're easy prey? Or for some other reason?"

"I spoke to a couple of prostitutes yesterday," I continue. "We could find them again, see if they know anything about this murder."

Rayne frowns. "We leave that sort of business to the CID. Our job is to find a demon."

"Surely—"

Cassius reappears in front of us. I jump and flash him an irritated look. Rayne crosses his arms over his chest, unperturbed by the sight of his demon popping in and out of sight.

"Well? What did you find?"

"This." He holds out his hand. Resting in his palm lies a dark violet shape that holds an odd sheen. A scale.

Steel strides over to us from the blood-stained palisade. "That could belong to anything," he says. "You didn't even find it in the yard."

"You're just jealous you didn't see it first."

I look at Steel for an explanation and he scowls. "He found it on the street. It's from a Stalker demon, but a Stalker isn't behind this."

"Stalkers are just as capable of murder as any other breed," Rayne says. "Good work, Cassius." The Phantom preens.

"Can you track it?" I ask Steel.

"There's not enough of a trace to follow it with any certainty, not in a place so crowded."

"I thought your kind were more talented than that," Cassius says, all sly smile and sharp canine teeth.

Steel shoots him a startled glance. "Even Hounds have their limitations," he mutters, after a pause.

"So?" Rayne demands. "Will you track it, or do you refuse?"

Rayne won't react well if Steel refuses. "Even if you can get us close," I add, "that would help."

"I'll do what I can," Steel says, after a moment. He pulls his hat down over his eyes. "This way," he says, and marches back through the house. Without waiting to see if Rayne will follow, I go after him.

CHAPTER SIXTEEN

We crawl through the streets of Whitechapel. Steel stops frequently, scenting the air and altering our direction. Everything smells the same to me—smoke and urine and refuse—but I keep close to his side.

"You said this was a Stalker demon, correct? They're copper class, like Hounds."

"Yes. They're the weakest of the class."

"Is that why you think the murderer isn't a Stalker?"

He eyes me as we walk. "This area of the city, packed full of people; it's perfect for them to hide in. They wouldn't want to draw attention to themselves."

"And this case is drawing a lot of attention," I murmur.

"Exactly." He stops and examines a narrow block of apartments. "It's in here. I think."

"You're not certain?"

"I told you," he says, dipping his chin into his collar. "The trail isn't fresh."

The building looks the same as every other one on this street: dilapidated and too small for its inhabitants. A good place to hide a killer.

Excitement thrums through me. I might catch him today, stop him committing any more murders. "Let's go, then."

Steel opens the door to the building. He moves inside, pausing again to scent the demon's trail. I wonder what the Stalker smells like.

Rayne and Cassius pile in behind us. "Have you found him yet?" the agent asks.

"Up here." Steel leads the way upstairs, to the second floor. The corridor is strewn with bits of musty-smelling straw. I tilt my head, listening, but there's none of the low murmur that comes with a building full of people. It's silent.

Without speaking, I point to the nearest door and raise my eyebrows at Steel. He nods, confirming. Rayne puts his hand on my shoulder, gently moving me aside. I bite my cheek.

Cassius kicks down the door and barges into the room. Rayne darts in after him, drawing the stiletto blades he'd wielded against Steel.

"Show yourself!" he demands.

I follow them inside. It's a small apartment, with a narrow bed and a jug of water in the corner next to a chamber pot. There's only one place to hide.

I crouch, peering under the bed. The wide eyes of a child stare out at me. I beckon, taking care not to get too close. "It's all right," I tell him. "You're not in danger."

The child creeps out from under the bed, one limb at a time. He has a mop of brown hair and vibrant blue eyes. His skin is yellowish, jaundiced, and under the strips of cloth that might once have been a shirt, his ribs are prominent.

"This is a *child*," Rayne says to Steel. "You led us to the wrong place!"

I examine the boy. Big, long-lashed eyes, a pouting mouth; innocence in living form. The eyes, though...that shade isn't natural.

"Why don't you show us your true face?" I ask. The child's gaze darts between us. "We only want to ask you some questions." I put my hand up as Cassius steps forward. "Isn't that right, Agent Rayne? We're not going to hurt him."

Rayne sheathes his dagger in a scabbard hidden under his jacket. "That's right," he says, making a show of pulling his hands back, fingers spread to show there's nothing between them. "We won't hurt you."

The child looks at Steel, then at Cassius. His throat bobs. The musty smell deepens. Abruptly the child hunches over with the crackle of snapping bones. I calculate the distance between the boy and me and take a step back.

The transformation takes less than a minute. The thing that now huddles on the floor bears no resemblance to the child it had appeared to be. Fur sprouts along thin, spindly legs—six instead of eight, so this one isn't mature yet—and forms amber patterns around eight bulbous eyes. Thank God I didn't have to partner with one of these.

Rayne reaches for his dagger. I yank at his sleeve. "We said we're not going to hurt him!"

The man stares at me. "*Look* at it!"

"It hasn't reached maturity," I reply, stonily. "At this age, the only mimicry it can handle with any level of realism is a child. It's not the murderer." The thing scuttles away as though it's going to dive back under the bed. "Wait," I call, releasing Rayne. "We're looking for a demon who might have something to do with the murders. Can you help?"

After a long moment, it speaks in a language that sounds like it's been constructed from gravel and iron. I blink and turn to Steel.

"No others are here," he translates.

"There are hundreds of people in the East End," I reply. "You can't be the only demon."

The Stalker speaks again, and Steel shrugs. "He says they were scared away by a Reaper."

Max. Monaghan was right; the Reaper's presence must have terrified the lower-class demons into fleeing Whitechapel.

"That's ridiculous," Rayne protests. "You're lying."

The creature cowers, stuffing itself into a corner of the room like a spider, its legs curled up to protect itself.

Rayne snorts. "This thing is just manipulating us. Next, it'll be demanding payment for its lies."

I eye the thing, the way it trembles at every shift we make. "I don't think so."

The agent throws his hands up. "More fool you, then. I'm not going to waste any more time here." He stalks out, Cassius at his heels.

"Why did you stay?" I ask the creature. "If the others left, why didn't you go too?"

It lowers its legs, and I realise why it didn't flee; one sticks out at an unnatural angle, and where the others are furred, this leg is covered in scales, still growing. Two of them flake off and float to the floor.

"It wouldn't have gotten far with a broken leg," Steel murmurs.

"Can you tell if he's lying?"

"I can't," Steel admits. "But Stalkers are built for speed, not strength. I can't see how he could have murdered this woman and then escaped over the walls. Not with that injury." The demon's front legs inch down and two of its eyes peek over the bristles.

"And Max?"

"Reapers intimidate copper-class demons," Steel replies. "Like a lion among a herd of gazelle. I wouldn't be surprised if they've fled the area."

Even if the thing *does* resemble a giant tarantula, the pathetic way it huddles against the wall stirs pity in me. "All right," I say to the Stalker. "Thank you for your help." I take Steel's arm and lead him out of the apartment, closing the door behind us.

"You're not going to kill him?" the Hound asks.

"He's only a child, and he hasn't done anything wrong. I'll notify Monaghan that he's here, and we'll involve ourselves if he proves a menace. Not before." Behind his tinted spectacles, Steel's eyes are thin slits. "Do you think that I should?"

The demon shrugs. "It's not up to me."

With that ambiguous response, he leads the way out of the building. We descend to the street in silence, and I emerge, blinking, into the morning light.

"If the murder was committed last night," I begin, as we make our way through the district, "and there were no copper-class demons in Whitechapel at the time, then our killer can't be one of them."

Steel hums in agreement. "Only the silver class or higher would remain under a Reaper's presence."

That narrows our hunt considerably. Silver class is rarer than copper, and comprises three breeds of demons: Reaper, Phantom, and the dangerous Blood Drinker. There's only one class higher than silver; the elusive so-called diamond. The only class the agency has never been able to summon.

"Is that why you don't like Max?" I ask, in an effort to control the line my thoughts are taking: speculation is useless without evidence. "Because he's a Reaper?"

"One reason."

"And the others?"

"Reapers are the ones you send to destroy us. Your Max has more blood on his hands than this Whitechapel killer. Besides," Steel adds, ignoring how I have frozen in place, "it may not be a demon at all."

I frown. "You heard how this woman died. How can you think it's not a demon?"

He gestures to the hive of Whitechapel. "Humans are just as capable of cruelty."

I want to object, but evidence to the contrary lies all around me. My mind shies away from the possibility. It's easier to think that this evil comes from a supernatural place.

Easier, but not right. A good agent cannot discount any possibility. I match my pace to Steel's, and we walk back to the agency together.

CHAPTER SEVENTEEN

"How long will you be gone?"

Jacob shrugs, giving me a rueful smile. "A few weeks, maybe. Not too long."

We stand in the entrance hall while Max loads luggage onto the waiting coach.

"Do you know what the case is?" I ask.

"A Blood Drinker nest, I think." The silver-class demon that the agency attributes to the myths of Romanian strigoi. Dangerous, in a pack.

"Be careful."

"I will. I'm excited—it's a real case." His smile doesn't quite reach his eyes.

"You have nothing to worry about," I tell him. "You're a brilliant agent." Behind me, Steel inhales. Before he can interject with a deprecating comment, I add, "And you'll have Max with you."

He looks through the open doors to the Reaper. "That's true. I'm sure he'll help me stay out of trouble."

The demon joins us and says, in his even-tempered voice, "The nest does not worry me." He says something else in Spanish, to which Jacob replies. Languages are divided among agents to ensure that the agency has a wide range of options. Max spoke Spanish when he was first summoned, so Spanish became one of Stewart's languages and, by extension, Jacob's. Lavender spoke French and Russian. I should ask Steel what he speaks.

"By the time I get back," Jacob says, when Max returns to the coach, "the professor might have forgiven me."

"You're not at fault for following orders."

He looks chagrined, and I wonder what Monaghan said to him. "Still, he was right. I should never have taken Max into Whitechapel."

The memory of the Stalker's words lingers in my mind. I redirect the conversation. "This case is a good chance to earn a name for yourself."

"If I can solve it," he replies, downcast.

"You'll be great."

He glances at me. "I should be the one reassuring you. I heard about the latest murder."

"Mm." Guilt seeps through me. I doubt I'll be able to get rid of the feeling. "We'll do our job, too."

"And we'll both be heroes," he says, flashing a grin.

Hero is not a word I've ever heard married to the agency. "No one knows enough about us to call us heroes," I say, smiling to take the sting out of the words. It may not have been why *I* joined the agency, but it's as good a reason as any, I suppose. "Are you taking your sketchbook?"

He lifts his case, a leather satchel with smart buckles and his initials inscribed in the metal. I push down a little surge of envy.

Hound agents have little need for such satchels. "I might even get to do some drawing, if it's not all blood rituals and demons."

"Show me when you get back? I've never been to Scotland."

"Of course." He gives me another smile. "I'd better go before we miss our train; Moss is meeting us at the other end. See you when I get back." With a wave, he climbs into the coach, where Max is waiting, and they drive away.

"He could have given us a lift," Steel mutters.

"Walking will hardly kill you," I shoot back. "It's not that far."

"It's far enough."

Instead of answering, I turn to the door, conscious of the clock ticking away the day. "Let's go, if you're ready."

"As I'll ever be, I suppose."

I keep my pace to a brisk march. When we arrive at Bethnal Green police station, I'm slightly out of breath but Steel has quit grumbling.

The police station is a large, imposing building. Officers in tall blue helmets go in and out in a near constant stream. Judging by the reaction I received at the crime scene yesterday, this won't be pleasant.

Perhaps that's why Turner dressed in male clothing; to make these encounters run more smoothly. I swallow, readjust my small-brimmed hat, and stride into the building.

At first, no one seems to notice me. I advance to the front desk and wait for the clerk to look up.

He eyes me. "Can I help you, miss?"

Instinctively, my shoulders curve inward, shrinking my height. "I'm here to see Agent Rayne." The clerk looks blank. "Or Inspector Abberline, if he's here?"

His gaze travels over my clothing and his lip curls. "And what do you want to see the Inspector for, miss?"

"It's regarding the Whitechapel case."

"I see." A sniff of disdain and he points me to a corridor on my right, away from the common area waiting room. "His office is at the end of the hall."

"Thank you." The clerk watches me leave.

The corridor moves with a slow trickle of police officers—all men. As I walk among them, conversation halts and heads turn in my direction. I keep my gaze on the floor, but that doesn't prevent me from hearing the whispers that start up as I walk towards the central offices.

"A woman," someone mutters. "What's a woman doing in here?"

One policeman walks past and clips me, sending a jolt through my shoulder. I straighten up, deliberately don't touch the ache there, and keep walking. The air feels large and tense behind me, like a pack of dogs at my heels. I want to look back to check, but that would telegraph my doubt. I keep going.

Another officer sees me coming and snorts. He steps into my path. "You're in the wrong place, miss."

"I'm here to see Inspector Abberline," I reply. "Please move out of the way."

The man arches an eyebrow. "The Inspector doesn't have time to waste with the likes of you."

Steel steps up beside me. From the corner of my eye, I see him grin. His white teeth flash, the incisors too sharp and too pointed.

The man balks and stumbles out of my path. I throw the demon a quelling glance.

"Be careful," I whisper. "We don't want them to try and burn you at the stake."

"Why do we have to deal with these humans?" he mutters, glaring at the officers we pass. It has an effect; the whispers stop dead. "Can't we do this investigation on our own?"

"Why so eager?" Perhaps he's looking for more opportunities to test our bond. The thought of fighting my supposed partner while also trying to solve this investigation daunts me. But then I remember his words, the other night. If *I'd* been the one summoned from my bed and dropped into a strange city, unable to leave, I wouldn't be keen on helping my new companions, either.

Steel doesn't answer my question. We reach Abberline's office and pause at the sound of voices. Striding into the middle of their conversation will not endear me to the Inspector.

I put my self-consciousness aside. This is for the case. I raise my hand to the door, then someone grips my shoulder and pulls me aside.

"What are you doing here?" Rayne glowers at me, drawing me to the side of the corridor. Cassius herds Steel along with us, though the Hound is bristling and baring his teeth like a wolf.

"I was looking for you," I reply, gesturing at the office.

"Well, you've found me."

"And? Have you spoken to the Inspector?"

"Yes. The inquest begins tomorrow, at the Working Lads' Institute. There's nothing else to do here."

"Perhaps we can interview the officers who found the body—"

"You shouldn't be here at all," Rayne interrupts. "This is a police station, for God's sake. You can't just wander in and do as you please."

My tongue sits heavy in my mouth as I search for something to say. "Turner—"

"Turner caused friction with the CID for doing exactly this. We need their help. We cannot afford to make them enemies."

"I'm not trying to make anyone an enemy."

"Yet you're succeeding."

I fall silent. The atmosphere in the station is tense, and the officers who pass by throw us—throw *me* wary looks. I'm drawing attention just by being here. "What should I do, then?"

"Go to Buck's Row. See what you can find there."

"The Nichols murder? It's been over a week," I protest. "Any trace of the killer will be long gone by now."

"Look anyway. We need to be thorough, to see if there's any connection to this Annie's murder, or—"

I hold up my hand. "Wait. The body's been identified?"

"The lodging housekeeper identified her as Annie Chapman. Another unfortunate."

A tight knot coalesces in my chest. Annie. The same Annie I spoke to a few days ago? "What—what does she look like?"

Rayne shrugs. "I haven't seen the body, but apparently they called her 'Dark Annie', for her hair." He holds his hands up next to his head. "Curly and brown."

Like the woman I met. I close my eyes. If I'd been there, if I'd stayed, if I'd done *something*...

"Miss Locke?" Rayne asks.

I bite the inside of my lip until the pain in my mouth is sharper than the ache of my guilt. "I see. Thank you."

"Perhaps this was too much." I open my eyes and find he's watching me with a frown. "A murder case is not for those of a delicate constitution."

I swallow the lump in my throat and change the subject. "What about Turner? Has anyone linked the case to her death?"

Rayne shakes his head, his mouth tightening. "Look," he says, as I go to interject, "I know you're concerned. We all are. But the Whitechapel murders are our priority. And a Hound is of no use in a police station."

Reluctantly, I nod. "Let me know if you learn anything."

"I will." He clasps my shoulder. "Report to me at the agency once you're done."

I turn and walk back along the corridor, avoiding the eyes of the police around me. Rayne's hand has left an impression on my shoulder, and I resist the urge to rub it away. It isn't until we're outside in the relatively fresh air that my breath comes easier. No one gives me a second glance out here.

"Buck's Row?" Steel asks, catching up to me.

"The site of an earlier murder," I explain. "Let's go."

"Walking, again?"

"Unless you can fly, yes."

He sighs, long-suffering.

"I didn't think a demon would be this lazy," I say, trying to distract myself.

"I'm full of surprises," he replies, dryly, and we lapse into silence.

CHAPTER EIGHTEEN

Buck's Row is a narrow thoroughfare just off Whitechapel Street. Its name crops up in the newspapers more than almost any other street in London. To find a body here isn't unusual.

Small cottages line the street, shadowed by the Board School, whose square turrets and bladed railings resemble a prison more than a school. The garage where Mary Ann Nichols' body was found squats between the cottages and the school, its face black with dirt.

It's late morning, edging into the afternoon, and there are enough people traversing the street that investigating will be a challenge. I move to the garage's doors, which are closed.

"She was found here," I tell Steel, pointing at the ground. "Her throat was cut, and she was disembowelled."

"Posed, like Annie?"

I'm surprised he remembers her name. "No. At least, nothing was reported in the paper, and I doubt they'd leave out something that sensational." Horror makes good entertainment.

Steel strides back and forth across the street. He lingers over the site where the body was found, then moves on. I remain by the garage, watching. At one point he draws close to the boundary of the spell, and I tense, but he merely scents the air and moves on.

Eventually he returns to my side. "There's nothing here," he says, examining the hard packed mud. "It's been too long."

"Nothing at all?"

He shakes his head in reply.

I clasp my elbows in each hand. He's avoiding my eyes, and uneasiness creeps over my skin. He could be lying, and I wouldn't know.

A drop of water lands on my cheek. I glance at the sky. It's burdened with thick slate clouds, and another drop of rain lands on my forehead.

I don't want to leave Whitechapel yet. I don't want to give the murderer another chance to kill again. "There's a pub near here called The Ten Bells," I recall. "We can stay there until the rain passes."

"A pub?" Steel asks, slanting a look at me. "I didn't think government agencies looked favourably on drinking on the job."

"I won't be drinking," I reply, heading for the tavern.

"That decision does not extend to me, I assume."

"I would prefer it if you didn't draw any undue attention."

"It will draw more attention if both of us go to a pub and neither of us drink," he points out.

I look at the sky again, praying for patience. "Very well. You may have a *small* amount of gin."

"I expect your measure of small and mine is going to be quite different."

I march towards The Ten Bells, ignoring his attempts to provoke me. Rain falls more quickly, a swift light drizzle that will turn into a downpour within half an hour. The pub sprawls over the corner of two streets. Loud voices and the clink of glasses pour from it, even at this hour. Its clientele ranges from local workers to men in more expensive suits, who might be business clerks or curious tourists. It's also a popular spot for working women.

The pub is full of small wooden tables crowded by chairs, with larger booths by the windows. The bar itself is paralleled by a line of men. No other women yet. I squeeze in at the bar and use the agency's allowance to order two drafts of gin. When I turn back, Steel has chosen a table out of the way of human traffic, seated in a position to watch both the bar and the door. I place our glasses on the table and sit next to him, with a view of the bar. I've barely taken a sip of the gin—sweet and heavily watered—when Steel downs his.

"How much is your allowance?" he asks.

"Not enough to drink the bar dry," I warn.

"Enough for a second glass, I hope."

With a sigh, I reach into my purse and give him a shilling. "That's your limit. I just got this allowance; I don't want to write up an expenditure report full of gin."

"That'll do." He takes my shilling and slouches off, keeping the brim of his hat low over his spectacles. I sip my drink and examine the pub's patrons.

The papers shared a description of the Leather Apron character they think is the main suspect, but it could fit half a dozen men in this room, and probably most of Whitechapel. I keep an eye out for any women who might be working the streets later. It's a tight-knit community; if Annie was here the night she was murdered, someone might have noticed.

Steel returns and plunks down a bottle of gin in the centre of the table.

"That costs more than one shilling."

"I supplemented your allowance," he replies, blithely.

"You *robbed* someone?" He pours another glass for himself and then tilts the bottle in my direction. I cover my glass with my hand. "I don't drink while I'm working." He looks pointedly at my less than full glass but says nothing. "If you were caught—"

"I wasn't," he interrupts. "I'm a professional demon agent tracker, remember? Or whatever it is you call us. What *do* you call us?"

"Partners," I say, glaring.

"Really." He sips his drink and scans the public house with apparent disinterest. Silver glints behind the smoky lenses of the spectacles. Reapers have an unusual amber colouring of the iris, but none of our demons have pupils like the ones that split Steel's eyes in half.

"Is it only male Hounds who have eyes like yours?" I ask, my curiosity getting the better of me.

Steel pauses, his glass halfway to his mouth. "Something like that," he says, and drinks.

"Do they mean something?" I curl my hands around my glass. To anyone who's watching, we're just a couple out having a drink. A couple with difficulties, by the way we barely look at each other.

"It means we come from…a different bloodline. A variation in breeding."

"That's not in the agency's files." Which doesn't mean much. Our records go into great detail on the nature of the summons ritual and how to call demons, but that's it.

"No doubt our history is not very useful." He pours another glass—ignoring the frown I send his way—and gestures with it at the bar. "You seem pretty comfortable here. I doubt many women in your situation would feel so at ease in a place like this."

"They wouldn't find themselves in my situation if they didn't."

"Why is that?" he says. "Why are you more comfortable in the slums of London than in your fancy agency building?"

I look away, taking a sip of gin to cover my reaction. That insight is more than I expected from him. More than I wanted. I take my time putting together an answer, examining my words for weakness before I set them loose.

"When I was a child, I lived at the workhouse on Whitechapel Road," I reply. "The professor found me there when I was fifteen and recruited me."

"You must have impressed him."

I pretend to take another sip to give myself a moment. It wasn't anything I did that impressed him. "Perhaps," I say. "Most agents come from places like that; places they aren't wanted."

"Orphans?"

"Some of them."

"Some of them," he repeats. "Not you, then?"

Careless of me. No matter: he could ferret out my history from Maia if he chose. "I'm not an orphan," I admit.

The demon leans back in his chair, regarding me. His gaze is keen, keener than three glasses of gin should make it. "I can't imagine any parent would give up their child so easily."

"The agency offers a diligence fee." I place my glass down and turn it a half-circle to the right, using the movement to avoid that gaze. The pub's still empty of other women. No excuse to escape this conversation. "It offsets the loss of wages caused by the child's departure. My parents used it to move to the country." I'm out of the workhouse. I have my own job, my own clothes, enough food that I don't go hungry. My family are better off. I haven't missed them for years. I refuse to feel ashamed for the fact.

"So, the agency buys you," Steel says, and I look up, startled.

"No, that's not—"

"They pay off your family and move them out of London." His mouth curls. "I bet that money keeps them from asking questions, too."

Suddenly, I get the impression that he's pressing me into dropping crumbs of my life so he can gather them up and use them later—though for what reason, I can't imagine.

"I have a better life, now," I say, with finality. I don't want to consider my childhood, those long dark days when I was always cold and always hungry. Monaghan gave me a new life. I will do everything I can to prove that I'm worthy of such an opportunity.

I stand, picking up my glass. "Wait here," I tell Steel and flee before he can form a rejoinder. At the bar, I elbow my way to the front and signal for the barkeep's attention.

"What can I get for ya, luv?"

"Information."

The man leans one thick forearm on the counter. "That'll cost ya, just the same." Of course it will. I flip him a shilling, which he examines carefully before pocketing. "What d'ya wanna know, then?"

"Did you know Mary Ann Nichols? Or any of the working girls who come in here?"

He shrugs. "They're in 'ere all the time. I don't know their names."

"Every night?" If Mary Ann or Martha were here before they were murdered, perhaps this was where they met the killer.

"Most nights, yeah. You'll have to ask them if you want more than that."

It's not much of a clue. "Thank you," I say, regardless.

A vulgar curse bursts over the congenial chatter that fills the pub. A curse in a familiar voice. I whip round.

Steel is standing, his jacket dripping wet and an empty tankard rolling over the floor. "What do you think you're doing?" he spits at a tall, heavy-set man. The stranger is flanked by three other men, all dressed for hard labour. None of them are as tall as Steel, but all of them are wider.

"Steel!" I call, but the men at the bar are turning to watch, nudging each other in anticipation of a fight. My voice is lost in their glee.

"Who the hell do you think you're talking to?" the man returns, squaring up.

Steel sneers. "Dross, it seems."

The man throws a punch. Steel dodges cleanly and then dives headfirst into the three others. The pub erupts with screams and the crash of broken furniture.

I edge around the eye of the fight and lurch to the bar. One of the strangers stands on the side lines, jeering. Behind him, a man holding a full pint tries to peer over his shoulder at the brawl. I dart forward and slam my hand into the bottom of his tankard. The man's beer spills all over the stranger's back. He yells a startled curse and I retreat as my victim draws three more men into the fight. The barkeep vaults over the bar and bellows for the police.

A large brass bell hangs on the wall. I grip its clapper and clang it as hard as I can. Shouts go up all over the pub.

"Last orders!"

"Last orders? What, you're closing?"

The entirety of the pub surges towards the bar. Abandoned by its owner, it's defenceless against the ring of people lunging to snatch free booze.

"Oi! Stop that!"

I weave through the crowd, shouldering them aside when I have to. The fight at the centre of the chaos is a confused whirlwind of arms and legs. I locate Steel, grab him by the wrist and yank him free. The hubbub around the bar keeps his opponents from noticing as I drag him out into the street.

"What were you thinking?" I demand. His collar is askew, and he smells faintly of gin, but that seems to be the only sign that I just pulled him out of a fight. His hat and spectacles are still on, though goodness knows how. "If they'd realised what you are, they would have hanged you from the church spire."

"I was just beginning to enjoy myself," Steel replies, smirking.

"You're risking both the investigation and our safety," I snap. "If they hadn't murdered you, we would have been arrested."

"Your agency would have rescued us. What's the point of them if not for that?"

"They wouldn't have *rescued* us," I shoot back. "They would have retired me and *killed* you."

"Are you always this judicious?" he asks, weaving a hiss into the words.

"You—" I stop, force myself to calm down. He's pushing me deliberately, trying to see if I'll crack. "We are here to work," I say, levelly. "Not to get drunk and start fights."

"*Win* fights," he corrects. "I never start something I can't win."

"You weren't winning."

"I would if you had let me *finish*," he mutters. But the stone in my voice seems to drain the wind from his sails. He looks back at the pub, which seethes with people trying to get at the bar. "What did you do, by the way?"

"I distracted them. If I'd have let you 'finish', as you call it, someone would have ended up dead."

His smirk broadens. He looks more relaxed than he did this morning, as if the fight has eased some tension in him. "So, you admit I would have won."

"It is not a contest when you have gifts from Satan himself."

"Satan is not generous with his gifts."

People in the street are staring at us, starting to put together the chaos at The Ten Bells with our rapid departure. There's no way we can investigate the pub, now; the killer would be an idiot to go anywhere near it. We'll have to wait for the inquest.

"We'd better head back to the agency." Irritation thrums through me, and I don't bother keeping it from my voice.

"After you, agent," Steel says, with a mocking bow.

CHAPTER NINETEEN

"Why do we need to sit in on this inquest?" Steel asks, as we approach The Working Lads' Institute.

"We might learn something from the witnesses."

"I didn't think there *were* witnesses. Isn't that the problem?"

"Hush," I whisper and, surprisingly, Steel falls quiet.

The building looms over Whitechapel Road, red brick and white stone. Its large gabled entrance is so ornate it should be inscribed with Dante's warning. At the entrance stand a handful of young boys. One of them gives me directions to the inquest, where I find Agent Rayne, along with three men I don't recognise.

Rayne glances up and frowns when he sees me. I try not to frown in response. "Good morning," I greet them. "Has the inquest begun?"

"The inquest?" one of them repeats, and they exchange glances.

"I'm Wynne Baxter," says another, a stern-looking man with a neat cravat. The coroner, according to the papers. "The inquest will start in a moment. Are you a witness?"

"No, sir. I'm here to observe."

"Is this a joke?" an inspector mutters. "One of you so-called agents is enough. We don't need a woman, too."

I look at Rayne, but the man avoids my gaze.

"We have enough spectators." The coroner throws a disgusted look at Rayne and the other two men. "And I will not allow a female reporter in my court. If you want entertainment," he says to me, "may I suggest the theatre?" He disappear into the room, shutting the door with a decided click.

"Please, go ahead," Rayne tells the inspectors. "I'll be right in." He takes my arm and pulls me away from the doors. The inspectors exchange another look and vanish after the coroner.

"Rayne—"

"I told you, yesterday," he says. "This isn't the place for you. What did you find at Buck's Row?"

I pull out of his grip, conscious of Cassius' ice-tipped gaze. "Nothing. There was nothing left."

"Then go back to the agency and focus on research."

"What am I supposed to research if not what I learn inside that room?" I whisper, hoping the door is thicker than it looks.

"Hound agents do not attend inquests." He looks scandalised even saying the words. "You are not a witness. Go home."

"But—"

"Go *home*, Miss Locke." Cassius is already opening the door for him, and, with a warning look over his shoulder, Rayne heads into the inquest room. The Phantom demon closes the door behind them.

I exhale through my teeth. If I can't even get into the inquest, how am I supposed to do my job?

There's a moment of silence, then Steel says, lightly, "Do you expect to solve this murder from out here?"

I give him a look. Regardless of my feelings, if I storm in there, they'll throw me out. I don't have much choice but to return to the agency and figure out where to go from there.

I squash a sense of defeat and stride from the building.

—ele—

Stepping into the agency an hour after I left brings that defeat surging back up. I jerk my hat off and stuff my gloves inside it.

"I don't think the hat is at fault," Steel murmurs.

Glaring, I place the hat carefully on the counter. "We'll go to the library," I say, in a growl.

"Hazel." Maia stops me as I place one foot on the stairs. "A letter came for you. It's from Bristol." She holds it out and I take it with excitement.

"Thank you."

"Bristol?" Steel asks, peering at the letter in my hand as we walk upstairs. "Who's in Bristol?"

"Another apprentice. A friend."

We reach the library and I go straight to my desk, folding into the chair and ripping through the wax seal. I glance at the signature first. It's from Eve. Relief fills me.

My condolences, she begins. *Monaghan sent a telegram on the 5th, but I didn't get a chance to write straight away. I never thought something like this could happen to Turner. I hope you're all right. Write to me when you can, won't you?*

Monaghan told us Lavender is missing. What's your new demon like? It must be hard, working with a new Hound. What have you called her?

Take care,

Eve

I flip the letter over, looking for more, but that's it. The brevity must be because of the case they're working on, not because Eve is upset that I became an agent before she did.

That's ungenerous and I shake the thought out of my head. It's nothing but petty to think Eve would feel envy about my situation.

I reread the note. Monaghan's telegram must have been sent before I summoned Steel. I pen a reply, explaining what happened at the ritual. I keep it brief; a list of facts, not feelings. Eve will meet him when she returns, and I want her to tell me what she thinks without colouring her opinion with my own.

Clara swans into the room with two plates. "Maia asked me to bring you something to eat." She drops one none-too-gently on my desk and hands the second to Steel with a dimpled smile. "Here you are."

The smile Steel gives her is something between fox and wolf. "Did you make it with your own hands?"

Clara looks nonplussed. "Ah, well, no…"

"Pity. I much prefer it that way. Perhaps, dinner?"

"I…well, I suppose I could make some soup…"

"Soup is best when it's cooked for hours," Steel says. "You should probably get started now, in fact."

Clara backs away, her smile uncertain, clearly sensing she's being manoeuvred and trying to figure out how. "Ah, yes of course." When she's gone, I purse my lips at Steel.

"What?"

"She's just doing her job. You don't need to mock her."

"I'm not mocking her. I told the truth. What she chooses to do with it isn't my fault. What are *we* doing, anyway? Are we going to stay in here all day?"

I sand and seal my letter, addressing it to the hotel in Eve's return address, and consider the question. The inquest is closed to me, and there's little more that we can find in Whitechapel. The only avenue that remains unexplored is the regiment that Turner was looking into, the soldiers who were with Martha the night she died. It's clear Rayne has no interest in pursuing the lead.

"We'll ask Monaghan for permission to visit the barracks," I decide.

"Now?"

"He's out of town. We'll have to wait until he returns."

Steel makes a sound of exasperation. "This is the reason you brought me here, isn't it? To stop this killer? So, why aren't we doing anything about it?"

I press my nail over the crease in the letter, ironing it into the paper. "The case is the reason I summoned you," I agree, slowly. Does he think we might let him go if he helps solve it? Is that why he's so keen to get out of the agency? Steel taps his fingers against the arm of his chair in a rapid staccato rhythm. He glances at the walls of books and the tall, barred windows. Or, perhaps, he just wants to be out in the open.

"Hounds don't stop criminals," I say. "That's the job of a Reaper. They're stronger, more aggressive; they can handle the kind of demons we get in Britain."

"*I* can handle them."

"The agency has a hierarchy. Rules."

"Those rules are not solving your case," he replies, sarcastically.

He's not wrong. The thought of sitting around for the next few days sits ill with me, too. I rest my head against the back of the chair and stare at the ceiling. What would Turner do, if she were here?

She wouldn't sit here, waiting. She'd find a way to discover the information she needed.

So, what information do I need? I've visited the crime scenes. I have as much of the police reports as I am going to get, which is the same amount that everyone else in London has, thanks to *The Times*. What I *don't* have is information on the bodies.

Of course, that means going into the morgue, alone, an experience that will at least match if not surpass this morning for discomfort. If women are not allowed into police inquests, they certainly won't be allowed into a morgue.

The ceiling says nothing in response to my glare. A real agent wouldn't hesitate. A real agent wouldn't let something as ridiculous as fear of what people thought stop her.

I can't help it, though. I do fear it. I fear the way they look at me, the scorn in their gaze.

And yet.

"We'll go to the mortuary," I say to the library at large. Three women have been murdered. Scorn seems a small price to pay for the chance to catch their killer.

CHAPTER TWENTY

S tepping into the grounds of the workhouse brings memories flooding back. For a moment I'm dressed in a white cap and apron, my fingers red and burnt from the laundry, my feet blistered and aching. I smooth my hands over my skirts, remind myself where I am, *who* I am. Not that person anymore.

The workhouse is a large, long building surrounded by thin black railings. It has tall arched windows and a huge entrance, as if it had been made deliberately large in order to fit all the destitute workers of Whitechapel. Holding my head high, I stride through the doors and into the courtyard, hoping an illusion of confidence will do as well as the real thing.

"This is where you lived?" Steel asks, gazing around.

I check his words for hidden sarcasm, but they only sound curious. "I moved in when I was nine, and stayed until Monaghan gave me a job. My family didn't have much space. Or money." He doesn't ask any other questions. "It's this way."

The morgue is more of a shed than a real building. Even the door hangs open. I grimace and step inside. There's a small entry space with a desk, and a door leads into another area, which, judging by the stench, is where they keep the bodies. It's supposed to serve the whole area, but most of the corpses come from the workhouse.

I greet the thin, whiskered man at the desk. "Good morning. I need to see the doctor in charge."

He tugs at his moustache. "You want the infirmary, round the back. This is a morgue."

"Yes, I'm aware." I lay my identification on the desk. "I'm from Her Majesty's Private Investigation Agency," I say, watching for any sign of recognition. A desk clerk in a workhouse mortuary shouldn't know anything about our work.

I'm right; he looks blankly at the card and then at me. "Are you an inmate?"

Steel muffles a snigger. I hold onto my patience with a tense grip. "No. This is the Home Office seal. I work for the government."

The man's eyes crinkle with suspicion. "Doing what?"

"That's classified," I reply, which is mostly true.

"Are you *certain* you shouldn't be in the asylum?"

I flatten my hand on the desk. "Look, I need to speak to Doctor Phillips about the recent murders."

The clerk sits up in his seat with an air of triumph. "Doctor Phillips isn't here. He's out doing rounds."

"Oh." I glance at the door. "Is there anyone else I can speak to?"

"Well..." He scratches his chin. "Green's here. He might speak to you."

"We'll only take a moment of his time."

He sighs and gestures at the door. "Through there," he says, reluctantly, and cranes his neck to watch us leave.

The morgue is dusted with straw and clouded with the stink of rotting flesh. I resist the urge to cover my mouth. Two parallel lines of wooden tables form an aisle down the centre of the shed. Most of the tables are occupied. A few rows down, a young man in a blood-spattered apron bends over an uncovered body. I ignore the lumps of white sheet on either side and advance towards him.

"Doctor Green, I presume?" I ask, when we draw within earshot.

He looks up, still bent over the corpse. The man can't be more than twenty, with smooth russet brown skin and a crop of black curls. "It's Mister," he replies. "Mister Green. I'm the mortuary assistant." He straightens up and wipes his hands on his apron. "Um. I'm not expecting—uh, are you here to identify a body?"

"No, I'm not. My name is Locke." I glance at his still bloody hands and refrain from offering my own, giving a small curtsy instead. "This is my colleague, Mr. Steel." Steel nods. He's examining the body on the table.

"Colleague?"

"I'm working with the Criminal Investigation Department," I say, deciding that ambiguity might serve me better than the truth. "I came to talk to you about the murders."

"The CID?" Green glances at the door behind me, his eyes wide. "I, uh—Doctor Phillips isn't here right now. I can…leave a message for him?" He wipes his hands on his apron again.

"Perhaps I could speak to you? I won't take much of your time. I appreciate that you're busy," I add, dropping my gaze to the corpse. It's a male body, so not one of our victims.

He darts a nervous glance at Steel. "Well, I mean, of course, if the CID—I'm happy to help if I can."

"Thank you. I assume that Mary Ann Nichol's body has already been removed from the morgue?"

"Yes. The funeral was the—the day of the second murder."

That's right: Annie and her friend told me about the funeral. "What about the other body? Annie Chapman?"

"Oh, we still have that one." He manoeuvres around the table and goes to another. He pauses beside the lumpy sheet on top and looks at me. "We've repaired most of the damage for the transfer to the church, but I—it's not a pretty sight." I nod and brace myself. He pulls back the sheet.

A cloud of sour-sweet rot billows up from the body, filling me with fresh nausea. The corpse is shrunken and riddled with black stitches where she was carved open and then sewn back together. Her hair is dark brown, and curly. It *is* Annie, the same Annie I met on Friday night.

I had suspected as much; the confirmation shouldn't throw me this hard.

It does, though, and I clench my jaw, remind myself that I'm here for a reason. This body is not a person, it's a thing. A thing cannot hurt me. I lock away my horror in an iron chest.

"Could you describe the injuries?" I ask, in a voice that thankfully remains steady. "I gained some information from the papers yesterday evening, but I would appreciate your analysis."

"Of course." Green moves next to the body and indicates the stitching on her neck. "Her throat was cut from left to right," he begins, straightening, more confident now that he's dealing with dead bodies rather than live ones. "A segment of skin was removed from her abdomen and placed near her right shoulder, next to the small intestines. Two other sections of the abdomen and the—the pubis—" He stammers and avoids looking anywhere near me. Monaghan gives all the apprentices a short introduction to anatomy when we join, to prepare us for the more gruesome cases, but it's still hard to separate the words from the horror they instil. I gesture for him to continue. "They were placed by the left shoulder. Sections of the abdominal wall are missing, including the navel, and the womb, the upper parts of the vagina and most of the bladder are also not present." He pauses and I clear my throat.

"I see," I say, my voice low. Missing—for what purpose would the killer take them? "Is there anything you can tell us about how they were removed?"

Green continues, clearly relieved to no longer be talking about the mutilation. "I—Doctor Phillips, that is—thinks the murderer possesses some anatomical knowledge, to account for the way that the woman's organs were removed. The blade itself was between six and eight inches, very narrow and thin."

"The kind of knife used in a slaughterhouse," I murmur, and he nods. Slaughterhouses are common in the East End, and a good source of work for many men.

"Yes, or a small amputating knife. They're easy enough to get hold of."

In a city as large as London, anything can be found for the right price. "And you say they might have some knowledge of anatomy," I say. "Two soldiers were seen with the first victim, Martha Tabram. Do you think a soldier could have done this?"

"I wouldn't rule it out," he replies.

I examine the woman's face. Annie looks as though she could be sleeping, if not for the odd, waxy tone to her skin. Why did the killer choose her? For a reason, or because she was in the wrong place at the wrong time? I think of the workhouse surrounding me and wonder what my fate might have been if Monaghan hadn't plucked me out of obscurity. If I could have been the one lying on this slab instead of Annie.

I draw my thoughts back. "You said her throat was cut from left to right," I say. "Was the killer left-handed?"

"It's a possibility."

"Or she could have been attacked from behind," Steel adds. His voice surprises me, but I tilt my head attentively. "He could have used his right hand to reach around her and cut her throat. Either way, it doesn't help us much."

If I was the killer, what would trigger such rage that I could commit these heinous crimes? I frown at the thought. That doesn't feel right. For Martha Tabram, perhaps: her killer didn't stop, kept stabbing her long after she would have died, overcome with fury. But Mary Ann Nichols and Annie...rage does not fit the cold calculation required to cut their throats and keep them silent while they died, nor the removal and arrangement of their organs. There is some dark purpose here I can't see.

Green touches his hands to his apron again. "I'm not sure how else I can help," he says. "I'm just an assistant. Perhaps you had best wait for Doctor Phillips."

I have everything I need to know. "That's all right, thank you. I won't keep you any longer." I curtsy again, and Green gives me a short bow.

"Of course, if that's—of course. I'm glad I could help."

I drop my gaze to Annie's body again, imprinting the image of her shrivelled corpse in my mind. I doubt I'll sleep tonight, but the memory will remind me of what's at stake.

We emerge into the daylight and I inhale deeply, clearing the rotten scent from my lungs. I realise I'm being watched—or, more accurately, like someone's trying to peel back my skull and pick apart the white noodles of my brain to uncover the secrets inside.

I swing my gaze to the demon. "What is it?"

"You don't seem disturbed," he says. "By the bodies."

"They're only bodies," I respond, repeating the train of thought I had earlier. "They're nothing to be feared." My mind goes back to the list of her injuries. "What do you think about the way she died?" I ask Steel, and he glances sharply at me.

"You want my opinion?"

"Of course," I say, nonplussed. "You're my partner, and you know more about demons than I do. *Do* you think this could be the work of a demon?"

He considers the question as we walk back to the street. "Possibly," he says, after a while. "The cut throat could be an indication of a Blood Drinker. But the organs—they don't make sense. The placement, and the missing pieces—that speaks of ritual, of magic, and there's only one class of demons who deal with magic."

"Which one?"

"Diamond."

I exhale. The one class we know nothing about. "Are you sure?"

"I'm absolutely certain. And if it is such a demon, this will only get worse," he adds, grimly. "Sooner or later the pieces they've taken will run out. And they'll need more."

I spend the rest of the day writing my report. My pen skips over the description of Annie's wounds, and I have to pause, and breathe, and build a wall around the memory. When I finish the report, I leave it with Miller and return to the familiarity of the library with Turner's journal. There must be some clue, something that will give me an insight into this case, or into Turner's death. Why else would she have written it in code? What was she hiding?

I let it fall open naturally, trying to find an entry often visited. The pages that greet me are drawn with the same coded script and a handful of unrecognisable doodles in the margins. All of the letters are evenly spaced, so I can't tell where to start. I flick through the rest of the journal. Turner's fingerprints dot some of the pages, smeared in tea or what I suspect is nicotine.

I spread out her collection of books. A few poetry volumes and a novel. I try the titles of poems as a cipher, then a few unusual words. I look for pages that are dog-eared, that Turner might have revisited, loved. None of them give me a cipher that cracks the code.

"You've been staring at books for hours," Steel mutters. "Do you intend to sleep?"

I look up and realise that the sun has long since fled, and the oil lamp on the desk is burnt almost to the wick. "I'm sorry. I didn't realise it was so late." I agree to leave and follow Steel up to our rooms. He departs into his own, and I pull my chair up to the vanity to continue.

Hours later, I give up and rub at my burning eyes. None of the poems work, and I've tried more than a hundred words from the novel. I'm missing something; a key to put the whole thing together. I search my memory for some clue that would give me a hint of what to look for, but there's nothing. Perhaps I didn't know her as well as I thought.

I rest my head in my palm, aware of the night creeping into morning outside. Sleep feels a long way away. I know if I try, I'll just lie awake thinking in code for the rest of the night.

Perhaps I'm just not that good of an agent. Perhaps Turner thought me more capable than I am.

The nib of my pen tears through the page. I put it down, flex my hand to feel the ache. What if I can't do it? What if, after all of this, I can't even break my own mentor's code?

No. I refuse to think like that. I have to figure this out, no matter how long it takes me. Turner deserves justice.

I open another book and try again.

CHAPTER TWENTY-ONE

Monaghan returns on Thursday. Once Maia has welcomed him with beef and kidney pie and a full bottle of red wine, I climb the stairs to his office. My heart beats quickly, shaking my body with nerves. I desperately want to get into the barracks myself and interrogate these soldiers. All I need is Monaghan's permission.

Tiberius greets me at the door. I pause and the demon's brows tick higher. He gives a slow half-smile, part welcoming, part amused. "The professor is inside," he says, in his low rough voice. His gaze slides to Steel, and he adds, "I assume I don't need to tell you that I won't tolerate misbehaviour."

"I'm not a child," Steel replies, his silver eyes narrowing. He's taller than Tiberius, but the Reaper has a presence that looms, regardless of Steel's height.

"Glad to hear it," Tiberius replies. "The agency does not recruit children." He stands back from the door and watches us enter. Steel tracks the Reaper with his gaze as Tiberius walks around us to recline against the far wall.

"Professor," I greet the man. "How was your trip?"

Monaghan grimaces. He gestures to the chair on the other side of his desk, and I take a seat. "Too much hunting for my taste; I'm a poor sportsman. But the Minister attended, and I think he might be persuaded to vote in our favour when the question of our independence comes up. We can't have enough allies in Parliament, at the moment; they'll be deciding on our future by the end of next month."

"I'm glad it went well."

He smiles, self-deprecating. "Forgive me; I shouldn't bore you with politics. I received your report." He taps his desk, and I realise that it's open in front of him. "I will ask Commissioner Warren to send over the reports from the CID as soon as possible. It's ridiculous that you aren't granted access to the inquests. They allow female witnesses; they have no reason to refuse our agents."

I look down at my lap, fighting an awkward flush. I can't help but feel the fault lies with me. "Thank you," I reply, gathering my damaged confidence, "but that's not why I'm here."

He folds his hands on the desk. "Oh? Then what can I do for you, Agent Locke?"

"I want to visit Wellington Barracks." Monaghan looks surprised, and I rush ahead before he can counter. "I spoke to the witness in Martha Tabram's case, Mary Ann Connelly, and one of the soldiers at the regiment was with the victim just before she died. I think there's something there."

Monaghan rubs the side of his neatly groomed moustache. "The police have already interviewed those suspects. The man has an alibi, I understand."

"Turner was investigating them. There must be a reason why, but I won't know until I can visit the barracks for myself."

"The Major wasn't happy about the police investigation," he says. "They won't be content to let you speak to them."

"Perhaps if your name was involved…"

"Ah: you want a letter of introduction."

I hold his gaze. "This is the last thing Turner asked of me. Please, sir," I add, when he says nothing, "I need to know."

He sighs. "Very well, then." He opens a drawer and pulls out a paper from a stack of preprepared letters. "But," he says, as he signs the bottom, "remember that you're on this case to investigate supernatural matters. Leave the police to follow up on human suspects. That is their job, after all. We are the only ones who can do ours."

"Yes, sir."

He hands me the letter. I grip it and he doesn't let go. "And be careful with your Hound," he adds. "I don't like letting agents wander into military facilities. Only the Major knows what we really are—don't let the rest of them see your demon for what he is. If they turn on you, you'll have nowhere to go."

"I understand."

"Good." He releases the letter and I fold it into careful quarters. "Send me your report when you return."

"Thank you, sir." I curtsy and leave.

"Why do we need his approval?" Steel asks, as soon as Tiberius has closed the door behind us. "Aren't you an agent, like that idiot with the fancy cuff links?"

"Do you mean Rayne?" The Phantom agent has a different outfit for every day, sometimes more than one. A product of his aristocratic past, no doubt, but I know little more about him than that. He never talks about his family. Not many of us do.

"I doubt *he* needs a letter of introduction," Steel says, grumpily.

"Hound agents work differently," I reply, although it's not only that fact that drove me to request a letter. It will be easier, with Monaghan's help. I was afraid of doing it on my own.

"Hound agents also get terrible quarters," he mutters.

I tap the folded letter against my hand. "We'll go tomorrow. Make sure you wear your hat."

CHAPTER TWENTY-TWO

Wellington Barracks is a small, squat facility in Westminster. Through its windows I can see the tall trees of St. James' Park, their leaves slowly turning bronze. I wait as the soldier on duty sends for the Major, Monaghan's letter gripped in my hand. I check Steel's hat, making sure the brim is pulled low over his spectacles and only his nose and mouth are visible.

At my searching look, the mouth curves into a smile. "So concerned," he says. "I would have thought you might appreciate being rid of me."

Unnerved, I pull at my own hat, tilting the brim unfashionably low so that Steel's doesn't look so out of place, and dig the hat pin into my hair to keep it there. "What do you mean?"

"If I'm killed, you'd have another chance at the ritual. You might even be able to find the demon you lost."

"Lavender." If Lavender *is* out there somewhere, she must have a reason for not returning to the agency. But the thought does not fill me with hope. Deep inside, I've already accepted that she's gone. "Monaghan won't give me a second opportunity to fail. Besides," I add, "if they turn on us, you have a greater chance of escaping than I do."

"Perhaps."

I eye him. "If *I* die, you're released from the spell."

"True," he says. "But I'd probably end up dying alongside you, in which case freedom won't get me very far." He smiles affably at me, the kind of smile that I feel like I should be suspicious of.

An old man with a greying beard and a sparse hairline approaches us. He wears regimental red and carries himself with stern, professional authority. "Miss Locke, is it? I understood that the investigation was closed. We are not a museum. You cannot just turn up and expect a tour."

I clear my throat. "I'm Agent Locke, yes," I say, "and this is my colleague, Mr. Steel. We just want to follow up on the police investigation." I show him my identification and his mouth tightens behind his beard. "And you are?"

Etiquette brings him back to cordiality and he gives me a shallow bow. "Major Hill, at your service."

"I understand that two of your soldiers were with Martha Tabram the night she died," I say, forgoing courtesy.

The man shifts his weight and glances around us at the wide-open corridor, and the soldiers stationed at the entrance. "Perhaps this conversation should be had in my office." He stalks away and I follow him to a small room just off the corridor. "Your colleague can wait outside," he says, as he opens the door.

I give him a bland smile to cover the sudden uptick of my heartbeat. Steel's head cants in my direction, his hat still over his eyes. "Very well." I advance into the room and the door closes behind me with a little click that sounds very loud in the silence.

The space is small, and sparse. Not much that I could use as a weapon, if I need one.

Steel is just outside, and there are guards stationed everywhere. The likelihood of the Major attempting something untoward is small. Still, I remove my hat and hold it, and my hat pin, in both hands.

The Major walks around me and gestures to a chair in the centre of the room, in front of a large ornate desk. "Please, have a seat."

I remain standing. "The two soldiers were identified by the witness, Miss Connolly, were they not?"

"Yes. They both have alibis for the night in question." Instead of sitting behind his desk, the Major opts to stand in front of it, leaning back on the wood. He gives me a smile that lingers on my skin.

"I see." I place my hat back on my head but keep hold of the pin, tapping it against my palm. I feel better—and more capable—with it in my hands. It's a good four inches long, and unnecessarily sharp. The Major's gaze falls on it as I speak. "Our reports state that one of the suspects spent the night with his wife, and the other returned to the barracks. I assume that you have a system for monitoring the entrance and exit of your soldiers." I give the pin a little twirl. Excessive, perhaps, but I'm comforted by the way his eyes follow its movements. Now I understand why Khurana hides a sword in her cane.

"I—yes, we have a ledger we use for this purpose."

"Excellent. I would like to see the entry for this soldier. Will you be so good as to show us the way?" I gesture at the door with my pin.

The Major swallows. "We cannot allow entrance to women in the soldiers' accommodation."

"I am an agent," I remind him, "not a woman." Internally, I wince. Perhaps there is a way to be both, but if there is I haven't found it yet. The man's gaze drops to my hands again. He's wavering. "It won't take long," I add.

"Very well," the Major agrees, reluctantly. "This way, then."

He opens the door for me, and I wait an uncomfortable moment for him to realise that I haven't moved. He coughs awkwardly and precedes me out of the room. I follow and join Steel outside.

The demon watches me slide the pin back into my hair. "Is that a blade in your hat?" he whispers.

"It's a pin." Never underestimate the power of a lady's toilette, Turner had told me once.

The Major takes us down a wide corridor. The walls are decorated with shields and coats of arms and trophies in glass cases. We turn away from the main aisle, down a flight of stairs and through a small passage of plain white plaster. Where the rest of the barracks had been quiet, this part of the building rumbles with low conversation and the occasional raised voice.

"Here. This is the ledger," the Major says, eyeing me with a gratifying level of wariness. He shows me a simple ledger that's been fastened to the desk with twine. "You can see today's date here—"

"Thank you." I step up to it and flick back to the date Martha died. I run my finger down the line of names. One is right at the bottom. "This is the soldier who came back to the barracks?"

"Yes."

I go back further, searching for that name over the previous months. Once I've found it, I check it against the night of the murder. The signature matches perfectly.

Disappointment wells inside me. But this is a good thing; it means we can confirm the police's decision and we have one less suspect to worry about. Still, I feel like I've wasted my time.

"The other soldier, who spent the night away. What is his wife's address?"

The man's fluffy brows arch up towards his hairline. "It is not appropriate to give out Private George's information."

"Sir," I say, turning to face him. "We are investigating multiple murders. Any attempt to impede this process could be considered an obstruction of justice. I have a duty to report any such incidents to Mr. Pemberton."

His cheeks redden above his beard. "I have no intention of obstructing your investigation."

"Then if you'll provide the information we seek, we'll be on our way."

After a moment's hesitation, he tears off a piece of paper and scribbles something down. "Here. His wife's address."

"Thank you." He makes as if to speak and I interject. "I will pass on my report to the Legal Secretary. Clearly, you run an organised barracks, sir." He blinks, digesting that. While he searches for a barb in my words, I take Steel and make our escape.

When we're outside, I reconsider. Making an enemy of a military officer might not be my wisest idea. I look back for Steel and find him trailing me.

"You were quiet," I say, pausing to let him catch up. "It seems rare that you have nothing to say."

"I was looking for traces." He taps his nose. "Couldn't find anything. I don't think there are any demons here."

I smooth out the paper the Major gave me. "Then we'll try here. Perhaps his wife can tell us something we don't already know."

CHAPTER TWENTY-THREE

The streets of the Hoxton district surge with people and the occasional determined cab. I dart out of the way of a trotting horse and stick close to the pavement. Private George's home is a tiny apartment on the second floor of a stack of flats.

I rap on the door. There's a long pause, then it creaks open a sliver. A woman frowns through the gap.

"Can I help you?"

"Are you married to Private George?" I reply.

"Yes." Long brown hair hangs over one side of her face and she touches it nervously, smooths it down. "What's this about?"

"We'd like to ask you a few questions. Can we come in?"

Her face closes off. "I've had enough of reporters."

"We're not reporters," I say, stopping the door with my boot when she tries to close it. "We work for a private investigation service. Please, we won't take much of your time." She hesitates, and I add, "Another woman has been murdered. We want to ensure no one else meets the same fate."

Mrs. George glances behind me at Steel, and back at me. Hesitantly, she widens the opening. "As long as you don't ask me no questions I can't answer."

I slip inside. The flat is little more than one large room, but the place is clean, and the aroma of stewing meat speaks of dinner not far off. I take a seat in a chair by the banked fireplace.

"Is your husband at home?"

"Not yet." She sits in the other chair, keeping her eyes on Steel. "He's due back any minute, though."

Steel goes over to stand by the window, and I'm not sure if his movement was prompted by her words or by the desire to give us space.

"Could you tell me about the sixth of August?" I ask, folding my hands in my lap and focusing my attention on her.

"What do you want to know that's not already in the bloody papers?" she mutters. She toys with the ends of her hair, the rest still covering her face. "He came home, he stayed all night."

"What time did he return?"

"I don't know; about ten, maybe. Eleven. I can't remember."

"And when did he leave in the morning?"

"About five, I think. It was before dawn." She tweaks at her skirt, an old, threadbare linen that has been darned and darned again. Her blouse, too, is old and much repaired. And yet they live in a clean, large apartment in a relatively safe district.

"Soldiers earn a good wage, don't they?" I ask. "What does he spend it on?"

"The usual things. Food, drink, things for the house." She exhales, and her breath dislodges a strand of her hair. She smooths it back into place quickly.

"How do you sleep here?" I gesture at the window. "It's not very quiet."

"Well enough." She glances at the fire, at the front door, at anywhere but me. "What's that got to do with anything?"

"Could your husband have left in the night without you realising?"

"What d'you take me for, a fool?"

I lean forward, trying to get her to meet my eyes. "Mrs. George, a woman was stabbed to death that night. Anything you can do to help us would be appreciated."

"There ain't nothing I can tell you." She meets my eyes for a moment and then looks away. The quick movement sweeps a little hair from her face, revealing a fraction of a dark bruise around her eye.

I sit back, regarding her levelly. "How often does he hit you, Mrs. George?"

She leaps to her feet, the visible side of her face flushed. "How dare you say that to me? Who do you think you are?"

I stand, raising my hands, palms out. "Is it true?" I ask, not letting my gaze waver. From the corner of my eye, I see Steel circling around behind the woman.

"I—" The woman shudders, all over, her slim body shaking. She wraps her arms around herself. "I think you should go."

"Mrs. George, please—"

The front door opens. "Sarah, the butchers were almost out, all they had was—" The man—the soldier, for he wears the red jacket unbuttoned and loose—stops on the threshold. He looks at me, my arms outstretched, and his wife, shaking. "What the hell are you doing? Get away from my wife!" He lunges forward and yanks me away.

"Mr. George—" I manage, but there's a flash of black and Steel shoves the man. The soldier skids over the floor and stumbles against a chair. Steel advances towards him, his body resonating with menace. I tug Mrs. George out of the way, to the window, but she struggles against me.

"No, don't hurt him!"

At her cry, the soldier swings at Steel, misses his face but catches his shoulder with a second blow. Steel moves with the punch. He jabs his own hand into the man's stomach. The soldier folds over the blow, and Steel grabs the back of his neck and yanks him upright. His fingers curl around the man's throat, his claws digging into unprotected skin. The soldier chokes.

"What are you doing?" cries Mrs. George. "For the love of God, let him go!"

The man's face flushes purple, and he gasps for air. I grab Steel's arm. "That's enough. Let him go." My voice trembles, shaken by the strength of my own heartbeat.

Steel glances at me, a cool, blank look. But his claws ease out of the man's throat. Bloody punctures stay behind. Released, the soldier drops to the ground, gasping.

Mrs. George flings herself down at his side, her hair in disarray and the bruise vivid over half of her face. "How dare you? I'll call the police!"

"Come on." I pull Steel out of the flat and drag him outside. I keep walking until we've put enough distance between us and the house. If he'd killed the man, what would I have done? "What were you thinking?"

"What was I *thinking*?" Steel shakes off my grip. His mouth is tight at the corners. "He's a wife beater and a murderer. Would you have preferred I let him kill you?"

"I would have preferred if you didn't almost *murder* him in his own house."

"Fine. Next time I'll take him outside."

I turn on him. "Steel, you can't do this," I tell him, keeping my voice hard, ignoring the part of me that thinks he might be right. If he hadn't intervened... "You're a member of the agency, now. I told you, we have rules."

"I do not give a damn about your rules," Steel replies, in the same tone. He meets my glare with his own. "I am not the one who's willing to let a murderer walk free when you have the power to stop him."

"I don't have that power."

"You have *me*," he retorts. "I'm your weapon, aren't I? Or your shield, or whatever the hell it is your agency claims I'm supposed to be."

"You're my *partner*," I say, when he pauses. "That means we work together. We take the same chances; we run the same risks. I understand why you acted—of course I don't want him to walk free—but I can't afford to lose you. I need you, Steel."

He looks at me as though I've just deposited a kitten in his lap; startled and bemused and a little suspicious. "You...need me."

"Of course I do. An agent is nothing without her Hound." It's the truth, and it costs me nothing to admit it. By the halted expression in his face, he hadn't seen it the same way.

"What about that man?" he asks, regaining ground quickly. "You're going to leave him there? Let him go?"

"Was he a demon?" I countered. "Did you sense anything that proves he or his wife were involved?"

A pause, then he shakes his head. "They were human."

"Then we can't do anything." I clasp my arms around my waist, clutching my elbows as I think aloud. "Judging by that bruise, Private George is a servant to his anger. If his wife is lying about his alibi, he could have been the one who stabbed Martha Tabram."

"So, why did we leave?"

"Because I don't think he killed the other women," I admit. "The way they were murdered is so different to Martha's death, it doesn't fit. And even if the man *is* a killer," I add, "the agency is forbidden from getting involved in human crimes. We have to give him to the police." Even though I dislike the idea as much as Steel does.

CHAPTER TWENTY-FOUR

The next morning, I approach Monaghan's study with trepidation. I hope the professor trusts me enough to overlook the proof I don't have.

His assistant looks up at us. "You can go in, Miss Locke. *You* must stay outside." The latter to Steel.

"Can I ask why?" Has Monaghan already heard about the fight?

A shrug. "The professor wishes to speak to you alone, Miss."

"Why am I kept out of the interesting conversations?" Steel mutters. He leans against the wall and crosses his arms. "I suppose I'll have to wait here, then."

Clearly, Monaghan wants to talk about Steel. It might be easier to defend the demon if he's not present. "I'll be back soon," I tell him.

He flicks his fingers in a dismissive gesture. "Take your time."

"Don't get into any trouble."

Steel only grins.

I enter Monaghan's study cautiously, conscious of the spell's border. He's not at his desk, this time, but seated on a chair opposite Tiberius. A chessboard is drawn between them. Monaghan gestures to a third chair set at right angles to them both.

"Have a seat, Locke."

The chair sits just outside the spell's limitation, so I pull it back a foot and then sit, examining the board. Both of their queens are lost, perched off the board, waiting. Tiberius has what looks like a lead, his knight three moves away from checking Monaghan's king. But one of the professor's pawns lies a square from the edge of the board. His next move will be to crown it, and from there winning will be simple.

I look up and find Monaghan's gaze on me.

He raises a finger to his lips and whispers, "Don't tell him." The professor is in his early forties, but the mischievous glint in his eyes makes him look half that age.

"You said you'd play with a handicap," Tiberius grumbles.

"I let you take my queen," Monaghan replies, spreading his hands wide. The hint falls on barren land: Tiberius just frowns.

"Should I come back?" I ask.

"No need. This will not take long."

Tiberius mutters something uncomplimentary.

"You have a report for me?" Monaghan asks. I wrote one up on our return last night, and I hand it to him. He puts it aside. "Tell me what you found."

"Private George claimed he was at home with his wife the night of Tabram's murder." My fingers twist painfully around each other, and I untangle them, smooth them out. "We went there and spoke to her. I think—that is, I believe he is Tabram's murderer."

Tiberius's left hand hovers over the board. Then he moves his bishop instead of his knight, sliding closer to Monaghan's king. The professor smiles and pushes his pawn to the edge. He swaps it for the queen and Tiberius scowls at the board.

"The first victim?" Monaghan asks. "What evidence are you using to make that claim?"

"He has been violent towards his wife. If he's violent towards other women as well, and found himself overcome with rage one night in Whitechapel when he was with Martha... It fits the aggressive nature of the crime."

"It's a good theory," the professor replies, "but it is only a theory. Without evidence, we cannot judge a man guilty of a crime he may or may not have committed."

"But I thought the police could arrest and interrogate him. If they press him, knowing that his wife may have lied, he might confess."

"And you want me to ask the Commissioner to do this?"

"Yes." He doesn't look impressed and my heart sinks. "Unless you don't believe me."

"It isn't that." Monaghan sighs. "Domestic violence is a terrible thing, but it is difficult to prove, particularly if the wife will not give a statement. Not to mention, getting him arrested in the first place won't be easy, not to mention his good conduct badges."

"What do you mean?"

"The soldier has three medals for good conduct. It was mentioned in the papers. The police will consider that a sign of good character."

I shake my head, frustrated. "His wife has a bruise over half of her *face*. How can he not be punished for that?" Monaghan watches the board, his expression distant. He doesn't reply. I take a deep breath, control myself. "Forgive me, sir," I say, dispassionately. "If the police saw what he did to her, they might be persuaded to reopen the investigation into his location that night."

"I will speak to the Commissioner. That does not mean they will arrest him," Monaghan cautions. "I don't have the political power to make that happen. But I'll do my best." He places his hand on my arm, for a moment, and then moves another piece across the board.

My skin stays warm from the brief touch. "Thank you, sir."

"Thank me if I'm successful. In the meantime, continue to pursue the paranormal element with Agent Rayne."

"Of course." If the soldier is arrested, then he'll be off the streets, unable to hurt his wife—or anyone else. My breath comes a little easier than it had this morning.

Monaghan brings his queen into the fray, forcing Tiberius to castle his king. The demon scratches at his half-grown beard. "I do not understand the point of this game," he mutters.

"This game is why I am the agent, and you are the demon," the professor replies and checkmates him.

"Sir," I begin, "is there a reason Steel had to wait outside?"

"Ah, yes." Monaghan crosses one leg over the other. "How are you finding that partnership?"

I hesitate, thinking of the way Steel tested the spell's limits, the way he'd almost killed Private George. If Monaghan has reason to doubt my ability to handle this case, he'll take it from me and give it to Khurana. This is Turner's case. Turner's killer. I'm not going to let it go.

"He's having difficulty adjusting," I say, carefully. "I don't think he's used to working with humans."

"That's always the case, at the beginning. Demons don't take well to chains."

Chains. The word fills me with nausea. I'd never considered the ritual in that way. Swallowing, I stare at the chessboard and not at Tiberius, though I instinctively want to look for his reaction.

"What about his abilities?" Monaghan asks.

"You mean, as a Hound?"

The professor rests his head in his hand, tapping his chin with his forefinger. "I'm not sure. The pupils are rare, you see." He indicates his eyes with his finger. "I looked over our records, after the ritual. No one has ever seen a male Hound, not even when the agency was first founded and we didn't understand the requirement for women. We were convinced the class bred Hound demons as female, and Sentinels as male. Yet now we have Steel." He exhales in a long sigh. "Perhaps I am seeing things that are not there, or perhaps our records are incomplete. But if there's one thing I've learnt during my time here, it's that demons are not to be trusted."

I do glance at Tiberius then, unable to help myself. He's watching me, not Monaghan, his expression inscrutable. The Reaper has always been good at hiding his thoughts. He must have learnt that from Monaghan.

"Do you think he's lying about being a Hound?" I ask the professor.

"I do."

"He tracked a demon in Whitechapel," I tell him. "We found a Stalker in a house nearby." Although since then Steel hasn't given any indication of sensing another demon.

"Hmm. So, he has a Hound's nose, at least."

I doubt Steel will volunteer any information about himself willingly. "What would you like me to do, sir?"

Monaghan straightens his cravat and stands. "For now, keep me up to date with your progress. On the case and with Steel. Tell me whatever you learn. If your demon turns out to be something new, something we've not harnessed before, I want to perform a full examination. If he's powerful, we'll be able to open up a whole new class of agents. An entire new department, even."

I rise, too, but I feel as though I've left my insides on the chair. "What kind of examination?"

"Nothing invasive," he clarifies. "I wouldn't want to incapacitate him. We will start with a blood sample."

I curtsy. "Thank you for your help, sir."

"Of course. Good luck with your case, Agent Locke."

I back out of the room and find Steel where I left him, all long limbs and sharp angles. I tuck away Monaghan's request and present him with a blank expression.

"Finished already?" he asks, peeling off the wall. "Let me guess; back to the library?"

The library is the last place I want to be, bogged down with research and wasting time.

Conscious of the assistant so close, I turn down the corridor. It's Saturday. One week ago, Annie's body was found in Hanbury Yard.

"What would you say," I begin, "if I said I wanted to go to Whitechapel?"

"I think that's an excellent idea," Steel says, immediately. "Let's go."

If nothing else, I might get a chance to learn what Steel really is. "All right. We'll wait until nightfall, and then we'll go."

CHAPTER TWENTY-FIVE

Whitechapel doesn't come alive at night so much as it transforms from starving stray dog into feral hunting wolf. Most reputable people have abandoned the streets in fear of the police's suspect, Leather Apron. The only sounds are the faint murmur of pubs, open at all hours, and the occasional meow of a stray cat. This time I'm prepared for the rain, armed with a sturdy black umbrella. I keep a tight grip on it.

"Do you smell anything?"

"Hmm?" Steel pulls his attention from a nearby alley and shakes his head. "Nothing yet."

I glance at him from the corner of my eye. He's distracted, glancing sideways at the buildings and the alleys that open up as we walk. "I hope you'll warn me before testing the spell again," I say. "I don't appreciate pain being sprung on me without notice."

For a second he looks guilty, then the expression is wiped away and replaced with a mocking smile. "I will endeavour to do so."

"If I'm killed, I promise the agency will bring you back." I tuck my umbrella under my arm. "As Clara's partner, no less."

"Touché."

"Consider it my revenge from beyond the grave."

"Death doesn't frighten you?"

I can't read whatever's behind his gaze. "Why should it?"

"Most people fear their own end."

"I have other things to be concerned about," I reply, scanning the road for anything suspicious.

"Corpses, for example," he continues. "You seem to be immune to the sight of them, at any rate."

"Dead things can't hurt you," I remind him.

"Some demons might disagree."

"Are you dead, Mr. Steel?"

"Not yet," he replies, irreverently, "though the night is still young, and that umbrella looks heavy enough to do the job."

I cast him an exasperated look. "You're here to track demons, not provoke me."

"I can do both."

Instead of encouraging this back and forth any further, I lapse into silence. It isn't a comfortable one, and I'm very aware of the demon's presence at my side, bound by the ritual. *Chains*, Monaghan had called it. Steel's words from a week ago come back to me in a flash: *Do you expect me to thank you?*

"Does the summoning hurt?" I ask, after a moment.

A pause answers me and we cross the street to reach another alley before he replies. "A little. It varies, by the skill of the caster."

I wince. I can't imagine I hold the kind of skill required to perform the magic without causing pain. "I'm sorry," I say, truthfully. "I didn't know."

He stares ahead, his eyes shadowed behind his spectacles and the brim of his Homburg. "Now, you do."

He doesn't trust me. And why should he? Have I given him a reason to? I stop in the middle of the road and face him. "Steel."

He stops and looks askance at me. "Why do I get the impression that you only address me as *Steel* when I'm in your black books?"

"The ritual was supposed to find Lavender," I say, groping for the right words, wishing I'd planned this conversation out before I dived in. "I didn't mean to call you here against your will, and I'm sorry for it, but four women have been murdered." Martha Tabram, Agent Helen Turner, Mary Ann Nichols and Annie Chapman. Names I'll never forget. "What do I need to do for you to help me catch the killer?" He stares at me for so long that I swallow and have to look away. "Please," I say, quietly. "This case is important. What can I do?"

There's a long, formidable pause, and then Steel says, "I will help you." My heart leaps, but he hasn't finished. "*If* you agree to break the spell afterwards."

It's my turn to stare. "What?"

"I refuse to stay at that agency for the rest of my life, being passed around like a family heirloom," he mutters. "I will catch this killer for you, but in return, you have to let me go."

Even if I wanted to agree—and the agent side of me doesn't like how quickly I *do* want to agree—I couldn't. There's no way to break the spell and live. It's been designed that way: a set of conditions that can never be broken.

"Where would you go?" I ask, stalling while I frantically think of a response.

"Paris," he answers. "I have business with another House."

The way he says the word makes the significance obvious: he doesn't mean a building, he means one of the demonic Houses, the familial structures that make up the demons' world.

"What business?"

"That is my concern, not yours."

I incline my head. I deserved that.

"Well?" he asks. "Do we have a deal?"

I weigh the deaths of four people against the cost of lying to this demon. Human lives will always come out heavier.

Still. He is my partner.

"If you help me solve this case," I say, "then I'll do everything I can to set you free."

His eyes narrow as he processes my careful wording. "And will you keep your word, Hazel Locke?"

I draw myself up, all my height and breadth to match his. "I will never go back on an oath." The words seal around me like their own kind of magic. I pray I've left enough space in my promise to keep it. And to deal with the fallout, when Steel realises the spell cannot be broken.

"Then let's move on, hmm?" Steel says, all mocking smile and glinting eyes. "A few copper-class demons have returned," he adds, as we resume walking. "I don't sense anything bigger than a Strike demon."

"A moment ago, you said you couldn't sense anything," I counter. "Were you lying?"

He gives me a sideways look. "I didn't have a reason to help you, before."

I rub my hand over my face. "Wonderful." Then I recall that he hadn't sensed anything at the barracks, or at Mrs. George's residence. "What about the soldier?"

"No. There was nothing there."

"How do I know you're not lying now?"

"I just revealed I was lying," he points out. "Why would I have done that and then lie again?"

I throw my hands up. "You didn't seem to have any issues about lying before. How can I understand how your mind works?"

"Before was different," he says, defensively. "I was a prisoner. Now, I'm a guest."

"I wouldn't describe it quite like that," I mutter. "The agency is not a hotel."

"Just as well: you'd have a terrible reputation."

Sighing, I head in the direction of Whitechapel Road. We're making a rough *M* shape in our path, tracking back and forth across the main road. So far, I've seen a handful of women who might be working, but no suspicious men, and plenty of constables. Just the sight of so many blue helmets might be enough to dissuade the murderer from striking again.

"Hmm." Steel stops in a small thoroughfare between two cottages. I halt and turn back to gaze at him.

"What is it?"

"I'm not sure." He scents the air, hound-like. The light from the street behind me reflects off his eyes, tiny twin mirrors among the shadows. My body gives a jolt of primal fear.

He's my partner, not a wild animal. Still, my hand goes to the strong shaft of my umbrella. I should remember that even with a deal, even with the spell, Steel isn't human. He's darkness cloaked in flesh.

"Hey. What's going on here?"

I turn around. Four young men filter into the alley. Each of them carries a stout stick and wears a pair of rubber galoshes.

"Good evening," I say, warily. Steel comes up beside me and the gazes of the four men go to him.

"Is this man bothering you, miss?" They advance, pushing us deeper into the alley.

They must be part of the Vigilance Committee, the unofficial group that's been patrolling the streets on the lookout for the killer.

"No, he's not bothering me." I put my hand on the demon's arm, squeeze a warning.

"It sure looks like he is." The group splits, two men edging around us to the right. Worry cuts through my stomach. All demons have some level of inhuman strength, but Hounds are among the weakest.

"I can assure you he isn't," I reply, my tone sharp. I pluck at Steel's sleeve, urging him to back away. He stands his ground. Foolish: these men are possessed by the idea of dealing out justice. One wrong move and they'll attack, regardless of whether their target is guilty or not.

"What were you doing then, eh? What do you want with this woman?" The man who spoke jabs Steel with his truncheon. The demon flinches under the hit, and his hat slides sideways.

I dart in front of Steel. "We were having a conversation. I know this man, gentlemen. I appreciate your devotion to the cause, but I can assure you he isn't the killer."

"Perhaps we should take him down to the station and let the police decide." The man jabs Steel again. I tense, waiting for Steel to lunge.

But the demon sighs. He lifts his hands, palms out. "I don't intend any harm. Take me to the station if you wish."

For a second I'm speechless. "Steel?" I ask, looking for the trick.

"Same chances, same risks, right?" he murmurs. "Although I hope you were wrong when you said your agency can't rescue us. If these idiots get us arrested, we're going to need rescuing."

"It won't come to that," I manage, trying not to reveal how completely he's stunned me.

"So, you admit it," the man calls, levelling his truncheon like a blade. "You want to be arrested. You *are* the killer."

"Sir, that's enough," I demand. "We will walk with you to—"

"He'll come with me. You lot, take her back to The Bells." He shoulders me aside. Another man grabs my arm and yanks me towards the mouth of the alley. The spell tightens painfully around my chest.

"Wait, you can't separate us—"

Steel steps towards me, bringing us back into range. Before he can get any closer, the leader intercepts him. If Steel doesn't do something—if *I* don't do something—

I'm pulled backwards again. I stumble, turn just in time to see the leader take a swing at Steel. The truncheon thuds into Steel's arm and he flinches, stumbling into the wall. His spectacles slide down his nose and his eyes gleam in the light of the alley, the unnatural elongated pupils visible even in the darkness.

The man scrambles away from us as though we shouted *Plague*. "A monster!"

We only have a moment before anger overcomes their fear. Shoving aside my doubt, I kick free of my assailant. My umbrella is thin, but its metal core is strong, and I whack it into the backs of his legs. His knees fold. A second hit to his head and he crumples. God, I hope I'm not doing any permanent damage.

Turner's philosophy was never to fight if it could be avoided, but if it couldn't, one good whack with a blunt instrument was all you needed. I don't think she meant an umbrella, but it's turning out to be more useful than I expected.

The others gawk at me for a second. Then they surge forward.

Steel finally moves. He snaps to the left and takes down one of them with a jab to the man's sternum and a quick punch to his stomach.

I stab the next man in the small of his back with the pointy metal end of my umbrella. He yelps and whips around. I go for his head, but he grabs the umbrella's canopy and growls a curse at me. He's too strong for me to wrestle it away. Instead, I release it. When he falls back, surprised, I dart closer and stab his arm with my hat pin.

He stumbles and a stream of blood runs from his hairline. Then he falls, revealing Steel behind him, hatless, his eyes metal slivers over his spectacles. He doesn't look like he's even broken a sweat.

"What happened to obeying the rules?" he asks.

I scoop up my umbrella. Tonight will certainly not be making it into my report. "I wasn't going to let you run all the risk," I reply. "Although, for the record, I would have preferred to run."

"Well, it seems we get to survive another night. So. Thank you." The words sound as though they hurt.

"You don't need to thank me." I tuck my umbrella under my arm. "I'm your partner as much as you are mine."

He hums thoughtfully. "You know, you're not as bad as I thought, Agent Locke."

Surrounded by comatose members of the Vigilance Committee, holding my irreparably damaged umbrella, I can't help but laugh. "Likewise, Mister Steel."

"It won't be long before the next policeman comes by," he adds. "We should leave."

With the number of patrols in Whitechapel tonight, the chances of the killer striking again are almost non-existent.

I waver. If I'm wrong, and someone else dies while I go home to sleep...

"This place is too busy for us to find the killer," Steel says. "Even a Phantom would struggle to get someone on her own."

Reluctantly, I nod. "We'll come out again tomorrow," I say. It's a promise to the killer as much as it is a promise to myself.

CHAPTER TWENTY-SIX

Maia greets me the next morning with a stern face. "Monaghan wishes to see you," she says, glancing at Steel, who is devouring his breakfast with typical ferocity.

"What for?" I ask, frowning. Has the soldier been arrested already?

"He did not say."

"I'll go now."

"He can wait for you to finish your breakfast," she replies, and mutters something in Hindi.

I pick up my spoon and make a show of eating, although my stomach churns at the thought of what Monaghan will say. As soon as Steel has finished, I clean up our plates, unable to stay seated any longer.

The demon is dressed in a waistcoat over his shirt, and I eye him in exasperation. "Where is your jacket?"

"We're inside, why do I need a jacket?"

I suppose I should be grateful he's wearing shoes. Hopefully Monaghan wants to see me, and not Steel.

Upstairs, there's no sign of Miller, so I knock on the door and wait for the professor's "Come in," before entering. The chessboard is packed away and Tiberius sits with a book in hand. Monaghan is at his desk, writing. It's a few moments before he looks up. His expression makes the lump in my stomach tighten.

"Agent Locke. I understand you ventured into Whitechapel last night. After dark."

I blink and reply, slowly, "Yes, sir. We—I thought it would be best for us to patrol, to see if we could find a clue as to the identity of the killer. Or even catch him in the act."

"Entering Whitechapel at night is too dangerous."

"I appreciate that the risk to women is high, but—"

"It's not only your risk, it's your demon's as well." He doesn't look behind me to where Steel is no doubt lounging against the wall, but I become very conscious of the demon's presence. "We only have two Hound agents. We cannot afford to lose either."

"I thought...I thought the potential gain was worth the risk."

"Not in this case." He sits back, sighing. "Even the most skilful agent can be taken by surprise, and Clara does not have the knowledge or experience to take over your role. Until she does, I can't let you take any unnecessary risks."

Cowed, I stare at my hands. "I apologise."

"No harm was done." I mask a grimace at the thought of the four Vigilance Committee members who might disagree. "But in the future, no venturing into Whitechapel at night. Not until this demon is caught."

"Yes, sir," I agree, subdued.

Monaghan shuffles the papers on his desk and puts them aside. "I do have good news, however: the Commissioner agreed to arrest Private George."

I exhale in relief. "Thank you, sir."

"Well," he adds, with a wry smile, "it's not as good a deal as I had hoped. They'll hold him until the end of the month. If they can't get a confession out of him by then, they'll be forced to let him go."

It's not what I want for the man, but it will get him off the streets and away from his wife. And if he confesses, she'll be free of him forever. "Thank you for letting me know."

"Of course." Monaghan gives me a smile. I return it, easing the tight grip I have on my skirt. "Although that is not the only reason I wanted to see you; we may have another case."

"In the East End?" I've only been paying attention to news of Whitechapel. Anything else that might have occurred has escaped my notice.

"No, in Pimlico. Someone found an arm on the bank of the river."

"A woman's arm? Could it be another victim?"

"I think so. The Pimlico division are not keen on letting us in on the investigation, however," he adds. "Which brings me to this." He holds out a strip of cream card.

I take it. Gold lettering covers one side: an invitation for dinner at the end of the month. "I'm...not sure I understand," I say, examining it.

"We need to better our reputation," he explains. "If we can garner more support for the agency, our work with the local police will be a lot smoother. Everyone at this dinner is aware of the agency's true purpose, and of our need for more resources. Rayne will be attending, and I'd like you to accompany him."

I don't know if I should thank him or curse him. Imagining myself in a big frilly dress, towering over the other guests, I flush. Curse him, definitely.

"I see," I say, toying with the card. It is soft against my fingers, and the lettering glitters. Expensive.

"I would go myself, but I have dinner with Pemberton that evening," he says, his wry smile reappearing. "The Legal Secretary prefers his reports in person." He waits for me to respond, but I can't find anything to say. "If you don't have anything suitable to wear, Maia can arrange something," Monaghan adds. "Do you have any questions?"

I smile to cover my dread. "No. Sir."

"Very good. Rayne can hire a carriage for the evening. It's an expense, but I think it will be worth it, given the importance of this dinner." Great. I can't afford to fail, then. "Thank you, agent."

At the dismissal I rise, tucking the invitation into my palm, creasing the fine card. I sweep out of the room, Steel already ahead of me.

"Dinner?" he says, before I've even closed the door behind me. "Are we to be put on display for them to stare at?"

"It won't be that bad." That's a lie; I'm sure it will be worse. Turner went to one of these dinners once. Monaghan never invited her back. "Parliament are aware of what we do. What you are," I say, in spite of my thoughts. "They won't be surprised."

"No, but they'll want to be entertained."

"Comfort yourself with the thought that you won't be the only one on display."

I make my way to our rooms, Steel trailing me like a wolfhound. I find Maia in my old apprentice rooms, sweeping. She stops when she sees me.

"What did he want?"

"We've been invited to a dinner," I tell her, gesturing at Steel and me with the invitation.

"Ah, yes, England's wealthy barons will be returning from their country estates," she mutters. She takes the invitation from me and examines it. "I would say perhaps we could have one of Turner's dresses tailored, but..." She looks at me and trails off.

"They're a little too short," I reply, reading the look.

"We would not want to scandalise these politicians," she agrees. "The twenty-ninth... I will send out to have one made. There is plenty of time."

I glance at the wardrobe beside my old bed. "Could you get a man's suit made, as well?" I ask, on a whim.

"You may be tall," Steel interjects, "but your dimensions still won't fit me."

"Not for you," I reply. "For me."

Maia looks surprised and she, too, glances at the wardrobe. "I can make the attempt. What colour?"

"Black." That shouldn't draw any undue attention.

"As you wish."

"Thank you." I turn back to Steel, and he sighs.

"Library?"

"Library," I confirm. If Private George murdered Martha Tabram, then someone else—some*thing* else—killed Mary Ann Nichols and Annie Chapman. I need to find out what.

CHAPTER TWENTY-SEVEN

The whole of Scotland Yard seems to be stumped by these murders. Even with police officers being drawn in from other areas of the city, they've still found no evidence. Not to mention that the witness reports are vague and inconsistent. It's like hunting for a rat on a plague ship.

At the far end of the library, the clock in the taxidermy room chimes. Another hour wasted. To think that a month ago I would have been sitting here, content to wait for Turner to return. Now, it's all I can do to distract myself from the time passing.

I turn back to Annie's inquest report. None of the statements reference anything that could indicate the presence of a demon, but it's the strangeness of Hanbury Yard that gives pause; the apparent invisibility of the killer, the body found in the late hours of the morning in a space the size of my bedroom. Someone would have had to be incredibly fast, or ridiculously strong, to commit the murder in the short space of time the Yard was empty.

Maia sweeps into the library, drawing me out of the report. Doyle trails behind her, carrying a tower of boxes. "Hazel," Maia says, "the clothes have arrived."

I examine the boxes doubtfully. "That looks like more than we ordered."

"I took the liberty of ordering you another day dress," Maia explains. "I thought you may need one, with how much time this case is taking."

"Thank you." Steel is asleep on the couch, his Homburg over his face. I wince at the thought of waking him just so I can go and look at dresses. "Can you bring them in here?"

"Into the library?" Maia shrugs. "Very well. Doyle, put them over there and then wait outside. I will need you to take them upstairs in a moment."

Doyle droops at the order. He deposits the boxes on my desk and traipses away. When he's left, I turn to Maia.

She nods before I can ask. "The suit is here, as well."

I open the package she directs me to, a simpler one than the sleek cream boxes tied with blue ribbon. This box contains a suit jacket, trousers, and two shirt collars, so I can wear my own blouse and swap the collars if I need to. I put the jacket to my shoulders. The fit is perfect. "Thank you, Maia, this is lovely."

Maia shakes her head and gives me a fond smile. "Why not look at the dresses, too?"

Cautiously I open the first box, prepared for a wild confection of bows and ribbons. Instead, the dress is green silk, trimmed with thin white satin ruffles that match a white border on the square-neck bodice. The only other embellishment is a small bouquet of silk roses on one shoulder. The silk is as smooth as water in my hands, nothing like the old wool I'm used to. Perhaps there might be something to look forward to about this dinner, after all. "Oh," I say, in a different tone. "This *is* lovely."

"The pattern had to be simple," Maia says, touching the silk, "because of the speed with which we needed it made. It comes with a flounced petticoat. Perhaps a little easier to steer than a full cage bustle."

"Much easier."

Opening the other box, I find the second dress; a coffee-coloured bodice edged in black lace with mother-of-pearl buttons and black cuffs. It has a matching skirt, drawn up at the sides over an underskirt of the same colour.

"You had best try on the green silk before Saturday," Maia tells me. "If something is wrong, we can get them altered. At least you will not disappoint Monaghan." Her smile is part teasing, part sadness, as though she thinks I expect something from the professor beyond what he's already given me. I know better: Monaghan's heart died years ago, alongside the woman he loved.

Still, my face betrays me with a flush. "Thank you, Maia."

"Stop thanking me," she says, gathering up some of the boxes. "It is the least I could do for Turner's apprentice." Her smile wobbles and she leaves to call back Doyle.

"Don't *I* get a new suit?"

I glance at Steel. He's peeking at the boxes from under the brim of his hat. "I thought you didn't want a new suit?" I counter.

"That was before I knew you were getting *three* new outfits."

"You can have one for the next dinner," I promise, packing away the day dress.

"If I'm still here," is his reply, and the memory of our deal comes flooding back.

The last murder was on the eighth of September, and it's nearly October; perhaps the killer has stopped. If my case is over, then soon I'll need to deliver on my end of the bargain.

I tuck that thought away with my new dress. When we've confirmed that the murders have stopped, I'll consider that avenue. And the way the investigation is going, that might be a long time yet.

CHAPTER TWENTY-EIGHT

I slide into the green dress and wait until I've pulled back my hair and pinched my cheeks before I look in the mirror. It's...good. The basque bodice makes my waist look smaller than it feels, even without much in the way of corset constraints. The square cut reveals my collarbones and conceals the breadth of my shoulders, and the soft green makes my unfashionably yellow hair look gold.

I put a hand to my chest, remind myself to breathe. It's better than I thought, but a new dress does not make a new person, no matter how pretty it is. I tuck a loose strand of hair behind my ears and advance out of my room.

Steel is waiting and he greets me with a question: "Do we *have* to travel with that demon?"

"Yes, he and Rayne are coming to this thing, too," I reply in an undertone, as we descend to the entrance hall. "Why, what do you have against Cassius?"

"Do I need to have something against him to not like him? Do *you* like Rayne?"

"My opinion on other agents is irrelevant," I reply, a shade too defensive. "We have a job to do. Monaghan needs us to boost the agency's reputation."

"In that case, you should have worn a dress with a lower cut."

Before I can think of a response, we reach the hall, where Rayne and Cassius are waiting. "You look lovely this evening," the Phantom says, with a smirk.

I hadn't hoped for a comment on my dress, but Cassius' remark brings an awkward heat to my cheeks and I resist the urge to tug at my bodice. "Thank you. Has Monaghan already left?"

"Not yet, he's going to Pemberton's shortly." Rayne holds the door open for us. "Are you ready? The coach is waiting."

I turn to grab our cloaks and find that Steel has already fetched them. I take mine and throw it over my shoulders, more comfortable when the expanse of green silk is covered. We climb into the coach and I tuck my skirt and petticoats around my ankles, gathering the voluminous material in my fist.

"How far is it?" I ask Rayne, who sits beside me.

"Not far," Rayne replies. His gaze drops to my bare throat and he adds, "A diamond necklace would suit that dress very well. There are jewellers in the city who can create cheap glass pendants, I've heard."

The insult is so casual and off-hand that I stutter to respond. "Do you know a lot about jewellery, Agent Rayne?" I ask, finally.

"A little. These are diamonds—heirlooms, from my grandfather." He proffers his hands and turns them so the stones in his cuffs gleam.

"They're very nice." Opposite me, Steel is grimly silent, as if determined to leave me to my fate. I struggle to think of something to say. "Do you know who's attending tonight?"

"Lord Arron and Sir Wolvesley," he replies. "And some lesser members of the Home Office, I believe. No one important."

"No one important," I repeat, dryly. If Rayne were Jacob, I'd suggest we approach each aristocrat together. But I have none of the comfortable ease with Rayne that I do with Jacob.

"I'll handle them," he continues. "When I was a Baron, we would mingle with Lords all the time."

"I thought you left the Baronetcy as a child?" I ask.

"Well—I meant the son of a Baron, obviously. I took on many of the responsibilities of the estate."

"I see." I wonder how often he introduces himself to strangers as Baron Rayne.

"Regardless, I need their support, so perhaps it would be best to leave the interactions to me."

"I'm sure *Professor Monaghan* would be grateful for their support," I remind him. We're not here for Rayne's political ambitions. He snorts and turns his face to the window. We spend the rest of the drive in silence.

Emerging when we stop, I'm greeted by a pretty townhouse with a white front and a black door, one of two dozen identical houses on a crescent overlooking a park. A cool breeze creeps down my exposed neck. At the door, a butler takes our cloaks and leads us into a large parlour, where we find a group of men and women gossiping over champagne flutes. Framed paintings jostle for position on green and gold wallpaper, and a legion of brocade chairs fill the spaces that aren't taken up by living bodies. Melodic piano notes drift through the room, dampening the clink of glasses and babble of conversation.

The butler bends to a grey-haired man in the middle of the party and after a whispered conversation the man advances towards us. "Agent Rayne, I assume," he says, in a deep voice. "And Miss Locke." He ignores the two demons behind us, his gaze skirting around them as if they're shadows. As high level Home Office employees, everyone here will know the agency's real function. "Monaghan told me to expect you both. Welcome."

"Lord Arron." Rayne shakes the man's hand. "I understand you just returned from your estate. Did you find good hunting?"

"I did, although I'm more of a fishing man, myself. Our lake has trout and pike, in the summer months."

"Fascinating. And your estate borders the river, does it not?" Rayne draws the man away, picking up a glass of champagne, at ease among the fine furniture and cordial music.

I cannot claim even a passing acquaintance with any of these people. If Monaghan expects this to be another aspect of my role, then I'm going to be very bad at it.

"Miss Locke." I jump and turn around. The man who greets me smiles. "Forgive me. Agent Locke, isn't it?"

"Agent Stewart," I reply, with more than a little relief. "I did not expect to see you here."

"Nor did I, to be honest," he replies, his eyes wrinkling in amusement.

At his side, a woman with high cheekbones and a broad nose mirrors his smile. Her hair is jet black despite the lines of age in her face. "I'm trying to persuade him to become a member," she says, "but he doesn't want to get into politics. Ah, my apologies. I'm Catherine Stewart. The wife," she clarifies, and I blink. It's rare for agents to have wives. I can't imagine the difficulty in balancing a home life with the demands of the agency.

I recall myself and curtsy. "It's a pleasure to meet you, Mrs. Stewart. This is Mr. Steel," I add, turning to introduce Steel. He stands a little apart, by the wall.

"Ah, yes. Jacob mentioned that your newest recruit was..." Agent Stewart trails off and nods at Steel. "I don't suppose you've had word of Jacob?"

Miller gets regular reports from the agency's regional hubs, and I seek to put to rest the concern in his gaze. "His investigation is proceeding as expected."

"Well, I look forward to seeing him when he returns."

"You must visit us, too," Mrs. Stewart adds. "Turner and I used to have tea once a week. When you can spare the time, of course—I know the professor keeps you all very busy."

"Not busy enough, for my taste," I reply, honestly. Another case might prove a useful distraction.

We exchange pleasantries for a little longer, and then the couple moves on to speak to someone else. I take the opportunity to seize a glass of champagne, more to occupy my hands than to drink, and wonder what to do next. Rayne is speaking to a group of men around a card table, his back to me. Cassius is seated on a chair just behind him, flirting with a few women. Wives, I assume. Hardly the kind of behaviour Monaghan would approve of. Although...

Perhaps I'm not giving Cassius enough credit. The professor wants us to get closer to the politicians. What better way than to endear ourselves to their wives?

Inhaling and mentally crossing my fingers, I approach two women a little older than me. They have glossy dark hair and pale skin, their waists so tiny that I could fit both my hands around them. I gulp, and scrunch lower so I look less Amazonian.

Far from the scorn I expected, they greet me with warm smiles and enquiring looks. "Miss Hazel Locke," I introduce myself, grateful that my dress hides my meagre class. They would look at me differently if they knew I was born in a room the size of a stable in the heart of east London. "I work with Dominic Rayne." I point him out and their expressions become very interested, very quickly.

"You work with Rayne?" one asks and the other taps her with her fan.

"Forgive my cousin," she says. "I'm Louisa Redville and this is Elena Tratheven. Dear Frederick is playing whist, at the moment." I look for dear Frederick and commit the face to memory in case he's one of the politicians we need to charm.

"How long has he been in Parliament?" The question unlocks a stream of information about Frederick's career aspirations, familial relations and nightly sleeping habits, down to the special gloves he wears to keep his hands soft. It takes a great deal of effort not to guzzle my champagne.

The cousin, evidently as uninterested in the state of Frederick's skin as I am, jumps in. "You said you work with Sir Rayne," she says. "What is it like?"

"*Sir* Rayne?"

"Son of Baron Rayne," she replies, eyeing me. "You don't use his title?"

"We relinquish our pasts when we join the agency," I tell her. "Is the Baron well?"

"*He* is, yes."

I don't miss the emphasis. "His wife?"

"She hasn't been well for years. Not since what happened to the daughter," the woman says, and her cousin tuts at her.

"Elena, please."

I shouldn't ask. It's none of my business, and if Rayne hasn't told me, he doesn't want me to know. My resolve lasts for less than a minute. "What happened?"

Elena pauses, and glances around, then leans forward as if to convey a state secret. "She drowned when she was a child."

"That's awful." All agents join the agency to escape something, but I had no idea Rayne's past contained a demon of its own. No wonder he never speaks of it. "How long ago did it happen?"

"Oh, fourteen, fifteen years, I think? The Baron's wife left him and his son not long after. They live separately, now."

That can't have been easy. I watch Rayne turn to say something to a lady sitting with Cassius. He wears a charming smile.

"We shouldn't be gossiping," says Louisa, fluttering her fan in agitation. "If agents are required to cut their ties to their inheritance—"

"I won't say anything." I shouldn't know, anyway. Rayne's reasons for fleeing his past are his own.

"Listen, they're calling us in to dinner," Louisa says, gesturing at the doors with her fan, where the butler has just made an appearance. "Miss Locke, perhaps we can continue our conversation later." They curtsy and I do the same, trailing after the stream of people to the dining room.

Pastoral tapestries mask the walls and a large embroidered rug softens our footsteps. The table seats twenty-four people, big enough for a banquet, and is laid with a dizzying array of silverware. The first course is served once we're seated, a fragrant bowl of shredded chicken soup. I sneak a glance at Steel. He's intent on conquering the dish, apparently as at home among the elegant tableware as he is in the agency's kitchen.

I dab my mouth with my napkin and mutter, behind it, "Which spoon should I use?"

He shrugs. "Whichever is closest. A spoon is a spoon." I glimpse the woman on his other side look at him, horrified.

The gentleman on my left is a better teacher, and I take silent direction from him, choosing the spoon on the outside. The soup is curried—overpoweringly so. Clearly the cook has little experience with spices.

"This is not as good as Maia's rice," Steel complains, echoing my thoughts.

"Someone will hear you," I say, from the side of my mouth.

"I think they're trying as hard as possible to believe I don't exist."

I cast a surreptitious glance around the table. No one is looking at Steel, or at Cassius. Their gazes skip past the demons as though looking at them might invite the devil himself to dine.

"We'll be done soon," I tell him; an attempt at comfort, perhaps.

It turns out to be a lie. Six more courses pass before the meal is declared to be finished. Then, there's an awkward moment when the women rise to leave and Steel rises with me. The titter of confusion is dispelled when Lord Arron stands and claims the gentlemen will accompany us. We all squeeze back into the parlour for more alcohol. I lose sight of Rayne and Cassius in the crush. Steel lingers at the edge of the room, steering clear of the other guests but staying close enough to me that the spell limit doesn't activate. I join my new acquaintances, smiling vaguely when they dive into a debate over the newest floral pattern that will be all the rage by Christmas.

The clock ticks sluggishly, creeping into the early hours of Sunday morning, and I wonder when we can leave. Cassius reappears from wherever he disappeared to, and I absently watch him cross the room. Then Steel steps into his path and I straighten. Cassius checks at the sight of the other demon. Steel stares him down. Hastily I make my apologies to Elena and Louise and approach the demons.

"—know how it works," Steel says, in a low voice. "You've been that man's servant for what, five years?"

"Servant is not the word I would choose," Cassius replies in a drawl, without the same apparent concern that he'll be overheard.

"It's a kinder one than the word *I'd* use."

The Phantom laughs. "Poor little dragon. I can't imagine how hard it must be for you." I step behind an ebony Coromandel screen, shielded from their view, and listen.

"What do you mean?" Steel replies, wariness making his voice slow and deep.

"You've never had to bend the knee, have you, last son of House Leviathan?"

A hiss. "You don't know me. Do not speak as though you do."

Through the latticework of the screen, I see Rayne standing at the far limit of the spell's boundary. His head turns towards Cassius, some unconscious connection to his demon sparking an instinct, and his eyes narrow.

"Ah, that's a sore topic, is it? You still haven't caught the ones responsible, I take it?" Cassius tuts. "And here I thought the Second House stood for something more than polluted bloodlines and useless magic. Seems I'm wrong."

"You—"

The Phantom demon continues, speaking over Steel. "It must have been galling," he says, "to see the House of *Flies* take your place. Better that your people not see that. They might have taken their own lives in despair."

Steel chokes. At once Rayne strikes out across the room, his expression darkening. I slip out from behind the screen. Cassius tilts his head in Rayne's direction without looking, wearing a mocking smirk as though it's his favourite suit. He's goading Steel. Whether through boredom or malice, I don't know, but if Steel attacks, Rayne will make sure he doesn't survive the night.

"Steel," I interject, striding up to them. I put my hand on his arm and blink at the tension that vibrates through him. "I need to speak to you. Excuse us, Cassius."

I extract my partner from the conversation, putting myself between the two demons, and propel Steel across the room. The demon is silent, but he trembles like a pot about to boil over.

"He was manipulating you." I watch Rayne engage Cassius in a heated exchange. "I expect he wanted to enliven the evening with a fight."

Steel's fists dig into his thighs. "Why did you stop him?"

"If you two get into a fight here, it's the guests who'll suffer. And you." I stare at him until he drops his gaze and looks away.

I know little of demon Houses, or hierarchy, but to be considered second among them all must mean this House Leviathan is important. *Was* important. What does that mean for Steel? I dearly want to ask, but guilt stays my tongue. He never intended for me to hear that conversation, and I will not earn his trust by forcing it out of him.

"Come," I say, drawing him away from the corner with gentle hands. "Rayne can have the carriage: you and I can walk home." It's not that far, and the night air will clear his head. Perhaps he'll open up on the way. I lead him out of the room and call for the butler, who attends me with a polite, distant expression.

"How can I help, miss?"

"We're leaving," I tell him, throwing on my cloak. "Please relay our apologies for our abrupt departure."

"Of course, ma'am."

There's a loud knock at the door. The butler, half-turned away to carry out my request, turns back. He opens the door a fraction, enough for me to catch sight of Doyle's frightened face.

"Doyle?" I step up to the door, frowning. The boy's alone, panting as though he's run a mile. "What's going on?"

"You need to come, miss," he huffs out. "There's—there's been another murder."

CHAPTER TWENTY-NINE

"Another murder?"

"Aye, miss. I was passing near the Tower and I 'eard the local police give up the cry. Miss Bhatt said you and Rayne'd be here and told me to come sharpish and tell you."

My stomach clenches into a hard knot. "Please send for Agent Rayne," I tell the butler. "Have him come here at once." The butler bows and leaves. "Where did it happen, Doyle?"

"The International Workers' Club, miss. Up by Berner Street."

"I know it. Thank you."

"Do you want me to take you there, miss?" He pales as he says it. I shake my head.

"Go back to the agency; wait for Monaghan. We'll find out what we can and join you there."

"Aye. Be careful, miss." He disappears into the gloom of the street and I yank on my gloves.

"Berner Street," Steel asks, donning his cloak. "Is that in Whitechapel?"

"On the district border." My hands are shaking. I still them by clenching my fingers together. Come on, Rayne. "If we get there in time, do you think you can track the killer?"

"If the trail isn't too obscured, yes."

Rayne materialises, finally. "What is it? I was in the middle of—"

"Doyle found us," I cut in. "There's been another murder. We need to go."

To his credit, Rayne does not ask questions, just grabs his cloak and gestures at me to lead the way.

It's almost two in the morning, and the city is quiet, but as our coach approaches Spitalfields the chatter grows. Berner Street, when we reach it, is clustered with people.

I jump out of the coach before the driver stops and stride over to the crescent line of police holding back the crowd. The place is lit with flickering gas lamps and faint mist curls over the air. I pull my cloak tighter around me. A body lies behind the officers, on the path heading into the yard.

"Officer!" I call to the nearest policeman. "What happened?"

The man glances at me, takes in my cloak and the green silk peeping out underneath. "Move along, miss. The street ain't a circus."

"We need to see the officer in charge," Rayne commands and flashes his identification. "I'm a government agent."

"You could be the Queen herself and you wouldn't be getting any closer. Move on, now." He pushes us back, his truncheon barring us from getting any nearer.

"These are City district police," I tell Rayne, taking note of their uniform. Berner Street lies on the other side of the district's border from Whitechapel. "They're not going to let us in."

Rayne mutters a curse. "If we can't get closer to the body, how can we find the killer?"

I turn to Steel. "What do you think?" I ask, keeping my voice low. "Can you sense anything from here?"

The demon gazes past the police at the heap of cloth and blood that's all we can see of the victim. "There *is* something," he says. "I'm not sure what class it is. But there's something."

"What are you waiting for, then?" Rayne asks. "Where is it?"

Steel glares at him and I touch his arm, draw his attention to me. "Can you follow the trail?"

"I'll try."

He steps away from the crowd, heading north. He walks slowly, placing his feet with care, Rayne, Cassius and I following. Ten minutes pass and I realise we're nearing Aldgate Station.

A cry sounds from somewhere ahead. "Murder! Murder in Mitre Square!"

"Mitre Square?" I repeat. "But the body was found in—" I look at Steel and see the same realisation in his face as it rips through me: *two* murders.

We race towards the shout. Mitre Square is a spacious gathering place surrounded by buildings. Police stand near a fence on one side, their faces glowing golden in the lights. Beyond them lies a body, the stone paving around it shining darkly.

"Wait." Rayne grips my elbow. "Stay here."

"But—"

"You shouldn't see this," he says, sternly, and joins the mass of spectators, Cassius at his side. I wait until they engage a policeman, and then go around to stand at the edge of the crowd, close enough to see the body.

Blood soaks the woman's clothes and spills onto the ground, running over the mud to my feet. Her throat is cut, just like the others, but her face—her face is unrecognisable. Her nose is a jagged hole and parts of her cheeks have been carved off, exposing bloody red muscle and white bone.

I push away a surge of horror and disgust. I don't want to remember this sight, to be haunted by it every time I try to sleep.

I know I will be, regardless.

Biting my cheek, I turn to Steel. "This is where the trail was leading," he murmurs, staring at the body. "The killer ran here and killed again."

Two murders in one night. I swallow bile, try to think. A doctor kneels beside the woman, categorising her injuries. A little way distant stands a young, dark-skinned man with curly hair. "Come on," I tell Steel, approaching the assistant. "Mr. Green. I'm glad you're here."

The man glances at me, then again. "I—Miss Locke. I mean, Agent Locke, my apologies. What are you doing here?"

"We were passing by," I lie, "and we heard the ruckus. Could you tell us how she died?"

"It's not—I'm not sure if..." He trails off, and I read the same concern in his face that drove Rayne to keep me away from the body.

"I appreciate your caution," I say, tamping down my annoyance, "but I need to know. It may help the investigation."

He nods. "Her throat was cut," he begins, "again, like the other victims. What's different this time... Well, judging by the wounds to her cheeks and nose, I would say he tried to slice off her face."

"Go on," I say, when he pauses.

"The—the intestines were removed and left near the body," he continues. "Her right ear has been cut. There appear to be more injuries to her abdomen, but we won't know much more until the post-mortem. I hope...uh, I assume that's what you wanted to know?"

Swallowing, it takes me a moment to speak. "Yes. Thank you, Mr. Green."

"Will I expect you at the mortuary?"

"We'll be there as soon as we can. I assume the police will get the report first, but I'd appreciate anything else you can tell us."

"Of course." The doctor calls Green to the corpse and he sketches a quick bow before he retreats.

"Do these injuries look like the work of a demon to you?" I ask Steel.

His mouth curls in distaste. "Possibly, though I can't think of any spell that would necessitate the injuries to her face."

Rayne joins us, then. "Who were you talking to?" he asks, glancing at Green as the man lifts the body onto the cart to be removed.

"The mortuary assistant. He told us what happened to her."

"I doubt an assistant would be able to comprehend the nature of this crime," he replies, dismissively.

"Were you able to speak to the doctor?" I counter. He opens his mouth, then closes it again. "For now, I suggest we search the area. Steel, would you mind?" I ask, before Rayne can protest.

"Perhaps you'll be able to find something before I do, this time," Cassius drawls.

I ignore the Phantom. "If there's anything you sense, let me know. The trail led here, so it must lead on."

He nods and pulls away. I watch him walk along the side of the street, shoulders hunched and head down. Cassius murmurs something to Rayne under his voice, and the Phantom trails after Steel, peering at the buildings on either side of the road. I start after them and find Rayne beside me.

"Your demon must learn to get along with the others," the man says. "He's not a stray dog, he's a member of the agency."

Needled, I reply with more heat than I intend. "Cassius has been griping at him all evening. If Steel chooses to reply with force, I can hardly stop him."

"This is not a fighting ring. I won't have them beating each other up."

"Then you should speak to your partner." I turn my back on him and go to meet the demons as they're walking back. Steel holds something in his palm. "You found something?"

He holds it out. The talon is thin and curved like an owl's.

"Seems your Hound is good for something, after all," Cassius interjects, and I cast him a swift glare.

Rayne plucks the claw out of Steel's hand. "Scout demons can mimic others, like Stalkers," he muses. "This might explain the various different suspects that the witnesses have identified."

"Scouts only mimic voices, or certain features," Steel replies. "They don't have the skill to hold a shape for as long as it would take to murder these women."

I examine the claw. "It also doesn't fit with what the Stalker demon told us: Scout demons are copper class. We're looking for silver."

Rayne shrugs. "The thing must have lied."

Steel looks as though he's about to say something, then pauses. I raise my eyebrows at him, and he shakes his head. "I will keep looking for a trail," he says, instead of whatever he was going to say. "Though it seems he's masked his presence so well I'm having trouble tracking him."

"See what else you can find," Rayne tells Cassius. "Look in the buildings, too. We'll be here for a while."

I tuck my cloak around me and settle in to wait.

CHAPTER THIRTY

We stay until dawn lightens the dark blue at the horizon. Steel's expression is grim, and I know we won't locate anything further tonight. We hire two hansom cabs, and I sit silently beside Steel on our way home. The image of the woman's body keeps flashing in front of my eyes, blood and muscle and broken skin. I blink it away.

The agency is dark and silent on our return. I go to put away our cloaks and pause. Two familiar coats hang in the closet, fresh with dirt. Eve and Khurana are back.

It's almost five in the morning. My eyes are hot and sore and desperate to close, but more than sleep I want to see Eve. I didn't realise how badly I needed to hear her voice until the urge sweeps over me.

"What is it?" Steel asks.

"Eve and Khurana have returned," I reply, over my shoulder, holding my skirts out of the way of my hasty feet.

We reach my old room and I hesitate on the threshold. It's a good four-hour train ride from Bristol; Eve won't take kindly to being woken at this hour.

I push the door open a crack. The fire is lit, casting a warm glow over the small metal beds—empty—and over Eve's hunched figure, sitting on the floor.

"Eve?" Her face is pressed to her knees, and my eagerness to see her drains out of me. "Are you all right?"

She lifts her head, and reveals a face stained with tears. "Hazel."

"Eve." I fold to my knees at her side. I've never seen her cry like this. "Are you hurt? Is Khurana hurt?"

"No, it's...nothing like that." She wipes her face and smiles tremulously at the floor. Her curls are coming loose; the oil she uses to smooth them into her bun lies unopened on the cabinet. As I watch, a shiver runs through her.

One of the beds is within reach and I pull off its blanket and throw it around her shoulders. "Tell me what happened."

"The case," she begins, haltingly. "It was—You didn't see it, you can't..." She sniffles and wipes her nose. "Babies, Hazel. They were just babies. They were..." She makes a gesture with her hands, forming a too tiny shape, then puts both hands to her face. "She strangled them. And then she dumped their bodies in the river."

I hug her tighter, press my face to her shoulder and hope the meagre comfort helps. "Was it a demon?" I ask, after a moment. I feel her shake her head.

"That's the worst part," she mutters. "She was human. No—she was a monster." I don't know what to say, how to take away her grief. I just hug her as close as I can. "I don't know if I can do this," Eve whispers.

What I saw tonight was awful, but the thought of what Eve must have seen brings tears to my own eyes. "You can," I say, blinking them back. "Now you know what people are capable of. Now you know what *you're* capable of."

She huffs a laugh and leans her temple against my forehead. "That's a good speech."

"Maybe I needed to hear it, too," I admit, watching the fire crackle.

After a long pause, Eve stirs and wipes her face. "Tell me about your case."

"It can wait. Why don't you go to sleep? We can speak tomorrow."

"Yes. I want to meet your new demon."

I glance over my shoulder. Steel stands in the corridor, at the edge of our bond. "I want you to make sure he's doing his job right," I tell her and Eve smiles. I wipe her cheeks with my thumbs, smoothing the tracks of tears away. "Come on, into bed."

Eve lets me hustle her into the nearest bunk without protest, even allowing me to smother her with blankets until only her face is visible.

"I missed you, you know," I say, sitting beside her. "No one else tells me when I'm being a fool."

"You're not a fool." Her eyes sparkle. "You're just stubborn."

"Pot; kettle," I shoot back. "Sleep. We'll speak at breakfast. Lunch," I correct, glancing at the sky outside.

Eve hums a response. I wait until her breathing evens out and slows down. Then, I bank the fire and slip out of the room.

I catch Steel in the middle of a yawn. "Sorry," I whisper. "We can go now."

He casts a curious glance over my shoulder but asks no questions, so I head to our rooms. He disappears into his, making straight for the bed, and I enter mine. I feel wrung dry, as if all the life has been twisted out of me.

I glance in the mirror and jerk to a stop. Scarlet stains reach up from the hem of my once-beautiful dress, staining the silk ruffles. Mud is caked onto the parts the blood hasn't touched, as though I'd waded through a stream.

My throat closes up. I rip the dress from my body. Buttons ping off and scatter over the floor. With shaking hands, I strip away the skirt and toss it into a pile on the floor, then peel off the bodice and fling it across the room. When I'm done, I clench my hands and suck in air until the pressure on my chest eases and the tears that burn my eyes recede.

I dress again in my old wool skirt and jacket, and sit by the window with Turner's journal, waiting for the light. I will not sleep tonight.

CHAPTER THIRTY-ONE

October dawns clear and cold. The few trees on the street are dusted with red and gold, and their crisp leaves carpet the pavement. It's been over a month since Turner died, and now three more women have joined her.

I must look as grim as I feel. When I enter the kitchen Maia shoves a cup of tea into my hand. "Sit," she orders. "I will bring you something to eat."

"Thank you." Eve is already at the table, her plate empty. I sit opposite her, leaving room for Steel beside me. "Good morning."

"Morning." Her voice is crisp, unladen with the grief she wore last night. She cups her own tea and regards Steel as he sits down. "So, you're the new Hound. The classless one. Is that why you're not a Sentinel?" she asks him. "Because they exiled you?"

Steel pauses, his spoon halfway to his mouth. "I suppose," he replies, and continues eating.

"Seems a little odd," Eve continues. "Three hundred years, and the agency has never met a male Hound. Why is that?"

"The effects of the spell are determined by the caster," Steel replies. "You should be asking your professor, not me."

Eve sets her elbows on the table, levelling Steel with a sharp look. "None of our demons have mentioned your existence. Why?"

"Why would they give up others of our kind to be captured and imprisoned, you mean?"

She frowns thoughtfully. "You're not going to answer any of my questions, are you?"

"I can't answer what I don't know."

"That's an evasion, not an answer."

He smirks at her.

"Steel has been helping me with the Whitechapel murders," I say. "He has no reason to deceive us." The lie is for Steel's benefit. If I'm to learn anything about him and his abilities, as Monaghan asked, then he can't think I suspect him.

"You'll be meeting Khurana, later. Consider this a rehearsal."

I nearly drop my cup. "Khurana?"

Eve looks regretful. "I meant to tell you: you're to meet her in the hall when you're done here. She's going to test Steel."

"Rayne already tested him," I protest. "Why does she need to do it again?"

"She wants to be sure, I suppose." Eve shrugs. "You know what Khurana's like. If she hasn't done it herself, it might as well not have happened."

They would only test him again if they had concerns about the ritual. Or about me. I rotate my cup, staring at the glassy surface of my tea. Khurana must think I'm useless. First to have summoned the wrong demon, and now to not have tested him properly.

"It'll be fine," Eve says, reaching out to still my hands. "If Rayne tested him and he passed, then he'll pass again. It's nothing to worry about."

"I believe *I* am the one who is going to be stabbed," Steel mutters.

I eye him. Of all things, this is not going to help him trust me, or convince him that we can work together. But I can't object. If she thinks there's a reason to test Steel, then there must be a reason. "If you're ready, we could go now," I suggest. "Get it over with."

He nods. "At least I'll have time to heal before we have to venture into Whitechapel again."

I place my hands on the table and push myself up. My feet are lead weights. "Let's go, then."

When we arrive at the hall, only Khurana and her demon are waiting for us. The agent's eyes are cold and hard. Her long dark hair is curled into a braided bun at the nape of her neck, and the only decoration she wears is the plain iron kara on her right wrist. She carries her sword-cane in her other hand.

"Agent Khurana." I swallow and Khurana's gaze drops to my throat, registering my nervousness. "Eve said you wanted to speak to Steel."

"Test him," the woman corrects in her clear voice. "Stand here, please," she adds, to Steel, pointing at a spot in the centre of the room with her cane.

The demon tilts his head, his gaze flicking between her and Isis. "Your professor seemed content with me," he says. "I'm not sure why you feel the need to second guess his decision."

"Is that what you think I'm doing?" Khurana's mouth widens in an amused smile. I try to signal to Steel that mocking the woman will not do him any favours.

"Aren't you?" he continues, either not seeing the minute shaking of my head or wilfully ignoring me. He puts his hands in his pockets and regards her, his silver eyes following her like a snake's.

"I am assuring myself that our new Hound is secure." She walks between us and I take a step back, out of her path. She continues to circle him, drawing a wide space around him. "We have just lost an agent. We cannot afford to lose another."

"Do you not trust your agents to perform their duties?" Where I would turn, following her, he lets her circle behind him, tilting his head to let his voice carry.

"I trust myself." Khurana grips the metal handle of her cane. I tense. "I can answer for no other."

"So, you *don't* trust them. Why is that, I wonder?"

"The question at hand," Khurana replies, "is whether I trust you." Her blade makes a soft hiss as she yanks it free. Steel catches it with his bare hand, inches from his face.

"This," he says, holding the sword, "will not change your mind."

With a scowl, Khurana pulls the blade free. Blood splatters on the stone floor and Steel drops his hand to his side. I step forward, objections crowding my tongue.

Eve grips my arm. I hadn't even heard her join us. Her expression is stern. "Let her finish."

I glance at Steel. The demon meets my gaze and drops his chin in the smallest of nods. Biting my lip, I wait.

Khurana levels her sword at him. "Do you understand the nature of the spell that binds you?"

"I cannot willingly harm any human member of this organisation," he replies, in a level tone. "Nor can I move more than twenty feet from Agent Locke. Although why your warlocks insisted on that amendment, I don't know," he adds, sardonically. "It makes things very difficult."

"Would you run, then, if you could?" Khurana advances, her blade holding steady. I brace myself for the pain to come.

"I would," Steel admits. He doesn't step back. "If you think I want to be here, you're not as good an agent as I've been told you are." The sword touches his chest, and still, he doesn't move.

"Steel," I plead. His lashes flutter but he does not retreat.

Khurana halts and raises a smooth brow. "I intend to test the spell's limit."

"I am not here for your amusement," the demon replies. "Do what you will."

"Isis was stabbed in the chest, once," Khurana muses. "She healed in a few days. Will it take you that long, I wonder?"

"Stop." My heart beats too quickly, making the word vibrate. "I'll do it." I walk backwards, tracking the distance between us until I hit the spell's invisible boundary. Pain ripples through my chest.

Steel exhales. "There," he says. "Are you content?"

Khurana regards him for a moment. "No," she says, and stabs him through the shoulder.

He cries out and folds forward, hunching over the blade. The agent pulls her blade free, showering the floor with more blood.

"Steel!" I rush to his side. "Why did you do that?" I demand. "The spell was working!"

"I had to see how he would react." Isis hands Khurana a pale blue handkerchief and the agent wipes her sword clean, then sheathes it. "If he had attacked me, I would know the spell had failed."

"But he didn't."

"No, he did not." She examines me and her voice goes icy. "Remember that your first priority is to the people of London. Everything else is superfluous." With that, she and her demon glide out of the room.

I hover at Steel's side, my hands fluttering around his shoulder. The stab had looked deep, and there's so much blood. "You could have told me she was going to be like that," I snap at Eve.

"Preparation would've given him an advantage," Eve says, frowning.

"To do what?"

"To deceive us."

"If you don't mind," Steel says, wearily, "I'd like to go upstairs now."

"Do you require bandages?" Eve asks, eyeing the demon.

"No," Steel attempts to straighten, but his injured shoulder slopes at an angle. He grimaces. After a moment's hesitation, I offer my shoulder for support. His expression flickers, but he leans heavily on me. "I would appreciate changing my shirt, however," he adds.

"Let's go upstairs." I cast Eve a look and she returns it coolly. "We'll talk about this later."

She shrugs. "If you like."

I wait until we're out of earshot before asking, "Are you sure you don't need bandages?"

"I'd prefer to be somewhere else before one of them changes their mind and tries to test me a third time," Steel replies, climbing the stairs doggedly.

His strides are longer than mine and I have to quicken my pace to keep up. We make it upstairs without running into anyone, and I help him into his room. "I'll get something for the wound," I say, lowering him into a chair. "Stay here."

In my own room, I tear a few strips of linen from an old blouse. When I return, I find that Steel has shed his jacket and is huddled in a chair. He takes the linen from me and holds it to his skin, under the shirt. His other hand, the one he used to halt Khurana's blade, is bleeding onto the floor. I clean the wound as best I can and wrap his palm.

"I'll heal quickly enough," he says, though he doesn't pull his hand away.

"She didn't need to stab you," I mutter. "It's been a month. If you'd wanted to kill me, you would have done it by now." A low current of anger pours ice into my chest, and I tamp it down. I tuck the end of the linen into his palm and sit back, finished. Steel turns his hand, examining my work.

"Her demon seems strong. I have to respect your agent for taming her, if nothing else."

"Khurana is our best. As good as Monaghan was, before he became Head of the agency. She's his heir. Well," I amend, "not officially, but she and Isis have helped solve more cases than any Phantom or Reaper agent. She's good at what she does."

We lapse into silence and I stand, awkward now that there's no practical application for my mind to focus on.

"You said we'd visit the mortuary." Steel slouches in his chair, keeping his wound covered. "I suppose that might be difficult, now."

I regard the red stain on his shirt. "I'll write to Green and ask him for a report," I decide. "We can visit him when you've healed. Likely the papers will have picked up the story by then, anyway." I perch in the room's other chair and rest my clasped hands on my knees. "What about the claw you found?"

"That does puzzle me," he replies, speaking to his bandaged hand. "Your friend's Reaper went into Whitechapel a few days before the second murder, and all the copper-class demons went to ground. If this is the same murderer, it stands to reason that it's not copper class."

"But?"

"But then we find this claw. First a Stalker's scale, then a Scout's claw. Two different breeds of copper-class demon. Odd, isn't it?"

"Could the Stalker have lied to us?"

"I doubt it. Max has a Reaper's aura," he says, with a shrug—then winces at the movement. "He'd terrify the district's less powerful demons."

"If it wasn't a copper-class demon..." I entwine my fingers as I think. "How normal is it for demons to lose their scales?"

"Not unusual for a Stalkerling. An infant Stalker," he clarifies, at my confused look. "At that age, scales shed like hair. But Sentinel claws are like a scorpion's pincers. They don't just snap off."

"So, it could have been planted." If it was, then following it is a waste of our time. Yet I can't afford to ignore any clue, at this stage. I rub my hands over my face. "He must have been interrupted at Berner Street," I say. "He didn't get a chance to carry out the disembowelment that he did with the others. So, he found someone else to finish the job."

"Which means that death is not his goal; the ritual is what he wants. Either the process of disembowelling these women, or the organs themselves."

I wait, but he doesn't follow with a conclusion. "It *is* a demon, then."

"I suppose it must be," he murmurs. "Though..." He trails off, pursuing some train of thought I can't follow.

"I didn't think you'd be this interested in the case," I admit. "Are you more concerned about humans than you let on?"

A wry smile turns his mouth up on one side, softening the hard lines of his face. "I enjoy a hunt, that's all."

"That's one way to put it." I should let him rest. "Let me know when you feel up to travelling," I tell him, standing. "I'll find out what I can from the police reports."

He hums and I leave him to rest, turning my mind back to the murders.

CHAPTER THIRTY-TWO

S teel's hand heals overnight, but the wound in his shoulder doesn't, so he turns large eyes on Maia and the woman brings him plate after plate.

I sigh. "Do you always eat this much?"

"I'm healing," he says, through a mouthful of cabbage and potatoes. "I need to keep up my strength."

"That sounds like an excuse."

He hesitates, fork halfway to his mouth. "I didn't get much chance to eat, before." I have to lean closer to hear him. "There wasn't really...I wasn't getting three meals a day. More like a quarter of one."

"Why?" But he shakes his head and resumes eating, the tiny window into his past closed once more.

The sound of quick footsteps keeps me from saying anything else. Eve strides into the kitchen, her mouth tense and her arms tight at her sides. All thought of Steel's eating habits slides away at the grim, focused way she walks. "You have a new case," I guess.

"I just came from Whitehall." She spreads open a piece of paper over the table. It holds three small sketches of an unfamiliar symbol; a collection of sweeping lines interconnected in complex harmony. "They're building the new Scotland Yard and they found a body part in the foundations."

"A body part? You think it's the Whitechapel murderer?"

"I don't know yet." She indicates the drawings. "They found a female torso with these tattoos. They're taking it to the city mortuary."

"Monaghan said an arm was found in Pimlico," I recall. I'd forgotten in the chaos of the double murder and the sensational way the newspapers reacted—calling the murderer 'Jack the Ripper', of all things, a name that makes me wince every time I read it. "Are they connected?"

Eve looks grim. "The doctor said there were signs on the torso that a tourniquet had been applied to the shoulder. So, yes, I think they're connected."

I feel sick. "If a tourniquet was applied, then the victim was still alive when the arm was cut off."

She nods, her expression stony. "Khurana's at the construction site, looking for a trail. I'm hoping I can figure out who made these tattoos, see if we can identify the body."

"There's no sign of the head?"

"No. Nothing."

"Decapitation is a common method for killing demons," Steel says, quietly.

The other girl taps her fingers on the table. "That might make things easier," she says. "Tattooing demons is tough work; they heal too quickly without holy water. If I can identify their style, we might be able to track the artist and have them identify the demon. They're old tattoos, though. They could have come from anywhere."

"Perhaps the Whitechapel murderer could have caught a demon by mistake."

"And scatter the body parts, to make it seem like a different killer?" Eve asks. "Or perhaps this *is* a different killer, and all of the activity around the new Scotland Yard building unearthed him from wherever he was hiding."

Steel pulls the sketch towards him. "That's the symbol of a demonic House," he says, and I inhale sharply.

"Which one?" Eve demands.

"Beleth. House of the Cat."

"For which demon?"

He shakes his head. "That House was destroyed years ago," he explains. "All its members are dead."

"So, a devotee, then?" I suggest.

"It helps narrow the field, at least. Thank you," Eve says, her mouth pursed as though she has to force out the words. Steel nods and turns back to his plate.

"We're stuck here for a few days while Steel heals," I say. "Can I help you identify some places to start? If this is the same killer, he's probably going to be local to East London."

Eve hesitates, but then shrugs. "If that's what you want to do."

She doesn't need my help, but I appreciate the gesture. It will give me something to do. She opens a map of London and together we lean over it, searching for places to find the artist she needs.

CHAPTER THIRTY-THREE

By the end of the week, Steel reports that he's healed. We visit the mortuary and Green recounts the information he gave us that night, and one more thing: the second woman's uterus was missing. The same injury, Eve tells us back at the agency, that was inflicted on the unidentified woman's torso.

"Wombs can be used in ritual spells," Steel says, outside Monaghan's office as we wait to deliver my report, "but rarely. And silver-class demons can't use magic, anyway. They'd have to be collecting them for someone else. Or making it look as though they are."

"To frame a higher class of demon?" But who, and why?

"Miss Locke. A card came for you." Monaghan's assistant holds out a slip of paper.

I take it and arch my eyebrows at the scribbled offer. "Mrs. Stewart has invited us for tea on Tuesday. And cross stitch," I add, bemused.

"Invited *you* for tea," Steel corrects.

"You have to come, too."

His face crinkles in dismay. "*Cross stitch*, Locke."

Penned under the invitation is a small sentence: *I have something for you.* Strange.

"Would you tell her that we'd be delighted to accept?" I ask Miller, and the man nods. "She was Turner's friend," I tell the demon. "I owe her this much." He sighs but doesn't protest further.

Monaghan's door opens. I straighten, holding my report in both hands, and the Legal Secretary walks out. I step back against the wall, out of the way.

"—my thanks to the department."

"Of course, of course." Pemberton pulls on his gloves. "Only three, remember, Monaghan. These murders are bad enough without a sudden influx of your lot flooding the streets."

"I understand, sir. And the declaration...?"

"My office will send it over as soon as the Prime Minister has signed off. Keep me updated." Pemberton shakes his hand, acknowledges me with a nod, and walks away.

I tear my eyes from him and stare at Monaghan. His mouth is soft, pleased. "Come in, agent." We traipse inside and the professor paces behind his desk, his hands at his back.

"My report, sir," I say and lay the folder on his desk. "Was that Pemberton?" I add when he doesn't acknowledge the work.

"Forgive me." He sits down, pushing my report aside. "I was planning."

"Planning?"

He sits down and puts my report aside. "The Prime Minister is granting the agency extended authority. We will have a place at his side alongside Commissioner Warren. We'll have access to police reports, resources, people—anything we need. It's excellent news. I just wish..." His gaze falls on the portrait that sits on his desk in its heavy silver frame. He turns it so that it faces him.

"They changed their mind because of the Whitechapel murders," I guess, and he nods, his expression turning grim.

"Yes. They're also granting me leave to recruit three more agents. The permission should come through by the end of the month. In the meantime, I can begin the search for new apprentices. Rayne will have to take one, whether he likes it or not. Horner, too. How are you doing with Clara?"

I can't think of a way to explain the tension between me and Clara without coming across as petulant. I force a smile. "Fine."

"Good. I'll have the jurisdiction to appoint another Hound, so I will promote Eve, as soon as I can backfill her position."

A real smile blooms over my false one. "She'll be delighted. She's wanted to be an agent ever since she joined."

"I remember. She saw Khurana fight off that Strike demon. A nightmare for me, trying to curtail public interest, but we gained one of our best apprentices, so I can't complain." He pulls a letter from a stack on his desk. "Now. The third murder, the first one that occurred last week—Elizabeth Stride, was it? Her death took place in the City's district. They're offering a significant reward for information leading to the killer's capture."

The East End has been pleading for the mayor to offer a similar reward for weeks. "How convenient they start to take notice when someone in a wealthy neighbourhood has been killed," I say, without thinking. Monaghan blinks at me. I duck my head, flushing. "Sorry, sir."

"Money makes the world turn when morals do not," the professor comments. "Either way, the police will be inundated with claims from people who think they know the identity of the murderer. Those letters in the papers are bad enough: this will slow their progress to a crawl. If you've received any assistance from them in the past, I expect it will stop now. We'll be on our own, at least until this structural change is approved."

"What about the soldier, Private George?" I ask. "Is he still in custody?"

The professor shakes his head. "He was released. The army is handling his punishment."

Bitter anger floods through me. "When was he released?"

"On the first of the month." Monaghan raises a hand as I open my mouth to interject. "He was in a cell the night of the double murders. The guards confirmed it. He's not our killer. Not *this* killer, at any rate."

"What about Martha?" I ask. "He might not be the Whitechapel killer, but all the signs point to the fact that he was involved in her death."

"It's out of my hands, Locke. I'm sorry."

Damn it. I do not want to admit aloud how much I want to see that man behind bars.

"Focus instead on what we *can* control," Monaghan adds, tapping my report. "I'll read this today and send you my notes."

Then I need to get back in the field—*we* need to. "In that case, I would like permission to return to Whitechapel," I say. "I would like to continue the search."

"As long as you stick to daylight hours."

"If this demon acts at night, we'll have a better chance of finding him in the dark."

"Regardless, I'd like you to avoid the Whitechapel district at night." The professor eyes me for a moment. "I know that you want this soldier to be punished," he adds, leaning forward over his desk, his expression kind, "but it's not our place. Our duty is to defend Britain from supernatural forces, not from its own people."

"I understand, sir." For once, the words take an effort to say.

"One good thing—the *only* good thing—to come from these murders is that we may be able to change that. It will be a slow, hard road, but now it's an upwards one. I just need you to be patient. I know you're good at that," he adds, with a smile.

It's little consolation. "I'll leave you to your day." He nods, and I do my best not to run from the room.

When we're outside, Steel arches an eyebrow at me. "What do we do now?"

I tuck Mrs. Stewart's invitation into my pocket. "Find out what Mrs. Stewart wants to show us."

CHAPTER THIRTY-FOUR

"**A**re you *sure* we have to visit this woman?" Steel asks, gazing at the modest, pedestrian townhouse.

"We can't ignore her invitation." I wear my new coffee-coloured day dress, the brown silk gleaming in the late morning light, the black ruffles soft on my wrists. A lace panel runs from the base of the bodice to just under my chin, holding off the cool morning wind. It's pretty and comfortable, a combination I hadn't thought existed.

"Why not?"

"It's not acceptable behaviour. And she's part of the agency, in a way." I ring the bell. "Besides, she said she has something for me." She and Turner were close. Could it be something of the agent's?

We're answered by the woman herself, who beams at us. "I'm so glad you were able to make it. Please, come in."

She urges us inside and into a small, cosy room already supplied with tea and lemon cake. At her insistence, I sit beside her on the couch. Steel hovers behind me.

"Sit down, please," Mrs. Stewart tells him. "Have some tea."

Bemused, Steel drifts to the chair she indicates and settles on its edge. He accepts a cup with an awkward nod and sits there blinking at it. I repress a smile.

"I'm so glad you could join me," Mrs. Stewart begins. "I thought you might be too busy for social calls." She sips her tea, waiting for me to fill in the gap she's left. Her expression is a little cool, a little assessing. It reminds me of Turner.

I run my finger against the raised filigree on the rim of the cup and consider the gap. Clearly, she knows about Steel, about demons, but I don't know how much Agent Stewart told her about our work.

"Not so busy we couldn't make time for a friend of the agency," I reply, cautiously.

Her mouth twists in a self-deprecating smile. "An old friend, if anything."

"Jacob speaks highly of Agent Stewart," I add, feeling my way forward. This kind of inconsequential conversation is not my forte.

Her smile softens at the mention of her husband. A love match, then. I wonder how they met, how Stewart found the time for romance.

"Well, it is nice to have Isaac's full attention. Not that Maximus isn't darling—you all are," she adds, reaching out to pat Steel on the knee, who immediately looks perturbed, "but it's a difficult thing, sharing a husband with the agency. I can understand why so few agents make the attempt. How *is* Jacob? Agent Horner, I should say."

"They're in Scotland, on a case with Moss. He's well, I believe. They both are." No word has come back otherwise.

"And you?" she asks, her dark eyes intent. "How are you coping?"

The directness of the question catches me off guard. I glance down at the amber liquid in my cup to grant me a moment to frame my response. "I'm well," I reply. "Steel has been a great help, already. I'm not sure what I would've done without him."

Steel glances at me narrowly, as if he suspects a lie. Part of me is surprised that it's the truth.

"I see." Mrs. Stewart regards the Hound. "And you, Mr. Steel? How are you coping?"

He blinks and then pushes his tinted spectacles up his nose as if he's just remembered they're there. "Less well," he says, after a moment.

"It is a difficult adjustment," the woman agrees. "Lavender found it hard, in the beginning. If not for Turner...well, Helen was the reason she joined, as well as the reason she stayed."

"Agent Turner was the reason?" She makes it sound as though Lavender had a choice. As though she wasn't bound by the same rules that Steel is, that I am.

Would Turner have left if Lavender had asked?

"I always thought so. They were very close." Mrs. Stewart sets aside her cup and then puts her hands on her knees. "I have to admit," she says, "that I brought you here on an ulterior motive. The agency hasn't told Isaac anything about its open cases. Apparently, it can't, now that he's retired. But Helen was a friend. I was hoping you might be able to tell me about her case; if you've made any progress." She looks at me, hopeful.

I put down my cup, mirroring her posture. "I will tell you everything I know, but I'm afraid that isn't much," I say, apologetically. "Her death doesn't match the murders that we've seen in Whitechapel, but she was killed around the same time that another victim died. It seems too convenient for their deaths not to be connected."

The other woman nods as I speak, and it's easy to imagine her husband coming home to her each night and relaying the details of his case, asking for her advice. "I see," she says. "And you have no suspects? The papers have named many."

"Nothing definite," I admit. "The evidence seems to point toward a demon being the culprit, so I doubt the police will be able to identify the killer." Even if the agency does, we'll have to keep that fact out of the newspapers.

"What have you learnt so far?"

I tell her about the murders, leaving out some of the more gruesome details. She doesn't blink as I relay the information, and I suspect that she's read every copy of the inquest reports in the *Times*.

"That *is* a difficult case," she says, with a hum. "I don't think Isaac had such a tricky one to deal with. But then, he didn't complete half the investigations that Turner did. She'd be happy that you're on her case, my dear." I look down to hide the ache that climbs up my throat. "Now, how about some more cake? Helen loved my lemon sponge."

I politely take a small slice. Steel doesn't need to be told twice and accepts a wedge of cake. My mind keeps returning to Turner, and to Lavender, and I put my fork down. "Did she say she was working on anything?" I ask the woman, unsure how to approach the message on her card. "Turner, I mean?"

Mrs. Stewart looks thoughtful. "Nothing in particular that I can recall. Not for the agency, I mean. When she came here, she wanted to work on her cross stitch."

"Cross stitch? Turner?" The invitation had mentioned it, but I didn't think she meant *Turner's* cross stitch.

"That's what I thought, too. She didn't seem the kind to spend her time with a needle. Oh, that's right, I meant to get it for you. Here, let me find it." She gets up and rummages through the drawers of her dresser. "Here we are," she says, and lifts out a large piece of muslin pinned to a round frame. "It looks finished, to me, but she always said she had more to do." She hands it to me, and I place it in my lap.

"This is what you wanted to give me?" I had been expecting...I don't know what. Not embroidery.

"Yes. It was the one thing she took out of the agency."

The centre is a small seed and surrounding it is an intricate circle of plants and flowers, different species depicted side by side, their branches intertwining. "It must have taken her months."

"Years." Mrs. Stewart shakes her head. "She was very particular about the threads—Helen was particular about a great many things."

"That describes her very well." I hold it out for her to take back, but she demurs with a wave.

"You keep it," she tells me. "Helen wanted you to have it."

That ache stings my eyes and I blink my vision clear. "I don't wish to take it from you, if you're fond of the memories."

"I have enough memories, and she cared for you a great deal, even though she may not have said it. Her demon, too. Tell me how Eve's doing," Mrs. Stewart adds, and I'm grateful for the opportunity to turn my mind away from Lavender, from Turner's death. "I worry about you girls in that place."

I talk about Eve, and Khurana, and then about Rayne and Monaghan. Mrs. Stewart updates me on the regional agents, who write to her husband more often than they write to the agency. We end up talking about the agency for another hour, the embroidery spilling over my lap. Finally, when the clock strikes again, I make my excuses.

"It was a pleasure," Mrs. Stewart says. "Come again whenever you like. If you need someone to talk to, or—any time." She smiles at me with a warmth I don't feel like I've earned, and I swallow a lump in my throat.

Outside, I hail a cab, unable to face the bare streets of London. Steel is a silent figure on my right and as the cab trundles us back to the agency I run my fingers over Turner's soft stitching. A couple of the threads are coarser than the rest. My fingers catch on one, trace a tiny pattern hidden among the embroidered flowers. A symbol.

I pause and glance down at it. It's one of the symbols from Turner's journal, picked out in a darker green than the stem of the flower it sits within.

My breath hitches and I run my hands over the thread with purpose. I find another symbol, then another, and another, all tiny and all hidden inside a stem or a leaf or a bud. The embroidery hides twenty-six of them, all arranged in a ring around the eye at the centre.

I'm biting the inside of my cheek hard enough to hurt. Exhaling, I force my body to relax. Twenty-six symbols. Twenty-six letters of the alphabet.

"It's an Alberti's disk."

"Excuse me?"

I stare at Steel, seeing not his face but the lines of script in Turner's journal. *That's* why she wanted me to have it. "This is the cipher for Turner's code."

He blinks at the muslin. "The what?"

"If we circle this ring with the alphabet, we can use it to break her code. We just match the symbol to the letter. Look, this is an ash tree," I explain. "And this is burdock root. Then cherries, then a daisy—"

"I'm not following."

"The images are the key, the outer disk." The words run together, tripping off my tongue. "Ash for A, burdock for B, cherries for C. We map these symbols against the images, starting with the ash tree. So, this symbol must be A, this B, and so forth." I should have seen it straight away.

Steel's eyes are a bit glazed. "I have no idea what you're talking about."

"It will make more sense if I show you." This is the cipher that will help me understand what Turner was working on and why she was so afraid of being discovered. I bang on the roof of the cab and urge our driver to hurry.

CHAPTER THIRTY-FIVE

At the agency, I head straight for my room. Steel follows me inside, scratching the back of his neck. "I'm still not sure I understand," he admits. "How can you use this to break a code?"

"Look." My blood thrums with adrenaline, the surge of satisfaction and delight that comes with a problem solved. I rip out a blank piece of paper and sketch the alphabet in a small circle. I fit it on top of the muslin, so the letters form an inner ring. "This is the ash tree, so this is where we start." I turn the paper, so the A of my alphabet sits underneath the symbol embroidered into the bark of the tree. "This symbol is an A." I draw the symbol next to the A. Burdock root follows, then the cherries. I keep turning the paper to align it until all twenty-six letters have a matching symbol. Now to see if it works.

I take the first page of the journal and write in the letters in pencil over each symbol. *T-H-I-S-I-S-T-H-E-P-R-O...* "This is the property of Helen Turner," I read, when I finish the first line, adrenaline becoming fierce joy. It feels as though she's here, as though I've captured a faint echo of her voice. "This is the cipher."

Steel takes a seat and rests his ankle on his other knee. "That journal is almost full," he says. "Are you going to translate every single page?"

"No, of course not. I'll start from the most recent entry and work my way backwards." I twirl my pencil, pleased at my progress.

He slouches down in his chair. "I'll make myself comfortable, then."

I turn to the last page of Turner's journal, her final entry. The code unveils each line as if they're gifts. Five sentences and a date:

31st August 1888

I took Lavender to the barracks today. The Major is a stuffed shirt and a prig, but his people don't have any trace of the supernatural about them. Perhaps I was wrong?

Still, something about this doesn't feel right. I'll go back out tonight, see what I can find.

That night she went out and didn't come back. I bite the end of my pencil and use the pressure on my teeth to ground me. She found the two soldiers, the same as I did, but no demons.

The next entry is just as brief:

30th August 1888

Locke's drumming up some data for me on the regiment. She might be a bit cautious for my taste, but her research is solid and she's not an idiot. I can help her work on the rest. She'll be a decent agent. Lavender will look after her.

Cautious, but not an idiot. My mouth twists in a wry smile. High praise, for Turner.

Lavender will look after her. Did she suspect that she might not make it through the case?

26th August 1888

That idiot Pemberton wants to shut us down. No doubt he'll start with me. His delicate sensibilities can't handle women working together. I just hope it doesn't happen yet. I need more time to figure this out.

In thirty years, only one in ten murders have been caused by demons, but our last five have all been supernatural. Five in a row, and that's just the London cases. It's too neat, too perfect.

I'll have to tap some of Lavender's old contacts, see if they'll talk. See if there's something more to these cases than mere chance.

Underneath this entry is a code. A book reference for the Reading Room, I realise, after staring at it for a few minutes. I look back over my scribbled translation. This entry is dated five days before Turner was killed. Had she visited one of these contacts? And this book reference—how does that tie into this?

I tap my pencil on the paper. The Reading Room won't take unannounced visitors. They only offer passes to writers or researchers, and I'm neither. I'll need a letter from Monaghan to get in there.

The click of my pencil as I put it down makes Steel stir and he peeks at me from under his hat. "Finished already?"

"We need to see Monaghan." I check the time. Nearly three o'clock. The museum closes at six. "Come on."

"What about lunch?" Steel asks, trailing me.

"You had an entire lemon cake."

"Cake is not food."

I sigh and change our path to the kitchen. Maia has made up sandwiches for herself and Miller and there's bread and cheese left over. I put together a sandwich each—and then a second for Steel, when he demolishes the first—and eat standing up. Then I herd Steel up to Monaghan's office.

"Where are we going?" Steel asks.

"The British Museum."

"Is this really the best time to visit a museum?"

"I'll explain in a moment," I say as we approach the assistant's desk. "I'd like to see Monaghan, please," I tell Miller. "As soon as possible."

He shakes his head. "I'm sorry, but the professor left early this morning. He'll be gone until the end of the week."

I stand there for a moment, Miller gazing at me and waiting for a reply. "Thank you," I manage. The image of the latest victim flashes through my mind. I can't wait that long. "I left something in his study. Would you mind if I go in to get it?" I ask, my heart picking up at the lie.

"Yes, of course. It's unlocked, go right in." Miller gestures to the door and goes back to his work, ignoring me.

Taking a deep breath, I enter the study, tilting my head for Steel to follow. He slips in and I shut the door.

He looks over his glasses at me. "I don't remember you leaving anything in here."

"We need a letter of authority for the museum, and I can't wait for the professor." My stomach contorts. Even if I justify this by saying it's for the case, for the women lying cold in the ground, it's still an abuse of my role. Monaghan could have me disciplined. Or worse.

"What kind of museum *is* this?" Steel mutters.

I open the first desk drawer: letters from the Home Office and copies of Monaghan's replies. The next holds a stack of the same letter he gave me for the Wellington Barracks, already written and awaiting a signature. I dip Monaghan's sleek black pen into the ink pot on his desk and copy his signature onto the letter, holding my breath as I do.

Steel picks up the portrait on the man's desk. "Who's this?"

I glance at it. The big frame makes the picture look tiny. "That's the daughter of the man Monaghan worked for, before he joined the agency. She was murdered by a demon, years ago." In the portrait, she has long blonde hair and a straight, freckled nose. It's easy to see why I'd stood out to the professor, over a hundred other girls.

It doesn't matter why Monaghan chose me. Only that I prove worthy of his choice.

I wince at the thought. Doing this is hardly going to prove that I'm worthy. The opposite, in fact. I sand the signature to dry the ink. "There. Done."

I put the pen and ink back where they were, lining up the pen with the grain of the wood, everything perfectly straight. Then I fold the letter and tap it against my other hand.

"Let's go."

CHAPTER THIRTY-SIX

Walking into the British Museum is like crawling into the veins of a titan. Huge walkways lead to a myriad of exhibits, with towering marble statues and elegant glass cases displaying artifacts plundered from countries all over the world.

The Museum's library is a haven of knowledge, brimming with toppling book stacks and a dry, dusty scent. The Reading Room is a circular walled structure at its centre, closed off from the bigger library.

Steel gazes around with raised eyebrows. "I'm starting to understand why you need a letter just to get in."

"Turner could have hidden a book among one of the stacks out here," I say, gesturing to the bookcases, the haphazard piles. "Why hide it in the Reading Room? Why go to so much trouble?" The letter is another barrier, like the code. Had she intended for someone in particular to break it? Me?

Or perhaps that's wishful thinking. I clutch the letter in one hand and lengthen my stride to reach the Reading Room. Inside is a far cry from the chaotic book stacks. Neat shelves line the circular wall, enveloping desks lit with stylish green lamps.

A few people sit scattered through the room, bent over their books. It is absolutely silent. I approach the desk at the centre.

The clerk is a man in his late fifties with coiffed hair and a magnificent white moustache. He examines me and sniffs. "Yes?"

I slide the letter over the desk. "I have special dispensation to review one of your texts."

He takes longer than necessary to open the letter. As he reads it, his brows draw together and his mouth droops. No doubt he was looking forward to showing me the door. "Write the reference here." He gives me a card marked with columns for the reference number. I write it in.

The clerk whisks it from me almost before I finish writing and sniffs again. "Take a seat. I'll bring it to you."

Is that how it normally works? Asking would reveal my ignorance, so I thank him and find a desk as far from the other visitors as possible.

Steel flicks out the tail of his coat and sits beside me. "So, this is where the Empire keeps its knowledge," he muses.

One of the men on the other side of the room looks up. "Quiet," I whisper. "This is a library."

Steel shrugs, unconcerned, and stares at the ceiling.

I put my hands on the desk and try not to tap my impatience into the wood. I watch the clerk, my eyes narrowing as he makes no move towards the shelves. Eventually he looks up and catches me watching. With apparent effort, he levers himself from his chair and lumbers over to the bookcases. Glancing at my code, he climbs up one of the wall ladders and pulls a large book from the shelf.

Not a book; it looks more like a folder. He brings it to our table. "We close at six," he says, dropping it in front of us. "You have two hours."

"Thank you." I pull the folder towards me and wait for him to leave before I open it.

The binder is made of leather and a date is inscribed on the inside cover: April 1861. Inside the binding are sheafs of paper, all different sizes, sewn or stamped into the leather to keep them together. Some pages are written in English, some in French or German, and others in Arabic and Mandarin. More are in languages I don't recognise. The pages I can read speak of demons: each one is a tale of a different breed.

I flip to the back. Tucked into the binder is a thick wad of paper. I unfold it and inhale. A map of London.

Not just any map, though; this one is marked with symbols. There are three that occur over and over again, dotted all around the map. One or two in west and south London, handfuls in the north and large clusters over the East End.

Steel leans over my shoulder, examining the map. "Those are alchemical symbols," he whispers. He looks at my expression and shrugs again. "What? I may not be able to crack a secret code, but I'm familiar with basic alchemy." He points to one, a circle standing on top of a small cross. "That means copper. This one that looks like a crescent moon, that's silver."

Copper and silver. "Demon classes?"

"I would guess so."

Those two symbols are everywhere on the map. "What about this one?" I point to one, a series of crossed horizontal and diagonal lines.

"That's an older form of the copper symbol. Maybe it refers to different types of demons within the copper class."

I flick back through the pages. They all have symbols on the pages, silver or one of the two copper icons. "This is a list of every demon in London." I peer at the map more closely. A fourth symbol lies tucked in among a group of copper and silver class, smack in the middle of the East End. Where the other symbols are repeated and scattered all over the map, this is the only one of its kind: a circle, with curved lines radiating from the sphere like tiny rays. "What's this?"

"That's gold," he replies, frowning. "But the gold class Houses are destroyed. They were all killed or cannibalised by—" He stops, his expression going remote.

"By what?"

He pauses and then says, "By what is now known as the diamond class." Another pause. "There is no symbol in alchemy for diamond," he adds.

I stare at the map, at the small sun. My heart has grown as cold and as heavy as a stone. "You're saying there's a diamond-class demon in London. In the East End." Spitting distance from Whitechapel.

"According to this, there was. This is thirty years old, isn't it? It might not be there anymore."

"Or maybe it's still there. Putting together components for its spells."

Steel sits back, crossing his arms. "If it's been there for thirty years, why is it *now* that these murders are taking place? I don't think much of your police force, but I find it hard to believe they wouldn't have noticed women being murdered in their own neighbourhood."

"We have to find it. That's the only way to know for certain."

He exhales. "The diamond class has magic. They can disguise themselves better than any other kind of demon. They'll be impossible to find."

I peel the map from the binder and fold it into a small square. "Not with this."

CHAPTER THIRTY-SEVEN

The map fits snugly in my pocket. It seems to make my skirt heavier, though I know that's a result of my stinging awareness of it rather than its actual weight. As we hurry back, a chill autumn breeze chases my thoughts. This map could make the agency's duties so much easier—finding and interrogating demons would be simple—yet it was locked away in a museum instead of in our own library.

And Turner knew about the existence of a diamond-class demon and hid that knowledge. Why? Why hand it to me after her death?

If only she was still here. If only I could meet her for tea and cake with Mrs. Stewart and unpick the details of this case together. But I'm alone.

Steel's footsteps click on the pavement beside me. Not quite alone.

The demon remains silent as we return to the agency. Eve's voice comes from the kitchen and I halt at the door. Khurana's there, too. This might be the first time I've seen her since the second test. She speaks to Maia in what sounds like Hindi.

I join Eve, who's perched against the wall nibbling a biscuit. "Working on the case?" I ask her.

"Taking a break. Monaghan wants to host a dinner when he returns, and he thought Khurana might help him organise it." She throws me a speaking glance and I grimace.

"I can imagine her reaction."

"We're going to make ourselves scarce. I suggest you do, too."

I nod. Monaghan won't return until the end of the week. Steel and I can patrol Whitechapel and escape the dinner at the same time.

"Where have you been all day, anyway?" Eve asks.

"We met Mrs. Stewart." The words to explain the map sit in my throat. I hold them back. Turner had a reason to keep all of this from the agency. Until I know why, I should respect that. Still, guilt curls through me. It's not just my case this might affect. "Do you still think there's a connection," I ask, "between your case and mine?"

Eve puts her biscuit down with a sigh and dusts crumbs from her hands. "Yes, we do. It would be better, in a grim kind of way, if it *is* the same person. At least then Khurana and I will catch him and know that all of it will stop. I dread to think of there being two of these murderers loose in London."

Steel has been sitting on a bench, watching Khurana, but at this he turns to Eve, smirking. "You're making the assumption that you'll catch him before we will."

Her mouth twists into a mirroring smirk, although hers has a hard, challenging edge. "What do you say to a wager?" she suggests. "First to catch him wins?"

Steel rests his chin in his hand. "What are the stakes?"

I sigh. "You're as bad as each other."

"I know," Steel continues, ignoring me, "the loser treats us to dinner."

"You mean *us*. And you're not going to win."

"This is not a game." Khurana's cold voice interrupts us, and Eve and I bow our heads, chastised. "It matters not who catches the man, as long as the killing stops. Our first duty is to the people of this city." Her expression matches the granite in her voice. Even if it's not a competition, I can't help but think that I'm going to lose.

The agent looks at me, her gaze piercing, as though she can see the secret I'm keeping. Dropping my eyes will project my guilt as loudly as speaking it, so I hold her gaze. With difficulty.

"It's getting late. We'll meet tomorrow morning," she tells Eve, who nods. "For now, you should all rest." She doesn't glance at Steel as she leaves, but her demon acknowledges him with a curt nod.

Eve jumps down from the windowsill, all long slender limbs and smooth dark skin. "I had best go, too," she says. "Our case isn't as widely published as yours, so Monaghan has persuaded the police to send over a copy of their reports. They saw me and decided to send everything they ever wrote, just to make my life difficult." She grimaces.

"If you'd like help—"

She cuts me off with a wave. "And rob me of the opportunity to make them look bad in front of the Inspector, when I dump it all back on their desks? I don't think so. Good hunting." She flashes me a grin and heads after Khurana.

"You didn't tell her," Steel murmurs.

Doubt gnaws at me under the guilt. "Do you think I should have?"

"It was hidden for a reason. No one else should know until we understand what that reason is," he replies, echoing my thoughts almost too closely for comfort. But his words ease a bit of the guilt. Eve will understand, when I explain it to her. When we find out what Turner was hiding.

CHAPTER THIRTY-EIGHT

The tiny sun hovers over a house on Flower and Dean Street. The building huddles in the middle of a dozen identical small brick cottages, and the hustle of people coming and going tells me each one will be overflowing with people. I wonder if Turner made a mistake.

"Would a diamond-class demon live here?" I ask Steel.

He watches the trickling stream of people. "It's a good place to hide."

I glance at the map once more, then tuck it away and knock on the door that I think is closest to the symbol on the map. No one answers for a long moment, then the door cracks open. An older woman, with two small children in the room behind her.

"Can I help you?"

"We're working with the Vigilance Committee," I reply. "We wanted to check on everyone in the neighbourhood. Have you noticed anything odd, recently? Strange behaviour from anyone you know?"

"Oh, you're talking about those murders." She leans against the door jamb. "You should go look at the Jones', at forty-eight.

They're right peculiar people. And the Harper family, over at fifty-two. They didn't go to church last Sunday. That's number fifty-two, yeah?"

"I see." I glance at Steel and he gives a minute shake of his head. "Thank you, we'll be sure to do that."

"You let us know when you catch him. It ain't right, being shut away in our 'omes like this." She closes the door and I look at Steel.

"Nothing that I could sense. Just human."

I continue to the next cottage. Steel draws a blank there, and at the next three. It's at the fifth, when a very old woman opens the door, that he stiffens. I keep my muscles as still as I can, watching the stranger. Her hair is sparse and white, and her eyes are rheumy. There's a raw scab on her jaw, red and weeping fluid.

"Good morning," I say. I lean subtly to the side to see behind her. The room's empty. "We work with the Vigilance Committee. May we come in?"

The woman's gaze darts between us and settles on Steel. "I don't know, luv," she replies, in a frail voice. "I'm a bit busy at the moment."

"Please, ma'am. It's important."

"It would be better," Steel adds, "to have this conversation inside."

The woman's mouth firms and she steps back from the door. "Well. You'd best come in, 'adn't you?" Her voice comes out hard and suspicious, nothing of the frailty she portrayed a moment ago. She holds the door ajar, and I have to breathe in deeply to slip inside.

The room is small, with a door on one side leading to another. It contains an old wooden rocking chair, an untidy bed and a lit hearth. A pot hangs in the fire, covered but emitting a putrid smell.

She closes the door behind us. "You're not part of the Committee. They don't 'ave your kind." She's looking at Steel.

"No, they do not," he replies. "But this woman's agency does."

"We're looking for a demon," I start. "They would have lived here thirty years ago."

She drops into the rocking chair, her knees cracking. "And you think I'm this demon?"

"She's silver class," Steel says to me, not taking his eyes from her. "She's not who we're looking for. And by that smell—what is that? Marrow?" He sniffs and grimaces. "She's a Blood Drinker," he adds, and I shiver.

"Bone and liver," she replies, lifting her lips in a gummy smile. "Oh, don't you fret none, luv. It ain't from those women. I'm too old to go jaunting about taking live ones. I get my dinner from the 'orse factories, before they turn 'em into glue. Much easier than cutting 'em up myself."

"Then you would hunt them," I say, barely restraining my disgust, "if you were younger?"

"Them?" she mimics. "Are you sure you don't mean 'us'? Unless you're so deep into whatever your business is," she says, jabbing a finger in my direction, "that you've forgotten 'ow to be 'uman." She continues before I can do more than gape at her. "But no, I ain't one for the dirty business, myself. That's the way to get caught."

"How do we know you're telling the truth?" I counter and she laughs, a sound that makes me think of a crow's caw.

"Bless you, luv. I mean, look at me. You think I could force some poor woman to the ground and cut up her insides? Go on."

Steel wanders over to the pot and lifts the lid. "It's horse, not human," he says. "She's telling the truth."

"You do 'ave a good nose, don't'cha?" the Drinker murmurs, watching him through lidded eyes. "I didn't think your lot had that kind of skill." My gaze shoots to Steel. He ignores the jibe.

"How long have you lived here?" I ask, putting that comment aside, for now.

"A while," the woman replies. "Long enough."

Perhaps I'm going about this the wrong way. "I apologise for jumping to conclusions," I say, starting again. "I'm Locke and this is Steel. What is your name?"

"You don't know much about demons," she says, "if that's your question. Names ain't something we'll give out on a whim."

I acknowledge her point. "Very well. We believe the demon who lived here may know something about the Whitechapel murders. We desperately need to find them."

"*Desperate*, is it?" Her voice is mocking, delighted.

I swallow and raise my chin. I hadn't meant to give that much away. But I *am* desperate. Every day it feels as though we take one step forward only to be pushed back three. Now we might have lost this lead, too.

"Desperate enough to bring the rest of the agency here," I reply. "And my fellow agents are not as merciful as I am."

The woman sucks her teeth, and then laughs. "Now that's more like what I expected." She shrugs. "I've been 'ere near on forty years. I've seen some things."

I step forward. "What things?"

"Well, there was a demon. Kept to 'erself for the most part, but I could tell what she was. Diamond class age half as quick as you 'umans. That and..." She glances at Steel and flicks her fingers against the arms of her chair. "Well," she says, again. "I could tell. You don't often see a Wraith round these parts."

Steel makes some kind of movement, but when I look at him, he's still. "A Wraith?" I ask. "What was her name? Where is she now?"

"She left twenty, thirty years ago. Disappeared, one night. I thought someone found out who she was. Folk round 'ere are a superstitious lot."

"So, you have no idea where she could be?"

"I ain't seen 'er. If she's still alive, you won't find her 'ere." The demon gestures to her chair. "Then again, I ain't the most mobile, am I?"

Great. How are we going to find this demon, now?

"If that's it, you can leave," the woman says. "I got to eat, soon. And I don't think you wanna see that."

I sketch a shallow curtsy. "Thank you for your help."

"Perhaps we'll meet again, luv." She rocks back and forth, her filmy eyes flashing like mirrors in the dim light. A shudder crawls up my spine and I hastily make my way out of the cottage.

In the open air, I snort out the scent of bone marrow and rotten meat lingering in my nostrils. "A Wraith demon," I say to Steel. "What is that?"

"It's a breed of diamond-class demon." His gaze seems distant, unfocused, although the tinted spectacles make him difficult to read. "They come from House Beelzebub. They used to come from House Beleth, too, when it existed. Wraiths are a distant cousin to Phantom demons; weak in physical combat, but they can turn invisible and they're excellent spellcasters—better than any human warlock."

"A candidate for our murderer, then," I muse. "If they can turn invisible, that would explain why no one's been able to see them leave."

"That does seem plausible," he admits, but his voice is slow, reluctant.

"Why wouldn't it be?"

"Why would a demon of that level be concerned about working girls in the East End? House Beelzebub is strong enough to take whatever it wants, whether that's money or influence or human organs. Why bother with all this?" He sweeps his arm to encompass the tightly knitted buildings around them. "The Houses exist alongside humans, hidden in plain sight. Drawing attention to them—to demons—will only risk what they have. It doesn't make sense."

"*Could* she be a member of this Beelzebub House?"

He tucks his hands into his pockets. "If she was a member of a House, I'd say she's Beleth. Thirty years ago was when that House fell and its last Wraiths died—or became classless." His throat bobs and he falls silent.

Classless. "Are there any other destroyed Houses?" I ask, casually, watching him from the corner of my eye.

"Not many."

I suck my lip between my teeth. Steel has never turned invisible, so he can't be a Wraith. Unless he's hiding that ability from me, maintaining this illusion that he's a Hound. And it *must* be an illusion. The Blood Drinker had been surprised at the strength of his nose, and that's a simple thing for a Hound.

If Wraiths come from House Beelzebub and Beleth, then what kind of demon comes from House Leviathan? What class of demon *is* my partner?

CHAPTER THIRTY-NINE

I lie awake most of the night, turning the Blood Drinker's words over and over in my head. Turner was searching for this Wraith. Now, it's down to me. I have to find this demon before she murders someone else.

First, I need to know everything the agency knows about Wraiths. Their abilities, their weaknesses—everything.

When morning finally comes, Steel greets me with raised eyebrows. "You haven't slept," he comments, and for a second I'm startled. Even Maia can't tell that quickly.

"My mind doesn't switch off." Even on a day without a case, I rarely find sleep when I bend my head to the pillow. Not straight away, and never for long.

We breakfast in the kitchen. Then, for lack of another option, I lead Steel to the library. To my surprise, he closes the door behind us. His expression is pensive.

I sit at my desk and consider him. "Have you thought of something?"

"Yes." He looks at me, a straight clear gaze. My muscles tense, and his next words confirm my unease. "I don't think you're going to like it."

"What do you mean? Why not?"

"I think the Wraith is here. At the agency."

"*What?*"

"Turner hid that folder from the agency," he points out, "from the people who needed it the most. Doesn't that seem odd?"

He's serious. I rise and walk to the window. "All that means is that she may have hidden some demons from us," I reply. "She adored Lavender; maybe she was trying to protect them."

"Or she was investigating someone at the agency."

"You're jumping to conclusions." I stalk back to my chair, unable to stand still. "No one here would do anything like what's happening in Whitechapel."

"I'm not saying they would," he replies, calmly. "All I'm saying is that one of them might be hiding their true identity."

"We would know."

"Would you? Has the agency encountered a diamond-class demon before? Do you even know what to look for?"

I fist my hand in the soft fabric of the chair. "We have no evidence that she suspected anyone here," I say, doing my best to keep my voice even. "Everything we have is coincidental."

"Can you rule out the possibility?" he counters.

No. Thinking the word is like being drenched in ice. I *can't* rule it out. "No," I admit, with more gritted teeth than I intend.

He doesn't push the point, just waits for me to realise that his conclusion has merit. I would prefer that he push it, that he rile me into snapping so I can dismiss the preposterous theory. But he doesn't. And I can't dismiss it.

If a Wraith *has* hidden themselves within the agency, then nowhere is safe. No one can be trusted.

I bite my cheek, hard, let the pain still the ripples of my mind. It's a case. It's a problem that must be solved. That's all.

Calmer, I return to my seat. Steel watches me and I clasp my hands on my lap, return his stare. "If that is true," I begin, "then one of our demons is diamond class."

He does not bat an eye at my acceptance of his theory. Of course he doesn't. "It may not be a demon."

I frown. "What else, then?"

"Wraiths are better than any other demon at imitating others," he replies. "They could be disguised as human."

"No," I say, more instinct than measured response. "That's not possible."

"Are you certain?" My stare is glacial. "*Are* you?" he repeats, unintimidated.

"If there *is* a Wraith here," I reply, turning the conversation away from that path, "how do we find it? How do we identify it?"

He sits back, crossing one leg over the other as though he has all the time in the world. "Diamond classes heal faster than others. A wound that might injure another demon for a couple of hours would leave a mark on them for mere minutes."

"And if a diamond-class demon was stabbed through the shoulder?" I ask, snidely. "How long would that take to heal?"

His mouth tilts up in a crooked smile. "It's difficult to say," he replies, not missing a beat. "Perhaps overnight. Perhaps days, if the wound was deep and the sword was blessed. "

Khurana is Sikh; perhaps she had her weapons blessed by a holy member of her order. But then, Steel never actually showed me the wound, after that first night. He could have been lying about how long it took to heal.

"So," I say, "what you're saying is we need to wait until they're injured, and see how fast they heal?"

"Why wait?" He shifts his gaze to a display case against the wall. It's filled with Celtic tribal jewellery, and half a dozen sturdy bone knives.

"You want us to stab the agency's demons?" I have to laugh at the absurdity of it.

"Not just demons," he reminds me. "And I'm forbidden from hurting the human agents, so you'll have to take care of them. Why don't we start with the Phantom agent?"

Sighing, I rub my face. "Just because you don't like Rayne doesn't mean he's hiding something."

"Everyone is hiding something. Our job is to figure out what."

"'Our'?" I repeat, and he shrugs.

"We have a deal. I aim to fulfil my end of the bargain." His level gaze is a heavy reminder of the promise I made.

I drop my head back against the armchair. "I can't go around hurting people just to see how long they bleed."

"Then what? What are you willing to do to solve this case?"

How dare he ask me that? "We search," I answer, crisply. "We find evidence, and we act on it. Not on some half-baked theory."

"Fully baked. I've been thinking about this for some time."

"You hate us. Why should I believe you?"

"I don't *trust* you," he corrects. "There's a difference. Are you that shocked, given how you brought me here?"

"No." My reply seems to catch him by surprise. He pauses, his lips still parted. "But I have to weigh the risks," I continue. "London—*Britain*—needs the agency. I can't put it in a position where it might fail."

If Pemberton and the Home Office thought that I'd turned against the agency, that I was acting in league with a demon, we'd be shut down. And I'd...I don't know what they'd do to me, but it wouldn't be anything good.

"We go back to Whitechapel this weekend," I decide. "We look for evidence. And we find the Wraith—whoever it is."

"Why are you so resistant to this?"

"Because they're my family," I snap. "Not that you would know anything about that."

There's a long silence. "No," Steel says, eventually. "I would not." He stretches his arms along the back of the sofa, his mouth twisted and his gaze icy. "Very well. We'll do it your way. But when this all comes crashing down around your head, don't say I didn't warn you."

CHAPTER FORTY

I stare into my wardrobe. Walking with Steel in Whitechapel last time had drawn the suspicion of the Vigilance Committee—perhaps if I go dressed as a man, we might draw less attention. I don't want to leave more unconscious bodies in our wake.

I braid my hair into a single plait that reaches the bottom of my shoulder blades, and pin it to the crown of my head. Then I slip out of my skirt and bodice, and into the man's suit Maia made for me. I keep my corset on—if we have to run through the streets of Whitechapel, I'll need the support—and the end result is curvier than I'd intended, but the loose lines of the jacket are enough to disguise my shape. I add a wide-brimmed hat over my hair. Luckily, I suppose, my face is broad enough that I could be mistaken for a young man at first glance. I straighten my lapel and emerge into the corridor, holding my breath.

Steel regards me for a moment, his face expressionless. The words of our argument yesterday linger between us. "Your collar should be buttoned," he says finally, pointing at the stiff white collar I'd left undone.

"It's too tight."

"Suit yourself."

Sighing, I do it up, wincing at the pressure on my throat. "It's very uncomfortable." My protest disguises the relief in my chest. I had imagined a much worse reaction.

"We all suffer for fashion," he replies, but the smirk that usually accompanies that mocking tone is gone.

I lead the way downstairs. The space between us yawns, regardless of the magic that sits there. I wanted to bring him closer, earn his trust. Instead we're further away than ever.

At the entrance, I don my coat in silence. I'm reaching for my hat when Rayne and Cassius descend into the hall. Rayne stops and stares at me. "What are you *wearing*?" he demands.

My cheeks go hot, and I get angry at my own reaction. "You said yourself, venturing into Whitechapel at night was too dangerous for a woman," I reply. "I thought this would be safer."

"This is not the stage, Miss Locke. You are not here to make a spectacle out of yourself."

I resist the urge to hug myself. "Turner used to—"

"Turner was a law unto herself, much to the detriment of the agency." Rayne glances over my suit and quickly looks away, as though the sight disgusts him. "Besides, clothing yourself in...dressing thusly does not change the fact that you are a woman, and the East End is no safe place for a woman. I will have your word that you won't go out at night."

"I—I don't think that's for you to decide, Agent Rayne," I stammer, struggling to recover my composure.

"Your *word*, Miss Locke." His gaze bores into mine as he waits.

I collect myself. I am not a child, to be reproved thus. "I will endeavour not to disappoint the agency, Mr. Rayne," I reply, injecting ice into my tone. "That will have to be enough to satisfy you." A downside to the suit is that I can't affect a dramatic sweep of my skirt and not-so-accidentally hit him with it as I leave.

My legs carry me for nearly a mile before I calm enough to slow down. "That was a mistake," I mutter.

"An entertaining one." I'd almost forgotten Steel was with me. "I'm looking forward to your next meeting with Agent Rayne," he says, his eyes glittering with a hard, cold light behind his spectacles.

"He's a fellow agent. I shouldn't be arguing with him."

"Another member of the family?"

"You don't understand—"

"You've made that quite obvious."

"Steel." I stop, remove my felt hat and run my hand over my hair. "I'm sorry. For what I said. I didn't mean it like that."

His expression doesn't flicker. "Are you going to listen to me?"

"That's beside the point." I resettle the hat firmly. "I *am* listening to you. I'm just choosing a different path."

"You're the agent. That's your prerogative." He says this in clipped, hard tones. Sighing, I resume walking.

The trousers feel odd against my skin, but warm. I can't help but glance at the people around me, checking my walk in windows as we pass to ensure I'm not moving oddly. No one looks twice at me. As a woman, my height is unusual if not downright strange, but as a man I'm commonplace.

The East End brims with policemen and members of the Vigilance Committee, all moving on a fresh surge of vengeance injected into the city's bloodstream by the two recent murders. I ignore them, hoping no one takes us for suspicious characters. The last thing we need is to end up in the station.

Night falls quickly, bringing a chill autumn wind. I'm grateful for my thick collar, now, and I dig my hands into my pockets for added warmth. Tonight, The Ten Bells churns with people; Committee members carrying black truncheons, labourers in leather aprons—my gaze lingers on them the longest—and a few small groups of women. The women cling to well-lit areas, chatting but glancing around every now and again, alert.

"What do you sense?" I ask Steel.

He scents the air. All I can smell is the foul stink of the slaughterhouses, brought to our corner on an unlucky wind. "Trying to track a demon in this city is like trying to sift for a fleck of gold in a river of filth."

Immersed in the stench of blood and death, I can't disagree. Two policemen march past us, lanterns in one hand and truncheons in the other. A clump of well-dressed young men follow them, craning their necks to peer into dark alleys. Tourists. To them, these dead women are just entertainment.

"Maybe we shouldn't have come." My outfit makes me practically invisible, but among all these people, so is the killer. "He would be an idiot to act tonight, in all this."

"Especially if he just saw you leave to patrol."

I stare at him. "Are you saying you think it's—you think the killer is *Rayne*?"

He tugs down the brim of his hat, hiding his eyes. "What I'm saying is, do not close yourself off to a possibility just because you don't want to face it."

That stings. "I've known Rayne for seven years," I reply, evenly. "He's a lot of things, but he is not a murderer."

Steel looks back at the pub. "You know him better than I do."

"I do." None of the agents can be the Wraith. None of them are capable of what we've seen.

A tendril of doubt winds through me.

"Do you want to stay?" Steel asks, with disinterest. "I doubt we're needed here."

"Yes. Just in case." Even if the likelihood that this 'Ripper' will kill tonight is slim, I can't leave. I can't take the chance, no matter how small.

The night waxes and wanes. People filter in and out of the pub, and eventually disperse to their homes. Whitechapel doesn't sleep, so the district never empties completely, but the clothing of its inhabitants gets cleaner in the pre-dawn light. By that time, I'm asleep on my feet, and Steel looks little better.

"Let's go home," I say, finally. He doesn't twitch at the words, but I correct them hastily: "Let's go back." No response, and he falls in line behind me instead of at my side. We travel back to the agency with only the murmur of the city as our companion.

When I enter the entrance hall, I shed my coat and look up. My heart gives a heavy thud. Rayne waits for me in the lobby, and he's not alone. Cassius and Monaghan stand between us and the stairs.

"There, you see?" Rayne says, watching me with cold blue eyes. "What did I tell you?"

Monaghan's face could be carved from marble. I swallow, my chest thick and heavy. "Sir—" I feel a presence at my elbow and look to my left. Tiberius emerges from the shadows and stalks past us to set his shoulders against the doors.

"It's almost dawn," Monaghan says, his voice slow and deep. It's not the tone he uses when he's angry. It's worse: he's disappointed. "Where were you?"

I inhale and lift my head. This is not about the agency—about me—this is about the case, the women who've died because we weren't there. "I went to Whitechapel, sir."

Rayne shifts. "You left hours ago," he says. "And dressed like that—"

"Dominic." The man stills at Monaghan's word. I look at the professor and my heart sinks. His expression hasn't changed. "I believe I told you that you were not to visit Whitechapel after dark," he tells me.

"I understand the risk, professor, but the threat to others is greater than any danger to me."

"Is it?" he replies. "From where I stand, I disagree."

I think of Catherine Eddowes' face and nausea bubbles up my throat. "If we don't find him, he might go after someone else," I say, "someone who can't defend themselves."

"How many people are in the city right now, looking for this killer? Enough that you're not needed."

"Sir, I'm prepared to face the risk—"

"I am not." He sighs, and his body relaxes as though he'd loosened his grip on it. "I am not prepared to lose you. To lose any of our agents. If the killer strikes again, Rayne will take you to the crime scene to pick up the trail. Not before."

"But—"

"No, Hazel. Go upstairs."

Tiberius watches me from the door, wariness in every line of his body. I feel Cassius' gaze on my face, gloating. Stinging with shame and frustration, I whirl around and stalk away. To the kitchen, as if that small amount of resistance means anything.

If we can't get into Whitechapel at night, there's no way that we'll ever catch this demon. What use am I if I can't protect my own city? My own people?

Clara is in the kitchen. She takes one look at the suit I'm wearing and her expression twists with scorn. "Couldn't you fit into a dress?" she asks, and my patience snaps.

"You have done as little as possible since becoming my apprentice." I'm distantly pleased that my voice comes out cold and steady. "Is that because you expected me to fail? Because you engineered it so?"

She takes a minute too long to reply. "I don't know what you're talking about."

"You switched my summons bag. Didn't you." Part of me recalls that I'd wanted to avoid this, that I'd been waiting for proof, but caution burns away in the wake of my anger and my shame. "You wanted me to fail."

"I—"

"You wanted to become an agent yourself," I continue, unable to stop. "So, you made sure I'd fail."

Clara draws herself up, lifting her chin to stare at me. The seven inches between us diminish to nothing in a heartbeat. "I *did* want you to fail," she replies, sneering. "Is it so wrong to want something more for myself? More than cleaning up after you and that old woman?"

"Then you admit it."

"I didn't swap the bags," she declares. "I only removed the wolf's tooth. Without a focus, the spell would have failed, anyway, and you would have been deemed incompetent. Why would I change the rest? I'm not an idiot, I'm not going to risk anyone's life, even yours." She strides past me, knocking my shoulder as she leaves.

The hot simmer in my chest freezes instantly. I shouldn't have—This will bring more tension to the agency. I drag my hands over my face.

"The night you called me," Steel says, "you said the spell used roses and anemones, not the flowers you'd prepared."

"So what?" I ask, tiredly. "Just tell me, Steel. I'm not in the mood to guess."

"If Clara didn't change them, someone *else* must have." His face is cold and hard, like Monaghan's. I can't look at him. "*Someone* at this agency meant you to fail."

"Enough." My voice cracks. "I can't do this, right now. I want to be alone."

"You'll never be alone," he replies, his mouth tight. "Not now you've called me. You'll never be alone again." The words are no comfort. He doesn't mean them to be.

CHAPTER FORTY-ONE

I exist in claustrophobic purgatory for the next few days. Cassius takes to following us around whenever the spell's limit allows him to, smirking at Steel. If I so much as approach the lobby, Rayne eyes me as though he thinks I might try to dive out the window and make a break for Whitechapel. I keep my spine straight and my head up and do my best to ignore them.

Steel doesn't deal with them as well, spitting back whenever Cassius strikes with a well-placed barb. As the days pass his mood gets surlier, and by the middle of the week I'm dragging around a tall dark thundercloud. I'm desperate for something to shatter the tension and I'm foolish enough to forget the adage; *be careful what you wish for.* Because when something comes, it's nothing good.

"Hazel-ji." Maia stops me in the middle of the corridor. Her expression, the one I have seen too much of as late, makes my stomach twist.

"Another murder?"

"No—not quite. It is not the Whitechapel killer," she corrects. "It is Khurana's case. They have found something."

The Whitehall mystery. I doubt that finding something means they've discovered evidence against the killer. More likely, it's another body part.

I'm right. Eve sits at my desk in the library, scribbling furiously. She doesn't look up when I enter, focused on her work. I stand at her side. It's not scribbles; it's a drawing of some kind. The books laid out beside her are botany texts.

"Is this a clue?" I ask.

"I think so. A reporter discovered a leg not far from where we found the torso." She exhales over her drawing. "I dread to think how many more body parts we're going to unearth before this is over."

"Are you all right?"

"I'm fine," she says, her voice curt. "This flower was tattooed on her calf. I haven't had much luck locating the artist from the ink on her torso, so maybe this will help." She pauses, glances at me and then back down at the drawing. After a moment, she slides it over. "Do you know it? I could use your help."

I blink. They must be struggling as badly as I am if Eve's asking for help. "Of course." I pull up a chair as Steel drifts closer and peers over the other side. Eve has drawn the flower multiple times. Something about it seems familiar, but the recognition is blurry. Slices of white bisect each drawing, leaving scars that mar the image. "What are these marks?"

"Wounds. The killer cut up her legs. He seemed pretty intent on destroying this, but he was sloppy. Rushed. After we wiped off the blood and the dirt, I managed to piece an image together."

I take up a pencil and sketch the flower myself, hoping the action will trigger a memory. The drawing is crude, and I wish Jacob were here. He could take a cramped pencil sketch and transform it into a masterpiece within an hour. Taking the paper, I fold over the pieces where the cuts were, matching the lines of pencil as closely as I can. The end result is a small bud with large, leaf-shaped petals that surround tiny, more rounded flowers. It's narrow, as though the real flower might be tall rather than wide.

My face goes cold. "It's lavender."

"Lavender's a sprig," Eve comments. "When is it ever drawn like this?"

"On Turner's grave," I reply, hoarsely.

Eve's eyes widen and she flattens her hands on the table. "You don't think…"

"Didn't you say that decapitation kills demons?" I ask Steel. He nods.

"The first body part, the arm," I say. "When did they find it?"

"The eleventh of September." Eve's fingers are white under her nails, in contrast to her brown skin. "She'd been dead for a little while."

"As much as a week?"

She shakes her head. "I don't know. Hazel, you can't be suggesting that this—that this is—"

"Lavender." The word sounds as though it's coming from someone else. I feel ill. "It's Lavender."

We fall silent for a long time.

"It can't be," Eve mutters, eventually. "Lavender is too strong, too smart. She would never have been caught."

"Then why didn't she come back?" I ask. Steel is silent, and I'm grateful. I can't handle his commentary right now. "If she was alive, and she knew Turner was dead, she would have helped us find the killer. She would have come *home*."

"Fuck," Eve mutters, putting her hand over her eyes.

I sit back, staring at the small flower. "How can we be sure?" I ask Steel. "Is there a way to know if the body is a demon's?"

"Holy water," he replies. "Or a blessed weapon. They usually leave a mark, but if the body's been dead for this long...it won't be conclusive."

"We should try it," I say. "It might—it might explain..."

"I'll ask Khurana," Eve says, lowering her hand. She interrupts me when I go to protest. "No, you shouldn't have to see that. I know how close you were to her. To both of them. We'll take care of it."

"Thank you," I manage. She grips my hand tightly, tight enough to leave an imprint on my skin. "If you—if you need anything—"

"Let me worry about it. I'll tell you, when...if we know."

I nod. Eve doesn't let go of my hand and I muster the control to curl my fingers around hers and take strength from her presence. We sit in silence until Eve has to go, and then I wait until dark.

The grief, when I let it come, visits me on the cold floor in my room as I press my knees to my face. Where no one can see me weep.

CHAPTER FORTY-TWO

On a day like today, the cemetery resembles something out of a Gothic novel. Craggy gravestones lurch out of the gloom like monsters.

Only the squelch of our boots accompanies the drumming of the rain as we follow the muddy path through the graves. Turner's is tucked away in a small plot near an oak sapling.

Two figures already stand there, draped in dark coats. Max holds a large umbrella like my own, sheltering him and Jacob from the spray. The young agent has a hand to his chest, over his silver hamsa pendant. He sees me and tucks it under his shirt with a rueful smile.

"I haven't prayed for a long time," he says, in greeting. "It's a difficult habit to get back into."

"I admire you for taking it back up." I glance over my shoulder at the church silhouetted against the clouds on the other side of the road and shiver. After walking so long beside demons, I've forgotten some of what it means to fear them. Evil isn't limited to demons, after all. "No one told me you were coming back," I add.

"Eve telegrammed me," he replies. "Told me about…told me what happened to Lavender."

The blessed weapon had indeed made a mark. Standing in front of Turner's grave, tracing the shape of the stone flower with my gaze, I have to admit the reality, as much as I would rather deny it with all my breath. Turner and Lavender are both dead. And, worse, Lavender suffered before she was killed.

Jacob sighs. The stone he put on Turner's tombstone weeks ago has fallen into the long grass at the side. He picks it up and places it gently back on top. "I wanted to come here, before I went to the agency."

"You were close," I murmur.

"I didn't spend as much time with her as you did, but, yes, in a way," he says. "She found a way to live, her and Lavender, that I admired. She knew herself, accepted herself. I guess I wanted that. I wanted to be brave, like she was." His hand goes to his sternum, where the pendant must rest.

Deep in my mind a memory surfaces, something Turner said to me years ago. "It takes one kind of courage to face down a pistol," I recite, "and another to stand up for what you believe is right, when everyone around you tells you it's wrong."

Jacob laughs. "She was wise."

"She was brilliant." I grip my umbrella, the metal handle cutting into my palm. "I wish we could have saved her."

"Monaghan doesn't want me out there, risking Max," he says. "But I'm going to help you find the monster that did this to her. To Lavender." Jacob holds himself with an easy confidence that he didn't have when he left London. Scotland was good for him. Getting away from the agency was good for him.

"I'm glad you're home."

"Me too." He throws me a rueful look. "And I'm sorry."

"What for?"

"For going into Whitechapel with Dominic. We caused you some problems," he says gesturing at Max. "We should have stayed out of it."

"It's done." In a way, it had helped, ruling out the copper-class demons who'd all fled because of them.

"This time, I'll help. We all will." Jacob looks at the grave again, his jaw clenched. "He won't escape all of us." He turns on his heel and strides away. Max hurries to catch up.

I watch them leave, Jacob tense and small beside the big Reaper. Rather than help me figure out what to do, this visit is leaving me feeling more lost.

"A Reaper demon has to learn how to control his presence early," Steel says. He stands behind me, scorning the protection the umbrella offers. "But your Max hasn't. An easy way to pretend to be something he's not, perhaps?"

"Don't." The umbrella trembles with the force of my reaction. I loosen my grip, take a deep breath. "Don't try to turn me against my friends. They're not suspects."

"Everyone is a suspect. Or do you not want justice for *this* friend?" He steps up beside me, into my line of vision, staring down at the grave.

"Don't," I say, again.

"You're blinded by your affection for Monaghan," he continues, ignoring me, "for what he did for you. But he didn't save you. All he did was open the door to another future. You don't need to be grateful to him."

"I will *always* be grateful to him. He took me out of poverty, out of starvation. He gave me everything."

"He gave you a choice. You did the rest."

I shake my head. I don't want to listen.

"A real agent would consider all of the possibilities."

My breath escapes in a hiss. "I *am* considering them."

"Then stop considering and *take action. Do* something about it."

"I *can't*." Turner's grave blurs. Would she have said that, to Lavender? Would she ever have said the words *I can't*?

I drop the umbrella to my side. Icy rain beats on the top of my head, slides under the collar of my jacket. A bead drips from my nose. More hang in my eyelashes. I let them run down my face, try to visualise my emotions going with them, washing away.

"These people are not just my friends." The words escape from a clenched place inside my chest. "They're my family. They're all I have."

But I have to weigh my personal feelings against the lives that have been taken, the lives that may *still* be taken. The cost is not enough to balance the scales.

I look at Steel and he returns my gaze levelly. His black hair is slicked to his head. "You're soaked," I say, uselessly.

"So are you."

I lift my umbrella and hold it over both of us. The drumming of the downpour echoes the quickened beat of my heart. It's time I stopped hiding. "I'm sorry," I tell him, speaking to the grave as much as to the demon at my side.

Steel inclines his head. "You were right," he says, after a moment. "My family...I don't—" He stops. Starts again. "You have so many people who want to help you. None of them want to tear you down and climb over your corpse to glory."

God. No wonder my words had hurt. "Not yet," I offer, a weak attempt to lift the weight from him, to help shoulder it. "I'm still young, though."

He snorts. "Is that supposed to be a joke? In a *cemetery*? Really, Locke, that's in poor taste, don't you think?"

"You are impossible."

"I know. I work at it." He seems to stand a little straighter, though, so perhaps my terrible humour did help. "What next?" he asks.

Inhaling, I tuck away the thoughts that are no longer relevant, harden my soul to what must be done. "If the Wraith can be anyone, then everyone at the agency is a suspect. Khurana, Isis and Eve were in Bristol the nights of the first two murders, so it can't be them. Rayne was with us at the dinner party—"

"Not all of the time," Steel points out. "And we should test everyone, just in case."

If we test everyone, then I can be sure that no one is a suspect, and my mind will quieten. "Fine." I nod to myself and the tension in me crystallises. If I'm going to do this—if *we're* going to do this—then I must be committed. No more doubting myself. No more second guessing.

CHAPTER FORTY-THREE

"We need to test Cassius first," Steel says, the next day. I don't dare have this conversation in the library, so I've pulled an extra chair into my room and converted my dresser into a makeshift desk. "He's the most likely suspect."

"How?"

"The spell doesn't restrict me unless my opponent is a human agent." His lip curls, communicating how he feels about that. "So, I'll test the demons first. We can pretend it's an accident."

"I don't know how attacking them is going to look like an accident," I murmur.

"We'll have to find the right opportunity."

An opportunity comes the next day: Jacob pokes his head in at the library door, Max at his shoulder. The agent's face is lit with a mischievous expression. "Are you busy?"

I look at him warily. "Why?"

He huffs a laugh. "I was going to ask if you wanted to come with us to the theatre. Drury Lane is showing a new play, and Max has never been to a theatre before. So, have you decided if you're busy?"

I refrain from wrinkling my nose. Jacob dragged me to Drury Lane once, shortly after I joined the agency, and the play had been a flowery, insipid thing that I'd done my best to sleep through. But this is the chance we need.

"We're not busy," I tell him.

Steel glances at me as if he'd hoped I'd say the opposite. "Are you *sure* there's nothing else we can do?"

"It's had rave reviews," Jacob replies, breezily. "And the lead actors are brilliant. Besides," he adds, and the grim determination I saw at Turner's grave flashes over his face, "I need to get away from the agency, for a bit. I think we could all do with a break."

"All right."

"Great. I'll see if Eve is free, too. It'll be like we're apprentices, again," he says, and grins at me.

Sighing, I agree to meet them in the lobby. "How is this going to work?" I ask Steel, when they're gone. "Cutting Max in the middle of a play isn't going to be subtle."

Steel curls his fingers one by one and his claws slice through the air. "I'll manage."

We head downstairs and are met by Jacob and Max, and then Eve. The woman tugs on her cloak, buoyant, though I notice her gaze slides over Steel as if he's not there. She still doesn't trust him. I don't blame her.

"So," she says, flicking her braided hair out of her collar, "are we sitting with the angels again, or have you managed to score us some decent tickets?"

Jacob grins. "We're in the stalls. They gave me a discount, because I said I worked with the Home Office." He looks sheepish and Eve snorts with laughter.

"Let's go, then," I say, shaking my head, "before Monaghan catches us and tells us off for abusing our authority."

We sweep out of the door, Eve linking arms with Jacob and Max. The Reaper scans the streets for trouble as we walk. I wind up behind them, with Steel.

My partner watches the Reaper, a faint downward slant to his mouth. He dogs Max's steps, and when he drifts closer the tension to his mouth increases and he frowns, drops back. Max's aura, I assume. Lavender once likened it to the deafening hum of a dozen beehives. The one weakness to offset a Reaper's tremendous strength.

The streets are too narrow for us to walk five abreast, so I raise my voice to ask Jacob about his Edinburgh case, turning his attention to me, away from Max.

"It was a Blood Drinker hive," Jacob says, turning to speak over his shoulder. Fine lines around his eyes that I don't remember seeing before crease. "I wasn't very useful, to be honest. Max did the real work."

"Not quite true," comes Max's quiet voice. "Jacob found the nest. I only destroyed it."

"It was hardly 'only'," Jacob says, throwing him an affectionate glance. "You took down five Blood Drinkers in less than an hour."

"It's good that you're both getting along," I add. Jacob gets along with everyone, so I shouldn't have been worried, but this will be a lifetime partnership. To have the easy camaraderie that they've built will make that partnership a whole lot easier.

Assuming that Max is not the Wraith.

Eve glances at me over her shoulder and tilts her head in a silent question. I smile and look away. That kind of rapport is beyond Steel and me. Civility will have to do, for us. When I glance back, Eve is glaring at Steel.

"How is Agent Stewart, Jacob?" I ask, hastily. "Do you plan to meet him while you're here?"

"I'll try," he replies. "We exchange letters frequently enough. Thank goodness. I'm not sure what I would have done without his experience to guide me." I fall silent. "I'm sorry," Jacob says, hastily. "I didn't mean—"

"It's fine," I say, even if my smile is brittle.

"Tell us about Scotland," Eve demands. "Where did you go?"

He launches into a vivid description of the Highlands, all lilac heather and rolling hills and expansive grey skies. The picture he paints washes over me, easing a tight spot between my shoulder blades. Before I realise it, we come upon the theatre. Large posters outside proclaim the new play: *The Armada: A Romance of 1588*. I raise my eyebrows at the depiction of the two actors.

"Augusta Harris is good, I've heard," Jacob says, eyeing them.

Eve shrugs. "I suppose we'll find out."

We join the queue and filter into the stalls. Our tickets get us within spitting distance of the stage, and I hope there's no actual spitting to come. The stalls are a series of long wooden benches, so I step forward to go first—me and Steel, then Max and Jacob—but Eve beats me to it.

"Come on," she says, dragging Max by the sleeve. "You should sit in the middle. It's the best seat."

Jacob squeezes in next to the Reaper and I smooth back a frown. There's no way Steel can get close enough to him to carry out our 'test'. Now, what?

"Hazel?" Jacob asks. He beckons me forward. "It's about to start. Hurry, sit down."

I reluctantly file in after him, Steel behind me. The bench is hard and unforgiving. "How long is this play?" I whisper, to Jacob.

"Just over three hours," he replies, looking delighted at the fact.

I glance at Steel, who grimaces at the stage. "Great," I murmur, putting my hands on my thighs, bracing myself.

Eve is whispering to Max, pointing out the candles set at the brim of the stage and the orchestra hidden in the pit. I sigh and settle in for a long wait.

CHAPTER FORTY-FOUR

The play comes to an end and I applaud politely with the others, not quite sure what happened, but the actors look happy, so I assume their night ended more positively than mine is going.

Jacob leans over. "That was excellent, wasn't it?" I smile and nod, hopefully concealing the fact I barely listened to it.

Eve stands and stretches. "I'm starving. Let's get dinner somewhere."

I look at Steel and he nods, brightening at the mention of food. "All right," I agree. It might give us another opportunity.

It's a short walk to Covent Garden, and already the sound of music and laughter can be heard. Above us the sky is a dark slate grey, full of smog.

"In Scotland all you could see were stars," Jacob says, following my gaze. "And the air was fresh." He inhales deeply and then coughs. "Not like this," he croaks.

"You were only there for a couple of weeks," I reply. "Do you miss it already?"

"It was pleasant. I think it would be a nice place to retire. If..." He trails off, the *if I make it* going unspoken.

"Don't retire yet," Eve says. "We have a lot of work to do."

"Oh?"

Eve includes the both of us in her gaze. "When Monaghan retires, *we're* the ones who are going to be calling the shots. So, we need to solve a lot of cases to help get us there."

I smile wryly. "I think Rayne would have something to say about that."

She waves her hand airily. "We'll send him to Ireland. Open a new branch in Dublin."

"He'd never go."

"He will if we call it a promotion," she shoots back, grinning.

"This was supposed to be a day when we don't talk about work," Jacob protests. "Plans for agency dominion fall into 'talking about work'."

"Fine, fine," Eve says. "I'll save the plotting for *after* dinner. Where are we eating?"

"What about over there?" Jacob suggests, pointing to a small Chinese restaurant.

Eve stands on her tip toes, looking down the street. "Are those jugglers?" Down the road, a handful of street entertainers are thrilling the crowd with wild acrobatics and flaming torches.

"Looks like it," Jacob replies, peering through the darkening shadows.

"Let's go see," she says, drifting ahead. I share an exasperated glance with Jacob, who shrugs and follows her.

A crowd has gathered around the entertainers. Murmurs of surprise and awe ripple through the throng with each new trick. Eve wriggles between people to get to the front. I skirt the edge until I can keep my eye on her as well as the jugglers. They're talented, and I gasp along with everyone else when one of the men slides a sword down his throat. I turn to share my awe with Jacob, but the agent is backing away from the crowd, his cheeks drained of colour.

"Jacob?"

"Let's go this way." He grips my arm and hauls me in the opposite direction.

"But Eve is still there." The agent keeps pulling me down the street. I hurry to keep up. "What's going on?"

"Oi!" Two young men peel away from the crowd and intercept us. They look a little older than Jacob, in their mid-twenties perhaps. Both wear ostlers' uniforms. "So, this is where you got off to, Jakey," one says. "Didn't *you* make out well?" he adds, sizing up Jacob and taking in his well-tailored jacket and shiny boots. Their faces are cold and hard and mean. I wish I had my umbrella.

The other one whistles. "Who did you bend over for to get your hands on that get-up?"

Jacob flinches. "Let's go," he whispers.

"And who's this?" They circle me, attempting to grab my skirt and laughing when I slap their hands away. "Didn't think you'd be the kind to take up with a woman, Jakey."

"Look," I say, dropping Jacob's arm and stepping up to them. "You—"

"Forget it." Jacob pulls me away. "It's not worth it. It's all right."

"It's none of their damn business, is what it is."

An actual smile tugs at his lips. "I think that's the first time I've heard you swear."

"Well, don't count on it happening again." We've put the crowd between us and those idiots, but Jacob's expression is still downcast. "Max, would you find Eve, please?" I ask, and the Reaper drifts into the throng of people, nudging the outskirts of the spell. "What would you like to eat?" I ask Jacob.

"Whatever you want," he replies, with a bland smile. I feel a fresh surge of anger towards those boys for destroying the happiness Jacob had found.

Eve flits up to us. "Sorry, sorry," she says. "I got caught up. Are we going to that restaurant you picked out?"

"No," Jacob says, instantly.

"We thought we'd try somewhere else," I add.

Max tilts his head and says, "Agent Stewart told me that venison was his favourite, but I've never had it. Do you think we could try it?"

"I've not eaten it, either," Jacob replies, looking intrigued.

"Perfect."

Eve's expression is curious, but she leads us away from the crowd. "That's settled then," she says. "Now we just have to find somewhere that serves venison and admits peasants like us."

Jacob rubs his jaw, running through a list of potential options out loud. I throw Max a grateful look, and he smiles at me, as though he's letting me in on a secret.

I drop back with Steel. The demon bends his head. "That was our opportunity. If it had escalated into a fight, I could've—" He flexes his clawed hand.

"I can't. Not tonight." I can't stomach the thought of my own distrust.

Steel sighs but doesn't protest. I will have to find another opportunity to carry out our test.

CHAPTER FORTY-FIVE

A few days later, Jacob bounces into the kitchen holding a large cream invitation. "A party on Wednesday," he confirms, passing me the card. "Halloween. Everyone in the Home Office is invited, as well as a lot of MPs. And so are we. Monaghan wants us to represent the agency."

I frown at the invitation. "Most lower members of Parliament don't know what the agency really is. You're sure Monaghan said we should go?"

"Pemberton won't be happy," Eve points out. "He wants us out of the public eye. This is right in the centre."

"There'll be masks!" Jacob says, cheerfully. "It's costume dress. Besides, the murders have stopped. And we could use a chance to relax."

This must be one of Monaghan's attempts to further the agency's cause. And it's not just an opportunity for him—it's an opportunity for me and Steel, too. "I think it's a great idea."

Eve sends me a sharp look. "*You* think it's a great idea? A costume party?"

"Why not? There hasn't been another murder in weeks. The killer might have given up." Or he knows that we're on to him.

My placid expression almost fails. I snatch at it, paste it onto my face. "If everyone else is going to wear a costume, it would look odd if we didn't."

"It would, wouldn't it?" Jacob adds, pouncing on the words. "We should order some. All of us." Jacob walks away with Max, their heads bent together, no doubt plotting what kind of costume they can get.

"I'm staying here," Eve says, standing. "Because unlike some, I have actual work to do." She shakes her head in Jacob's direction and slinks away.

I notice that Steel is quiet. "Not a fan of costume, Mr. Steel?" He's gazing off in the direction Jacob and Max went, a faint frown between his eyes. "What is it?"

"Nothing," he says, dropping his gaze to the invitation. He slides it over the table towards me. "This is a good opportunity," he adds. "In the heat and chaos of a party like this, anything can happen. People can get hurt." He means more than what we have planned. The risk that the Ripper will strike again.

"We'll be on our guard," I reply.

"Indeed, we will."

CHAPTER FORTY-SIX

B y Halloween, I'm less concerned with the time passing than with simple logistics: how can I get Steel close enough to the agency's demons to injure them without drawing attention, while also shedding enough blood that we can measure their rate of healing? It seems ridiculous, and even as I help Steel into his new black tailcoat I wonder if I'm wasting my time on this while the real killer wanders the streets.

Steel grunts and curses. "This goddamn jacket—are you sure it's the right size?"

"It's supposed to be this tight," I reply, helping him shrug it on. "It's the kind of coat you need a valet for."

He finally gets the thing on and turns to face me, flattening the lapels. "How does it look?" The coat has a slim, fitted waist, its severe black lifted by soft velvet lapels and thin piping. His waistcoat is of the same material, dotted with tiny silver buttons. A dark violet cravat is the only splash of colour on him. Suddenly, I understand what the phrase *devastatingly handsome* is supposed to mean: Steel could break hearts with no more than a glance.

Something in my stomach flutters. I squash the sensation immediately. Romantic relationships between humans and demons are forbidden, but more than that, Steel is in my power. Developing an attachment to him would be at best inappropriate and at worst reprehensible.

"I think you'll fit in," I say, dryly.

"Thank goodness for that," Steel replies, in the same tone. He dons a black and silver half mask shaped, ironically, like a devil with curled horns. Gauze hides his eyes, just in case one of the guests gets too close. His other mask, the one I purchased in secret, has the same protection. "It's been a long time since I attended a masquerade." He touches his devil's horns and gives a low, sardonic laugh. "At least this time I'm dressed appropriately."

"What do you mean?"

"Nothing. A bad memory."

Someone knocks on Steel's door and he calls for them to enter. "Here you are," Maia says, out of breath. "I have been looking for—You have not changed!"

I glance down at my coffee and black lace dress. The green silk I wore a month ago is ruined. "What's wrong with this?"

"It is not an evening dress, nor is it a costume."

"I don't have anything—"

"I know you do not, which is why I ordered one for you. If you had been in your room, I could have told you that an hour ago," she says, pulling me to the adjoining door. "Now, you must hurry. The coach will be here in half an hour." I cast a beseeching glance at Steel, and he smirks at me until Maia shuts the door on him. She pushes me to the bed. "There. Put this on. Quickly."

I stare at the fabric draped over the sheets. The bodice is amethyst satin trimmed with ribbon sashes. It has a simple scooped neckline and draped sleeves, and it fits perfectly over my corset. The skirt is a heavier taffeta in the same purple colour. When I pull it on, the hem sweeps against the floor. Impractical, but I can't help swishing it to feel it move.

"Here." Maia hands me a pair of violet kid slippers with a slight heel. I frown at the height. "You will need them, to keep the skirt out of the mud," she advises me. "And if you stick close by Steel, no one will notice."

"More like everyone will notice," I reply, sitting to put them on. The two of us will tower over all the other guests. An aspect of our plan that I hadn't considered: even with a different mask, it will be difficult to hide Steel's height.

A pair of full-length black gloves and a black half-mask with a hawk's pointed beak complete the outfit. Staring in the mirror, I have to pinch logic back into my head. It's only a dress. My focus must be on other things, tonight.

"Now you look the part," Maia says, turning me in a circle. "You will make the professor proud."

I smile over the twist that gives my heart. I doubt that Monaghan will be proud of what I'm doing tonight.

Steel waits for us outside. I can't see his expression behind the mask, but he tilts his head. "You almost look like a fashionable lady, Agent Locke," he says, an amused lilt to the words.

"And you look more human by the minute, Mr. Steel," I counter.

He acknowledges my hit with a dip of his head. Then, dropping his voice, he adds, "Are you ready?"

"I believe so." As much as I can be.

"Good." He offers his arm. Amused, I take it, and we follow Maia down to the entrance.

Jacob and Max wait for us. Max wears a black suit stitched with silver bones and a skull mask that hides all but the golden skin of his jaw. Jacob's suit is gold and green, topped with a mask that looks like a serpent coiling around his eyes. Its forked tongue sits over his nose. He flashes me a toothy grin. "What do you think?"

"You look brilliant. You both do," I add, including Max.

"As do you," Jacob replies. Politely, I'm sure, as my pretty but simple dress pales in comparison to his jewelled emerald. "Rayne and Khurana took the first coach with the others. Shall we follow?"

I inhale and smile at him, conscious of the Reaper at his shoulder and the so-called Hound at mine. "Let's," I agree, and precede him out of the door. Whatever this night will bring, I hope I'm ready for it.

CHAPTER FORTY-SEVEN

The house we arrive at is more of an estate. It's surrounded by lush gardens shrouded in late evening fog and sparkling with dew. Inside, the rooms are filled with the bubble of pouring champagne and the murmur of conversation. Wooden panels on the walls flow with ancient animals and hunting scenes, moving under the light of a thousand candles.

Silk-adorned guests roam the plains of the house in stylised costumes, their hair moulded to look like doves, or swans—or, in one highly ambitious case, a fully antlered stag. Their outfits glimmer and glisten, each designed to look as though it came from a distant country, the more exotic the better. I suspect most were cut from a template by West End drapers. The place throngs with people and the chance of finding a politician seems slim. It's as if the whole of London has been invited.

I lean closer to Jacob. "What are we supposed to do here?"

"I suppose we just speak to the MPs," he replies, uncertainly.

Steel's voice is a murmur in my ear. "We should locate the others." I nod and repeat the words to Jacob. He agrees and follows me into the crowd.

Heat simmers under a layer of perfumed incense, a mixture of warmth from an excessive number of candles and the even more excessive number of bodies squeezed into each room. In one, animal skulls climb tables topped with dripping tallow candles, and in another, a woman draped in dark cloth and wielding a cloudy crystal ball holds court over the crowd. A third is empty save for a group of people clustered around a table at the room's centre. I sidle up to get a better look.

An old wooden Ouija board lies in the middle of the table, held steady by half a dozen pairs of hands. As I watch, the needle jerks sideways. Everyone screeches.

"Is there anything supernatural about this?" I ask Steel. I don't want to discount the possibility, even if I find it hard to believe a spirit would choose this party to spend their next life at.

"Yes, but not a ghost. Look."

I watch and a moment later Cassius slides out of thin air behind the crowd, wearing a smirk. He flexes his fingers and moves away to talk to Rayne, unnoticed by the group. "He shouldn't be using his powers like that," I mutter.

"No doubt he finds it amusing to toy with others."

One of the women at the table closes her eyes. "Are you still there? If you're there, give us a sign." They wait, but the needle does not move.

"Tell us your name!" shouts a man.

The woman giggles. "Perhaps we already know your name," she calls. "Perhaps the spirit of one of the Ripper's victims is with us tonight! Annie, is that you?"

Disgusted, I turn away. These people come from a different world, a world in which they don't have to fear darkness. They don't know what darkness is.

I find Khurana standing against the far wall beside Isis. They have both declined to wear masks and are dressed in simple black. I walk to them, my heart beating faster as I remind myself of our goal. We should test Isis, if we want to be sure.

The pair stand with a small group of women who wear elaborately ruffled dresses and masks embroidered with tiny jewels. One lifts a platter dotted with small mouthfuls of meat speared with fresh fruit. "Here," she says, "won't you try one of these?"

Khurana eyes it. "I am *shakahari*. Vegetarian," she clarifies, when the woman stares at her, uncomprehending.

The woman smiles thinly. "This venison is the best that London has to offer. I insist. Eat." The last is a snap of a word. A command. This woman has no idea who she's dealing with.

"If that is the best London has to offer," Khurana returns, in a voice cold enough to freeze the stack of candles beside her, "then I am severely disappointed in this city."

The woman splutters over a response. I take a glass of wine from a passing server and jerk forward as though I've been pushed. Crimson splashes over the woman's expensive silk dress. It was a full glass, too.

"Forgive me," I say. "Perhaps you should see to that before it stains."

With a flounce of indignation, the woman drops the tray on the nearest table and stalks away with the others. I take a fresh glass and take up a position beside the agent. Isis stands on her other side, her back to the wall and her pale eyes on the crowd. We won't get to her here.

"Have you seen the others?" I ask Khurana.

She shakes her head. "I expect Rayne is with the mayor, or if not, the next most influential man here," she adds, with a dry twist to her mouth. I swallow my own smile with a mouthful of wine. "The professor is here, too. It seems that the government is beginning to think the Whitechapel murderer is done."

"What, captured?"

"Or that he has been scared away, perhaps. They have little intention of continuing their investigation beyond the next few weeks."

My appetite for the wine vanishes and I put down my glass. "I see."

"And I assume your partner has made no progress?" Khurana asks. She doesn't look in Steel's direction, her gaze on the crowd, but I sense her attention shift to him. Steel does, too, by the way he stiffens.

"Not yet."

"Pity."

"And you?" I ask. "Have you found anything for your case?"

Her gaze drops a little. "Not yet," she echoes. "But we will. I will not leave this city until we find the killer responsible."

There is something reassuring in the quiet force of her conviction. Even if something happened to me, or if I couldn't end this case, I could rest easier knowing Khurana will find him.

If I told her about the Wraith, about what Turner was up to, would she help?

But Turner didn't hide the code with Khurana. I can't risk exposing her secret just yet. Not until I know more.

"I should find the professor." Khurana nods and lets me walk away with Steel. I glance in a large ornamental mirror as we leave the room; Khurana has not moved, but Isis watches us leave. A shiver runs down my spine for no reason that I can identify.

Professor Monaghan is in one of the quieter rooms, sitting in an armchair opposite three other men who all wear the same kind of smart, pristine suits: government officials. These must be the people he wanted to impress. I drift around the edge of the room with Steel, pretending to admire the carved mahogany walls, and listen to their conversation.

"It's too soon to make this decision," Monaghan is saying. He sits with one leg propped on his other knee, his elbows resting on the arms of his chair, apparently at ease, but I see tension in the lines around his mouth. "It's only been a month."

"Exactly," another man replies. His gaze flicks to Tiberius, who looms behind the professor's chair. "The other murders all took place within a few weeks. It's been a month, and there's no sign of him. He's gone."

"We've had policemen on twelve-hour shifts," adds another. "Twenty-four hours they've been covering that district. We simply do not have the resources to keep this up."

Monaghan shakes his head. "The quiet we've had is likely due to the extra police presence in the East End. You cannot draw them out now."

"They've already been drawn out." The man sits back, flicking the lid of a gold snuff box, open and shut and open again. "Commissioner Warren gave the order this morning. All the men that Abberline called in from the city districts are being redeployed back to their regular beats."

Monaghan presses the backs of his fingers to his mouth for a moment, then taps his lip and adds, "Did Commissioner Warren receive my last report? Does he understand the kind of creature we might be dealing with?" These men must be important politicians if they know about the agency.

All three of the men steer their gazes away from Tiberius. "If you ask me," says the third man, "I don't think he does. I think he's bungled this."

"Linde—"

"No, hear me out. It was Inspector Abberline who asked for the patrols, not Warren. Warren was the one who kept petitioning the Secretary for a reward, and look where that's got us. Now he's pulling out as if we've caught the man."

"I'm sure the Commissioner knows what he's doing," Monaghan says.

"He doesn't," the man replies. "We'd do better with someone like you, if we're being frank. You have an awareness of this...this other world. And the Commissioner's due to retire any day now. If I were you, I'd consider throwing your hat into the ring for his replacement."

The professor laces his fingers together and gives the man a rueful look. "I wouldn't know what to do with that many departments. No, the paranormal is my area of expertise."

I've made a full circuit of the room. If I linger any longer, I'll be noticed. I duck out. With the police presence reduced, it will be that much easier for the Ripper to find his next victim. I need to move quickly.

I head back to the seance room, but Khurana and Isis are no longer there. Clicking my tongue, I stop. "Can you sense the others?" I ask Steel.

He cocks his head. "Only Max. He's outside, near the front."

I hand Steel his second mask, black and carved to resemble a raven. One thing this dress is useful for: hiding things in the voluminous material of its skirts. Steel hides the devil mask behind a stack of occult books and replaces it with the new one. It covers his whole face, and his suit is black and nondescript—all I need to do is to ensure no one sees me.

Outside, the breeze is cool, and the night sky is dark but clear. One or two tiny stars glitter against the smog and the lights of the city. Out here, the laughter and conversation become louder, swapped between coach drivers and servants. Jacob stands with Max, who's bending over a late-blooming chrysanthemum.

"Do you think you can get to him?"

Steel snorts. "Easily enough. You'll need to stay close, so we're not outside the limit."

"And you have a weapon?" We decided against using claws, this time. It would be too difficult to hide his identity. He digs into his cuff and brings out a slender needle. Not a needle; a hat pin. "Is that mine?"

"It seemed to deter that Major well enough." I frown doubtfully at his raven's beak. "I'll be quick. Just keep an eye on Jacob."

He fades into the shadows before I can respond. Clasping my hands together against the cold, the thin material of my gloves little protection, I circle the two of them. The amethyst of my dress catches the candlelight spilling out of the building's windows. Perhaps this is not the best outfit for skulking around in the darkness. I take in a deep breath scented with horses and woodsmoke, and drift close enough that I should be able to see the wound, if Steel strikes hard enough.

Four young men spill from the street onto the mansion's grass. They shout at the coach drivers, stumbling against each other, drunk. They weave up to the steps that lead to the front of the house. One of them pauses.

"You again," he calls, staring at Jacob. "Theatres *and* fancy parties, is it? What did you do to deserve this?" he asks, with a sneer.

With a shock I realise they're the boys from Covent Garden, from Jacob's past. I stiffen.

"*Who* has he done, more like," another boy sputters. They line up in front of Jacob, big enough to block him from the street and the coaches. The agent takes a step back. I pull my gloves up to my elbows. Steel will have to wait for another opportunity; I can't stand here and watch.

Then Max puts a hand on Jacob's shoulder. The young agent visibly inhales, and replies, "What I do or who I'm with are none of your business."

"That's not what you used to say," the first boy says. He sways closer. "Shall I repeat what it was you used to tell me?"

Jacob punches him. He looks as surprised as the other boy to do it, and there's a moment of tense silence as they all stare at each other in shock. Then Steel materialises from the shadows and slugs one of the others. Someone yells and there's a sudden surge of arms and legs and screamed curses as they collide into each other.

I rush to help them—or stop them, I'm not sure which—but by the time I cross the short space between us it's over. Max drops the last one, piling the unconscious boy on top of the other two, who grunt. Jacob rotates his wrist carefully.

"Are you all right?" I ask, gripping his arm.

Steel takes off his mask and tucks it out of sight. "We were passing," he explains. "I hope I didn't overstep."

"Not at all," Jacob replies, grimly. "I should have done that years ago." His gaze goes to Max and his eyes widen. "You're hurt."

The Reaper grimaces. "It's just a scratch." Blood drips along the edge of his hand. I sneak a glance at Steel, and he quirks his brow. So that fight wasn't purely for Jacob's sake.

"Let me see it," I offer and take his hand. I peel off one of my gloves and dab the blood away. The scratch is long, but not deep. I take longer than necessary to clean the skin, waiting, but the scratch remains. "Will it heal?"

"In a few hours," the Reaper says. He seems unconcerned about it. I let go and toss my glove away. Another item of clothing ruined by blood. I strip off the other one and wind it around my wrist, just in case someone else bleeds tonight.

"And you?" I ask Jacob, indicating his bruised knuckles. "Do you need me to look at that?"

"It'll heal. In a bit more than a few hours, perhaps, but I'll be fine." A shaky smile winds over his face. "Although right now I think I need a drink. Will you join us? Toast our victory?"

"I would love to," I reply, returning his wide grin with a small one of my own, "but I'm looking for the others."

"Ah, I think I saw Rayne in the rear gardens, with the mayor." Jacob flexes his hand again and turns towards the building. "Better find him soon, before he's recruited into Parliament."

I wave him into the house. When they're both gone, I turn to Steel. "Well?"

"A Wraith would have healed that in an instant," he confirms. "I don't think it's Max."

"You don't *think*?"

"Well, it's not a conclusive test. It's only an indication."

"You couldn't have told me that before?"

"Would it have changed your mind?"

"It might." I blow out a breath. "Probably not, but still. You should have told me."

"I didn't see the need to explain," he says. "You'll confront them and they'll confess. You'll get the same result, either way."

"I don't think you understand the idea of innocent until proved guilty," I mutter.

"That's a human proverb."

Sighing, I move through the gardens. The lawn encircles the house, surrounding it with an elegant tree line and the illusion of privacy. The grass is heavy with dew and even with the added height from my kid slippers, my skirt soaks up the water like a sponge. Oh, well. Better than blood, I suppose.

A series of chimes ring through an open window. After the twelfth, a cheer goes up. Steel skitters sideways like a startled horse. "What was that?"

"Midnight. They call it the witching hour."

"If they knew anything about magic, they wouldn't be so keen on celebrating it," Steel murmurs.

I cut through a rose garden that's mostly thorns save for one or two late-blooming buds. The gardens are abandoned, no doubt due to the icy wind that seems intent on finding as many ways as possible to reach my skin. I move quickly, hoping Rayne is distracted by the mayor enough that he won't notice if Steel bumps into Cassius with a needle. And hoping the damage is light.

Then I stop. Silhouetted under a white arbour some distance from the house stands Khurana. Her long braid of hair and straight stance mark her as the agent, but something about her image halts me in shock. For a moment, I can't figure out what. Then I realise: around Khurana is at least forty feet of empty grass. Isis is nowhere to be seen.

CHAPTER FORTY-EIGHT

Within seconds, Isis comes striding over the lawn and into the gazebo, but the moment when they'd been apart hollows out my insides. I slide behind a large laurel tree, slowly enough that my movement doesn't catch their eye. Hidden, I exhale and clench my hands.

Steel ducks into the laurel with me, its big bushy leaves nestling over his shoulders. "That's impossible," he mutters. "She shouldn't be able to go that far under the binding spell."

"Could a diamond-class demon break it?" I ask him.

He frowns through the laurel to where Isis and Khurana were standing. "The ritual is centuries old: it would take a tremendous amount of power to undo it. It's not impossible, but it wouldn't be subtle."

I cast my mind back to the night of the ritual, to the blood patterns carved into the stone. The faded streak of blood I'd seen, washed away. "What if they didn't undo it? What if they just...changed it?"

He glances at me. "What do you mean?"

Khurana and Isis must still be in the arbour, but they'll have to come this way to return to the house. We can't stay here.

"Come on." I lead Steel back the way we'd come. The wind dips under the neckline of my bodice at my back and I rub my arms.

"What do you mean, change it?" Steel asks again.

"When I performed the ritual to summon you," I explain, "I saw something on the floor. It looked like another segment of the spell but...wiped away, as though someone had washed it clean."

"It *would* be easier to modify the spell than to undo it completely," he says, slowly. "Still, it would take a lot of power, a lot of experience...I would struggle with it."

"*You* would?"

"I mean..." He stops and scowls at the ground.

I don't want to force him into a confession: the rapport we've built isn't strong, and I need him for what's to come. But silence pools between us, filling the hole that contains his secret. We can't keep going like this, pretending it's not there.

"I know you're not what you say you are," I begin. "If there's anything you can tell me that affects this case, I need to know. Anything else..." Turner wouldn't be happy that I'm saying this. She'd tell me that all information is useful, even if you don't think it will be.

I don't want someone who'll fight every decision I make, who'll make me feel alone even when I'm not. I want a *partner*. Selfish, perhaps, but I can't solve this case by myself. "Anything else can wait," I say, finally.

After a moment, Steel inclines his head. "That's gracious of you. Considering."

"I hope I don't regret it," I add, and the man has the audacity to smirk at me. I huff. "The spell," I remind him.

"Only the diamond class have that kind of power," he says, easily moving past our exchange. "And it would have to be a strong demon, to craft an extension of the spell that doesn't conflict with the rest of it. Magic is like music," he continues, shaping a smooth curve with his hands. "Add the wrong note, the wrong instrument, and the whole thing will crack. The right notes, and it will resonate beautifully."

"Only diamond has that kind of power." Part of me wants to take back what I just promised.

Steel flushes. "You said if it didn't relate to the case—"

"I know." I shake my head again, more at myself than at Steel. "Fine. How do we know if the spell was modified?"

"I'd have to see this stain you mentioned."

The ritual room is locked when not in use, a way to protect the agency from the remnants of any magic left simmering after the spell is cast. Only Monaghan's key can open it without risking a painful death.

"We'll go to the professor tomorrow," I say. "Ask him for permission to inspect the ritual."

Steel pulls a delicate gold fob watch from his pocket—I'm pretty sure Maia didn't give that to him, so he must have swiped it from a guest—and tilts his head, his raven's mask making the action almost comical. "Today, you mean. It's almost one in the morning."

I pull off my mask so I can give him a dry look. "Today, then."

He drops the watch back into his pocket, regarding me. "And if he doesn't believe us? What will you do?"

"I'll cross that bridge if we reach it."

Maia wakes me before lunch, picking up my dress from the chair I'd draped it over and tutting over the wrinkles in the satin. "You take well enough care of your other things; I would expect you to take better care of this."

"I'm sorry," I reply, getting up to wash and don my old wool jacket and skirt. "I forgot about it." My response is absent, my mind turning over phrases to use for Monaghan, ways to explain what I saw.

"Is everything all right?" Maia asks, gazing at me with sharp eyes.

"Yes. Of course." I hold her gaze, my suspicion against Isis squirming in my chest, a living secret.

"Are you having lunch?"

"Yes. Of—in a few minutes," I say, stopping myself before I parrot my own response.

Maia's gaze is appraising, and I doubt I'll be able to keep much from her for long. She's been here for too many years not to smell a secret. "I will see you in a few minutes, then," she replies. Once she hangs up my clothes, she leaves, and I knock on Steel's door.

He opens it almost immediately, dressed in a navy suit with a cravat that pools over his chest like a waterfall of churned cream. Whatever was about to say is diverted by the sight. "Are those new clothes?"

"I asked Maia for a couple more suits when you weren't paying attention. You've been getting so many new dresses, I felt left out."

"We have better things to do than dress up."

"Is that why you're wearing that old thing?"

My lips threaten to turn up in a smile. "No. My new dress is being cleaned," I admit and turn on my heel to the sound of his breathy chuckle.

Steel follows me through our wing to Monaghan's study on the first floor. My heart beats rabbit quick. Once we tell him what we saw, he'll give us the key. He has to, even if that means drawing down suspicion on his own agency. What other choice does he have?

But when we reach Monaghan's study, Miller shakes his head. "I'm sorry, Miss Locke. The professor is at an event with the Home Office. He won't be back until late."

Stupidly, I hadn't prepared for him not to be here, and my mouth hangs open. Steel recovers quicker. "We just have to leave him a report," he says. "We can drop it on his desk."

"I'm afraid he has locked the study and taken the keys with him," the assistant replies. I can't help but remember the introduction letter we forged for the library. Did Monaghan notice something out of place?

"When will he return?" I ask.

The man shrugs. "I don't expect him until the early hours of the morning, if at all."

I set my teeth. The delay means yet more time when the killer—Isis—could strike again. "Do you have the agents' schedules? I'd like to ask them for some advice on the Whitechapel case."

"Uh, yes, I do." He shuffles a few papers around and then hands me a sheet marked with pencil grids and notes in his tiny, cramped hand. "Let me know if you'd like me to schedule a meeting."

"Thank you, I will." I incline my head and walk away, examining the schedule.

It's a table marked with the days of the week and the dates. Agents' names run down the column to the left, including my own, right at the bottom. Khurana's squares for the next couple of days are blank. At least she'll be here, where we can keep an eye on her.

"Now what?" Steel asks, reading the schedule over my shoulder.

I hand it to him. "Lunch. Then we'll come back tomorrow."

Steel hums. He walks with a light spring, a kind of buoyancy I don't remember seeing before.

"You're enjoying this," I realise.

"I like a hunt, and this is shaping up to be a good one." He winces. "Not that I mean the murders, just that—I didn't think solving them would be this interesting."

"Welcome to my world," I reply, with a tiny smile. I recall Monaghan's instruction to report back on Steel's abilities. The demon's knowledge of magic would certainly be of interest to him. I file that thought away, unsure yet how to tackle it. If the professor thinks Steel might be able to help maintain and improve the ritual, he won't be inclined to set him free.

"That doesn't mean I'm going to change my mind," Steel adds, "about our deal."

"I know." We both fall silent. If the ritual *can* be changed to allow for demons to travel beyond the boundary limit, then there's no reason why I couldn't do the same for Steel. I put that thought right next to the other one. I'm not ready to face it. Not when the Ripper is still out there.

We pass Clara on our way to the kitchen, carrying a tray for Miller. She scowls at me and sweeps past so quickly that I have to duck out of her way or be bowled over.

If it wasn't Clara who changed the ingredients of my spell, then it must have been Isis. To prevent another Hound from being summoned? Was she that afraid of being sniffed out?

Maia isn't in the kitchen when we arrive, but Eve is. I take a bowl of fragrant stew, but instead of the potato parings and wilting cabbage that I expect, my bowl is filled with diced lamb, fresh tomatoes and carrots. Another, smaller pot holds what looks like diced potato and onions. "This is impressive," I murmur, making my way to Eve, who's already finished and is now laying out a series of playing cards.

"It seems that Head Office has given us a bonus," Eve says, examining the layout of her cards. "Maia went out this morning and bought more meat and vegetables than she knows what to do with."

I eat quietly, watching her sort cards into their suits. My stomach ties itself into a clump of suspicion and guilt and finally I put my stew aside. "I need to ask you a question."

Eve glances at me. Her hair is loose, today, a dark cloud around her face. "Oh? What?"

The suspicion crowds into my mouth, desperate to burst out. No one is closer to Khurana than Eve, so I doubt she'll take my accusation lightly. I wouldn't, if it was Turner. I phrase my question as carefully as possible. "The nights of the first two murders," I begin, "Nichols and Chapman. Khurana was in Bristol then, wasn't she?"

Eve's hand pauses in laying down a card. She taps its edge on the table. "Why are you asking me this?"

I mirror her posture, returning her look for as honest a one as I can. "You know why."

"I don't," she replies, as sharp as a sabre. "Because if I did, I'd think that you suspect her of something. *Khurana.* The greatest agent we've ever had."

"It's not Khurana I suspect." I hadn't wanted to come at this so directly, but it was out, now. "Was Isis there? On those nights?"

"*What?*" Eve stands and a handful of cards go fluttering to the floor. "You suspect *Isis*? Hazel, you know what the spell does; it's impossible for demons to leave us." She gestures at Steel as she speaks.

The demon is watching her. "True," he says, "but you haven't actually answered the question."

Eve snorts. "Because that question does not deserve an answer."

"Were they with you the whole time?" She turns on me and I raise my hands. "I have to know, Eve. I have to do my job."

"I know them better than anyone," she replies, stiffly. "She wouldn't do this. You're just clutching at straws because you haven't caught the killer yet. You'd accuse anyone if it meant you could get justice for Turner."

"Eve—"

"Perhaps you should stop listening to him," she overrides me, pointing at Steel, "and start listening to the people who *know* you. Or did you come up with this theory all by yourself?" She laughs at my expression; a hard, scornful laugh. "I didn't think so." She strides out of the kitchen, leaving her cards scattered over the floor and her words hanging in the air.

I sigh and slump over the table. "That was not how I'd hoped that would go."

Steel gathers up the cards and shuffles them with a flicker of dexterous skill. "I didn't realise letting her in on our suspicions was part of the plan."

"It wasn't." I shouldn't have said anything. "Now she'll tell Khurana."

"I don't know." He lays out the cards in a new game. "Telling her would mean turning against you. I'd say we have a few days for her loyalties to go to war before one of them wins out."

"That's not comforting."

"Isn't it? My apologies."

Now we have another reason to get into the ritual room sooner rather than later. I watch Steel discard a series of hearts and pick up a diamond. He was right, though: she never did answer my question.

CHAPTER FORTY-NINE

Monaghan doesn't return that night, or the next. The hours trickle by, a finite amount of sand that will run out before I can capture the killer. On the third day, I rise with determination and the faint trappings of a plan. I can't wait any longer; we need that key.

I go to the library first, to the small weapons display near the component room. It holds a handful of serrated knives of varying lengths and widths, as well as a bunch of small metal stalks, each with a shaped tip. I take them all and drop them into my jacket pocket. Steel is clearly intrigued but seems content to follow me to the kitchen in silence.

"Maia." The woman steps back from the fire and from the steaming pot hanging over it. She's alone. "I need to ask you for a favour," I add.

"A favour? That does sound ominous." Her smile dies at the expression on my face. "What manner of favour?" she asks, seriously.

"Can you call Miller down here for lunch? Or to the dining room?"

"Clara takes him a tray," she replies. "He does not like to leave his desk."

"I know. That's why I'm asking."

Her eyebrows arch up towards her hairline. "And the professor is not here."

"Yes," I confirm, though it wasn't a question.

She wipes her hands on her apron and regards me for a long moment. Then she nods. "Very well. I will make up some excuse. He eats little, though. You will not have much time."

"Can you stall him?"

Maia clicks her tongue. "For an hour, perhaps. I do not think he will stay any longer."

"We don't need much time, we just—"

"Do not," she says, raising a hand. "It is better if I do not know. Be careful, yes?"

"We will."

I hurry back to the first floor—I want to be nearby when the man's called away. We need as much time as we can get. The back of my neck burns under Steel's gaze.

"What is it?" I ask, without looking back.

"Are you planning what I think you're planning?"

"That depends. How good are you with locks?"

He draws level with me as we reach the first floor. Together, we dip into a small parlour before Miller sees us. Steel flexes his hands. "I can break one, if that's what you mean. It won't be subtle, though."

"I suppose I should know better than to hope for subtlety from you," I reply, and he mutters a semi-aggrieved, "Ouch."

We'll have an hour to take the key, inspect the ritual, and return it without Miller discovering us. If I can do it without breaking the lock, we won't leave a trail, and if we get back in time, no one will be any wiser.

My stomach coils. That's far more ifs than I'm comfortable with.

We wait inside the parlour, the door ajar. Maia arrives a little past eleven, wielding a tall wooden duster that bristles with tawny feathers. She drifts down the corridor, making a light effort at sweeping up non-existent cobwebs. I watch through the gap of the door as she reaches Miller. They exchange a few words; the assistant frowns and she shrugs. He shrugs back and smiles at her. She nods and moves on with her dusting. He returns to his work. I lean against the wall and wait.

An hour later, when Steel has paced the length of the room, its width and then its diagonals, twice, Miller shuffles his papers. I tilt my head to the corridor and Steel comes up beside me. The man taps the sheets into alignment and then stands. A few more adjustments—he's as fastidious as Monaghan—and then he walks down the corridor towards us. I retreat from the open doorway and hold my breath as he passes. Steel goes to move, and I fist a hand in his jacket, wait for the click of footsteps to reach the bottom of the stairs. Then I nod.

We move swiftly down the passage. The door to Monaghan's study looms at the end. I fish out the lock picks I took from the library.

"Can you use those?" Steel whispers.

"We'll find out."

I kneel in front of the door, holding two of them in hands that tremble. I fit one into the lock and twist the other inside. All apprentices have a go at locks, when we first arrive, but it's been years since I last practised. Turner had never been big on lock-picking. She'd always bribed or blustered her way through a locked door, so I don't have the skills with the tools that I should. I bite the insides of my cheeks and hold my breath.

The pick clicks against the metal of the lock. Each click makes me think it's the one, that it's the lock turning. Each one is a disappointment.

Steel pulls out his stolen watch. "It's been three minutes," he says, calmly.

My pulse speeds up in response. We still need to find the key, get down to the basement, examine the ritual and then get back up before Miller returns. I try a different pick with a hook at the end. Push in, twist, hold my breath.

"Five minutes," Steel murmurs.

Damn it. I strain my ears for the sound of the lock, and my knuckles go white where I'm clutching the picks tightly enough to feel the slightest vibration.

"Seven."

It's taking too long. Even if I somehow stumble onto the right pressure point, I have no idea how long it will take to find it. I make a decision and stand. "Break it," I tell Steel.

He quirks an eyebrow even as he drops the watch back into his jacket. "Are you sure? We won't be able to hide it." He's already moving to the door, and his confidence in my direction eases some of the tightness in my chest.

"I'm sure."

Steel wraps pale fingers around the handle. He yanks, and the door clacks and shudders in its frame. The handle comes away in his palm. "Uh. Well, the door's unlocked," he says and pushes it open with a finger.

"Yes, I can see that," I mutter and slip inside. "Honestly."

I survey Monaghan's study. His large mahogany desk looks the same as it always does, and the shelves are lined with books and ledgers. If I wanted to hide the key, I'd put it somewhere safe, somewhere important. Somewhere no one would expect it to be.

I rifle through the drawers of his desk, find a handful of opened letters, most stamped with the Home Office seal. No sign of a key. There's a slender, pretty vase on one of the shelves; it's empty. I realise Steel is examining the room with the same keen gaze.

"The books?" he asks.

If it were me, I might hollow out a book and place the key inside, but that doesn't feel like Monaghan's style. My gaze I drawn to his desk. There's only one important thing in the room.

I pick up the portrait on his desk in its heavy silver frame, stare at the girl's brown eyes and golden waves. Swallowing, I turn it over and unhook the back. Between the frame and the painting is a delicate key. I meet Steel's gaze.

He nods. "Time to go."

"Right." I fasten the frame back on and place the portrait where it was. Steel pulls the door closed behind us and awkwardly wedges the handle in place. I pull him away. "That'll do for now. We'll come back." I'll figure out what to do with it, then.

We rush downstairs. A murmur of voices come from the dining hall: Maia and the assistant. I slow our pace. Inching closer to the open door, I peer around the threshold. Maia holds a plate for the man, who's sitting at a table, waiting. She talks solidly, gesturing with her other hand, not letting him get in a word edgewise. He reaches for the plate and she goes to hand it him. It slips out of her grasp at the last minute and hits the floor, splattering food over the floor.

"Oh, I am so sorry," she says, loud enough I can hear her from the corridor. "I will clean this and get you a fresh plate." Miller waves off her apologies, his cheeks flushing pink.

She bends to pick up the shards of porcelain and I pull Steel across the corridor to the basement door. The key fits smoothly into its lock and the door opens with a faint creak, the magic that clings to the wood dispersing. I hold it steady as we enter the tunnel and then push it shut.

The torches are unlit, the passage silent save for our breathing. "I can't see anything," I mutter.

"Here." Steel takes my arm and places my hand on his shoulder. It's a slight stretch for my muscles and I'm reminded again of his height. "My eyes are more suited to this."

He leads me through the pitch-black tunnel. I grip his shoulder, trying not to squeeze too hard. In dim torchlight, this place was unnerving; in darkness, it's frightening.

Steel walks and I stumble down the slope that leads to the ritual room. Then a pressure in the air vanishes and I sense a large empty space around us.

I let go of Steel's shoulder and shuffle into the middle. The urn's cold metal rim bumps against my thighs.

"We'll need light to see the ritual," I say, crouching and sweeping my hand underneath. Ah. "Here." I lift the small box of tinder and flint.

Steel takes it from my hand. A moment later comes a hiss and a flare of light. One of the torches nailed to the stone columns lights up. Steel pulls the torch from its bracket and joins me at the urn. Blood patterns fan out around us, whorls and angles and symbols I can't begin to unpick.

"Show me what you saw," he says.

I take him to the place I'd stood when we performed the ritual. The memory leaps fresh into my mind with the crackle of fire and the scent of ash and decaying roses. I swallow and squat by the urn. "Here."

The faint outline of blood is still there. Steel brings the torch closer, and its light reveals the muted contours of a symbol, stained into the stone.

"It's relatively recent," Steel says. "Maybe twenty years or so, but it's been used at least once more since it was first inscribed." He runs his hand over the stain. "Demon blood," he adds. "And...human, too. A powerful mix."

"How much farther does it extend the boundary?"

He frowns. "It's not an extension," he says, mapping the symbol with his fingers. "I think it's a trigger."

"For what?"

"To dissolve it." He rests his elbows on his knees. "With this, the spell itself remains intact but the boundary no longer exists."

"So, when the ritual was performed, a demon was summoned without a boundary?"

Steel stands instead of immediately replying. He circles the urn, examining the bloodwriting. "I don't think it would be limited to a summons ritual. Someone could have performed the spell outside it."

"I'm not sure what you mean."

"It could have been performed after the demon was summoned," he explains. "It could have been performed any time in the last—however long Isis has been here."

So, she *could* have returned to London without Khurana, to commit the murders. But why?

I glance up at Steel to ask the question. He stares at the glyphs with a look on his face that can only be described as yearning. I swallow the question. "Could you replicate it?" I ask, instead.

His gaze darts to me. "Yes." His throat bobs. "At least, I believe I can."

I hesitate, and then say, "We have to get this key back to the study before anyone finds out we took it."

Hope seeps from his expression.

"Our first priority is the case," I remind him, keeping my thoughts from my face. The answer to our deal is right here: Steel's freedom. I can't withhold it from him. "But I haven't forgotten our deal, either," I add. "Once we've caught Isis, we can return and perform this ritual."

The look he gives me is unreadable. "You'd let me leave?"

"I don't want to keep you here against your will." I trail my hand over the rim of the urn. The cold bites into my fingertips. I try not to think beyond Steel's freedom, try not to wonder what it will mean for me. "Now that we have the power to change that," I say, "I'm hardly going to deny it to you."

"That's a promise?" he asks, with a mocking lilt to the words that I suspect is a shield rather than a sword.

"It's a promise," I agree. "Now, let's get out of here."

"Couldn't have said it better myself."

Steel snuffs out the torch and we sneak back upstairs. I don't know how long we took in the ritual room and Steel doesn't pull out his fob to check. Quickly I replace the key in its portrait and get out of the study. The handle, though...

"You weren't lying."

Steel shrugs. "Subtlety does not come easily to me." There's no way to disguise or conceal it. Miller will be able to tell as soon as he returns, and he'll suspect anyone in the agency.

So, we need to not be in the agency. "Mrs. Stewart," I say aloud and Steel cocks his head.

"The agent's wife? What does she—"

"Hurry."

"Hurry *where*? What are we—"

"I'll tell you in a minute," I whisper. "Just go."

I rush him down the stairs again. We make it to the entrance just as I hear the assistant's voice drift closer to the door of the dining hall.

"Thank you, Maia, but I really must return to work—"

I push Steel outside, closing the front door as quietly as I can behind us, and drag him down the road. He grumbles a complaint but keeps pace until we're a few streets away.

"*Now* will you tell me what's going on?"

"We left before lunch," I reply. "We weren't there when Monaghan's study was broken into."

Steel considers that. "He won't buy it. We've been asking to see him for three days, and now his locked door has been mysteriously opened? It's too coincidental."

"It doesn't matter if he suspects us, it only matters if he has evidence. And he doesn't." I tuck my hands into my sleeves for warmth. The winter chill has hit the city hard, and I expect we'll see snow by Christmas. "Speaking of evidence," I add, "we need it. For Khurana."

"The ritual wasn't enough?"

"Not to convict her demon of multiple murders. We need absolute proof."

"I assume you have a plan for how to get it," he says, eyeing me sidelong.

"Not a great one. We'll have to search her rooms." And if we're caught, she'll have a good reason to turn her blade against us.

Steel pulls out the agent schedule that the assistant gave us a few days ago. "She's at New Scotland Yard on Wednesday," he reads. "They'll both be away."

"Wednesday, then." At least we won't have to wait long.

CHAPTER FIFTY

Swallowing, I smooth down my wool jacket. It's half past ten and Khurana's appointment at New Scotland Yard was on the hour. She should be gone by now.

The muted sounds of the street accompany us as I lead Steel through the corridor and to the other wing. I pass Turner's old room and my skin prickles with gooseflesh. I hope she's proud of me. Even if I am turning against one of our own.

Next is Khurana's room. I stop outside her door, and press up against it, listening. Nothing. I glance at Steel and he shakes his head. Bracing myself, I grip the handle and push.

The door swings open on an empty room. My chest deflates in a rush of breath. No celebrating yet—that was the easy part.

I move inside, pushing the door to, but not closing it. It's a small room warmed by a lit fire, and the furniture is basic, cheap. There aren't many places to hide a secret.

"If you hear anyone coming—"

"I'll let you know," Steel replies, before I can complete the sentence. "What are we looking for?"

"Something to tie Isis to the site of the murders. Blood on her clothes; a weapon; something like that."

He nods and starts rifling through a small wardrobe. I approach a pallet bed that's been set up under the window. Its bedding is pulled taut around the mattress, as if it hasn't been used in days. I push my hand underneath, search in the space between the mattress and the wooden frame. My hand comes back empty.

"I don't think there's anything here," Steel mutters. He shakes free of a generous silk skirt and scowls at it.

"Try the books." There are a handful, stacked in a pile by the bed.

I hurry to the dresser. A metal bowl filled with clear water sits beside a horsehair brush and a handful of pewter cosmetics tins where metal peacocks strut over fields of lotus flowers. I search each drawer, finding blouses and a few silk chemises. All clean, all normal.

"I can't read these."

Steel stands with a book open in his hand. At my look he flashes me the pages. It's a Punjabi script.

"I don't know it," I admit. "Leave them, we don't have time."

He nods and moves on to the next book, shaking it to see if anything falls out.

The bed lies nestled in a corner next to a small hearth. Its low fire crackles, heating my skin. Unlike the pallet, the bed is made, but rumpled. Both pillows hold an indentation. I sweep my hand under them and my fingers meet a book. I pull it out.

It's a miniature notebook, smaller even than Turner's, designed to be kept close. I let it fall open and gasp. A charcoal woman stretches over the pages. The sketch is a silhouette, hinting at the curve of her hip and the swell of naked breasts. Desire permeates each black line. But it's the long, unbound hair and the simple bracelet around her wrist that catches my eye. This is Khurana.

I look at the bed again, the indentations in both pillows, the pallet bed that hasn't been slept in.

"What is it?" Steel comes over to stand at my shoulder. "That's...racy."

"They're involved." If Monaghan knows about this...

He can't know. He would have separated them by now, if he did.

"Perhaps that's why they changed the ritual," Steel suggests. "To allow Isis more freedom."

"Or she manipulated Khurana into thinking that way." Silence answers me and I realise how that must have sounded. "I doubt that's the case," I add, quickly, "but we should consider the possibility."

"Perhaps."

I flip through the book. More sketches, and what could be poems in a variety of languages. Then, near the back, a double spread of pages filled with looping black curves. "Wait. Look." It's the same image that's sketched in blood five floors below us—the same except for one additional symbol, a glyph I've never seen before.

Steel holds a corner of the book, peering at the image. "That's interesting. I hadn't thought to—" He seems to become conscious of my gaze and swallows. "This is the alteration."

"Could you—"

"What are you doing?"

I whip around. Rayne stands in the doorway.

For a moment I can't speak, my throat a vice. I cough and stride from the bed, tucking the notebook into the small of my back to hide it. "I thought I heard something," I lie. "We came to investigate."

Rayne examines me and then Steel. "Is that so?" He takes a few steps into the room, the firelight catching on his sable hair. He's alone.

I stiffen, but before I can move there's a brush of air at my back.

"What's this?" a voice whispers in my ear. The book is plucked out of my hand.

"Cassius—"

The Phantom demon materialises between me and Steel and pads over to Rayne. He rifles through the book as he walks and his eyebrows climb towards his hairline. "Well, this is interesting."

"Stealing from another agent?" Rayne says. "I thought better of you, Locke. I'll have to report this to Monaghan."

"This isn't what it seems."

"Oh? And what is it *not*, in that case?" the Phantom asks, his blue eyes glinting.

We have to tell them. I glance at Steel. He's glowering at them, his eyes little more than silver slits. "Turn to the end," I direct. "Khurana changed the ritual spell to allow Isis to break the distance limit."

"That's impossible," Rayne replies, but Cassius is already flicking through the pages.

"Now, this *is* interesting." He shows the page to Rayne, who takes the book, frowning.

A long moment passes in strained silence as I watch his gaze move over the two pages. "Amending the spell is impossible," he says.

"Not for a Wraith demon," Steel interjects, his voice low and steady.

"We believe that Isis is not a Hound," I clarify. "We think she's one of the diamond class demons."

Rayne looks between us as though he suspects we're about to reveal the punchline of this joke and he's trying to figure out what it is. "*You* believe this?"

"It's there in the book," I say. "That glyph was painted into the stone downstairs and wiped away. I saw it."

"Wait, you saw it? How? When?"

I fold my fingers into the wool of my skirt, pressing them against my thighs. "We...stole the key to the ritual room."

"*Borrowed*," Steel murmurs.

"This is a lot to take in." Rayne shuts the book and strides to the hearth, stares into the fire. Cassius tilts his head and watches the man with an amused slant to his mouth. "Say that I believe you," Rayne continues. "This drawing isn't evidence of anything, and you cannot accuse another agent without proof."

"I know," I reply, my pulse kicking up. He believes us. "That's why we came. We can keep looking—"

He holds up the book, stopping me. "Before we do anything else, we need to speak to Monaghan," he says. "This is an internal investigation. He needs to know."

"Very well." It will be a relief to tell him. It's already a relief that Rayne knows. That I'm not alone in this.

"He's due to return tonight. Meet me outside his study at ten this evening. We'll tell him together."

"Thank you."

He gives me a wry smile. "I wish you'd come to me sooner, but then I suppose I didn't give you reason to." He taps the book against his other hand. "I'd like to examine this ritual drawing, if it's all right. I'll bring it to the study later."

I nod. "We'll see you at ten."

"At ten," he confirms.

I tow Steel out of the room, leaving them in silence.

"If he gets all the credit," Steel mutters, as we descend to the first-floor library to wait, "I'm not going to be happy."

"Credit isn't important. Catching the killer is." And with my own words I'm reminded of what's at stake, of the potential repercussions of what we're about to do. What will happen to Khurana, when we tell Monaghan?

I can't suppress the feeling that somehow I've failed.

CHAPTER FIFTY-ONE

At ten that evening, I cross the agency to Monaghan's study. The building has been burdened with silence all day, and every breath I take feels loaded.

Miller isn't at his desk—he must have retired for the night—but Rayne and his demon are waiting outside Monaghan's study. Cassius sees us and murmurs something to the agent.

Rayne greets me with a smile. "There you are."

"Are we late?"

"No, you're right on time." He runs his hand through his hair, dishevelling its pomade. "Well. Let's get to it. Start with what you saw, the night of the party," he advises.

I nod, taking a deep breath. This is my chance to prove that I deserve to be here, that I have earned the right to stand next to Rayne and call myself an agent.

He and Cassius enter the study first, and I follow them inside.

Monaghan sits at his desk, both hands clasped together over the wood. The portrait on his desk is gone. Movement at my side draws my attention: Tiberius closes the door behind us.

He regards me with an impassive stare. I move to stand beside Rayne.

"Sir," I greet.

The professor acknowledges my greeting with a dip of his head. "Agent Locke." He glances at Rayne and then at me, a faint frown between his brows. "Why don't you tell me what this is all about?"

I exhale slowly, shed any emotion that might colour my theory. Stay clear and concise. "At the party on the thirty-first of October, I saw Isis outside the spell's boundary," I begin. "I believe that she is a Wraith demon, and that she amended the ritual. I don't know why," I add, "but in light of the recent murders, we have to investigate this fully."

Monaghan's frown deepens. "If I understand correctly, you are insinuating that Isis—and by extension, Khurana—has something to do with the Whitechapel murders?"

"Possibly, yes."

He sits back, one hand spread on the desk as if to anchor himself. "This is a serious accusation."

I swallow and rub my fingers against my thumbs. "I am aware of that, sir. I would not make it without due cause."

"Locke," he says, after a long moment, "I appreciate your passion, but Khurana has been with us for years. Do you have any evidence to back up your theory?"

It's understandable he'd doubt me. *I'd* doubt me. "Yes. I found a book in her room that details the amendment to the spell."

Interest flickers over his face. "Really?"

"Yes." I turn to Rayne. "Show him."

Rayne's brows crinkle. "Show him what?"

"The book I gave you in Khurana's room," I reply, bemused.

"I'm sorry, sir," Rayne says to Monaghan. He spreads his hands, palm up. "I don't know what she's talking about."

The world slips sideways. My chest hollows and fills with cold.

"I requested this meeting," Rayne continues, ignoring my stare, "because I found Miss Locke and her demon snooping around in Khurana's room. I was concerned. Now, I see that I have reason to be."

"No, that's not—" My stomach tries to make a break for my throat. I press a hand to my abdomen, try to hold myself still. Calm. "Professor, we found a notebook that demonstrated the change in the spell. I gave it to Rayne."

Rayne makes an apologetic face. "I'm sorry, Miss Locke. You gave me nothing."

My gaze flicks to Cassius.

The demon shrugs. "It's news to me," he says, no sign of a lie on his face.

"They're both lying." Steel steps towards Rayne and Tiberius jerks him back, Reaper strength in every line of his body. "Let *go*, you—"

"Silence." Monaghan's gaze, as hard as emerald, dismisses Steel and returns to me. "This agency does not tolerate baseless accusations."

"They're not baseless, I—"

"Sir," Rayne cuts in. "I think we need to consider the fact that this case has been too much for Miss Locke."

"What?" I can't contain the edge of breathless confusion in the word.

"When I came across her in Agent Khurana's room," he continues, "she told me that she broke into your study and stole the key to the ritual room."

Monaghan looks at me. "Is this true?"

"I—" I look frantically between the two of them, the professor's stony gaze and Rayne's falsely apologetic one. "Sir, I had to see the spell to confirm—"

The professor draws his hands away from the desk. "I see."

"Not to mention this habit of dressing in male clothing," Rayne adds. Why is he still speaking? "Breaking into your study, then Khurana's room, and now this paranoia. Did you suspect the rest of us," he asks me, "before you came up with this story about Isis?"

"That's—" I can't even say it's not true. "You're twisting everything."

"This case is highly disturbing," Rayne goes on. "I did my best to keep Miss Locke from experiencing the worst, but she continually put herself into situations where she'd be confronted by the gruesome nature of these murders. I fear the images have overpowered her mind."

How dare he? How *dare* he? "You don't know what you're talking about." My hand trembles against my stomach. "I worked so hard on this case—"

"Which we understand," Rayne soothes. "I'm sure you thought the work you were doing was helpful."

"It *is* helpful."

The agent raises his hands in a calming gesture. "Please, Miss Locke. There is no need to become hysterical."

"I am not hysterical!"

"You were an apprentice for seven years, weren't you?" Rayne asks. "You felt it was too long to wait. You wanted the attention that came with being an agent."

"No, of course not—"

"I wouldn't be surprised if you sabotaged your own ritual." He shakes his head, as if he's disappointed. *Disappointed.* "God," he says, then, his eyes widening, "you didn't—did Turner find out you wanted to take her place? Did you...did you *do* something to her?"

I slap him.

The sharp crack cuts through my fog of anger. Monaghan is on his feet, staring at me. Horror swells in my chest. What have I done? "I..."

"Physical violence is often the first sign of insanity," Rayne says, touching his cheek and wincing. "I should have known better than to let her visit the crime scenes. The sight of the bodies—I apologise, professor."

The floor has fallen out from under my feet. Everything is unravelling. "That's not true," I say, but my voice is thin and high and weak.

"Locke," Monaghan says and then goes silent, shakes his head.

"I think we should put her in her room." Rayne's pale skin is blooming with red. With the imprint of *my hand*. "At least for a day or so," he adds. "Until we can summon a doctor."

"I do not need a doctor," I reply, shaking all over. "Monaghan, sir, I—"

He raises a hand, stops me mid-sentence. "I think it's for the best," he says, lowly, and my stomach drops into my shoes. "We cannot allow this kind of behaviour in a government establishment. Rayne, will you escort her?"

"Yes, of course."

Steel makes a sharp movement towards the desk. "Down, dog," Tiberius growls, with more malice than I've ever heard from him. "If that is what you truly are."

Rayne's hand lands on the back of my neck like a collar. I shudder. "Come along," he tells Steel. "Let's not make this unpleasant."

"It will only be for a few days," Monaghan adds. He does not meet my eyes. "I will summon a doctor as soon as I can."

If we try to fight, we'll lose. If we try to run, we'll lose.

Swallowing, my eyes burning, I whisper, "Steel."

He looks at me, his mouth tight. At first I think he's going to ignore me, but then his posture eases. "Fine," he mutters and glares at Tiberius. "But I won't forget this."

Cassius collects him, pulling him out of the room. "Come along, little dragon."

Rayne's hand is a guiding pressure on my nape. I try to look back at Monaghan, but he propels me outside and shuts the door on any hope of rescue.

CHAPTER FIFTY-TWO

My stomach curdles with rage and shame and shock. Everything I did, everything I'd planned so carefully—all of it played right into his hands.

"What did you do with the book?" I ask, through gritted teeth.

Rayne walks beside me, his hand still a heavy sickening pressure on my neck. "I don't know what you're talking about."

"Are you going to try and use it?" No, that's not his style. He wants Cassius where he can control him. I recall the way he'd tapped it against his hand, the light of Khurana's hearth warming his face. "You burnt it, didn't you?"

Rayne's gaze slides to me, cool and amused.

"You *monster*."

"Please, Miss Locke," he says. "This really is for your benefit."

We reach our corridor and my heart lurches. Standing by our rooms are Jacob, Max and Eve. Thank God. They can help us. "Eve—" I say, desperate.

"Thank you for meeting me," Rayne interrupts, in grave tones. "I understand how difficult this must be for all of you."

What?

"Are you sure this is wise?" Jacob asks, shifting from foot to foot. "I don't think—"

"Eve, you heard her accusation towards Khurana, didn't you?" Rayne inclines his head towards her. "Do you really think Miss Locke is in her right mind? Would the girl you know ever suggest that Khurana betrayed us?"

Jacob drops his gaze, avoiding my eyes. Even Max stares at a point over my head.

I stare beseechingly at my friend. Eve rubs her lips together and sighs. "She needs to see a doctor," she tells Jacob. "If nothing else than to rule out an illness."

"Precisely." Rayne opens the door and brings me inside. I hear Steel and Cassius' footsteps behind me and then the click of the door. I'm released.

The anger has burned through me, leaving only dread. And betrayal. "You thought of everything, didn't you?"

He puts his back to the door, arches his eyebrows. "I am an agent. It's my job to think of everything."

I shut my eyes, but the threat of him looms in the darkness so I open them again quickly. The one question that reverberates through my whole body is *why*, but even as I think it an answer comes back. "It's you, isn't it?"

"You know," Rayne says, "I don't think I would have been surprised if you *had* killed Turner. You always were too smart for your own good. Until now, it seems."

"I would *never* have hurt her. How could you think I would?"

"How do you think he became an agent?" Cassius says, all sharp smile and mocking delight. "I helped, of course. If I'm going to be chained, better to be chained to someone moving up in the world."

"You're a disgrace to your own kind," Steel mutters. He stands with his shoulders drawn tight, his hands clawed.

"Did you sabotage my ritual?" I demand. "Was that you, too?"

Rayne laughs. "Monaghan is an idiot if he thinks having female agents is anything but a disaster. Clara, at least, would have been easy to control. You, on the other hand." He flares his nostrils. "You would have taken this case away from me, would have made the old man think twice about making me his heir."

"That's what this is about? You want to take the agency from Monaghan?"

"Oh, I'm going to take more than that," he replies, silkily. "Monaghan's days away from being appointed Commissioner. It'll be a simple thing to take that, too."

"And then on to Home Office, is that it?" I ask. "The Mayor? The Prime Minister?"

"We'll see."

"I will stop you."

He laughs. "And that's exactly why you're here. I thought you would trip up, sooner or later, but this—you built your own cage and walked right into it. All I had to do was turn the key." He holds up the key to my room, smirking.

"You bastard."

"You never swear, Hazel," he replies and tuts. "Another sign of the dreadful influence this demon holds over you."

Steel flexes his hands. "You can say what you like, but that door won't hold me."

"I don't expect it to." Rayne doesn't even look at Steel, keeps his gaze on me. "It doesn't *need* to. Jacob and Eve will be in that room." He points to the adjoining door. "And they have orders to stop you, if you try to escape. At *any cost*. You wouldn't want either of them to get hurt, would you? Violence, after all, is one of the earliest signs of insanity," he says, again, and his mouth curves into a smile that doesn't reach his eyes. "And we are not equipped to deal with that kind of thing here."

Ice seeps through my veins. "You wouldn't."

"Asylums are not very nice places," he says. "I suggest that you don't give me a reason to put you in one."

"They won't listen to you," I reply, clutching at my last thread of hope.

"Won't they? Won't they believe that your so-called Hound has turned you against us? Made you paranoid and delusional?" He tilts his head. "Really, Miss Locke. You're smarter than that."

Cassius backs away from Steel. "We should go," he says to Rayne.

"I should thank you," he tells me, straightening. "Now that you're taken care of, I can use this conspiracy theory you've dreamt up and be rid of Khurana and her pet." His smile morphs into a flash of white teeth. "Remember. Don't do anything foolish."

With that, he and Cassius leave. The lock of the door is a gunshot in the silence.

The threat against Jacob and Eve forms a more effective prison than any wooden door. I cover my face with my hands. How could I let this happen? Why didn't I see it?

Tears wet my palms. Steel's footsteps are a steady drum as he paces around the room like a caged cat. I wish I was alone so I could break, so I could let the cracks running through me rip me into pieces. I take thin, controlled breaths, hating the wheeze that runs under every exhale.

I don't notice when the pacing stops until fingers brush my shoulder. I jump, feeling the imprint of Rayne's hand on my nape.

It's Steel, leaning over me with a frown. He takes in my tear-stained face without comment. "You should sleep," he tells me.

"I don't know what to do." The words spill out of me. My mind is slow and stupid and hugs the memory of Rayne's smug face as though it wants to impale itself on his teeth.

"Sleep," he says, again. "We can plan in the morning."

I don't want to sleep. I want to sit here and carve my stupidity into my skin until I learn from my failure.

But Steel's right. Such thoughts won't help me. Rest will reset my mind, give me the distance I sorely need. I climb into bed and curl up against the pillows, tucking my arms and legs around me. I'm aware of Steel's presence, but all he does is go to the window and lean against the wall. He stays in my field of vision and I watch him until my eyes drift shut.

Sleep is fickle and gifts me with nonsense dreams that I can't look at too closely. They are thankfully absent of Rayne. Perhaps my mind knows how stretched my control is.

Morning brings a faint light through a gap in the curtains. Steel is curled into a chair, its back to the adjoining door. He must have drawn the curtains in the night. I rise and wash dream sweat from my face. I check that he's asleep and quickly change my clothes. Then I sit with my legs tucked under me on the bed and think. We need to get out of here. We need to find Rayne before he finds Khurana.

Steel stirs, blinking into wakefulness. He stretches, yawns, and stumbles to the window. "We're too high," he murmurs, in a voice still hoarse from sleep. "You'd break your legs if you jumped."

A very small tinge of amusement seeps under the cold dead weight of the rest of me. "Are you awake or sleep walking?"

"Awake." He stretches again as if to emphasise the fact. "I thought we might try the window," he explains, more clearly, "but it's too high." He prowls around the room again, checking both doors. They're still locked. After his circuit, Steel collapses back into his chair.

I lean my head against the wall, watching him from under my lashes. "They'll give you to someone else," I realise, thinking aloud. "Monaghan won't let Rayne get rid of you. You're too interesting—too valuable. He'll give you to another agent."

"And here I thought it couldn't get any worse."

I'm grateful that he's here, that I'm sharing my captivity with his dry humour. "I won't let that happen."

He looks at me with interest. "You've thought of a plan?"

"Not yet." I rub my hands over my face. "Not *yet*," I repeat, with conviction. "I'll think of something." I have to.

A knock interrupts any chance of planning. It comes from the door to the corridor. "Come," Steel orders, rising.

The lock clicks and the door opens a fraction. Maia squeezes through, carrying a tray. Instantly the door shuts behind her.

"Maia," I say, with relief.

"I cannot come any further," she says, with a scowl, and places the tray on the floor. It holds two cups of water and a plate of food. "They told me to leave the tray and go."

"I'm not insane," I tell her, leaning forward, praying she'll believe me. "I never wanted to hurt anyone, Maia."

"I know." Maia's expression is sad but kind. "But Rayne showed us his face. If the others had needed more convincing that you were not acting like yourself, that was enough. I fear there is nothing I can do."

I try to hide my disappointment. "I understand."

"But," she adds, and I look up. "Khurana and Monaghan are with Pemberton tonight. If one was to attempt an escape, that would be the time to do it." She gives me a speaking glance and then raps on the door. It opens and she slips out.

I wonder who's on the other side, if it's Rayne or if it's one of my friends. Despair threatens to overspill the precarious equilibrium I've pieced together, and I discard the thought.

Pemberton lives not far from the East End. Rayne said he wanted to be rid of Khurana. If he's chosen her as his next victim...

Steel picks up the food and offers me the plate. My stomach is twisted into knots. I shake my head.

"We don't know when they're next going to feed us," he points out. "You'd better eat what you can, now."

Reluctantly I take it: bread, cheese, ham, fruit. Nothing we need cutlery for. I eat less than half and hand the rest back to Steel. I watch him eat, a plan—or an idea, not quite a plan—unfolding at the back of my mind.

"Will you tell me what you are?" I ask, when he's finished.

He rests the plate on his knees. "I thought you weren't going to ask me unless it was relevant."

"It just became relevant."

He glances at the window, and for a moment the only sound is the clopping of hooves as a cab passes. I tie my questions to my tongue and wait him out.

"I told you that the old classes were destroyed," he says, frowning at the grey sky. "There was a purge, over a century ago. Whole groups of demons were wiped out. Six Houses remained at the top, all diamond class—the royalty of the demon world. Lucifer's descendants rule, of course. They're a Dragon breed, so they looked on House Leviathan with favour. My House."

"So, you *are* diamond class," I murmur, forgetting my determination to remain silent. I eye him, his long limbs and serpentine eyes. I wonder how I could ever have thought he was a Hound.

He nods. "Leviathan was the second most powerful House in our world. Four months ago, someone changed that." Anger glitters in his expression.

"What happened?"

"My House was murdered. All of them, in a single bid for power." His mouth twists in an unhappy smile. "Now, I'm the only one left."

"And you want to stop the demons who killed them? Keep them from becoming more powerful?" I ask.

A laugh escapes him, dark and strained. "I don't care who sits at the top, I just want vengeance for the people I loved. The rest of them can rot in Hell." He turns a suspicious, resentful look on me, as if he regrets telling his story. "How is this relevant?"

"Can you cast magic?" I ask, instead of replying.

"Not as well as a Wraith, better than a Revenant," he replies, as if that's an answer I'll understand.

I get up, brush non-existent crumbs from my skirt. "We need to escape before Rayne gets to Khurana." There's still the question of Isis, the Wraith, but I can't let Rayne hurt anyone else. We have to find him, first.

"And how, exactly, are we going to escape?" asks Steel, his earlier look dissolving under a flash of amusement.

"Draw the ritual," I tell him. "Use the spell to break the boundary limit. If you leave, the others will be distracted, and I'll escape."

Steel regards me for a long, quiet moment. "Leave?" he repeats.

"Leave," I confirm. My stomach gives another twist at the word, but I have the power to free him, and no reason for him to stay. Even if it means I have to go after Rayne alone. "You said I'd break my legs if I jumped," I continue, gesturing to the window. "But you can make it, can't you?"

He nods.

"They'll chase you, but they won't follow you to Paris. The agency's jurisdiction ends at the sea."

"And what will they do to you," he asks, "when they come back and realise you've escaped?"

"I'll worry about that later." It takes effort to shove that concern aside, and it lingers like cigarette smoke, trying to wind through the tenuous grip I have on my courage.

"I hope you're not expecting me to say no," Steel says, standing. I have to look up to hold his gaze. His face is as expressionless as the night I first summoned him.

"I'm not." I offer him a wry smile. "I wouldn't, if I were in your position."

He inhales through his nose and then lets out a slow breath. "Very well. Let's begin."

CHAPTER FIFTY-THREE

"What do you need?" I ask and Steel circles the room, examining the furniture with a critical eye.

"Blood. A lot of it."

"Oh."

"And space."

That is an easier request. I put my shoulders to the bed and push it up against the wall. Its metal feet scrape over the wood floor and I pause. The door remains closed. I sigh in relief. If someone comes in now, I couldn't form an explanation that anyone would believe. They'd lock Steel into the adjoining room and keep us separated. I can only assume they haven't done that yet because Rayne doesn't expect us to try and escape.

And because they don't believe that I *could*.

Everything feels distant, as though I'm directing someone else to move the bed, someone else to stand out of Steel's way as he walks the lines of the spell. As though it's someone else defying the agency, not me. My pulse beats rapidly but where I expect my hands to shake, they're steady.

What will happen if I *do* catch Rayne? Will Monaghan let me stay? Could I partner with another demon if the ritual is still tied to Steel?

Would I want to?

"All right," Steel says, saving me from answering that question. "Now for the blood." He shoves open the window a few inches and tosses out the water I use for washing. Then he sets the bowl on the bed and indicates that I should sit next to it.

I perch on the blanket by the bowl. The copper looks dark in my shadow, black and bottomless. I gulp. "We don't have a blade," I say, stuck on the practicality of the thing, trying not to think about how it will feel.

"We don't need one." Steel grips the plate in both hands and snaps it into two pieces. He breaks one of the pieces with a crack, and then again, until he has a jagged slice of sharp porcelain.

"Ah. I see."

He holds his left wrist over the bowl, takes the triangular edge of the porcelain and runs it down the line of his vein. His skin opens in its wake, a thin river of blood. I glance at his face, but any pain that he feels is tucked away behind an impassive expression. Blood pours over his arm and into the bowl. *Lots* of blood.

But as I think it the skin closes up, following the line the porcelain took.

"You heal quickly."

"Mm."

Then I frown. "Your shoulder took days to heal."

His mouth twitches. "Her sword is blessed. And I may have exaggerated." I glare at him and he shrugs. "You would have suspected me much sooner."

"That hardly helped my investigation." I'm stalling. Swallowing, I hold out my hand to take the makeshift knife.

"I would do it for you," Steel says, "but…"

"You can't hurt me. I know."

He exhales and hands me the shard. "The spell will heal you, but we shouldn't go too deep." He grips my wrist gently to brace my arm. His gaze is intent on my skin, metallic eyes glinting from between long strands of dark hair. I hadn't forgotten that he was beautiful, but I'd discarded the thought as irrelevant. Now that he's on the edge of freedom, it returns to me abruptly—uncomfortably, given how close his face is to mine.

I box away my trepidation and start cutting. The slicing pain drives any thought of beauty from my head. I flinch instinctively and his grip tightens, holding me over the bowl so my blood mingles with his.

"Sorry," Steel says, as if *he's* the one carving into my skin.

"Does it need to be human and demon?" I ask, trying to distract myself.

"It works best when it's the blood of the warlock who is casting, and the demon who is being summoned. The binding is stronger."

"But it's the same as the ritual, isn't it? It won't affect us any differently." A pause and I shoot him a look. "Won't it?

"I don't think it will," he replies, in that flippant tone I'm starting to recognise as a bad sign.

"You don't *think* it will."

"Like I said: not as good as a Wraith. That's enough," he adds, before I can give voice to my frantic budding questions. He pulls the shard from my hand (delicately, but my grip is so tight the sharp edges are imprinted into my palm) and tosses it aside. Then he shreds a pillowcase into strips of linen and wraps them around the wound. He takes the bowl, half full with thick crimson liquid, and stands.

I go to stand with him and my head swims. Blinking, I sink back onto the bed. "I don't think I'm going to be much help," I admit.

"This won't take long."

Steel dips his fingers into the blood and crouches to spread it over the floor. He maps out the spell on the wood panelling, smaller than the one downstairs, but the same shape. Our blood pales as he spreads it thin enough to draw all of the symbols. By the time he gets to the final glyph, the odd one that we'd seen in Khurana's notebook, the bowl is almost empty. I clutch my wrapped arm, hoping he doesn't need more.

He stands back from the bloodwriting and nods to himself. "That should do it. Though I would prefer a bull's heart, or a liver, at least." He discards the bowl. "Do you remember the words?"

"Yes." I committed them to memory, that night, and they swim up from my subconscious.

"Good."

He offers me his hand and I take it with a small flicker of sorrow. This is not how I had predicted our partnership to end. Part of me is sad that it is, but the rest...I can't begrudge Steel his freedom.

"Stand here." He positions me within a curl of blood that blooms from the central sphere and then stands inside the sphere, facing me. "I will help direct the magic," he says. "You just need to say the words."

Curling my arm to my chest, feeling its sting, I inhale. Exhale. Remind myself why we're doing this. That the Whitechapel killer is still out there.

I speak the words of the spell quietly, soft enough that no one outside the room will hear. The bloodwriting at our feet flickers. Red blood and gold light, until the red is all gone and there's just a soft glow that lightens the hard lines of Steel's face.

A force tightens around my ribs, as thick as a band of metal. I murmur the last sentence, and gradually the tension dissolves until I can breathe again. The gold fades. Blood is just blood.

I blink, trying to see if anything is different. Then I realise that my arm has stopped stinging. Hastily I unwind the linen. A white scar runs up my inner arm, the only sign of the wound.

"That's interesting," Steel murmurs. I glance up but he isn't looking at me. He tilts his head, his gaze distant. "I see."

"See what?"

"It isn't just a modification to unhinge the boundary," he says, still with that distant gaze. "It's removed the restriction on my magic."

"But you just performed magic."

"Not this kind." He holds out a hand and a few drops of blood, still wet, drift up from the floor and come to rest in his hand, floating an inch over his palm. He exhales, a sigh that seems to come from deep in his core. "That's better."

"You can control *blood*?"

"I control water. Blood is just another form of it, when it's like this." He flicks it away and the blood splatters on the floor. "It's a skill of House Leviathan."

It's the same demon. The same Steel. Just because he can do things like *that* doesn't mean he's changed. Still, unease curls up in my stomach like a stray cat come home.

"It's not a very powerful skill," Steel adds, looking at me. "I can hardly part seas or shift rivers. It's more of a magician's trick."

"Some trick," I say, through a dry mouth.

Something heavy clouds the air, a storm about to break. The bloodwriting flickers again and one of the floorboards buckles. Wood splinters under invisible claws.

Steel mutters a curse. "This room isn't designed to hold magic. It's clinging to the blood."

I seize the cup Maia brought and toss water over the floor. The liquid smears the writing, darkening the wood, until all that's left of the spell is a few dark smudges. The light fades and whatever threatened the air dissolves with it.

"Is it...gone?"

"Enough of it," he replies. He raises his hand to his face, and, under my gaze, his serpentine pupils fatten and grow round, human—or very nearly. They're a fraction too large and the irises a fraction too vibrant.

"More magic?" I ask.

"Just a little." Steel glances at the door, then the window. "Best to get on with it before someone decides we've earned another meal."

I face him. "Are you ready?"

He grins at me with a smoothness I've never seen before, as though a weight has been lifted. I file the image away in the back of my mind, one to pull out when I'm old and grey and want to reminisce about the mysterious, sardonic creature who walked so briefly at my side.

"Are you?" he counters.

"When you break the window, I'll scream," I tell him. "You won't get much of a head start."

He rolls his shoulders. "I don't need one."

"Be careful," I reply, exasperated. "Max is a Reaper, remember? Even if he can't perform magic, he's stronger than you are."

"He's not as fast, though." He actually *winks* at me.

"Fine," I reply, too wound up to roll my eyes. "Just...don't get caught." I hesitate, unsure what a farewell between us should look like. Perhaps it looks like this, a fond wish that he not be captured.

"I hope you find Rayne," he says, seriously.

I give him a half-smile. "Good luck in Paris."

He gazes at me, and I wonder if he, too, is crystallising this moment in his mind to revisit in years to come: the agent who trapped him in a bid to catch a killer. I hope he remembers me kindly, even if I do not deserve to be.

Then he turns and strides to the window. I draw a deep breath, brace myself. He smashes his fist through the glass, and I scream.

CHAPTER FIFTY-FOUR

Steel leaps through the broken window and vanishes. Any sound he might have made hitting the ground is lost as the door crashes open.

Max surges into the room, Jacob crowding in after him. "What is it? What happened?"

I make my breathing shallow and shaky. "The window," I cry, pointing. My hand is too steady, so I pull it to my chest. I stumble backwards until I hit the bed, fold onto it. "Steel, he—he—" I mask the rest with a gasp. The window is broken, and Steel is gone. They should be able to add two and two together and come up with four without my poor acting muddying the situation.

Sure enough, Jacob rushes to the window and leans out. For a second, I fear he'll find Steel's broken body on the pavement, that the demon somehow misjudged the height.

But Jacob curses. "He's gone. Max, can you—"

"I will find him," the demon promises from the doorway, coolly confident. The door he'd burst open dangles from one hinge, and even that is starting to peel off the wall. I pray Steel has enough time to get away.

"Eve, stay here," Jacob commands. "Send word to Rayne that the demon got loose. We'll bring him back." He flees, Max close on his heels.

Eve steps out of his way, and her gaze flicks over the room. Over the floor. "How did he leave?" she asks me, her eyes narrow and her mouth thin.

I tense. "He jumped out of the window—"

"Don't give me that," she snaps. "You know the ritual. You know he can't leave you. So, how did he do it?"

"I don't know."

Her nostrils flare. "What about this?" She waves a flat hand at the floor, at the faint traces of blood just visible on the drying wood.

There's no way to disguise them as anything other than what they are. I stand and reply, evenly, "It's the same spell that Khurana used to release Isis."

Eve shakes her head. "Rayne was right. You're delusional."

"How else can you explain how Steel jumped through that window? Isis isn't who she says she is." I take stock of the room. The bowl Steel had filled with our blood is on the floor, between us. Solid copper. I could knock her out and get away. I flinch at the thought.

"So, you think she's the Ripper?" Eve drags her hand over her forehead. "Or Khurana? They would never do that."

"You're right," I agree. "Rayne is the killer."

"Oh, it's Rayne, now? And how much longer before you think it's Jacob? Or me?"

"Eve, you're not listening—"

"I'm trying to, but you're talking about *agents*. It's not possible, Hazel."

"The evidence—"

"There *is* no evidence," she interrupts. "You're so desperate to find whoever it is that you're turning on *us*."

The words might as well be daggers. "You don't believe me."

She spreads her hands. "How can I? If I had come to you and claimed that Turner was behind this, what would you have said? Would you have believed me?"

No. I knew Turner better than that. The same way she knows Khurana. I glance at the window. The thick bank of clouds glows orange above a setting sun. There's not enough time.

"Please," I say, "let me go."

"I can't." She sucks her bottom lip between her teeth. "I can't disobey the agency. I don't have a choice, Hazel."

"Of course you have a choice—"

"No, I *don't*." She gestures at her face, her textured hair. "Do you think anywhere else would make me an agent? A police officer, even? Do you think they'd let me through the front door? I hate having to rely on Monaghan to *permit me* into his sphere, but if I want to become an agent and protect my people, there is no other way. I don't have a choice, not like you." Eve stops, breathing heavily, her words floating between us like the embers of a banked fire.

"Eve…" I trail off. I don't know what to say; if there *is* anything I can say.

"Look," she says, slowly, holding out her hands as though I'm some wild animal she needs to tame. "When the others return, we'll speak to Khurana and Rayne. We'll get to the bottom of this."

If Rayne comes back and finds Steel gone, he'll have me committed. And by then, it'll be too late. Khurana might already be in danger.

I snatch the porcelain shard from the bed and level it at her. "Let me leave."

"Hazel." Her expression doesn't change, and she doesn't drop her hands. "Don't be a fool."

"I will use this if I have to."

"No, you won't," she replies. "I know you, Hazel. You won't hurt me."

I grit my teeth. *Damn it. She's right, I could never wield this against her.* I turn the blade on myself. It nestles coldly at the base of my throat.

Her eyes widen. "What are you—"

"I told you," I reply, watching her, "I will use this if I have to." I have no intention of slitting my own throat, but I know *her* just as well as she knows me. She won't take the chance. "Turn around," I order.

"Hazel—"

"Do as I say." The porcelain's edge is sharp, and it takes little pressure to prick my skin. A bead of warmth drips to my collarbone.

"Just—for God's sake." Eve whips around, her hands clenching and unclenching at her sides. "Don't do this."

I back away to the open doorway. "My summons bag was changed," I tell her. "Who do you think did that? Who had access to roses and anemones if not the people in this agency?"

She protests but I don't stop to hear the words. I fly down the corridor as quickly and quietly as I can, the makeshift blade clutched in my palm. For whatever reason, whether by my threat or my words, Eve does not follow.

CHAPTER FIFTY-FIVE

Pemberton's house is about two miles from Whitechapel. I keep my head down and cut through the narrow alleys and back streets that wind through the city's heart. A hansom cab trots down the main road and I raise my hood, turning away. The cab might get me to my destination faster, but it won't be hard for the agency to circulate my description to the cab stands.

The stone buildings grow smaller and closer as I near east London. And darker: the sun has dropped out of sight and a cold wind seeps through the fabric of my cloak. I hasten my step.

Gas lamps cast gloomy yellow light over Pemberton's house, turning white stone ghastly pale and shaping the door's knocker into a gruesome face. I grip it and crack it twice against the door.

A young butler answers. His face lifts in surprise at the sight of me. "Can I help you, miss?"

I push back the hood of my cloak. "I'm here to see Agent Khurana and Professor Monaghan. Please can you let them know I've arrived?"

"I'm sorry, miss. They've already left."

Damn. The route I took from the agency was off the main roads; I must have missed them. "Did they leave in a coach?"

"Professor Monaghan and his companion took the coach," the man replies. "Miss Khurana and her friend walked."

"Walked? Where?"

"They headed in that direction, I believe, although I could not inform you as to their intention." He points east. Had Khurana gone into Whitechapel? "Is there anything further that I can—"

I'm already turning away, pulling my cloak tighter around me. "No. Thank you." I toy with the notion of asking him not to inform Pemberton of my presence, but the very act of asking will make my presence seem more suspicious. Instead, I stride in the direction Khurana took.

The shadows grow and I weave through the dwindling streams of people making their way home for the night. The Ripper hasn't struck for weeks. Perhaps Khurana is worried that will change tonight.

If Rayne is out there, she might be right.

It takes longer than I like to reach the East End, and a nearby church bell tolls the late hour. Yet people still linger in the streets, with no sign of the fear that haunted the district a month ago.

Whitechapel is a labyrinth. If Khurana is trying to find the killer, she must be dogging places that he might strike. I turn in a circle and examine the dark alleyways that branch off from the streets. He could attack anywhere, and I can't be everywhere at once.

Gritting my teeth, I head for The Ten Bells. If I were Khurana, I'd start there.

The pub rumbles with conversation and the occasional clink of glassware. Under the smell of ale and gin is the fainter scent of stale sweat. I see the table in the corner that I brought Steel to, where he'd almost got into a fight and broken our cover. His absence is a hole at my side.

I shake off the sensation. Steel is on his own, now. As am I.

The barkeep looks up at me as I lean over the bar. "Quarter of gin, is it?" he asks.

"I'm looking for two women," I call, over a group of men laughing. "An Indian woman with a long braid and a tall woman with white hair. Have you seen them?"

He squints at me. With a sigh, I slide a shilling over the counter. He takes the coin, taps it against the counter, and pockets it. "Saw two women like that," he replies, filling a glass with dark ale. "They left a little bit ago."

"Do you know where they went? If they said anything?"

He shrugs. "Looked like they were heading up Commercial Street."

I leave the pub and hasten after them. Khurana and Isis must be combing the streets one by one, as Steel and I did. And if I can find their direction that easily, so can Rayne.

Commercial Street is a wide, popular road lined with comfortable housing. It's not the kind of place the Ripper—Rayne—would haunt. However, the wedge of houses between Commercial Street and Whitechapel Road is much smaller, much closer, and its people more vulnerable. Khurana must be going there.

I branch off Commercial Street and cut left into the first lane. Another body among the small cottages would be accredited to the Ripper, even if the woman isn't a working girl but a government agent.

Walking quickly, I scan the streets, looking for a flash of pale hair or Khurana's long braid. In the dark, I have to look twice at every woman who passes, and as the minutes tick by unease crawls over my skin. I duck into another alley, and another. A church bell chimes, and I exhale, my breath misting out in a foggy cloud.

People glance at me as I pass, but no one tries to stop me. The Vigilance Committee are nowhere in sight, their force reduced to a skeleton of protection.

A shift of movement at the other end of the lane makes me pause. That was white hair. Isis.

I snatch up my skirts and run to the mouth of the alley. A labourer swears at me and stumbles out of my way. I can't spare the breath for an apology. I reach the end, and the street splits into three dark passages. I stop, panting.

Hands flash from the shadows and yank me into the darkness. I hiss, grappling with the arm that snakes around my throat. The figure pressed up close to me is tall and wiry and female. I make myself go still, grasping her arm with one hand, my other fluttering over my skirt towards my pocket.

"Who are you?" I demand. My throat is stretched by the woman's arm and the words come out thin.

I get no answer, but I don't intend to wait for one. I drag the plate shard from my pocket and slash at her arm. The woman yelps and releases me. I whirl and brandish my makeshift blade at her. It's Isis. Blood streaks her forearm.

I glance between her face and the wound. It bleeds freely, not healing. "What are you doing?" I ask. "I'm an agent."

"So is Khurana," the demon replies, in her light voice, "but you still seem to suspect her."

Air shifts to my right, in the shadows. I whip around, moving backwards to put space between us. Khurana levels me with her direct gaze.

"So, now you're following me," she says. "I cannot help but question if the Ripper is male, after all."

I narrow my eyes. "I'm not the killer."

"But you think I am?" Khurana grips the top of her cane in one hand, ready to draw. My porcelain knife will do nothing against her blade.

"I think you're in danger."

"Somehow I find that difficult to believe."

Isis makes a sudden, strained noise and we both turn. Steel stands behind the Hound, one hand on her throat and the other holding her wounded arm. My heart skips.

"Still bleeding," he says, as calmly as if he'd always been standing there. "So, she's not the Wraith."

If Steel is here, and not on his way to Paris, then Max and Jacob won't be far behind. What is he thinking, putting himself at risk?

He smirks at me.

The only sign of concern that escapes Khurana's control is the whitening of her knuckles on the cane. "If you hurt her—"

"Steel," I say. "Let her go."

The demon releases Isis. She gives him a dark look and glides to Khurana's side, ignoring the blood that drips from her arm.

Khurana stares at me, an arrested expression in her eyes. "You thought Isis was the Wraith?"

"You know about the Wraith?" I return.

After a moment, Khurana lets her arm fall to her side, lowering her cane. She looks at Isis, who shifts and cups her elbow. "I'm not a Wraith," the demon says, quietly.

"But you can separate," I interject. "I saw you, on Halloween, and we found your book."

Khurana sighs. "So, that is what happened to it."

"Rayne burned it, when he found me with it." I bow my head. "I'm sorry."

"It is done."

Steel draws closer to my side, and the warmth of his presence eases the nerves in my stomach. Isis examines us, and I see her gaze flick to the street. Mapping the distance that Steel must have travelled to get here. More than twenty feet.

"If you're not the Wraith," I say, "then who is?"

"Lavender," Khurana says. "Turner found her hiding in the East End, after her House had fallen. She persuaded Lavender to join the agency. Then, when Turner realised how we..." The woman glances at Isis and hesitates. "Lavender taught us the modification and helped us to cast it."

"The House Beleth tattoo," Steel murmurs. "I didn't even think about it."

Wise and careful Lavender. A poignant ache winds through my chest. I wish Turner had trusted me with that knowledge. "Then why did she keep it from the rest of us?"

"She suspected something wasn't right at the agency." Isis speaks slowly, eyeing Steel as if he'll lunge for her. "That there was something more to our cases. Most of them were Rayne's, and Cassius has been stalking around our rooms for weeks, invisible, trying to catch us out."

"I thought the party would be distraction enough to hide our own investigation." Khurana's expression twists with self-deprecation. "I was careless."

"You were following him," I realise.

She gives me a small smile that's little more than an upturn of her lips. "As were you, it seems."

I shake my head, shame curling through my stomach. I was so wrong. "I didn't know who to suspect." But Khurana believes me. The cold knot that was eased by Steel's presence dissolves further. I tell her what Rayne said, when he locked us up, and a delicate frown forms between her brows.

"If he *is* the killer," she says, "then we need to find him before he finds his next victim."

"He was looking to make *you* his next victim," Steel points out.

Khurana smiles, a glittering flash of white teeth. "I hope he tries."

Isis gestures at the dark, quiet cottages surrounding us. "We should split up. We can cover more ground, that way."

"Is that safe?" I ask.

"Safer for the other women who are walking abroad tonight," Khurana says. In a smooth movement she flips her cane, so she wields it like a baton. "None of them have demons to protect them."

"I'm worried about *you*," I tell her. "If Rayne is after you—"

"That is sweet," she replies, smirking, and I flush, feeling the weight of her years of experience against my two months.

Steel breathes out a soft snort through his nose. "How can we find you," he asks, "if we do run into Rayne?"

"Call for us," Isis replies. "I'll hear you. I'm the Hound, remember?"

Khurana pulls a fob from her jacket and frowns at its face. "The Ripper seems to strike in the early hours of the morning, but that doesn't mean we should lay idle until then." She slides the watch away and gives me a nod. "Good luck, Agent Locke."

I stand straighter, square my shoulders. "And you, agent."

The woman sweeps past me into the street. Isis follows, throwing Steel a sharp look as she goes. Within seconds, they've disappeared into the gloomy shadows.

I turn on Steel. "You were supposed to be halfway to Paris. What are you doing here? It's not safe."

"Nowhere is safe."

I should persuade him to leave, for his own safety. "Steel—"

"I made a promise, too," he says, cutting me off. "That I'd help you catch this man. And..." He sighs and looks away. "I didn't want to see the newspaper tomorrow and read your name in the headlines. Not if I could have done something to prevent it."

I wince, a faint thread of guilt worming through me. If I had not trapped him here, he wouldn't have had to make this decision.

But if I hadn't trapped him here, I might never have discovered the truth.

"I'm glad," is all I say. "But it's still dangerous."

"I left Max a trail. He'll be chasing a ghost for a few hours yet."

"I'll help you," I promise, searching for some way to pay him back. "Once we find Rayne, I'll do everything I can to help you find the person who murdered your family."

He grins, knife-edged and hungry. "Let's catch your killer, first, before we worry about mine. Where to, Agent Locke?"

I pack away my gratitude and the parasitic guilt attached to it and focus on the streets around us. "North, towards Buck's Row." An agent on the killer's trail would revisit past crime scenes to try and piece together a pattern. Rayne would expect that and be waiting. I slide my porcelain dagger into my pocket and flex its imprint from my hand. "We'll start there."

CHAPTER FIFTY-SIX

Buck's Row is almost pitch black. Not empty, though: two dockworkers walk down it in the opposite direction, and an older woman with a shawl drawn tight around her shoulders makes for home, her head down and her stride fast. There's no sign of Rayne.

"We could wait here," Steel suggests. "See if he comes back."

There are four Whitechapel murder sites, if we ignore Martha and Turner. Buck's Row is only one of them. "Let's go to Hanbury Street." The site of Annie Chapman's murder. From there, we can cut down to George Yard.

We move west through small houses that loom over narrow streets. Lights spill out from a couple of the businesses, despite the sliver of moon that has reached its peak over our heads. Here, it's busier than Buck's Row.

"Your hat," I remind Steel.

He pulls its brim down until it almost touches his nose. "They're less noticeable, now," he replies, glancing sidelong at me. His pupils are still round, still human-looking.

I eye the space between us. "What happened to the rest of the spell? Is there anything left?"

"I'm not sure. The ritual was designed to bring me here and then bind me to you. The first has already happened, and we undid the second. All that's left might just be residual magic."

I don't like the sound of *might*, but without any knowledge on the subject, I have no competing theory to offer. It may not even matter; Steel will leave for Paris, and I'll no longer be an agent. I try to ignore the heaviness in my chest. I didn't think I would miss it this much.

"Can you sense demons?" I ask Steel, pulling my mind back to the present, to the cold wind that stings my cheeks.

"Not as well as a real Hound, but enough."

"What about Cassius?"

"There are a lot of demons abroad tonight," he murmurs. "It's difficult to pick out anything beyond that. I'd need to get closer."

I nod and turn us off the main street into the alleyways. This way will take longer, but if Rayne *is* going to attack, he's not going to do it on the wider, more populated roads. We weave through the small, dark side streets towards the site of Annie's murder.

A figure appears at the end of the alley that leads to Hanbury Street, blocking our route. I check, my heart juddering, but the man is too thick-set to be Rayne, too short to be Cassius. Sliding my hand into my pocket, I approach him warily.

Instead of walking past us, he stays where he is. A felt cap perches on the crown of his head and he wears a neckerchief tucked under his chin. Something in the broad bones of his face chimes against a memory, but it isn't until a streak of dull moonlight illuminates his checked suit and the wide lapels of his jacket that I recognise him.

"The Vigilance Committee," I mutter. The ones we left unconscious. Of course, my luck is that bad.

The man pushes his cap back even further and squints at us. "You, there. What's your business?"

"We have no business with you," I reply. "We're just passing by."

His curious gaze lands on Steel and turns sharp with suspicion. "I know you. You were the ones that attacked us, before. Isn't that right, Laughton?"

Footsteps cross the alley behind us. I turn to see another man, older, stride towards us from the far end of the street. "Aye, I remember." He pushes up his sleeves and glares at us.

"We don't want any trouble," I say, holding up my hands. Steel has moved to put his back to the wall, keeping his eyes on both of them.

"That's twice we've seen you skulking round these streets in the dead of night." They close in until they flank us. I flatten my hand against my thigh, over my pocket, but they don't come closer.

"We don't want any trouble," I say, again.

"I'm sure you don't. We'll let the police decide if they wanna make any trouble out of you." He turns sideways and shouts for someone to fetch the nearest bobby.

I glance at Steel, who meets my eyes. If we attack them again, the police will have more than enough reason to come after us. Then all we've done will have been for nothing. But if we stay here, we risk being delayed. I shift my weight, uncertainty keeping me from striking one way or the other.

A moment later, a police officer joins us and we lose our chance to get away.

"Constable," I greet, before the Committee men can get a word in. "I'm sorry to disturb your beat. These men thought it best they ask for your advice."

"Right," the officer says, doubtfully, eyeing the four of us. "What's this about, then?"

"They attacked us," says the first man.

The policeman lifts his lantern to examine the man. "You look all right, to me."

"Not now, a month ago. They've been hanging round Whitechapel. Suspicious, if you ask me."

I fold my hands at my waist and regard the men. "I apologise if our behaviour seemed odd. We were just trying to get home."

"'We'," the policeman repeats, regarding Steel, who keeps his gaze averted.

"Yes. This is my—brother," I say, and then curse inwardly as the policeman looks at my long yellow hair and at Steel's straight dark locks. "Half-brother," I correct, hastily.

The constable frowns, drawing closer. His hand drifts to the truncheon that dangles from his waist. A couple of people are lingering at the mouth of the alley, whispering. Any longer and we'll draw a crowd.

"I apologise for causing any unease," I continue. "If you would just let us be on our way—"

"It's my duty to interrogate any suspicious characters, miss," the policeman interrupts. "Perhaps if you and your...brother would come down to the station, we could get this cleared up."

"We don't have time—"

"It won't take long. And I'm sure you can appreciate that it's better to be safe, in days like these."

I swallow, try desperately to think of a plan that won't get us dragged to the station anyway. Then Steel jerks towards the other end of the alley.

"Reaper," he says. "Shit, how did he get here so quickly?"

Max. We're running out of time. "Can you take them out without killing them?" I ask him, ignoring the startled exclamations from the Committee members.

Steel nods.

"Do it."

The police officer grabs his truncheon. Before he can tug it free, Steel is at his side. The demon yanks it from his grip and slams it over his head. He turns with the movement and strikes the Committee member, who hits the wall with a dull crumpling thud and slides to the ground.

I duck into the third man as he lunges forward. He stumbles around me, off balance, and Steel wraps an arm around his throat. The man gasps for air, his face going purple, and finally goes limp.

"You didn't—"

"No, he's still breathing," Steel replies, letting him fall to the ground.

The people who were watching us have made themselves scarce. Fights are common enough in Whitechapel, but when the next policeman comes across the bodies, there'll be witnesses telling him who to look for.

"Where's Max?" I ask.

"I...don't know." Steel frowns. "I sensed him, for a moment, but now the trace has vanished. I can't tell where he is."

"How is that possible? Max can't shield his aura."

The shrill sound of a whistle cuts through the hum of the street. I grab Steel's arm and pull him in the opposite direction. I only realise after I do it that we're heading *towards* where Steel sensed the Reaper.

We race west, winding through dark alleys until the distance grows and the unconscious bodies are long behind us. We reach a block of apartment buildings crammed around a tiny square. The streets behind us are empty.

I stop, press a hand to my stomach and try to catch my breath. Water lands on my shoulder, then a drop on my cheek. Spots of rain drum against the earth, muting the noise of the city. There's no sound of pursuit.

"Locke."

I almost don't register my name, for a second; I've never heard Steel use that tone before. "Yes?"

Steel is gazing into the window of a ground floor apartment near us. The glass is dark, and I see nothing beyond the pale reflection of his face, but that reflection is tight with shock and horror.

My stomach sinks. "What is it?" I whisper.

He doesn't answer. I creep closer, my instincts telling me to stop, to stay still, to do anything but approach that window.

Up close, the glass is smudged and bleary, and smears the details of the scene beyond. All I see through it is blood.

CHAPTER FIFTY-SEVEN

Another murder. We're too late. We didn't stop him.

I have to see if it's Khurana. Swallowing, I reach for the door.

Steel catches my wrist. "I don't think you should."

"I need to know who it is."

His gaze flickers between my eyes. His pupils are serpent-thin again, as if the control he had on their shape has slipped away. I do my best to keep the fear from my face. It must work, because he releases me.

The door is stuck. There's a small hole in the windowpane, just big enough for a hand. I reach through, scrabble at the door until I grasp the latch, lift it. It opens with a nudge.

Death rolls out of the room in a blood-scented cloud. I close my throat, hold my breath, and step inside.

For a moment, all I can think is that I won't know if it's Khurana, because there's no way to recognise the woman lying on the bed. Pieces have been carved from her body and deposited around the room. Her face has been peeled away entirely. Blood is *everywhere*.

A sound escapes me. I put my hand to my mouth to suppress it, to push down the bile that clambers up my throat. The hair. I should look at the hair.

I take another step inside. Slices of skin lie stacked on a cabinet next to ale bottles filled with scarlet liquid. The woman's organs are nestled around her own body. Most of them. I can't tell what's here and what's missing.

The hair. I tear my gaze from the corpse. Strands of the woman's hair cascade over linen that must have once been white. Pale brown. Not deep enough to be Khurana, not light enough to be Isis. This is not an agent; this is another woman. Another Ripper victim.

I spin and stumble outside. Clean cold air seeps into my lungs, fights with the tang of blood. I bend at the waist and vomit into the gutter.

Standing, I wipe my mouth with a trembling hand. Steel pulls the door shut and reaches through the window to relatch it. "We can't be found here," he says. "We have to go."

Something beyond shock, beyond anger, coils through me. The weight of it pins me to the ground, but it clears my head of everything but the need to find Rayne. Find him and bring him to justice.

"They were here," I say. "They must have been. Can you sense them?"

Steel pauses, scents carefully, and then shakes his head. "There's no sign of a Phantom."

"We have to find him."

He looks up at the dark sky. Rain soaks his face, making it shine under the light of a gas lamp on the corner of the square.

"I have an idea," he says, a grim expression on his face. "I might be able to bring him to us."

"How?"

He raises his hand, and the rain stops. Drops of water hang in the air all around us, glittering. Between one heartbeat and the next they flow to Steel's palm. He curls his hand and the water twists upwards, a thin tower of glass that ripples as it climbs, touched by yellow gaslight and silver moonlight.

"That's distinctive," I murmur, taking refuge in a calm I do not feel.

He grins a wolf's grin; ravenous, savage. "Cassius will know what it means."

"That you have magic again?"

"That I am free," he replies, and a jolt of mingled guilt and fear goes through me. Guilt that I trapped him, fear of the water that bends to his will.

"What *are* you?" I whisper, unable to stop the words.

He doesn't reply, but an answer floats from the shadows. "The last son of House Leviathan." Cassius steps from nothing and curls his mouth into a smirk. "You are awake, I see."

"I knew you weren't a Hound," Rayne says, standing at the Phantom's shoulder. "At least you've chosen somewhere quiet for this. That will save me some trouble."

Steel releases the column of water with a strained sound, and the rain pummels into the ground. Others might have seen his display. We won't have long.

I plunge my hand into my pocket and grip my porcelain shard. I wish I had a real blade so I could stab it between his eyes. "Why are you doing this?"

Rayne flexes his hand and I realise he holds his stiletto dagger. Not a gun, at least, but far more deadly than my shattered plate. "When I tell Monaghan that you and your demon are the ones who've been committing these awful murders, and that *I* caught you... Well, he won't have a choice but to make me his heir."

"That's why you murdered another woman? To have the agency?"

"What woman?"

I tighten my hand and warm blood seeps into my palm. "Turn yourself in. Tell Monaghan the truth."

He tilts his head, frowns at me. "Why would I turn myself in, Miss Locke? I have nothing to hide."

"*Agent* Locke."

"Shall we get on with it?" Cassius asks with a lazy grin. He vanishes.

Raindrops splatter against his invisible body. Cassius swears. Steel is a blur of movement in the corner of my eye.

I intercept Rayne as he starts towards Steel and slam the edge of my hand into his inner elbow. The stiletto blade clatters to the ground. Swearing, he bends to grab it. I kick it away, and the knife skitters over the flagstones. He spins to face me.

"You should have stayed in your room," he mutters, "like a good girl."

Anger fuels each thunderous beat of my heart. I punch him. The impact ricochets down my arm, but he cries out and clutches his face. I lunge for the dagger.

He grabs me by the waist and hauls me against him. I kick out, miss his leg by inches. He steps backwards, jerking me with him. Writhing in his grip, I reach over my shoulder and claw at his face.

"*Fuck*," he swears and his hold on me loosens. Before I can reach for the blade, he hits me, his fist slamming into my temple.

I hit the ground, hard. Spit out dirt and try to shake the ringing from my ears. Somewhere Steel and Cassius are fighting; my chest reverberates with their growls, but I can't see them.

Rayne's shiny black shoes appear in my vision. I grab his ankle with both hands and yank. He folds to one knee with a shout. I use his jacket to try and pull myself upright, but he grabs my arm and bends it until I scream.

"If I kill you," comes Rayne's voice, from far away, "it will be in self-defence. They can't hang me for it."

The blade shimmers on the ground, less than three feet away. Three feet too far. I scrabble in my pocket for the uneven shard. Rayne yanks my shoulder and whips me around, reaches for my throat. The porcelain sinks into his chest as smoothly as a steel knife. Warmth bursts over my hand, pooling over my skin. My whole body recoils at the feeling and I let go. Rayne paws at the shattered enamel speared in his chest. A gurgled noise escapes him. Slowly, he collapses backwards onto the ground.

For one eternal moment, all I can do is stare at his motionless body. Only for a moment, and then the world spins again.

Cassius falls to his knees, shuddering. "That," he says, hoarsely, "did not go as well as I'd hoped."

Steel's clothes are ripped, and blood darkens his hairline. "The ritual is broken," he mutters, watching the Phantom demon.

Cassius grins. His teeth are red. "Now, I, too, am free."

The rapid click of shoes darts towards us and Khurana races into the square, her sword bared, Isis at her side. The agent takes in Rayne's body and levels her blade at Cassius. "Perhaps you should rethink your position," she says, coldly.

The Phantom glances between the four of us and wipes his mouth. "I was never interested in being tethered, anyway," he says, and disappears.

Khurana strides forward, but the air where he'd stood is empty. "Now we must deal with that one, too," she mutters.

My gaze returns to Rayne's inert body, to his dull, dead eyes.

"Are you all right?" Steel asks, his voice distant.

Tremors of pain run up my arm and I can't seem to see straight, but I can stand. Walk, even. "I'm fine."

His gaze flicks to Rayne. To Rayne's corpse. "I don't think fine is the appropriate word."

"I would have liked the opportunity to do this myself," says Khurana, standing over the body. "Still. Now Turner has justice."

I swallow. "There's another body." I tilt my head at the house, at the window. "We couldn't prevent his last murder."

Isis drifts to the window and curses. "We cannot hide this from the police," she says.

"I will stay." Khurana kneels beside the body. "The last thing we want is for the agency's involvement to be splashed over the papers, and someone will have to explain away your rain trick." She looks up at me. "Go back to the agency. Tell Monaghan what happened and ask him to meet me at the station."

"Shouldn't I stay? Help?"

"I can sense Max on his way," Isis says, joining Khurana. "It may be safer if you weren't found at the crime scene."

Her words make sense, but leaving them after what I did feels... I am guilty of murder, too.

"You did what you had to do in order to survive," Khurana says, reading my thoughts in my face. "But now you need to leave, agent. Quickly."

Steel clasps my elbow, draws me away. "We'd best go," he murmurs.

Swallowing, I nod. With effort, I turn my back on Rayne's too-still body and go with him.

CHAPTER FIFTY-EIGHT

As soon as we get onto the main street, Steel summons a cab. I don't object. No doubt the police will have stumbled onto the unconscious Committee members by now and will be looking for us. We need to get back to the agency as fast as possible.

In the cab, I stare at the street as it blurs past. My right hand, I realise, is wet. I look down at it, knowing what I'll see and dreading the sight.

Blood stains my skin. I fold the fabric of my skirt and rub my hand. The wool does little more than smear the crimson over my fingers. I scrub harder.

Rayne's face swims in my vision, distorted by rain. The twist of shock and pain ripples through me again as his blood gushes over my hand. I scrape the wool over my skin and try to push the image from my head.

"At least you've chosen somewhere quiet for this. That will save me some trouble." His voice whispers in my ear as though he sits beside me.

A memory of his voice. It's not real.

But the words catch on something in my chest, a small pebble of emotion: doubt. We stumbled upon the victim out of sheer luck. We didn't choose the location. *Rayne* chose the site of the murder, not us.

"You'll scrub your hands raw." Steel's voice drags me out of my whirling thoughts.

I pull my hands apart. There's no more sign of blood on my hand, though a large patch on my blue skirt is now dyed black. I spread my fingers over my knees, so I don't have to feel my own skin.

"Thank you," I tell him, tearing my gaze from the stain. "For coming back. I don't think I thanked you, before."

His mouth is rueful. "I don't think we had time before."

More words tread through my chest, words that need to be said but keep disappearing like smoke when I try to articulate them. I frown and keep it simple. "I'm sorry for summoning you against your will. I didn't say that before, either."

He draws his gaze away from my hands, but he doesn't quite look at me. "Thank you. For saying it now."

"Once we've seen Monaghan," I add, "you should leave. If anyone finds out what you can do...they won't want to lose a valuable asset." If they discover Steel's abilities, a twenty-foot restriction will seem like paradise in comparison to the chains they'll put on him. "In fact, perhaps you should leave now."

"I'll come to the agency. Your professor might not believe you, on your own." *Then, I'll leave.* The words are unspoken, but I hear them clearly. I want to ask him if I can still help him, but that's a request I may not be able to deliver on anymore, so I keep it to myself.

A few moments later, we pull up outside the agency. I pay the driver with the last of my coin and dart inside. The drumming of the rain echoes through the dark, empty lobby. I wonder where Eve is, if she went after Jacob when I left.

"Monaghan will be in his room," I say, leading Steel upstairs.

The professor's bedroom is on the floor above his study. I stand in front of his door, take a deep breath, and knock. Monaghan answers. He's dressed, though his cravat is undone. I glimpse Tiberius behind him, a coat slung over his shoulders that sparkles with rain.

"Agent Locke," Monaghan says. "What are you doing out of your room?"

"I need to speak to you, sir. Urgently. It's about Rayne."

His eyes narrow but he nods. "Meet me in my study. I'll be there in a moment." He shuts the door before I can say anything else.

The door to Monaghan's study is unguarded. I go inside and stand in front of his desk. Steel drifts to the window.

With only the patter of rain to distract me, my mind wanders. I try not to examine the doubt sitting in my chest, growing in weight with every breath. If I acknowledge it, then I have to acknowledge that something's wrong. And if something's wrong, then I made a mistake.

I can't have made a mistake. Because Rayne is dead. And I killed him.

The pebble of doubt does not go away.

I pace around the desk to stand by the window, trailing my fingers over the wood. A letter stamped with the Home Office seal lies unfolded beside the open ink pot. I pause, something in the words catching my attention.

Dear Prof. Monaghan,

We are delighted that you have chosen to accept the position as Shadow Commissioner. I'm sure you can appreciate that, with Warren's resignation yesterday, we will need to appoint a replacement in name, if not in role, who can act the part for the papers. Please be assured that your position will be working directly for the Prime Minister, and, consequently, the Queen. Your dedication to the investigation of these murders has been clear, and the Prime Minister is very interested in your ideas for expanding your agency.

The letter goes on, requesting a meeting to discuss the details. In my chest, the doubt blossoms.

Monaghan keeps Home Office correspondence in the first desk drawer. I saw it, when we stole the letter for the barracks. Guilt stays my hand. Monaghan was the one who took me out of destitution and gave me something to live for. Am I really suspecting him?

There shouldn't be any reason he'd keep secrets from us, from the agency. One look and I can put my suspicions at ease.

Resolve overcomes my hesitation and I pull the drawer open. The first few letters are simple reports of the police progress into the Whitechapel and Whitehall cases. Underneath them is a small note containing two short sentences:

1st October 1888

Monaghan,

I do hope you've recovered from your bout of sickness on Saturday. Perhaps we could rearrange our dinner for later this week?

Pemberton

The first of October—that Saturday would have been the twenty-ninth of September. The night of the Home Office dinner, and the night of the double murders. If Monaghan was not at Pemberton's, and he wasn't here, then where was he?

"At least you've chosen somewhere quiet for this. That will save me some trouble."

"What woman?"

I scour my mind, try to remember if Monaghan was here on the dates of each murder. I can't. The Reaper that Steel sensed for only a moment—Max can't shield his aura, but Tiberius can, *Tiberius can...*

The door clicks open. I look up, the pebble in my chest as heavy as a granite plinth. Monaghan's gaze alights on the letters in my hands.

"Ah," he says, with a lift to his mouth. "I see you've found my secret. I'm to be promoted."

It takes me two attempts to speak. "A promotion." I force myself to let go of the letters. "Is that your only secret?"

"What do you mean?"

Tiberius closes the door and sets his shoulders against it. I glance at Steel, who looks at my expression and stiffens.

At least you've chosen somewhere quiet for this. I was wrong. I was *so wrong.*

"I came to tell you that Rayne was the Ripper, and that he was dead," I say. "But now I think I'm wrong."

Monaghan straightens his cuffs. "Do you?"

"Rayne never confessed to the murders. I thought—" I assumed he was the culprit because of what he did to me. I didn't bother looking for another explanation. "I thought he was the killer. But he wanted to *catch* the Ripper. He wanted to prove he could be your heir."

"Perhaps that was why he committed the murders," Monaghan suggests. "So he could be credited for solving the case he created."

"Murders that would make the agency indispensable to the Home Office," I reply, groping my way through what feels like dense mist, grappling with the sheer enormity of the pieces that are just now fitting together. "Murders that netted you a position second only to the Prime Minister."

Monaghan exchanges a glance with Tiberius, and my heart thuds.

"It was you, wasn't it?" I ask Tiberius. "Max can't mask his presence as a Reaper, yet, but you can, can't you? Except for tonight."

"That was you I sensed, then," Steel murmurs. "Not Max."

The Reaper shrugs. "Masking my presence takes energy and concentration. I must have slipped."

"Tiberius." Monaghan's voice is calm but ice-cold.

"It's true, then?" I want him to tell me I'm imagining things, that Rayne was the one who'd committed the murders, that Monaghan had been on the other side of the city when it happened. "You're responsible for the deaths of these women?"

Monaghan sighs. "They were going to shut us down, Hazel. Britain cannot defend itself without an organised response. Now, our position is secured, and the country is protected."

I sway and have to grasp the desk to stay upright. "At the cost of *seven lives*?"

"Turner was not supposed to get in the way." The man flicks a glance at Tiberius, anger in his expression.

"I made it a quick death," the Reaper says, as though that's a comfort, as though murdering her without carving her up was *mercy*.

"And Lavender?" I ask.

"A Wraith is a threat we cannot afford."

Steel faces him, uses the movement to shift closer to me. "So, you tortured and killed her. For what? The spell?"

"Lavender was a source of valuable information," Monaghan replies. "It was a rare opportunity to learn about a class we've never encountered. What makes them tick. What makes them bleed."

I flinch. "She was one of us," I whisper. "One of your own people."

"No," he replies, his voice hard. "Demons are not people."

"The women—" It takes effort to push out the words. "The way you killed them—"

"It had to look demonic. What good would it do if they blamed a human for the murders?"

Breathe. Breathe, and *think*. I will have time for pain and grief later; if I let them overcome me now, we're as good as dead.

The room has one door and Tiberius stands between us and it. Perhaps there's a chance that Steel can overpower the demon using his magic, but I'm not strong enough or fast enough to defeat Monaghan alone.

Tiberius' attention is on Steel, but Monaghan watches me. Waits to see what I'll do. I search for ways to distract him, to stall for time while I think of a plan.

"That's why you sent Khurana to Bristol, isn't it? So she wouldn't find out what you were doing."

"It would have been difficult to hide this from her," he agrees.

"She'll catch you." I grasp onto that thought. "Khurana will find out what you've done."

"Thanks to you, she believes the killer is dead." Monaghan raises his hands in a small shrug. "And when I tell her that your demon demanded we free him, and then turned on you when we refused—well. Tiberius had to stop him, no matter the cost. It's a shame we were too late to save you."

I curl my hands into fists on the wood, staring at Monaghan, the man I thought I knew better than my own family. "How can you do this?" My voice is small, defeated. I wish it was a pretence.

"Demons are dangerous. They need to be put down." His gaze flickers to the desk, to where the portrait of his lover once stood. "I cannot do that without the support of the government. Sacrifices were necessary."

"Sacrifices." I feel sick at the thought that I once revered this man, that I cherished his approval. "Is that all we are to you?" Something else occurs to me, and my mouth twists. "This is why you put me on the case. Because I was untried, inexperienced. I wouldn't have caught you."

"You *haven't* caught me," he replies, mildly, and anger flashes through me, makes my arms tremble.

Calm. I have to stay calm. Think. Plan.

The window. Monaghan's office is on the first floor, close enough to the ground that I shouldn't break anything if I jump. But I'll have to break the glass, first, and that moment is all

Tiberius will need to strike. I need to distract them; buy us the seconds we need to get away. I need a partner.

I need Steel.

I bite the inside of my cheek, hard, and then spread my fingers on the desk, as though I'm using it to prop myself up. "I feel as though I'm sleep-walking," I mutter, glancing at Tiberius again. From the corner of my eye, I see Steel tilt his head towards me. "What will you do with us?" I demand. "Break our legs so we can't leave?" It's clumsy, and I hope it's enough. I can't think of any other way to clue him in without giving away my plan.

"No one will believe you when you're in Bedlam," Monaghan replies.

"And Steel?"

"Steel will go to Eve." He advances until he stands on the other side of the desk, meeting my eyes with a flat gaze. "She will replace you as our next Hound."

"And you'll buy her loyalty." I scowl at him. "Like Pemberton bought yours?"

"I hardly think—"

I don't wait for him to finish. I snatch the ink pot from the desk and hurl it at him. Black ink splashes into his eyes and he shouts, raises his hands to them. At his cry, Tiberius lunges.

I grab the chair and at the same time, Steel flips the desk over and hurls it across the room. It hits Tiberius with a loud splintering sound—maybe Monaghan, too, I don't see—as I smash the chair through the window. Glass and wood shatter on the pavement a floor beneath us. Steel grabs me, an arm around my shoulders and another around my legs, and leaps.

He lands with a bone-jarring crack, crushing glass and stone under his feet. The chair is in splinters beside us. I glance up and Tiberius' shadowy figure leans out of the window. His eyes are shards of reflected light. I grab Steel's hand and flee.

CHAPTER FIFTY-NINE

A few miles from the agency, I collapse against a wall, panting. Tiberius might have been the one to commit the murders, but Monaghan masterminded them. He was the one responsible for the women's deaths. For Lavender's. For Turner's.

I swallow bile. All this time, and I was *working* for the man the papers called Jack the Ripper.

"Shit," I mutter.

Steel lets out a low, grim laugh. "I echo the sentiment."

"I should have seen it. I should have realised—" I trail off, shake my head. Rayne is dead, because of me. Because I was happy to believe that the man who'd locked me up could be just as guilty of murder.

"You couldn't have known."

"Maybe." Maybe not. Already my mind is dragging up memories, searching for any hint of what Monaghan truly was. But we don't have time for that.

I look around. We're hidden in a dark alley, somewhere west of the agency. It's stopped raining, but the stone is slick with water.

"They're not coming after us," Steel says, gazing back the way we'd come.

Gulping, I catch my breath and stand up straight. My stomach wants to pin me to the floor. "It serves them better not to," I manage. Steel glances at me and I explain, "We're alone, conspicuous, and penniless. In a few hours, our likenesses will be plastered over every paper in London. He'll call us Ripper suspects. He won't need to come after us himself." It might play better for him if he doesn't. He could tell Khurana that we ran, that I left the agency to free Steel. He could tell them that *we* were the ones behind the murders. Khurana might even believe him.

Either way, he'll come after us. He'll need us silenced before he takes up his new role. A part of my mind sinks its claws into my memory of him, curls it close like a grudge.

I run my hands over my hair, smoothing it out. There's a little fleck of rust on my fingernail. Rayne's blood. Dropping my hands to my side, I turn my gaze to the sky. Later. I cannot fall apart now, not yet.

"We need to get out of the country," I decide. His blood stains my skirt, but I can pass that off as dirt or oil. The lack of baggage will be harder to disguise, but our first problem is the lack of money.

"And go where?" Steel blinks and his pupils widen, soften. He seems human, but his looks are distinctive enough that he won't go unnoticed.

Perhaps we can use that to our advantage.

I step towards the main street, glancing at the sign nailed to the building on the other side. Lime Street. We're not far from

Tower Hill. I start south. "We need to get across the river to London Bridge Station."

"We're taking a train?"

"Not exactly." I lead him across Fenchurch Street and cut down Philpot Lane, sticking to the side streets. "We need money before we can do anything," I add. "How are your pickpocketing skills?"

"Not bad," he replies, sending me an intrigued glance. "I'm fast."

"Then let's see if we can find a mark."

The river glitters under the night sky as we emerge onto Lower Thames Street. For a second, I'm back at the docks, staring down at Turner's body. Gritting my teeth, I look away from the water. A tall man in a nice suit walks towards us. A decent enough mark.

"This one," I whisper to Steel, and lengthen my stride so I pull ahead. I bump into the man, knocking him off balance so he swings to the side, his gaze sliding away from Steel and to me. "I'm so sorry," I murmur, raising my hands. "I'm afraid I didn't see you."

"Uh, no problem at all." Flustered, the man touches his cap. "It was my mistake."

Steel sweeps up behind him, mutters, "Excuse me," and touches the man to manoeuvre him out of the way.

I dip into a shallow curtsy and put on a friendly smile. "Good morning to you."

"And—and you." He nods at me and continues on his way.

I catch up with Steel. The demon has a wallet in his hands.

"Have you considered a career in petty crime?" he asks, one of his teasing smirks curling at the corner of his mouth.

I wince. My career—what little of it I had—is dead, and no doubt I'll soon be a wanted criminal.

"Sorry," Steel murmurs. He rifles through the wallet and clicks his tongue thoughtfully. "We have about six pounds. That should cover us for two tickets, shouldn't it?"

"More than enough."

We cross London Bridge. More people are traversing the big stone bridge, and I tuck my hand into Steel's elbow. Anyone who sees us will assume that we're on our way to work. Two half-constructed towers loom across the water to our left, the new lifting bridge. I may never get to see it built.

The realisation sinks through me. I didn't think I was attached to this city, but the thought of never seeing it again makes my stomach plummet. London is no longer my home. I don't have a home anymore.

There's nothing I can do about that now. What matters is the present moment, the problem of our freedom. The future—I can worry about the future later.

London Bridge Station is a sprawling mess, guarded by a large brick facade and a spear of a bell tower. Already, a handful of pedestrians are making their way through tall archways towards the platforms.

I weave through the entrance and make my way to the gated ticket booths. Only one of them is open, but there's no queue.

Steel pulls on my arm. "If Monaghan traces us here," he whispers, "he'll know where we're going."

"I'm counting on it," I reply, and march up to the booth.

The man behind the railing is half asleep, but he sells me two tickets to Brighton and takes a long enough look at us that I'm confident he'll remember when they come to question him.

Steel sidles close to me as I walk away, clutching the tickets. "What's in Brighton and why are we going there?"

"Sand and pebbles, and we're not." I tear the tickets into small pieces and slide them into my pocket.

The big station clock reads three thirty in the morning. By now, Monaghan will have sent runners to the local police stations. Rayne's body and the murder of that poor woman will distract them for a while.

Unless Monaghan prioritises our capture, in which case we're already running out of time.

"We're going to St. Katherine's Way." We reach the bridge and I point across the river, the way we'd come. The Tower squats on the bank like a giant toad, huddling between London Bridge and the docks. Its huge grey walls are dark, but its presence looms over everything. I try to trace our steps as closely as possible so the scent trail doesn't waver.

"What's in St. Katherine's Way?"

"A steamer to Boulogne."

"So, we're going to Boulogne?"

"Yes." I cast a nervous glance over my shoulder as we reach the middle of the bridge. The sky is pitch black, threaded with smoke and thin clouds. The crescent moon has vanished behind one of them, and there's no moonlight. My heart drums in my chest, marking every second that goes by, and my pace quickens. "It won't hold them off forever," I reply. "They'll catch on when they search the train in Brighton. But by that time, we'll be on the water." That's my hope, anyway.

"Boulogne is just north of Paris," Steel says.

I cast him a glance and find him eyeing me in return. "*Just* may be an underestimation," I reply. "It's four hours by train. I think; I've never been to France."

"So...we're going to *Paris*."

Despite the urgency thrumming through my blood and the nausea that twists my stomach, a smile tugs at my mouth. "I did promise I'd help you, remember?" The weight of what I owe him leans on my shoulders. Well, if my career as an agent is done, at least I can try to make up for what I have cost Steel.

"You already did, by freeing me," Steel replies, as we pick our way across the quay along the Thames' shore, in the shadow of the Tower. "I don't expect more than that."

"I have nowhere else to go," I admit, quietly. "At least let me help you. And I have a debt to pay, I believe."

He arches his eyebrows. "That's not how I'd put it." Then he sighs. "If you're sure. I certainly won't stop you."

St. Katherine's Way appears in front of us before I can reply, its docks rustling with quiet activity. A big steamship bobs on the waves, puffing smoke up into the night sky. Someone's nailed a timetable next to the advertisements on the walls of the marina:

BOULOGNE AND LONDON

From LONDON: 5th; 12 night; 7th; 2 a.m.; 9th; 4 a.m.

Four in the morning— "That's our ship." A steamer agent in a smart cap and gloves is standing by the gangway, dealing out tickets.

Steel hisses and stops in his tracks. "A Reaper is here."

"What? Where?"

He looks over his shoulder, back at the semi-visible line of the bridge. "It's Max," he says, narrowing his eyes. "I don't think he knows where we are. He's walking towards the station."

Fear plucks at my heart as though the organ is a harp. My distraction won't mean much if they find the branch in our scent trail. I run to the officer at the gangway. "We need a fore cabin, please," I request, counting eight shillings into the man's palm.

"The ship leaves in a few minutes," the man says, eyeing us and our lack of anything resembling baggage. "Are you ready to depart?"

"Our friends are on board," I lie. "They have our things. We just wanted to say goodbye to the city."

The man's face creases with patriotic sympathy. "Of course, of course. Bon voyage, as they say over the Channel."

I manage not to wince at his accent and hope there aren't any native French speakers on board. "Thank you." I turn to Steel, but he's staring at the bridge. "Steel. Hurry, or we'll miss the tide."

"Pity," he mutters, glaring at the dark expanse of water. "I almost *want* them to catch us. I feel like I owe them for chasing me across London."

"Let's pay them back another time, all right?" I steer him up the gangway and onto the ship, our cabin ticket crumpled in my sweaty grip. On deck, I clutch the railing with white-knuckled hands.

A few moments later the call goes up from the marina and the sailors retract the gangway. I watch the quay, holding my breath, waiting for Khurana or Jacob or Eve to burst out of the shadows and order the ship to stop.

But no one comes. The steamship bobs out of the dock and points its nose downriver. London, and all of its glittering lights, slides away.

It's only when the unrelieved black of the Northern Sea opens around us that I relax my grip. We'll be in Boulogne in ten hours. That's plenty of time to come up with a plan for what happens next.

Plenty of time to deal with the yawning pit in my chest.

"So," Steel says, leaning his forearms on the railing. The sea breeze ruffles his coat. "I didn't fulfil my end of our bargain."

"What?"

"We didn't catch your killer."

I sigh and lean against the side, watch the waves crest and fall under the ship. Behind us, the city's lights fade and gradually wink out. "No," I reply. "No, we didn't catch him."

"And now we're on the run. Really, I just made things worse."

Part of me wants to huddle into a ball against the cold wind and cry myself to sleep, but the rest of me can't help but listen. I wonder if he knows that. "You don't need to sound so happy about it," I mutter.

He gives me a one-shouldered shrug. "I'm tracking my own killer, and now I have you to help me. I'm not going to shed a tear about that," he says. "The more time goes by, the more I think I might actually need your help."

"What do you mean, *actually*?" I shoot back with the ghost of humour and he grins.

"I'll try and find a puzzle for you to solve."

"It was a code, not a puzzle."

"Same principle."

I roll my eyes, but a thin thread of amusement is winding through my chest, melting the chill. I don't know how he accomplishes it, but the churning nausea that has been present since Monaghan's study eases to a dull lurch. Whatever awaits us in Paris, part of me—a *big* part of me—is grateful that he's here.

"I need to know more about your family," I tell him, softly, "about this case."

"I know." He gazes out at the endless sea. "Later. It can come later."

I tuck my hands into my sleeves and stand beside him, watching the black waves roll past, waiting for the dawn. For the dawn, and for Paris. And whatever future they may bring.

READ MORE IN THE SERIES

Thank you for reading *The Agent's Demon*, book one in the *Locke & Steel* series. If you enjoyed it, please leave a short review. Your feedback will help other readers to decide whether to read the book, too.

Read more about Hazel and Steel's journey in the second book in the series, *The Rose and the Ghost*, available now from most online retailers.

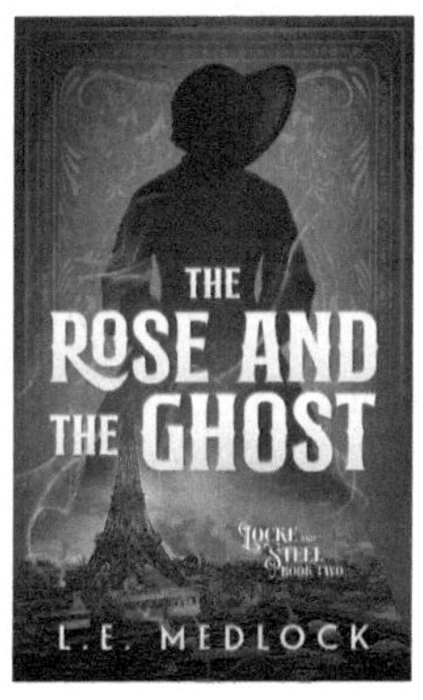

THE CITY OF LIGHT CASTS A DARK SHADOW...

After fleeing the Agency, Hazel and Steel travel to France on the trail of the demon who killed Steel's family. Their only clue leads them to Paris, and to rumours of a mysterious spectre terrorising the opera house...

Acknowledgments

First, I want to thank the brilliant people who helped me in the publishing process. To my wonderful beta and sensitivity readers, for their guidance and advice on improving this story and helping to make it what it is. To the brilliant designers at MiblArt, a huge thank you for your support and endless patience. To Nicola, my editor, for pointing out those cliches I always struggle with and making sure my hyphens are em dashes (en dashes??), not to mention eliminating those pesky extra spaces.

Then, to my friends, who are all beacons of support and joy (even when I don't message you back as quickly as I should!). To Leslie and Jason, for reading drafts of older novels while trying not to fall asleep on the tube. To Lulu and Haha, for feeding me the most delicious three course meals and enduring all my talk of writing with little to show for it. To Elaina, for accepting me as a the Cantankerous Wife I am and growing older together, apart.

And I owe a huge amount of gratitude to my family, who never tried to persuade me not to write, something not every author can say. I appreciate all of your support and I always will. To Kevin, for inspiring an interest in Jack the Ripper (thanks I guess?!). To Becky & Liam, for being game buddies and making me laugh. To Dad, for your sage business advice and for nudging me out of my comfort zone into growth.

Finally and particularly to Mum, who always supported me when I said I wanted to write, even when it meant giving up other options, and for soldiering through an early draft of this to give me her English teacher honed feedback. This wouldn't have been possible without you. Thank you.

About the Author

L. E. Medlock has been writing stories since her first school writing assignment, and reading books long before that. She initially decided it wouldn't make a great career choice and went to University to study Egyptology and Classical Civilisation, but the writing never stopped. At the end of her master's degree, she decided to try and turn professional. Some fourteen years and six novels later, she published her debut, The Agent's Demon (the "light-hearted" one). She enjoys stories about flawed gods and monsters who look like us. She's much too addicted to video games and dreams of one day being a cat owner.